# THE ETERNITY PROJECT

DEAN CRAWFORD

SIMON & SCHUSTER

London · New York · Sydney · Toronto · New Delhi

A CBS COMPANY

First published in Great Britain by Simon & Schuster UK Ltd, 2013
A CBS Company



1 3 5 7 9 10 8 6 4 2

Simon & Schuster UK Ltd
1st Floor,
222 Gray's Inn Road
London WC1X 8HB

www.simonandschuster.co.uk

Simon & Schuster Australia, Sydney
Simon & Schuster India, New Delhi

A CIP catalogue record for this book is available from the British Library

B Format ISBN 978-1-47110-257-8
Trade Paperback ISBN 978-1-47110-258-5
Ebook ISBN 978-1-47110-259-2



Typeset by Hewer Text UK Ltd, Edinburgh
Printed and bound in Great Britain by CPI Group (UK) Ltd, Croydon CR0 4YY

To the fans of the *Ethan Warner* series

# THE ETERNITY PROJECT

# I

# ANCRE RIVER, THIEPVAL, THE SOMME, FRANCE

*November 1916*

'Stand tall and show an imposing front!'

Private Oliver Barraclough staggered to his feet as a thunderous blast shook the deep earthen walls of the trench towering around him. A shower of dislodged soil and stones pelted down onto his helmet and splattered into pools of icy water beneath his boots. His uniform was drenched and plastered with mud, and the sullen gray sky above was weeping thin veils of freezing rain that ran down his face. Dozens of soldiers clambered to their feet all around him, pale with exhaustion and cold, hands clenching the stocks of long-barreled Lee-Enfield rifles.

A screech shattered the air and Oliver hurled himself against the slimy wall of the trench as a mortar shell crashed down nearby. The blast hurled chunks of earth and rock mixed with torn limbs and ruined weapons that crashed down in their midst. The shockwave from the blast rattled Oliver's eyeballs in their sockets, his vision quivering. Oliver blinked and shook his head as his ears rang from the infernal noise, droplets of moisture stained crimson now dripping from the rim of his helmet.

A distant stream of keening, agonized screams echoed up and down the trench as medics struggled to make their way through to the injured men. An officer's voice rang in Oliver's damaged ears.

'Stay on your feet! Stand your ground!' he raged, a silvery moustache lining his upper lip like twisted bayonets and his blue eyes piercing the early morning gloom like searchlights as he stormed down the trench. 'Fix bayonets!'

Oliver scrambled with hands too numb to feel anything and unclipped his bayonet from its sheath on his webbing. He twisted it into place on the end of the rifle's barrel and pulled hard, ensuring the weapon was securely fixed, then turned to where tall ladders were being placed against the twelve-foot-high walls of the trench. The soldiers gathered around the ladders, huddled against the cold and fear that permeated their miserable existence.

Puddles of partially frozen water filled the muddy floor of the trench, the ice crunching beneath their boots. Oliver could feel his feet likewise crunching inside his boots, victim to the trench-foot and frostbite that was slowly rotting away the blackened flesh of his toes. He could no longer feel them but it was better without the searing pain haunting his every step. A tiny part of his mind had hoped that one day soon he would no longer be able to walk and would simply fall over, to be sent to the rear to convalesce and perhaps never return to this living hell. But he had seen others try the same trick only to be shot in their dozens at dawn for cowardice. The Somme was no place for hope.

Now, there was no time left for his feet to rot further. The troops lined up against the ladders as mortar rounds thundered down across the mud-churned fields above and rained more debris down into the trench to mix with the bitter rain. Oliver clutched his rifle more tightly, his knuckles shining white beneath the skin.

'Stand by!' yelled the officer.

Oliver's teeth chattered in his jaw and his body shivered with the cold as amid the chaos a brief image flashed into his mind. Home. He saw in his mind's eye a tiny hamlet in Somerset, remembered the warm summers of his childhood; the school and parish; his parents waving him goodbye with pride in their eyes as he left home for the first time in his life.

Oliver Barraclough was six days short of his seventeenth birthday.

From somewhere deep within him came a choked cry as tears spilled from his eyes to mix with the mud-stained rain trickling down his face. His legs quivered, the strength gone from them as he felt other soldiers lining up behind him, huddling together for warmth and comfort and blocking his only chance of escape. Suddenly, with all of his heart, he wanted to be home.

'All arms!' the officer bellowed. 'Up and at 'em!'

A ragged cheer soared from the trenches and, before he could think about it, Oliver was clambering awkwardly up the ladder, trying to keep his fingers from being crushed by the boots of the man above him. The soldier crawled off the top of the ladder as Oliver popped his head above the trench wall for the very first time.

The man before him stood up and his tin helmet flew off with a metallic twang as he toppled backwards into the trench, his face a bloodied mess of bone and tissue. As Oliver dragged himself up off the ladder, he heard cries of pain as the lifeless body slammed down onto the men below him.

Time seemed to slow down as he scrambled onto a gloomy wasteland of churned mud and freezing snow. Ranks of men charged into a thick, swirling, yellowish morass of smoke that drifted like phantoms up ahead where twisted lines of barbed wire coiled like thorny metal snakes across the desolate expanse of no-man's-land. Gunshots crackled out and Oliver saw several more men fall before they had even cleared the trenches, toppling back on top of their comrades below or collapsing flat onto their faces on the freezing ground.

Oliver ran forwards, slipping and staggering through potholes and around craters with his rifle cradled in his grasp. Mortar rounds blasted the frigid earth around him and sprayed rocks and stones into his face but he kept running because to turn back was to die. Tears streamed from his eyes and he both cried with fear and screamed in outrage as he powered forwards through the hellish battlefield, lifting his rifle to aim at whoever came at him from the writhing veils of smoke.

He saw figures like ghouls stalking toward him through the fog ahead, saw his comrades running ahead of him and firing at the enemy lines, their rifle shots snapping and cracking. And then, as though cut down with an invisible scythe, they toppled as one and tumbled into the dirt and the ice.

Oliver's brain registered the hellish cackling chatter of the enemy's machine guns and saw a scattering of bright flickering forks of fire spitting death toward him. Oliver shouted something unintelligible as he sprinted faster and took aim at a figure close to the guns. And then his chest shuddered as a salvo of bullets tore through him.

Oliver was lifted off his feet as the massive bullets shredded his lungs, smashed through his bones and tore chunks of flesh from his body as they passed through. The world spun and he landed flat on his back in the mud. Chunks of ice trickled down his neck as his unfired rifle slapped down alongside him.

Oliver blinked, not entirely sure what had happened. And then he tried to breath. Raw pain seethed through his chest but no air reached him. He tried to cry out in horror but no sound came from his throat as he coughed and choked and realized that he was drowning in his own blood. In terror and fear he clawed at his own chest and his hands came away thick with blood. Fresh tears tumbled from his eyes and he stared up into the bleak clouds above as the cries of mankind's hymn of war raged around him. His vision starred and then began to turn black as with the last vestiges of air in his lungs he screamed silently for the one person he wished dearly he could lay his eyes upon one last time.

His mother.

*

## BRIDGWATER, SOMERSET

*November 1916*

Pennie Barraclough sucked in a lungful of air and sat bolt upright in bed as though a bolt of electricity had surged through her chest. Her heart pounded as her eyes adjusted to the gloom of a winter's morning peering through the curtains of her bedroom.

She looked down beside her and saw her husband still deep in sleep.

Pennie felt cold seeping through her bones despite the warmth of the sheets, unease lying heavily across her shoulders as she stared across the room. Slowly, she climbed from the bed and walked to the bedroom door, unhooking her gown and slipping it over her shoulders as she walked out onto the landing. The stairs beckoned and she walked with unthinking reflex downstairs and into the hall, then turned and drifted almost dreamlike toward the front door.

As she reached out for the handle, she could see through the frosted panes of glass a figure standing on the other side of the door waiting for her. She flipped the latch and turned the handle, then opened the door toward her.

A waft of bitterly cold air swept into the hall, touched with the scent of early morning frost that enveloped her in a freezing embrace and seemed to reach into her very bones as she looked into the eyes of her unexpected visitor.

Oliver, her son, stood before her on the porch of their home. His face was splattered with a gruesome mess of mud, blood and dirt. He was wearing his full battle uniform, the material thickly smothered in mud and ice, and, as she stared at him, her stomach plunged in despair as she saw a half-dozen ragged bullet holes torn through his young body. Fresh blood soaked the coarse material of his uniform.

Pennie opened her mouth to speak but no sound came forth. The cold morning air seemed frigid and utterly silent as though time had come to a stop. She stared at her son, his brown eyes looking into hers, and Oliver smiled softly as though he were suddenly old and wise beyond his years. He slowly reached out toward her with one muddied hand and then faded from view until he vanished into the misty air before her eyes.

Pennie felt a sudden, wrenching loss as though her own life was being ripped from her and she sank down onto her knees on the porch.

She knew without a shadow of doubt that her Oliver had died.

# 2

# DEFENSE INTELLIGENCE ANALYSIS CENTER, JOINT BASE ANACOSTIA–BOLLING, WASHINGTON, DC

*Present day*

This would be the last time he would visit this place.

Douglas Ian Jarvis was flanked by a pair of security guards in an elevator that was making its way with an efficient hum up to the seventh floor of the DIAC building, the headquarters of the Defense Intelligence Agency. The producer of military intelligence for the Department of Defense, the DIA employed almost six thousand staff and worked on a budget that was largely shielded from congressional scrutiny. The DIA was more clandestine than other celebrated partner agencies such as the FBI or CIA, chiefly because it handled all intelligence that passed through the myriad of Pentagon departments via the ultra-secretive National Security Agency.

Doug Jarvis had seen much of that intelligence. He had begun his career serving with the US Marines in South East

Asia and later in both the Gulf Wars, before resigning his commission in order to serve his country on home soil. His chagrin at being unable to continue a field posting due to his advancing years had been replaced by a stoic patriotism as his increasing authority and experience peeled back layer after layer of military secrecy. In recent years, his work had unveiled a Pandora's box of extraordinary discoveries, many of which now languished under military protection in locations kept secret even from him.

Jarvis's last mission within the DIA had been to create a small but efficient department of investigators that were willing to scrutinize cases that other agencies rejected as *paranormal* or the work of fraudsters. He had relinquished the chance to take the DIA director's chair in favour of starting the new unit, and had hired a former United States Marines officer with whom he had served some years before. The fact that the said officer had been a drunken recluse at the time had not endeared him to the Joint Chiefs of Staff or the Pentagon, but the results he achieved had. In fact, they had been so spectacular that the CIA had begun taking a great interest in seizing the department's assets, and had eventually done so with customary zeal.

A congressional investigation into malpractice at the CIA, started eight months before by a Democrat senator in DC, had initiated a brutal manhunt by CIA agents desperate to conceal their own abuses of power. In the aftermath of the investigation's closure, Jarvis had seen his authority and security clearance revoked, the director of the CIA cleared of all charges via a Pentagon inquiry that nobody trusted and Jarvis's two best investigators forced to go underground for fear of assassination attempts. Put simply, everything had gone to hell in a hand-basket and that mightily pissed Jarvis off. So much so that he had spent the last six months collating evidence to clear his own name and that of his colleagues, all of it contained in an envelope in his jacket pocket that he fingered subconsciously.

For the last three months of his personal crusade, he had repeatedly been denied an audience with his former boss at the DIA. Hence, he had not expected to be summoned urgently to that very office this morning and was still none the wiser as to why. There was a fire under somebody's ass and Jarvis presumed he was about to be accused of lighting it. He ran a hand through his thick white hair and lifted his chin. Confidence was everything. *Semper fi*, as they used to say in the corps.

The elevator reached the top of its climb and Jarvis stepped out with his escort onto a carpeted corridor. A secretary looked up at them from behind her desk and pressed a button: Jarvis knew that it would illuminate a discreet light on the director's desk, alerting him to the arrival of his guest. The two guards took up flanking positions either side of the door to the DIA director's office. Jarvis tightened his tie before knocking.

'Enter.'

Jarvis walked into the office and was struck by the unexpected desire to bow. DIA Director Abraham Mitchell, a three-star general, sat behind a large desk, his burnished-mahogany skin glistening. With him were seated the Joint Chiefs of Staff, the senior officers from each of the services forming neat lines of gray hair and polished medals: Army,

Navy, Air Force and Marines. Alongside them were the JCOS Chairman and Vice-Chairman, and, most remarkably, the Director of the Central Intelligence Agency, General William Steel, the man directly responsible for Jarvis's demise. Between them there was enough brass to fit out an orchestra and enough authority to influence and perhaps even overrule the President himself.

'Good morning, gentlemen,' Jarvis said, deciding to leave the chip on his shoulder outside the room.

'Jarvis,' Mitchell rumbled, and gestured to the only remaining empty seat.

Jarvis sat down and was relieved to find that the chair wasn't wired to the mains for the amusement of the most powerful men in America. Even with his recently revoked authority, Jarvis would have been a small fish swimming in a shark tank.

'Thank you for coming, Doug,' said Admiral John Griffiths.

Jarvis felt a rush of gratitude toward the admiral for his unguarded familiarity, born of their working together in the past. The mood in the office changed instantly as the other chiefs took note of the admiral's tone. Only DCIA Steel retained a stony silence.

'No problem,' Jarvis replied. 'Why am I here?'

'Where are your people, Doug?' Mitchell asked.

'By my people, I suppose you mean Ethan Warner and Nicola Lopez?' Jarvis asked and was rewarded with a nod. 'I've been asking without success for an audience here for months. Now you drag me in here at a moment's notice. What's the deal?'

Mitchell turned his gaze to DCIA Steel. The podgy man, his face glowering with supressed rage, looked at Jarvis.

'We think your people are murdering CIA agents as an act of revenge,' he said. 'They're hunting them down one by one.'

Jarvis's jaw dropped. He could have anticipated any number of responses, but that was one he would never have seen coming. 'How many men are down? When did it happen?'

'Where are they?' Mitchell asked Jarvis, ignoring his questions. 'I mean, right now?'

'I don't know.'

'What do you mean you *don't know* where they are?' Admiral Griffiths was looking at Jarvis as though he had gone insane.

'They're not my assets now,' Jarvis said defensively. 'My agents felt that they needed to stay off the grid until they could figure out what the hell was going on. They went dark just as I was removed from my post. I haven't heard from either Warner or Lopez since.'

'You don't have a contact protocol?' the chief of the army asked.

'The last I heard from them they were being bombed by the National Guard,' Jarvis snapped at the chief, '*your* people dropping bombs on American citizens, in case you didn't know. There wasn't much time to arrange niceties, and, seeing as I was forcibly retired, how the hell would you expect them to contact me?'

'Your relationship with Warner was close,' Mitchell replied. 'It is reasonable to assume that he might try to contact you.'

'He hasn't,' Jarvis said, and then looked around the room. 'You all think he's behind the murders?'

'As you've pointed out, he has a motive,' Mitchell said. 'Revenge.'

'I take it everybody else in this room knows what happened six months ago in Idaho?' Jarvis asked.

Mitchell nodded. 'I briefed the Chiefs about the unfortunate turn of events.'

'Is that what you're calling betrayal and treason?' Jarvis asked.

'What were your people doing in Idaho?' the chief of the army demanded. 'There's nothing there.'

Jarvis let a brittle smile crack across his face.

'There's nothing there *now*,' he corrected. 'The CIA had an operation running up there, using National Guard assets to protect it. Warner and Lopez were sent to investigate a series of murders and realized that whatever was killing people wasn't *human*. It turned out the CIA had been conducting experiments, for want of a better word, under the banner of a top-secret program called MK-ULTRA, and something got out.'

'*Something?*' the chief of the army echoed.

'A species not quite like us,' Jarvis said without elaborating. 'Ultimately, the entire operation was destroyed in an attempt to remove evidence, and that included removing Ethan and Lopez.'

'This is ridiculous,' the chief of the army snapped. 'I'm aware of no such operation by Guard assets. I've served my country for over forty years and I've never encountered this kind of conspiracy crap.'

Jarvis glared at DCIA Steel. 'Will you tell him, or do I have to?'

Steel kept his beady black eyes focused on the table top as he spoke.

'A paramilitary team from the 24th Special Tactics Squadron was deployed to destroy a CIA facility in Idaho. When the operation failed, the National Guard was deployed to blow the site using A-10 Tankbusters. The strike was recorded as a training exercise, and the aftermath as a gas explosion in an abandoned mine. An exclusion zone remains around the site under the guise of public safety.'

The chief of the army stared at Steel in horror. 'Jesus Christ, what the hell has been going on here?'

'The persecution of patriots,' Jarvis growled, 'by elements of the CIA trying to cover up abuses of power going back decades.'

'Warner and Lopez escaped the aerial attack, and now they're taking their revenge, and killing CIA agents?' the chief of the Marines presumed.

'They escaped,' Mitchell confirmed, 'and have been on the run ever since. The CIA managed to cover up events in Idaho but was looking to tie up a few loose ends.'

'Those loose ends,' Jarvis said, 'being my two agents. 'I've conducted a six-month investigation into CIA corruption; corruption that has led to the deaths of several US servicemen and civilians.'

Jarvis produced from his jacket pocket the envelope containing his research. He laid it face down on the table, tantalizingly close to each man and yet just beyond their reach.

'Your investigation is meaningless,' Steel pointed out, 'conducted without authority or oversight.'

'People who have served this agency with distinction are now being forced to live in hiding for fear of assassination attempts,' Jarvis replied, and looked each of the JCOS in the eye. 'Patriots, people whom you would be proud to be associated, hounded by operatives who swore to protect them, and not just my people either. At the same time as the events in Idaho, three members of the Government Accountability Office in DC were attacked by CIA assets, two of them fatally.'

A moment passed as the JCOS exchanged glances.

'What's the link with Warner and Lopez?' asked the admiral.

'Ethan Warner's sister, Natalie, was one of the GAO targets,' Jarvis said. 'Natalie Warner moved departments afterward, but the closing of the investigation removed her as a threat to the CIA, along with her colleague Ben Consiglio, who was also the victim of an attempted homicide. However, what the CIA doesn't know is that both of these individuals can identify the CIA agents in question, the men responsible for the murders.'

The JCOS looked at each other again and General Steel glared at Jarvis, but it was Director Mitchell who spoke.

'You're sure?' he asked Jarvis. 'And you're sure that these individuals can be tied to the murders?'

'One hundred per cent sure,' Jarvis replied without hesitation. 'We were even able to obtain genetic material that can be matched to them should they be brought to trial.'

'You investigated the site?' General Steel asked in disgust. 'You infiltrated a federal crime scene and—'

'I was on the scene when the murders occurred,' Jarvis snapped. 'You don't think I wouldn't have taken any useful evidence with me?'

The chief of the army shook his head.

'There would be utter outrage if this got out,' he murmured. 'Our capacity for unhindered intelligence-gathering would be blown out of the water by Congress.'

'The ensuing court cases,' Jarvis confirmed, 'would result in virtually every major defense initiative in this country being hauled out into the open for congressional scrutiny. Our ability to make hard choices to defend our nation would be compromised beyond repair. It would, essentially, be the end of covert intelligence-gathering in the continental United States.'

'All the more reason,' Steel insisted, 'that this remain a closed affair.'

The JCOS remained silent for a long moment, before Admiral Griffiths gestured to Jarvis's envelope.

'What's in there?' he asked.

Jarvis opened the envelope and let a series of pictures fan out onto Mitchell's desk.

'Copies of CCTV footage in Washington, DC, internal cameras at the GAO and several images shot by Natalie Warner from her vehicle traveling in the Capitol. Each shows one or other of the two men responsible for CIA-sanctioned killings of congressional aides and American civilians who were survivors of the original MK-ULTRA program in the 1970s. These images, along with the genetic evidence obtained from the crime scenes, are enough to convict beyond all reasonable doubt those responsible.'

The JCOS leaned forward, examining the pictures, as Jarvis leaned back in his chair and waited. DCIA Steel scowled at him as he gestured to the photographs.

'They're nothing,' he said, 'pictures taken by amateurs that wouldn't hold up in any court. They could have been working in unrelated projects in DC.'

'True,' Jarvis replied, finally looking at the DCIA. 'And the blood sample retrieved from the site of the murder of GAO worker Guy Rikard, that will match the blood of a CIA agent and assassin you call Mr. Wilson?'

Steel glared at Jarvis but said nothing. The JCOS stared at the pictures in silence.

'Warner and Lopez are not behind this,' Jarvis said. 'They're both patriots, always have been. They wouldn't kill: they'd want to apprehend, to see people brought to trial.' Jarvis glanced at Steel. 'Especially you.'

'They're liabilities,' Steel shot back. 'Warner is a former Marine officer who was virtually a hobo when Jarvis hired him. Lopez is a former DC detective with known loyalty issues. These people are exactly the kind of rogue agents we all fear.'

Jarvis peered at Steel with interest. 'You're getting quite hot under the collar there, William. Wondering if you're next, are you?'

'This is ridiculous,' General Steel raged at the JCOS. 'All of this is true but all of it's been twisted to fit this man's fantasies of a conspiracy. The CIA was cleared of all wrongdoing by an independent Pentagon investigation.'

'Which was guided by the CIA,' Jarvis growled back at him. 'I offered my services in order to expose what had really happened but, surprise-surprise, I was removed from my post by your people. That investigation was toothless before it even began.'

The JCOS all seemed to sit back in their seats as the chief of the Marines cast a glance in Mitchell's direction.

'How many investigations have Warner and Lopez conducted for the DIA, in total?'

'Four,' Mitchell replied. 'All have been spectacularly successful, although major questions have been raised in the past about the exposure of civilians to classified projects during the course of those investigations.'

Admiral Griffiths looked at Jarvis. 'Warner and Lopez, can you bring them back in? We need them in custody.'

'You need their *help*,' Jarvis countered. 'They're not killers.'

'It could be anybody,' the chief of the army pointed out, 'given that the CIA has ruffled so many feathers over the years. An escaped prisoner from one of their overseas black prisons, perhaps? But would they have a trail they could follow?'

Jarvis shook his head. 'They'll be in the black budget. There won't be a paper trail, so it has to be somebody with inside knowledge.'

Jarvis knew that the United States Department of Defense concealed within its black budget almost $60 billion of funding, a tremendous sum in addition to the annual defense budget. MK-ULTRA's various experiments and programs were a tiny drop in this vast financial ocean and that was no doubt how the CIA had kept such a perfect veil over its operations: the paper and money trail was so well hidden that finding it would have been like trying to track an animal burrowing underground by sight alone, at night, from the air.

'Do Warner and Lopez know anything about MK-ULTRA?' asked the chief of the Marines.

'No,' Jarvis replied, 'at least they didn't when I last heard from them.'

'Either way,' Steel said, 'this isn't something that can be resolved through the courts or ever reach the public domain.'

Admiral Griffiths rubbed his temples wearily.

'We don't have any other means to properly investigate and expose whoever is responsible for targeting these CIA agents without attracting too much attention.'

Jarvis smiled. 'Yes, we do. I can task Warner and Lopez to do it.'

The JCOS eyes flew wide as one as they stared at Jarvis.

'Are you serious?' Steel uttered.

Jarvis gathered his thoughts. 'There is one person who may have sufficient motivation to actively hunt down a specific set of CIA agents.'

DCIA Steel sat bolt upright in his seat and pointed a fat finger at Jarvis.

'That's enough,' he growled. 'You're speculating.'

'Am I?' Jarvis challenged the director. 'You know damned well who I'm talking about, don't you?'

'The CIA is perfectly capable of handling it,' he blustered.

'Doesn't seem that way,' Jarvis mused out loud. 'Several agents down in just a few days, I'm presuming?' he said to Mitchell. 'I last requested a meeting with DDIA Mitchell about ten days ago, and was turned down flat in the usual manner. Now I'm sitting here. These agents must have been killed in quick succession to have got me here at all.'

The Chairman of the JCOS directed a stern gaze at DCIA Steel. 'In total, six agents have been killed. Are you aware of who might be responsible for these slayings?'

Steel slid behind a wall of national security. 'I am not at liberty to answer that question, sir.'

The Chairman slapped a hand down on Mitchell's desk. 'This is ridiculous. You've come here for help and now you're refusing to supply us with information?'

DDIA Mitchell spoke softly.

'The individual in question is an American citizen, abducted several years ago,' he informed them. 'It would seem likely, given Director Steel's reticence, that the individual's disappearance was orchestrated and that they may have suffered at the hands of MK-ULTRA operatives or assets in the field. Her name is Joanna Defoe.'

Jarvis chose his words with care as he spoke.

'She was Ethan Warner's fiancée, hence the assumed motive. Disappeared from the Gaza Strip four years ago,' Jarvis confirmed. 'The abduction was never solved, but she represented a high-profile critic of government policy overseas and of the unaccountability of the intelligence community. Silencing Joanna and preventing her from investigating the CIA could have both been achieved by abducting her.'

DCIA Steel squirmed uncomfortably as Jarvis addressed the JCOS.

'What evidence do you have that this individual you refer to could be capable of such acts, or that they're even on the loose?' General Steel demanded.

'Footage retrieved from Project Watchman,' Jarvis explained. 'Our satellites spotted Joanna during an Israeli incursion into Gaza City. Her abductors were killed but Joanna disappeared.'

'I can see why the CIA disagreed with your policies on civilian exposure to military hardware,' the chief of the army pointed out. 'Project Watchman is one of our most prized resources and classified COSMIC.'

'Ethan's exposure to Watchman resulted in him being able to thwart a serious attempt to enslave our government to the machinations of a powerful corporation,' Jarvis explained. 'Believe me, he's the best man for this job.'

'Which may not be what we want,' Mitchell rumbled. 'Ethan Warner has a habit of leaving a trail of destruction behind him. Tenacious does not even begin to describe this guy.'

Jarvis opened his hands in defense.

'It's all of you that have put him in this position,' he said reasonably. 'If you give me the resources I need then I can set him on a course to resolve the problem. Right now, all I need is for the CIA to pull their people out and let us get started. Can you do that?'

The JCOS looked at each other in silence and then turned to look at the CIA's director. Finally, General Steel spoke.

'I can.'

'Good,' Jarvis replied. 'All watch-teams, surveillance both human and electronic and flag references in the intelligence database must be removed. Where was the last CIA operative murdered and when?'

General Steel ground his teeth in his jaw. 'Two days ago, in New York City. Aaron Lymes, a retired operative who was based near Gaza City at the time of Miss Defoe's abduction. Police and FBI are on hold until our say-so.'

Jarvis looked at Mitchell. 'I'll need my department back up and running along with all previously revoked security clearances and a four-man field team to accompany me to New York.' He glanced at Steel with a smile. 'Just in case.'

Mitchell nodded slowly. 'It will be done.'

Jarvis stood up and straightened his jacket.

'I'll find a way to locate Ethan and Lopez and get them assigned to this. It's in their interests as well as our own for this situation to be resolved, and, if I know Ethan, he'll be following the same trail we are. Now, if you'll excuse me?'

Jarvis turned for the door but was held back by General Steel's voice.

'There is just one more thing, Mr. Jarvis?'

Jarvis turned and looked down at the DCIA, who was staring at him once again with his cruel little eyes.

'In the interests of national security, I insist that if Joanna Defoe is apprehended by your people, that she be immediately passed to the CIA's custody.'

Jarvis shook his head. 'That's not part of any deal that I—'

'This isn't a negotiation,' Steel snapped. 'You want to keep Ethan Warner and Nicola Lopez free from prosecution for their exposure to classified material then you hand over everything you find to me, or I'll make sure Joanna Defoe spends the rest of her life rotting in a Supermax facility. Use

Warner and Lopez to find her if you must, then make damned sure that she ends up at Langley.'

Jarvis looked at Mitchell for support, but the DDIA shook his head.

'It's a trade, Doug,' he said. 'Joanna Defoe likely knows far too much about MK-ULTRA and its methods and could expose it at any time. This has to stay out of the public eye. Find Warner and Lopez and keep this all quiet.'

Jarvis clenched his fists at his sides, but managed a stiff nod before he turned and stalked from the office.

# 3

# GRAND CENTRAL STATION, EAST 42ND STREET, NEW YORK CITY

Crowds.

Thousands of people rushed to and fro in a miasma of coats, hats, legs and commingled voices that rose up into the soaring ceiling of the station amid shafts of sunlight beaming down through the iconic windows far above. Countless footfalls hammered out a symphony of mankind on the move on the vast polished flags, all on their own personal journey and yet surrounded.

Ethan Warner had never in his life felt so alone.

He leaned against a towering pillar on one side of the central atrium, watching the milling crowds. It was a strange sensation, to be a citizen in one's home country and yet feeling like an imposter no matter where he traveled. Ethan felt as though he were standing in a stranger's house or in a foreign country without a passport, not inside the main station of one of America's largest cities.

Staying off the grid, away from any kind of observation or transaction that would allow those in power to locate and apprehend him, was harder than Ethan could ever have imagined. He had once read that many thousands of people disappear every year in America, simply vanishing from existence. Although some were probably the victims of crimes such as homicide, the majority just got up and left their homes, lives, jobs and families, never to return. To do so wasn't necessarily the hardest part: staying hidden was what tested even the most determined of absconders. The majority of runaways turned up sooner or later; sometimes living in different states or even different countries and having made errors that exposed them: habits and hobbies, loose talk or even just the mention of a hometown or friend that placed them elsewhere in the country. Others were spotted as a result of campaigns by concerned relatives. Some just couldn't stay away and returned of their own accord. But a small minority vanished and managed to maintain entirely new lives, never once returning to those they left behind.

Insider knowledge helped, but common sense was also a valuable weapon and Ethan knew how to hide in plain sight. Wearing a hoodie would attract attention from innocent civilians fearing a mugging and suspicious cops sensing the chance of an arrest, so attempting to conceal his face was out of bounds. This would normally expose him to the ever-watching eye of government agencies. His eyes flicked up to myriad watching cameras that scanned the crowds, but he knew that any facial-recognition software being run by the NSA or the CIA would be unable to identify him beneath his simple but effective disguise.

Most of the high-tech facial-recognition programs used anchor-points, features on the face like eye and eyebrow position, the shape of the ear, width of the jaw and so on. Ethan had donned sunglasses with light-sensitive lenses that obscured his eyes. He had grown his hair longer, letting it cover his ears. He shaved rarely, thick stubble concealing his jawline and chin, and he had used a dye to speckle his hair with streaks of gray that aged him by a decade. He wore faded jeans and a T-shirt emblazoned with the name of some rock band he'd never heard of and a jacket that was a size too large, concealing his physique.

In short, he looked like a middle-aged, slightly overweight dropout: anonymous.

Ethan had accumulated extensive knowledge of what it took to remain hidden in the modern world, not through his own experience but through his search for a woman who quite likely lived as he did now: off the grid, anonymous. Joanna Defoe, his fiancée, had vanished from Gaza City, Palestine, four years previously. Ethan had believed her dead, but just a year ago had seen a remarkable piece of footage captured by an Israeli drone showing her alive, escaping an attack on Palestinian militants by Israeli forces. That footage, now almost two years old, had started him on a new mission to locate her, much to the chagrin of his family and friends. He had been making some progress when everything had gone to hell and he'd found himself on the run with his partner.

A young man weaved his way toward Ethan through the crowds. He wore a Yankees baseball cap over dark hair, a long winter coat with a high collar and carried a large backpack slung over his shoulder that further concealed his shape. He held a cellphone to his ear, shielding his features from the cameras high above as he moved to stand next to Ethan. A faint five-o'clock shadow was visible against the dark skin of his jaw as Ethan looked down at him.

'You need a shave, son.'

A pair of dark, exotic almond eyes peered up at him from beneath the cap, going purposefully boss-eyed as the young man spoke with a remarkably feminine accent into the cellphone.

'We'll be there.'

Ethan heard a tinny sounding reply from the cell, and then the young man shut it off and slipped it into a pocket before looking up at him.

'Thanks, *Dad*,' Nicola Lopez uttered. 'Start acting like a good parent and take my bag.'

Lopez let her backpack fall from her shoulder and thump down onto Ethan's foot. He smiled as he picked the bag up. 'Insolent juvenile. I'll send you to bed with no dinner.'

'I'd rather go hungry than eat your cooking. How much longer are we going to keep this crap up? You should have seen the ticket man's face when he got a good look at me. Probably thought I was a lady-boy.'

'It's enough to fool the cameras,' Ethan replied evenly. 'That's what they'll be using to search for us, narrowing our location down before moving agents in, and the resolution won't be enough to expose you. We keep this up, we stay off their radar. Once Jarvis gets in touch, we'll hopefully be able to quit with the disguises.'

'It's been six months,' Lopez grumbled, rubbing at the make-up she'd used to mimic stubble. 'He's been retired off the DIA, there's nothing he can do for us.'

'He'll come through,' Ethan insisted. 'He always has.'

'With conditions,' Lopez pointed out. 'There'll be something that he wants in return. There always is.'

Ethan didn't reply. Fact was, Lopez was right, but, as they stood, almost anything was better than living the way they were now: endless nights spent in run-down motels; eating in crumbling diners on the edge of obscure towns; and running with no clear idea of where they needed to go. Maybe living that way worked for crime-fighting loners in novels, but in real life it was an impossible existence. After six months of following dead-end leads and struggling to find money and digs as they wandered aimlessly across the United States, finally a solid lead had presented itself.

In rural Wisconsin, a thirty-six-year-old man had been murdered in an apparent robbery gone-wrong. Stripped of his possessions, the man's unfortunate demise might have remained a footnote in the records of county police if not for one major factor: the man was identified as a former employee of the Central Intelligence Agency.

The murder hit the news state-wide, having gotten out before the CIA could close the lid on what had happened. Before the familiar veil of silence had settled on the case, Ethan and Lopez had seen it on the news and thus been alerted to a possible thread that they could follow in what felt like an endless and equally hopeless quest to clear their names.

'You got a rent?' he asked her.

'It's a motel across the river in Williamsburg,' she replied. 'Not perfect, but we're not going to get anything we can afford on the Lower East Side or Manhattan.'

Ethan shook his head. 'Don't worry about it; right now, the more anonymous our accommodation is, the better.'

Ethan followed Lopez out of the station and onto the crowded streets of the city. Heavy traffic, swathes of pedestrians and a wall of noise filled the air as Ethan craned his neck back and looked up at the buildings soaring up toward the cold sky above.

Lopez turned to him on the crowded sidewalk. 'You think we can track her down here in New York?'

Ethan nodded as an image of his long-vanished fiancée drifted like a ghost haunting the deepest recesses of his mind.

'The trail led here,' he said. 'If she's following the same information that we are, New York's a great place to disappear and get some work done at the same time. Nothing like eight or nine million people to make it easy to hide in plain sight.'

Fact was, the leads that Ethan was following were tenuous in the extreme.

Six months previously, he had approached his sister, Natalie, after learning that Joanna Defoe was alive. Asking her if she would be willing to use her influence within the Government Accountability Office during a congressional investigation into CIA corruption, Natalie had gone on to uncover evidence of an immense covert operation named MK-ULTRA, used to abuse unwitting American citizens both within homeland borders and abroad. Whatever it was, MK-ULTRA was definitely illegal and represented the core issue that had landed Ethan and Lopez in their current mess.

Joanna Defoe's name had been connected with the program, as had her long deceased father. Harrison Defoe had worked in the Far East as a translator during the Vietnam War and had suddenly gone on the rampage in Singapore, shooting dead several leading opponents to the US intervention in the conflict. Her father had served time in a Singapore jail for his crime and had become a vocal opponent and critic of the CIA afterward. He represented the likely source of Joanna's determination to root out corruption at government level as a journalist.

That same determination, it now seemed, was what had gotten her abducted. If they could find Joanna, she might possess enough evidence to expose MK-ULTRA and clear all of their names.

'What's the next move?' Lopez asked, as they walked.

Ethan scanned the thousands of faces and the dense city skyline.

'We start digging and hope that we get lucky.'

# 4

# LOWER EAST SIDE, MANHATTAN, NEW YORK CITY

'If it's going down, it'll be within the next ten minutes.'

The car in which Detective Karina Thorne sat was parked by the sidewalk on the corner of Broadway and Pike, looking across the intersection toward a Pay-Go cash-checking store where a trickle of customers were filing in and out, many of them with envelopes in their hands.

Karina kept her hands in her lap, preventing herself from checking her sidearm for the twentieth time. Anxiety twisted her stomach muscles and her gaze flicked back and forth from the store to her wing mirrors, catching a glimpse of her long dark hair pinned back in a ponytail. Her features were a little too stern to be called attractive, the line of her mouth thin and her jaw a little too wide.

'Relax,' came a voice from beside her. 'No need to get twitchy until something happens.'

Jake Donovan, a twenty-year veteran of the New York Police Department, glanced sideways at her with a wink and a smile. Donovan was in his mid-fifties but could still bench-press two-fifty for five and was surrounded by an aura of competence that commanded complete loyalty from his team. Karina let some of her tension out in a long sigh.

'It's a big deal if it goes down, is all,' she replied.

'They're all a big deal,' Donovan said, 'especially when we catch them in the act.'

Karina nodded but did not share her boss's confidence.

Over the past two months, several major bank heists had rocked the east coast from Pennsylvania right up to Maine. It was considered almost impossible to hit a major bank successfully these days: accounts at all American banks were insured by the Federal Deposit Insurance Corporation, bringing such heists under federal jurisdiction and involving the FBI. Federal Sentencing Guidelines mandated long prison terms and there was no parole in the federal prison system. Coupled with biometric markers on bank cases – dye-emitting sensors that rendered stolen cash useless – the massive resources of law enforcement and the involvement of the media in pursuing and catching violent gangs ensured that few such criminal enterprises succeeded for long.

But the gang that had hit four armoured trucks in New Hampshire and Connecticut were a different breed. Wily, patient and yet supremely violent, their genius was a blend of deception and simplicity. They wore disguises, but not just clothes. Instead, they wore complex, expensive latex headpieces and gloves most often seen in movies, that completely altered their features and even their skin color. Using these skillfully crafted latex masks, no law-enforcement agency yet had been able to identify any of the gang members. All of the men were of similar height and build and conducted themselves in a manner that seemed to suggest a military background. But with the United States having been on a war footing for over a decade and with the heists occurring across several states, the number of disgruntled former infantrymen who could be suspects ran into the tens of thousands.

In short, it had been the perfect crime. No evidence. No leads.

Until now. An informant had tipped Donovan off a week previously that the gang was rumored to have moved even farther south, losing themselves in New York's population with a plan to hit one of the countless cash-checking centers located all over the city. A further tip put the target as the Pay-Go on Broadway. It was a good target, sitting on a broad intersection with multiple egress routes across to New Jersey, up into Midtown and Harlem or out across the East River to Queens and Long Island. If the gang hit either the Pay-Go or the armoured truck due to make its daily collection and were able to give police the slip, then they would have multiple opportunities to transfer vehicles, split up on foot or just hunker down somewhere and wait for the dust to settle.

A car pulled in ahead of them, a dark blue Prius with three occupants: one woman, one man and a young girl in a child seat. The man got out and kissed both the woman and the child goodbye. The Prius pulled away and the man walked to Karina's car, opened the rear door and climbed in.

'We need more units,' he said as he closed the door.

Tom Ross was a young but dedicated service officer who had joined the department in his late teens and was now

Karina's partner. A firearms and forensics officer, he'd made detective by his twenty-sixth birthday, an extraordinary achievement by any standards. In the rear seat alongside Tom sat Glen Ryan, Karina's boyfriend of the past five years. Glen was a former soldier who had joined the NYPD two years previously, all buzz-cut hair and square-jawed efficiency. It was like dating the Terminator, minus the sense of humor. Iraq and Afghanistan had drained Glen of his zest for life and he viewed most of humanity with a disappointed disdain.

'We haven't got the resources,' Donovan replied to Tom, 'not with the presidential debates going on.'

The city was host to the incumbent president and his challenger's first live television debate in the run-up to the elections, and half of the goddamned force was on high alert at the Hofstra University on Long Island. The fact that the most wanted gang of thieves on the east coast had possibly chosen today to hit a target in Manhattan, during a period of reduced police activity and after a massive reduction in law-enforcement manpower, wasn't hard to understand.

'And it's based on a tip-off and a hunch,' Glen added, 'not exactly rock-solid grounds for deploying the entire department, Tom.'

Tom Ross shrugged and checked his firearm. 'These aren't Boy Scouts we're up against. Five cops against four psychopathic thieves isn't my kind of odds.'

'You should've seen Basra,' Glen began, 'you'd have—'

'All right, Glen,' Donovan cut him off, 'we've heard it all before.' The old man looked across at Karina. 'Is Neville in position?'

Karina keyed a microphone concealed low under the dashboard. 'You ready, Nev?'

The voice of Neville Jackson, an African-American cop and the team's fifth member, came back over the radio loud and clear. '*I'm on Grand. If they run north, I'll pick them up.*'

Karina scanned the Pay-Go one more time, and then Glen tapped her on the shoulder. 'Here comes the armoured truck.'

Karina resisted the urge to glance over her shoulder at the traffic flowing down Broadway, instead looking down at her wing mirror to see a brief glimpse of a dark blue Freightliner easing its way toward the intersection.

'We got any lookers?' Karina asked.

All three men shook their heads. Nobody had been seen acting suspiciously, no lingerers on the intersection watching the Pay-Go. Karina searched for parked vehicles or motorcycles running up as the cash truck approached, but nothing untoward was happening.

'Maybe they got wise to us and took off,' Tom hazarded.

It was possible, Karina reflected. A gang as methodical and experienced as the one they sought might have found a way to discreetly observe the Pay-Go and noticed the unremarkable gray sedan parked a hundred yards up from the intersection. At the least, they would have monitored the Pay-Go's daily pickups. Most all armoured cash vehicles these days ran varying routes to avoid having regular daily collection times, all of which helped to confuse potential heists, but, with Pay-Go stores, there had to be at least one daily collection to avoid the vaults overfilling. A patient gang would wait for the right moment to strike.

'That's a big truck,' Tom said.

The Freightliner pulled into the sidewalk alongside the Pay-Go and one of the armed personnel aboard climbed out, methodically locking the door behind him as the driver waited with the vehicle.

'What's the truck's position on the round?' Glen asked.

'Fourteenth pickup,' Donovan replied without hesitation. 'Average pickup is worth about a quarter million bucks.'

'Three and a half million,' Karina said. 'Well worth hitting, if you've got a plan.'

'They'll have to hurry up,' Glen said. 'Courier will be out of the store real quick, and, once he's back aboard, there's no way they can reach the cash.'

Armoured trucks were notoriously tough, and the drivers never had access to the money inside. They simply transferred the aluminum bank-cases into the vehicle. The cases were later retrieved at a secure depot.

Karina watched as the door to the Pay-Go opened and the armed man walked back out with a steel-gray cash box handcuffed to his left wrist. He strode into the cold, bright sunshine, toward the Freightliner's side door, as the driver leaned forward to press a button to unlock the external cash-box door.

Karina knew the drill. The door would unlock. The guard would open it and insert the case into a locking mechanism, half in and half out of the vehicle. Secured, he would then uncuff himself and push the steel case fully inside, before shutting the door and climbing aboard.

There was no access to the cash from the vehicle cab.

There were no other access doors, no other way to get inside.

'It's not going down,' Tom said. 'He's already at the door.'

Karina saw the guard disappear from sight as he reached the armoured truck, but she could see his reflection in the windows of the Pay-Go as he reached out for the door and slid it back to reveal a steel cage. He reached down, lifted the case and inserted it into the dock.

'It's off,' Glen agreed. 'They can't hit them now.'

Karina was about to reply when a screaming engine howled past them down Broadway. She turned her head as a huge, battered old Kenworth truck thundered through the traffic and across the intersection, black smoke pouring from its exhaust stacks.

Karina's jaw dropped in disbelief as she realized what was about to happen.

'They're not hitting the store!' she yelled. 'They're hitting the truck!'

'Get out of the car!' Donovan bellowed. 'It's on!'

In a moment of time frozen in Karina's mind, the Kenworth roared through a red light across the intersection and, with a deafening crash of rending metal and shattering glass, it crashed into the parked armoured truck like a missile through an eggshell.

# 5

Karina grabbed her door handle and leaped from the car as the Freightliner was hurled across the sidewalk amid a shower of splintering plastic and glass that sparkled in the bright morning sunshine. The immense mass of the charging Kenworth lifted the Freightliner momentarily off its tires before smashing it aside.

'Cover the left!' Donovan shouted. 'I'll block the right!'

Karina, Glen and Tom all ran down Broadway as vehicles screeched to a halt and pedestrians hurled themselves clear of the two massive vehicles.

The Freightliner's tires hit the sidewalk and squealed as it was smashed to the right and spun out of control. It plunged through a fire hydrant and came to rest alongside the intersection amid a fountain of high-pressure water that sprayed down across the street. The chassis was twisted beneath the vehicle where the Kenworth had struck it, the axles warped, and the metal body of the truck had been ripped open like sharp metal leaves. From the split side of the vehicle spilled a dozen or so aluminum cases, the cage within ripped apart by the tremendous force of the impact.

The Kenworth plowed onward and smashed into the Pay-Go store, the broad windows shattering as half the vehicle plunged into the building to a crescendo of screams from within. As the Kenworth came to rest with white smoke billowing from the cab and the hood buried inside the store, Karina saw the flailing body of the guard spin through the air and land on the hood of a Mercury that screeched to a halt outside the Pay-Go. The body slid down the hood and landed with a dull thump on the asphalt below.

Donovan screamed into his radio as they ran. 'All units, robbery in progress, corner of Broadway and Pike, request back-up immediately!'

Karina dropped one hand instinctively to her sidearm as the four officers sprinted toward the Pay-Go. Karina dodged past pedestrians who had stopped to stare at the terrific impact, her pistol held low and her thumb fingering the safety catch as she ran.

'Take the store!' Donovan shouted at her. 'Glen, Tom, the Kenworth. I'll cover the cash truck!'

Karina dashed out across the intersection, the traffic frozen as though immobile as a fountain of white foamy water sprayed up into the air near the cash truck and thick, oily smoke smouldered from within the Pay-Go store.

She switched the safety catch off on her pistol but kept the weapon low as she slowed, the Kenworth's rear wheels pinned a few inches off the sidewalk and spinning slowly. The smell of gasoline and burning rubber tainted the air as she saw figures in the smoke hurrying out of the Pay-Go and covering their faces with their hands.

'Weapon!'

Karina heard the cry, Tom Ross's voice, just as the clattering of an automatic rifle crashed out from the far side of the crashed Kenworth. Karina changed direction to see a man in a latex mask firing three-round bursts at her colleagues as they dove for cover behind the vehicles crowding the intersection.

Karina aimed without conscious thought and fired at the man, the bullets puncturing the fractured windows of the Pay-Go as around her she heard the screams of pedestrians dashing for cover into shops and behind vehicles.

The man ducked down, turned and fired back in one smooth motion. Karina hurled herself down onto the asphalt and rolled behind the ruined Kenworth as rounds crunched into the chassis and sprayed sparks onto the cold air. The vehicles on the intersection began reversing wildly away from the sudden and unexpected gunfight as panicked civilians struggled to escape the crossfire, their engines wailing above the cacophony. Karina covered her head as another salvo of shots battered the Kenworth, rounds zipping past her head toward pedestrians cowering in a nearby service alley. Chunks of brickwork sprayed onto the sidewalk as the shots ricocheted away into the distance. Karina rolled back out and aimed again at the gunman, firing double-handed at the largest target she could find, his torso.

The gunman's rifle spun from his grasp as Karina's second shot hit the vehicle beside him and he whirled aside in surprise, slamming into the rear of the crashed Kenworth with an audible clang of bone against metal. Karina saw him go down, and then ducked as a fresh wave of bullets smashed across the Pay-Go beside her.

A pale gray Ford F-150 pickup screamed toward her as it skidded in alongside the Freightliner, and a hail of bullets sprayed across the front of the Pay-Go as two men lying in the back of the vehicle opened up with assault rifles.

'Jesus Christ!' Glen yelled from nearby. 'We need back-up!'

Karina remained flat on the sidewalk, unwilling to take on two assault weapons with her meager 9mm pistol. She heard shouts and the metallic clang of what she assumed were aluminum cases being hurled into the pickup, and then suddenly the vehicle screeched past her in a cloud of burning rubber as it accelerated away down Broadway toward the southeast.

Karina scrambled out of sight as the two men in the back fired randomly, spraying the intersection with gunfire as the truck swerved between stranded vehicles and accelerated away.

She scrambled to her feet as the shooting stopped and sprinted instinctively for their car as the sound of approaching sirens howled through the streets. Donovan shouted at them from where he stood beside the ruined Freightliner.

'Corner them on the bridge! I'll direct units in from across the river!'

Karina reached her vehicle and yanked the door open, Tom and Glen close by as they piled into the rear of the car. Karina hit the gas and swerved out across the intersection and back east.

'Vehicle in pursuit,' Glen snapped with military efficiency into the radio. 'Suspects heading east on Delancey for the river.'

Karina looked up ahead and saw the truck swerving between slower moving vehicles all heading for the Williamsburg Bridge.

'They're taking the lane for Brooklyn,' Karina said.

The truck was heading for the outside, southernmost lane of the bridge that excited into Brooklyn and turned south.

'Christ, are they insane?' Glen said. 'They'll never get across before we close the bridge off.'

Karina knew that the police in Williamsburg and Brooklyn would already have been alerted by Donovan to the truck's location, and squad cars would converge on the four lanes of traffic exiting east off the bridge. She glanced down at the cold gray water of the East River as they approached.

The bridge was mostly encased in steel girders and mesh, protecting the six central lanes of traffic and the metro. But the outside lanes were exposed, just a low concrete wall with a steel rail between the traffic and the plunge into the bitter East River far below.

'They're going for the water,' she said with clairvoyant certainty.

'No way,' Tom argued, 'it's too far to drop. They won't make it.'

The pickup accelerated past the traffic slowly climbing up onto the bridge, barging past a family car as it fought its way forward. Karina slipped past the same vehicle a few moments later as the city beside them dropped away and vanished as they drove out across the churning waves below.

'No boats beneath us,' Glen yelled, peering down through the rear window. 'That's not their play.'

Karina frowned in confusion as she steered the vehicle in pursuit of the flatbed. 'This isn't right. They haven't planned their escape.'

Glen didn't reply as Karina fought to pass a lumbering four-by-four blocking the lane ahead. Karina hit the switch for the lights and sirens and instantly the vehicle swerved aside to let them through.

In the same instant, a crackle of gunfire clattered across the steel girders and beams of the bridge around them as their quarry opened fire again.

'Shit!' Karina yelled as she flinched.

Karina slammed her foot down on the gas and swerved the car protectively in front of the four-by-four that they had just passed. The car accelerated wildly, and she heard both Glen and Tom shout in alarm as the car bore down on the pickup. A salvo of shots zipped off the bodywork as she struggled to maintain control, and a round shattered the windshield into a frenzied web of splintered glass.

Karina, her boot slammed against the throttle, saw in a brief moment the rear of the flatbed and the two men lying in it, and then they vanished as the splintered windshield buckled.

With a crash of metal and crumpling plastic, her car slammed into the rear of the pickup. The pickup swerved violently to one side and crashed into the concrete barrier before the wheels locked up in a cloud of blue smoke as the front axle collapsed under the impact. The pickup skidded sideways and then its wheels gripped again and it flipped up and over, rolling through the air as the two men in the rear were hurled clear.

Karina instinctively hit the brakes and swerved to one side to avoid hitting the outside wall of the bridge. Her fenders smashed into the inner wall and scraped along it in a shower of bright sparks as, through the opposite window, she glimpsed the truck slam down and roll over, spilling aluminum cases out over the railings and down toward the river below. The car shuddered as it skidded to a halt sideways across the lane, the truck barely fifteen yards away as it landed hard on its wheels with smoke pouring from its hood.

'Incoming!' Glen shouted in horror as tires began screeching behind them.

Behind them a line of startled traffic began screeching to a halt in a chaotic frenzy. Karina winced as she heard a terri ble crash of vehicle after vehicle plunging into each other, and saw countless shards of glass sparkling in the sunlight as windows and windshields imploded.

Horror knifed into her heart as she saw dozens of people scrambling from their vehicles as a huge articulated tanker's wheels locked up and it jack-knifed behind the wreck. The huge vehicle hit the barrier wall amid a shower of sparks as its tires screeched along the asphalt and it plowed into the stationary vehicles. A cloud of metal panels and glass were blasted into the air as the entire train of trapped vehicles shuddered. The tanker smashed its way through them as its cargo ruptured and a flood of inflammable liquids burst in a torrent that spilled across smouldering engines and burst batteries.

'Fire!'

Glen leaped from the car, his pistol in his hand, and rushed toward the smouldering wreckage of the flatbed, as Karina got out and sprinted in the opposite direction toward the cries and shouts from panicked civilians trapped in their vehicles.

'Fire!'

As she rounded the back of the four-by-four behind them, she saw that its rear had been crushed by a smaller vehicle that was itself pinned in place by a Lincoln. Behind that, four more cars were crushed in by the tanker. Karina's pounding heart seemed to stop in her chest as she saw the bodies in the trapped, crushed vehicles. Bloodied. Still. Slumped across steering wheels behind splintered windshields.

A sinister blanket of flame burst from the vehicle nearest the tanker and snaked its way across the wreck.

'Forget them!' she yelled back at Glen and Tom. 'Get over here!'

Even as her brain fired neurons ordering her to call for ambulances and fire trucks, so she saw the final vehicle down the line, crunched into a barely recognisable pulp of twisted metal by the huge tanker. Dark blue Prius. Two occupants. A woman and a child in a baby-seat. Both motionless. Karina felt a terrible fear as she scrambled up across the hoods of mangled cars, but she wasn't even close before the Prius was engulfed in a sheet of writhing flames that spat a boiling pillar of black smoke into the pale blue sky.

As Glen and the others raced to join her, so she saw Tom Ross lay eyes on the burning vehicle.

'No!'

Tom hurled himself onto the mountain of twisted metal and plastic. Karina threw herself into him and they slammed down onto a Lincoln's warped hood. Tom fought her with the strength of a fallen angel, screaming as he hurled her aside and scrambled to his feet.

Glen and Jackson tackled him down before he could enter the writhing flames that seethed around the Prius.

Karina knew it was already too late, even through the tears that stung like acid in the corners of her eyes.

# 6

# WILLIAMSBURG, QUEENS

'*We've got them. Two males heading north, just passing us now.*'

The voice came through a radio transmitter fitted to the vehicle's dashboard, designed to look like a cellphone. The agent in the front seat glanced out of the tinted glass of his window and spotted the two figures strolling down Union Avenue. Both wore clothes that looked normal enough but could also be used to conceal their identities and physiques; one wore a hoodie while the other wore a baseball cap, shielding their faces.

'They look like the same ones from the CCTV footage in Grand Central,' said the driver. 'You sure one of 'em's a woman?'

The two men sitting in the front of the vehicle watched as the two suspects ambled along, pointing at shops and chatting.

'Like they haven't got a care in the goddamned world,' said the man in the passenger seat.

'Don't be deceived,' came a voice from the back seat of the vehicle. 'They're professionals. We need to disarm them quickly or this will all go very wrong.'

The agents in the front both looked over their shoulders at the old man behind them. A senior intelligence officer, his word was highly respected, but even so . . .

'There's only two of them,' the driver replied.

The old man nodded. 'That's all they need.'

'What's the plan then?' asked the other. 'Call in the Marines?'

The old man grinned bitterly but shook his head.

'We let them get to wherever they're going, circle them to prevent an escape, and then we close them down.'

'They're onto us.'

Lopez's voice betrayed no concern as she walked alongside Ethan down Union toward the motel they had booked.

'Where?' Ethan asked.

'Ten o'clock, corner of South 2nd.'

Ethan didn't look up immediately as he walked with a bag of groceries tucked under his left arm. He feigned a chuckle and nodded as though Lopez had muttered a gag, kept looking the way they were walking. But his focus switched immediately to an SUV parked near the sidewalk, maybe thirty yards away on the opposite side of the street.

'Looks like government,' Lopez said as they walked, pointing randomly at a furniture store on their side of the street. 'Too damned clean.'

Ethan did not reply but he agreed. The vehicle's windows were tinted with a film that concealed enough of the occupants' features to make it suspicious.

'Check our tail,' he said, and stopped on the sidewalk to examine the interior of his bag of groceries.

Lopez stopped alongside him, reaching into the bag as though searching for something within but scanning the sidewalk behind them. As they started walking again, she spoke quietly.

'Another one about a hundred yards behind,' she confirmed. 'It's not crawling, just sitting there.'

'Anybody on foot?' Ethan asked.

'Not close enough to be a threat.'

Ethan felt certain that anybody wanting to take them down would not be foolish enough to open fire in broad daylight in New York. Even a drive-by shooting from the relative cover of a vehicle would present numerous risks if those responsible were identified in any way. No. If they were going to make a hit, it would be at the motel and probably through more covert means than a shooting disguised as a drug or gangland dispute.

'How the hell did they find us?' Lopez asked. 'We've barely stayed still for six months.'

'Maybe a lucky break,' Ethan hazarded. 'Or somebody anticipated our next move.'

Lopez shook her head. 'I doubt that. What are we going to do about it?'

Ethan didn't look at the SUV as they passed by, instead thinking about angles and distances. 'We have to assume they already know where we're staying,' he said, 'and that we haven't just spotted them.'

'Could be a team waiting,' Lopez cautioned him.

'Yeah, but if we don't keep going, they'll know we're onto them.'

'You want to fight it out?' Lopez asked, looking up at him.

Ethan shook his head. 'No, but let's see if we can't vanish again.'

They walked across the lot of the motel and passed the foyer. Ethan glanced inside the small waiting room as they passed and saw nobody waiting for them. As he looked up he saw a cleaning lady wheeling her trolley of laundry down along the rows of apartment doors just past their own.

Lopez led the way to their motel-room door, fumbling for the keys as she did so.

'We're virtually inviting them in for coffee,' she said.

'I think they're hoping to corner us,' Ethan replied. 'But they didn't have anybody out on foot, so that means they were in vehicles when they spotted us. But if they'd pulled in ahead of us now they'd have risked being spotted by us. So my guess is they'll let us get inside, quietly surround the motel, and move in.'

'Which helps us how?' Lopez asked as she opened the door.

'Because we won't be here.'

'*They're inside, room 27.*'

The old man in the rear seat of the SUV reached up to one ear and pressed a tiny button on the microphone that he wore.

'Block all exits, secure the room and take them down!'

The driver started the engine and pulled out, just as the second vehicle passed in front of them on Union. They pulled in behind and followed it to a weary-looking motel a couple of hundred yards down, drove into the lot and parked a short distance from a block of rooms that ran east–west along one side of the lot.

The old man climbed from his own vehicle and followed his agents as they converged on the door marked with plastic numbers: 27. Three of the four agents pulled pistols from shoulder holsters and checked the mechanisms before looking at the old man for orders. The fourth man held a black iron door ram cradled in his arms.

'Any chance of exit from the rear?' he asked them in a whisper.

Two of the men shook their heads and the old man gestured to the door. 'Do it.'

The agent with the door ram moved into position and hefted it up before smashing it into the door right alongside the lock and jamb. The door shuddered and splintered at the lock with the first blow, and with the second it smashed through as the door swung open and the five armed men plunged into the room.

The old man walked in behind them, to see them staring about in amazement.

The room was entirely empty.

Ethan followed Lopez through the sparsely furnished surroundings of room 28. The room smelled of fresh linen and cleaning fluids. He turned to a large cabinet that stood against the wall opposite the bed.

'Help me shift this one,' he said.

Lopez grabbed the cabinet and, with Ethan, hefted it away from the wall and turned it sideways. 'What, you think you're going to find the gateway to goddamned Narnia behind one of these?'

Ethan smiled as he examined the wall and tapped it lightly. 'Near enough.'

Cheap motels had thin stud walls, built with timber and often not more than six inches thick. Ethan rapped his knuckles on the wall until he found what he was looking for and then lifted a boot and pushed it hard against the plasterboard wall, close to the thinly carpeted floor. The wall bowed and then with a soft crack it folded inward and exposed a gaping hole. Ethan swiftly pushed it out and knelt down. The timber frames in the wall were built in a cross-hatch pattern that created two-foot square gaps. Ethan got down onto his butt and slammed his boot through the wall of the adjoining room, smashing the plasterboard aside and then scrambled to his feet.

'Off we go, quickly. They'll check the adjoining rooms. Ladies first.'

Lopez shook her head and hurled their backpacks through the hole before she scrambled through it and disappeared.

Ethan turned to the bathroom and hurried through, reaching up for one of the dressing gowns hanging from the door and pulling the waist tie from it. He quickly dragged the cabinet as close to the wall as he could while still leaving enough room to wriggle through the hole he had created, and then looped the gown's tie around the base of the cabinet.

Ethan climbed backwards into the hole in the wall and through into the adjoining room, then hauled on the robe tie. He heard the cabinet shuffle back into place an inch at a time, until it bumped gently against the damaged wall, concealing the hole. Moments later, he heard two dull thumps, a loud crack and a rumble of heavy feet bursting into the room.

Ethan released one end of the tie and then yanked on the other, pulling it through the gap. He got to his feet, dusted his hands off, and looked at Lopez with a bright smile. 'You're welcome.'

Lopez raised an eyebrow. 'Are we going to be doing that all the way down the block?'

Ethan shook his head.

'The rooms have just been cleaned,' he said, 'that's why I knew these would be empty. My guess is that our government friends want to be discreet, so they'll ask the cleaner instead, who will confirm that the rest of these rooms were empty when she cleaned. I'm hoping they'll think we gave them the slip.'

Another series of loud crashing sounds came from outside, and Ethan hurried to the window. Through the aged blinds, he saw a group of suited men barging their way into Room 28, pistols in their hands.

'That's a big chance to take,' Lopez said as she heard the scene unfolding outside.

'Not that big,' Ethan said, and suddenly opened the front door of the room and stepped out into the lot.

# 7

Ethan covered the few steps to room 28 in silence as he saw the back of an old man peering into the deserted room. He drew his pistol from where it was tucked into his jeans and rammed the barrel under the old man's ribs as he reached across and wrapped his other arm around the man's throat, pitching him backwards and off-balance.

'Jesus!'

Ethan held the old man firmly in place, the pistol pressed securely against his torso, as the four agents in the motel room spun and aimed their pistols at him. He heard Lopez rush to his side, her own weapon drawn as she saw what Ethan had done.

'Jarvis?' Ethan turned the old man slightly until he saw both the recognition and the relief in the old man's eyes.

Jarvis waved his men down. 'Lower your weapons,' he snapped.

Ethan released Jarvis and glared down at him. 'Looking for someone?'

'Both of you,' Jarvis nodded, somewhat shaken but quickly recovering as he glanced at Lopez. 'Good to see you, Nicola, you're looking well.'

Lopez forced a crooked '*up yours*' smile onto her face. Ethan decided to do the talking.

'Coming in a little heavy, don't you think?' he snapped as he gestured at the agents in their motel room. 'You trying to clean something up here, Doug?'

Jarvis raised his hands in placation. 'I had no choice,' he replied. 'You're under suspicion for multiple homicides and we didn't know if you were responsible or not. For all we knew, you might open fire on us.'

'What homicides?' Ethan demanded.

Jarvis turned to his men. 'Form a perimeter, quietly.'

The four men hurried out of the room and crossed the lot to their vehicles, as Jarvis walked with Ethan and Lopez into the room and closed the damaged door behind them as best he could. He looked at them both.

'Are you okay?' he asked. 'You look tired.'

'We're fine,' Lopez snapped. 'Just cut to the chase.'

'Several CIA agents have been murdered in the past few days,' Jarvis said promptly. 'The CIA believes that you're responsible.'

Ethan shook his head. 'We're not. But we did hear about one of the murders, out Wisconsin way.'

'That's what I thought,' Jarvis replied. 'And it's what I told the Joint Chiefs of Staff.'

'You're back at the DIA?' Lopez asked.

'I wasn't until this morning,' Jarvis admitted. 'I got a call to come in. Turns out the DCIA is finally getting his just deserts and is in a world of hurt over MK-ULTRA. The rest of the intelligence community is keen to see the whole thing shut down, but there are loose ends and none of it can be brought to public trial.'

Ethan rolled his eyes.

'So we get to carry the can and the rest gets swept under the carpet, right?'

'That's what the CIA wants,' Jarvis said, nodding, 'but I've managed to reach a compromise with them. I've got our department up and running again and you're both in the clear.'

'In exchange for what?' Lopez demanded.

'They want you to find out whoever's responsible for the deaths of the six agents, and bring them in.'

'*Six* dead agents.' Ethan repeated.

'Last one was killed in New York yesterday,' Jarvis confirmed. 'I'm assuming you figured that might happen.'

'There seemed to be a hint of a trail of slayings being covered up,' Ethan replied, 'crossing states and pointing to the east coast. New York seemed like a good, crowded place to hide.'

Lopez peered at Jarvis suspiciously.

'You've got your entire department up and running and agents with you right now, but you want *us* to go and sort this out for you.'

Jarvis shrugged apologetically. 'Deniability,' he said. 'You're sub-contracted to the DIA, but since you've been off the books for six months if things go wrong they can simply deny any knowledge. There's no paper trail.'

Ethan rubbed his face with his hands.

'Perfect,' he said. 'And if this all goes to plan, how can we trust the CIA to stay off our backs?'

'MK-ULTRA is finished,' Jarvis promised. 'It's been far too compromised to continue its work. Even William Steel wants it shut down. He fears that any public exposure now could be the final nail in the CIA's coffin, to the detriment of our intelligence-gathering capabilities, and, for once, I agree with him. Once this is done, you're both free.'

Ethan shook his head and Lopez sounded equally unconvinced. 'MK-ULTRA is dead? You're sure about that?'

'It can't survive everything that's happened,' Jarvis explained. 'It'll be signed to an Executive Order for classified materials and buried for at least fifty years.'

An Executive Order was a directive signed and sent by the President of the United States and a policy that could transcend administrations. Any such order directed at projects concealed within the black budget would have been carried out without the knowledge of any American public office or the people, regardless of how long it continued.

'I want to know everything,' Ethan said. 'Up until now, all we've heard is mention of this mysterious MK-ULTRA and no hard details. Fill us in so we know what we're up against.'

Jarvis sat on the edge of the bed and spoke quietly, as though even here in a lonely motel room there might be people listening in.

'MK-ULTRA is the name of a covert project run by the CIA under various different guises over the last four decades,' he explained. 'Its origins were founded during Operation Paperclip, the rounding up of German scientists after the Second World War Two who had been responsible for torture and brainwashing programs run by the Nazi regime. Project Bluebird grew out of this operation with a purpose to study mind control, behavior modification and interrogation techniques. It in turn was renamed Project Artichoke in

1951 and run by the CIA Office of Scientific Intelligence, finally becoming Project MK-ULTRA in 1953. The cryptonym name of the program indicates that it was run by the CIA's Technical Service Staff, via the designator "MK", and that it received the highest security classification rating, "ULTRA".'

'And what, exactly, did this project do?' Lopez asked.

'It began with the study of hypnosis, forced morphine addiction and withdrawal, the use of chemicals and deprivation of sensory stimuli to produce amnesia and general vulnerability in subjects,' Jarvis explained. 'There was a memo, dated 1952, where a senior officer states the project's main goal as being to ask: "*Can we get control of an individual to the point that he will do our bidding against his will and even against fundamental laws of nature, such as self-preservation?*"'

Ethan frowned. 'Mind control?'

'It went on through the 1960s,' Jarvis said, nodding, 'with experiments on unwitting American subjects both in the military and as civilians: drugs like LSD injected into drinks and water supplies, hallucinogens administered without the subject's knowledge or consent, and so on. It progressed eventually to full-blown deep-hypnosis programs designed to create unwitting assassins posted in politically volatile countries who would, upon a given command, carry out attacks on enemies of the state. Their actions could be explained away as psychosis or similar, divesting any shred of blame on the USA.'

'Roving sleeper-assassins,' Lopez said. 'Similar programs were uncovered in Russia after the Cold War, right?'

Jarvis nodded.

'MK-ULTRA also had an overseas arm, MK-DELTA, which was responsible for the contamination of food supplies and the spraying of aerosolized LSD onto the village of Pont-Saint-Esprit in France in 1951. The event resulted in mass psychosis, the deaths of at least seven French citizens and thirty-two commitments to mental institutions. One of the CIA operatives involved, a man named Frank Olson, developed a crisis of conscience after the events and also after witnessing a terminal interrogation in Germany under Project Artichoke. He resigned his position and was later found dead after a suspicious fall from a Manhattan building.'

'You're kidding?' Ethan gasped. 'CIA-sanctioned murders, just like those my sister witnessed in DC?'

'The same,' Jarvis confirmed. 'In 1975, our government admitted that Olson had also been dosed with LSD and that the CIA and the state of New York had been covering up the details of his death for almost a quarter of a century. The government settled financially with Olson's family, out of court.'

'How come this hasn't come to light before now?' Lopez asked.

'The CIA canned the project and literally burned the evidence in 1973 after a congressional investigation attempted to gain access to files relating to MK-ULTRA,' Jarvis explained. 'However, it appears that not all of the project's programs were shut down. You ended up in the middle of one when you went to Idaho. You all saw the news reports after you escaped, I take it?'

Ethan nodded. A major embarrassment for the administration, there had been widespread accusations of a cover-up but as usual no evidence had been forthcoming. He knew that was nothing to do with a lack of evidence: those involved simply wanted to stay alive.

'Okay,' Ethan said finally to Lopez. 'So we're being asked to hunt for the assassin, in order to get our own asses in the clear. You up for this?'

Lopez shrugged.

'It could be worse,' she said, 'at least this time we're searching for something human.'

'What about Joanna?' Ethan demanded. 'We've been trying to track her down for six months. I figured that she may have something to do with the homicides.'

Jarvis nodded.

'So did I,' he admitted. 'The DCIA would not admit to anything when I spoke with the JCOS, but all of the CIA murder victims had at one time or another been posted to a safe-house in Gaza City.'

Ethan took a pace forward as anger surged through his body.

'You're saying that the CIA was involved in her abduction? That she's been killing these agents?'

'It's not something that you didn't already suspect, Ethan,' Jarvis said, 'after all of the agency's connections with arms companies working in Gaza. Joanna may have embarked on a revenge mission of some kind and her next target might even be the director himself. If we're right and she's behind it, all she's doing is exposing herself to a federal prison sentence that will never end.'

Ethan ground his teeth as he realized that he had no choice.

'So we have to hand her over in order to save our own skins.'

'Joanna will never be prosecuted,' Jarvis replied. 'She could hardly be tried without the reasons for her rampage being broadcast. This is better than the alternative, Ethan, which is the CIA finding her first. They'll spirit her into Eastern Europe under extreme rendition, then have her tried before a military court as an enemy combatant. You think she's been missing for a long time right now?' Jarvis shook his head. 'Believe me, this case is now so sensitive that nobody will ever see her again.'

Ethan shook his head in disbelief as he stared at Jarvis.

'All of that time, Doug,' he murmured, 'all of that time you could have helped me find her and you didn't, and now it's come to this.'

Jarvis jabbed a finger in Ethan's direction.

'I'm not her mother!' he snapped. 'I've done all I can to help, but it's Joanna who's gone around shooting former patriots, not me. I can't be held responsible for what happened to her or her response.'

'No,' Lopez agreed, 'but you sure as hell could have made it easier for us.'

Jarvis's anger blustered away and he sighed.

'I've already made contact with somebody who can help us,' he said. 'You may not like everything that he has to say, but if you're willing to come with me, we can meet him tomorrow morning. What he knows may help us figure out where Joanna may go next.'

Jarvis reached into a pocket and produced a slim cellphone that he handed to Ethan.

'Burner cell,' he explained, 'untraceable and linked to my own phone. You can call me securely on that, anytime, without fear of the CIA tracking the call. Let's go.'

# 8

# EAST VILLAGE, NEW YORK

'You there, Tom?'

Karina Thorne stood at the door to the apartment block near the corner of East 10th and peered up at the fire-escape ladders as she spoke into the entry panel on the wall. The low sun glinted off the metal railings, but she could see that the windows to Tom's apartment were shut and the blinds drawn tight across them.

No reply came from the device and she was about to turn away and pull out her cellphone when the entry door's locking mechanism suddenly buzzed. Karina turned and pushed the door open.

The apartment block had been recently renovated, the foyer clean and hushed as the door locked shut behind her with a sucking sound, the noise from the busy streets instantly deadened. She turned and climbed up the stairs, avoiding the elevator as she always did. Karina was claustrophobic, probably due to her having grown up in the open wilds of Blackwater alongside Chesapeake Bay. She had never quite got used to the towering steel-and-glass blocks of New York City.

She reached Tom's door and knocked softly. For a long time no sound came from within but finally the door clicked and opened. Karina saw the apartment in shadow within and Tom's eyes staring out at her, black and devoid of emotion.

'Can I come in?' she asked, her voice almost a whisper.

Tom turned away from the door without a word and walked into the shadows. Karina followed him in and shut the door behind them.

As a cop, Tom would not have earned enough alone to afford a two-bed in the East Village, but his wife Donna had been a doctor and together they had been doing okay. The apartment was neat and tidy, the décor clearly chosen by a feminine touch. The only thing out of place was Tom's disheveled hair and the cushions that had been scattered off the couch.

Tom slumped down onto the couch and stared into the darkness, his hands hanging limp between his legs, his eyes as black and vacant as deep space. Karina knew what shock looked like – she had seen it many times before in the eyes of gunshot victims and automobile-wreck survivors, when the face lost all expression, the brain shutting down due to an emotional overload.

Karina stood immobile in the center of the lounge and chose her words with care.

'Have you been back to the hospital yet?'

Tom did not respond. He had frantically followed the ambulance carrying his wife and child after they had been cut from the tangled wreckage of the Prius, screaming and hurling away anybody who tried to approach him. Even Jake Donovan had been unable to restrain Tom, instead enforcing a ten-foot exclusion zone around the distraught officer lest he toss somebody clean over the railings and down into the East River below.

Karina knew that racing the bodies to the hospital was most likely a futile gesture, as nobody could have realistically survived the wreck and the fire. By the time she had got there, Tom had already left. A duty nurse informed Karina that Donna and Sarah Ross had both died instantly from massive head and neck trauma from both the initial impact into the pile-up and then the second impact from the truck that piled into them from behind. Neither would have known what had happened or had the opportunity to feel a thing, but there was no such mercy for Tom, who for entirely understandable reasons had been prevented from seeing them one last time.

Karina felt tears pinching the corners of her eyes again as she sensed some tiny fragment of the colossal pain that Tom was enduring. Her voice croaked as she spoke.

'They're gone,' she said. 'I know you can't deal with it right now, so I'm going to leave you in peace. I just wanted to let you know that the duty nurse confirmed that they would have known nothing about it. It was instant.'

Tom remained motionless. Karina sucked in a short, quivering breath as she felt something trickle gently down her cheek.

'You're on compassionate leave, effective immediately,' she added. 'Donovan has said that you can take as long as you need. The department will send somebody to see you when you're ready, a counsellor.'

Tom did not respond, still staring silently into blackness. For a moment, Karina wondered whether he was actually breathing, he seemed so still. She knew that no words would be adequate, that no action could even begin to replace the vacuum torn into Tom's soul by the uncaring hand of fate, but she also knew that to just walk away from him wasn't an option.

'Is there anything I can do, Tom?'

Tom remained silent and still, the silence drawing out until it weighed heavy in the darkness. Karina sighed softly enough that Tom would not hear it, and then she turned for the door. 'You know where I am, if you need me. Just call, anytime.'

Karina reached out for the door handle when a faint voice reached out for her, sounding monotone as though the life had been ripped out of it to leave only a bare shell of sound.

'Is that it?'

Karina hesitated, then turned to look over her shoulder. Tom had not moved, sitting still as though carved from granite. Then, slowly, his head turned and his black eyes stared into hers from across the room. 'They're just gone?'

Karina let go of the handle and turned to face her partner.

'They're gone,' she whispered, 'gone from here.'

Tom's features remained turned toward her, but his eyes were focused on some distant place far from where he sat in the present.

'Gone where?' he asked.

Karina had the sudden impression that she was talking not to an experienced detective but to a small child, as though the tremendous trauma had regressed his age.

'I don't know,' she answered, unwilling to commit herself any further.

Tom seemed to focus on her for the first time. His mouth was slightly open, as though his jaw were too heavy to hold up, and the lack of life in his eyes suddenly scared her, as though he too were already gone, his body merely running on what remained of his strength like a discarded toy that needed new batteries.

'I don't know what to do,' Tom whispered. 'I can't feel anything.'

Karina realized that in all of her life she had never witnessed a human being so completely scoured of all emotion. Murders, rapists, serial killers – all of them harbored somewhere within them the same humanity with which they had been born, no matter how deeply buried. But Tom seemed completely devoid of any psyche, an automaton incapable of feeling the pain that must now be rising up like a tsunami inside of him.

Karina slowly walked toward her colleague and sat down carefully on the edge of the couch near to him, instinctively knowing not to move too close and invade his fragile personal space. Tom stared at her with those unblinking eyes and she was forced to look away, unable to bear the thought of whatever lay behind them.

'These things take time,' she replied finally, trying to be sympathetic and pragmatic at the same time. 'Try not to force anything, Tom.'

He didn't react to her words, still enveloped in a haze of confusion. Karina knew that in his apparently senseless state, he might become a suicide risk. Devoid of any sense of future or consequence, he could be suddenly overcome with grief when the shock finally wore off and take his own life in some unspeakable act of self-mutilation.

With a start of realization, she recalled that Tom's parents had passed away a few years previously. An only child, he had literally lost the only family he had left.

She reached into the pocket of her jacket and lifted out a brass key. Gently, she reached across to Tom and took his hand. Tom looked down vacantly as she opened his hand and pushed the key into his palm.

'My apartment,' she said. 'Use it. Doesn't matter how upset you feel or what time of the day or night it is, you go there and you find me, okay?' Tom stared down at the key. 'Okay?' Karina pressed him.

Tom looked slowly up at her and gave her a barely perceptible nod.

'Good,' she said. 'Do you have a spare key for here?'

Tom's head turned and he looked at a clear plastic bag lying on a table top a few feet away. With a sickening feeling, Karina realized that it must have been the possessions of his wife and daughter, recovered from their bodies or from the wrecked Prius.

Slowly, Karina got up and walked across to the bag. Inside was a purse, some credit cards, a set of keys on a ring and, to her dismay, a small doll dressed in pink clothes, its blonde hair carefully platted.

'Jesus.'

Tears drenched her cheeks as she opened the bag and unclipped the apartment key from the ring.

Karina slipped the key into her pocket and walked back to Tom, who was staring now at the bag on the table. Karina belatedly spotted pictures hanging on the opposite wall of the lounge, images of Tom with Donna and Sarah and others of Sarah as a tiny baby and toddler. She struggled to keep her own emotions in check as she knelt down before Tom and grasped both of his hands in hers. She desperately wanted to insist that she stay the night, to keep him company, to prevent him from doing something that he might regret, but she somehow knew that right now all Tom wanted to be was alone. She would have felt the same.

'Keep in touch,' she insisted. 'Don't let go, Tom, okay?'

Tom stared at her for a long beat before offering her another silent nod.

Karina stood and walked to the apartment door, glancing back as she left to see Tom still sitting in the darkness and staring at the plastic bag on the table nearby.

# 9

# HELL GATE, QUEENS, NEW YORK

'Shut up and keep moving!'

The whispered voice was harsh in the night, as was the calloused hand that cracked across the back of Wesley Hicks's head. The impact echoed across the docks and out over the glistening black surface of the East River. Wesley ducked and his gloved hand flew to his head as Connor Reece, his older and altogether more unstable partner, rested a pair of bolt croppers alongside an old chain-link fence.

'I don't like it out here, is all,' Wesley complained.

Reece, his shaven head covered by a black cap, did not reply as he hefted the croppers to waist height and settled them around a thick chain padlocking a set of gates together. With a groan of effort that puffed clouds of his breath onto the cold air, the croppers bit through the steel chain and it clattered down onto the asphalt. Wesley winced at the noise and glanced furtively back up the road. There were no cars and certainly no pedestrians out here at night, but he could both see and hear the traffic flowing over the Robert F Kennedy Bridge just a couple of hundred yards to the north, its lights twinkling in the chill misty air.

'This way,' Reece snapped.

The older man yanked back the rolling gate by a couple of feet, just enough for them to slip through. Wesley followed him and then pulled the gate loosely back into position before looping the heavy chain back into position. If any security guards or cops did patrol down here, they would have to look closely before realizing that the chain was severed.

Reece led the way across an old disused parking lot to a large building, its loading bays all boarded up. A handful of scattered Dumpster bins lined one wall, some of them overturned, probably by vagrants searching for an easy, if unpleasant, meal.

A set of rusting iron steps led up to a solid-looking door. Reece reached into his pocket and produced a thick key, cast from what looked to Wesley like solid iron. In the darkness, the key looked unusual, old-fashioned.

'Where did you get that from?' he whispered.

Reece did not reply. Instead, he shoved the key into the lock and turned it. Wesley heard a heavy revolving sound as the key turned, as though the big old door had stood here for centuries, its mechanisms forged in another age. The lock clicked and Reece turned the handle and pushed. The door swung smoothly open, no sound emanating from its aged hinges.

Reece moved inside, Wesley following and trying to control his grating nerves as he was swallowed by the absolute darkness within the old warehouse.

'Push the door shut,' Reece ordered.

Wesley obeyed, leaning against the door behind him until the locking mechanism clicked. Satisfied, Wesley heard Reece searching through the pockets of his jacket. Then a bright beam of light burst into life as he turned on a small but powerful flashlight.

'This way.'

The flashlight beam illuminated a cavernous warehouse that was largely empty. Lines of racking stood against the opposing walls, scattered bits of old paper and wrapping littered the floor and the light from the nearby bridge glimmered faintly through dirty windows caked with the filth of decades.

Wesley followed Reece closely, the building's abandoned, sombre atmosphere chilling his bones as they crept through the darkness, the flashlight scything a path toward the very rear of the building.

'Do we have to go right back there?' Wesley asked.

'You don't shut up, you'll be staying here for a very long time, you feel me?'

'I feel you,' Wesley replied quickly, not wanting to upset his volatile companion any further. 'Just feels like we're not on our own in here.'

'I fuckin' wish I was,' Reece muttered.

Wesley said nothing more as they walked, looking up instead at the soaring ceiling above them and wondering what this building had been used for. Maybe the docks when they were busy back in the day, storage for the big old ships that used to unload here. Now the docks were mostly silent and filled with the rusting hulks of shipping containers and parked haulage wagons.

'Here.'

Reece's voice snapped Wesley out of his reverie as the older man peered into the gloom at the very rearmost corner of the warehouse. There, tucked in behind the rickety old shelves and racking, was a canvass sheet draped over something on the ground. Wesley watched as Reece bit the flashlight between his teeth to free his hands and then yanked the sheet aside with a flourish.

A cloud of dust particles spiralled up through the flashlight beam as Wesley stared down at three heavy-looking metal containers, each about the size of a large suitcase. Reece flashed him a wicked grin as he yanked the flashlight from his mouth.

'Pay dirt,' he said.

Wesley smiled back and was about to reply when a faint whisper of movement somewhere behind him raised the hairs on the back of his neck. He whirled and peered into the gloomy darkness. He saw the flashlight beam flick around to point past him into the warehouse as Reece searched for the source of the sound.

'Man,' Wesley whispered, 'I tol' you there was someone else in here.'

Reece reached out and grabbed Wesley's collar in one chunky fist, yanking his face to within inches of the older man's grizzled, pockmarked features. In the harsh light from the beam, he looked even more demonic than normal.

'Only thing in this building you need to fear is me, you got that?'

Wesley nodded, his eyes wide and quivering in their sockets. Reece pushed him roughly away and then turned back to the metal cases. 'Help me with these. We've got to get them out of here tonight or this is all for nothin', you understand?'

Wesley stepped forward, reached down and grabbed the handle on one of the cases before hauling it backwards across the floor. The corner of the case screeched against the ground, and Reece whirled and thumped a thick forearm across Wesley's chest.

'Quietly, you idiot!'

The impact hurled Wesley onto his back, and as he fell he saw the flashlight beam arc up into the darkness above them. There, in the harsh white light, he saw the clouds of dislodged dust swirl as though an aircraft had sailed through them, spinning in tight vortices as the cloud folded over itself and then vanished from sight as the beam passed by.

'Shit!' he whispered and pointed up above them. 'There's something up there!'

Reece barely glanced up as he hefted one of the steel cases up off the ground with one hand.

'What's up, Wes?' he inquired with a twisted, mocking scowl. 'Pigeons gonna getcha?'

Wesley struggled to his feet and stared at Reece, as the older man snickered in delight and turned toward the far end of the warehouse. He made two paces when suddenly his feet lifted off the floor and he was hurled onto his face on the ground, the metal case crashing down alongside him. Wesley flinched as the sound echoed and bounced through the warehouse like rolling cannons.

Reece leaped to his feet and whirled to face Wesley as he pulled a snub-nosed pistol from beneath his jacket and aimed the weapon directly at him.

'You think that's funny, you little shit?' he raged as he stormed toward Wesley.

Wesley did not move. His legs would not respond and his voice was entrapped in his throat with a terror that he could never have believed existed. He felt his neck trembling, felt saliva pooling in his throat and his heart fluttering in his chest as though afraid to go on.

Reece halted in front of Wesley, suddenly taut as he registered the blind terror etched into every pore in Wesley's face. With a monumental effort, Wesley managed to rasp a few words in a voice that sounded thin in the darkness.

'It wasn't me, Connor.'

Reece winced uncertainly, but his eyes flicked left and right around them. Wesley felt something cold fill the air, as though somebody had opened the door to an enormous icebox right alongside him. His quivering breath condensed in a cloud before his eyes, billowing blue-white in the flashlight beam.

Both his and Reece's eyes fixated on the cloud of moisture as it suddenly was sucked up out of the light as something raced past in the darkness above their heads.

Reece shouted something unintelligible as he whirled and aimed the pistol up above them. Wesley staggered backwards and away from him, and then Reece screamed as the pistol and flashlight fell from his grasp and he was yanked up into the darkness.

Wesley heard a cry of terror break free from his own chest as his legs crumpled beneath him. He crawled forward on the ground as he heard Reece issue a strangled cry of unbearable agony from somewhere far above him. A terrible ripping sound echoed across the warehouse and Reece fell silent as Wesley managed to grab the pistol in one shaking hand and the flashlight in the other.

A loud thump surprised Wesley and he hurled himself sideways as he aimed the flashlight into the darkness. He almost gagged as he saw Reece's face staring back at him, lifeless like a waxwork in the harsh light, his face forever contorted in terrible pain and his mouth open wide in a silent scream.

Wesley turned the torch and saw thick blood draining from Reece's entrails as they snaked across the warehouse floor and curled steam onto the cold air. In the distance, across the warehouse, he heard two faint thuds and glimpsed Reece's legs tumble to the ground. Wesley began sobbing as he felt his bowels loosen and spill into his pants in a hot, thick mess.

The darkness seemed to close in on him and he cried out in terror as he kicked his way backwards and away from the grisly corpse until his back hit the wall.

'Jesus, save me,' he whispered through his tears. 'Please save me.'

Something whispered through the air directly above him, and in panic he aimed the flashlight and the pistol up into clouds of dust motes swirling through the beam. A demonic face glared down at him with primal fury as it rushed from the darkness. Wesley fired the pistol over and over again, and then quite suddenly he felt a terrible wrenching pain surge through his chest as though he had been impaled.

He lurched to his feet to flee, but the pain suddenly intensified until it filled his universe as he folded over at the waist and dropped to his knees.

Then his world went black and he felt nothing.

# 10

# WHITE PLAINS, NEW YORK

'So who are we going to see?'

The SUVs drove north in the pale dawn light and crossed the East River up towards Westchester, near the border with Connecticut. Ethan and Lopez had said little for the duration of the journey, knowing better than to try to draw information from Jarvis when he was on a roll, but now Lopez was getting impatient.

'You'll see,' Jarvis replied. 'We're nearly there.'

Whatever the old man had discovered, Ethan could tell that it wasn't something he physically possessed otherwise he would have produced copious files by now. Which meant that it was something outside of the DIA. Jarvis had claimed to have been working tirelessly for months to secure evidence sufficient to free Ethan and Lopez from the specter of a CIA-sponsored witch-hunt. Ethan guessed that whatever he had up his sleeve was waiting for them at their destination.

The SUVs slowed and turned onto the gravel drive of a moderately sized colonial house, all white paint and porticoes. Lopez peered through the rain-streaked windows and raised a mocking eyebrow at Jarvis.

'Been moving up in the world since your retirement?'

'If I'd moved up this far,' Jarvis muttered, 'I'd have stayed retired.'

The SUV pulled up outside the house and they disembarked as a man walked out of the front door, dressed in a smart pullover and slacks, his gray hair cut short and smart. Ethan recognized him as a military man at first glance, the bearing and poise as clear to him as if the man had still been in uniform.

'Ethan, Nicola,' Jarvis said, 'this is Major Henry Greene, former United States Army. He worked with the CIA on many operations back in the day, mostly in South East Asia.'

Ethan introduced himself, the major clearly impressed by his background as a Marine officer and Lopez's experience as a detective. Major Greene invited them into the house and led them to a drawing room. A large reading table was surrounded by ornate cabinets and a couple of decent-size canvasses of major historical engagements. Ethan recognized one as Gettysburg, and wondered not for the first time why anybody would want images of slaughter plastering the walls of their home.

'Major Greene has information that may be of use to us,' Jarvis explained as they sat down around the table.

'You worked with the CIA during the Vietnam conflict?' Ethan asked.

'1969,' Greene confirmed. 'I was a greenhorn back then, got myself sent straight into the Tet Offensive.'

'Baptism of fire,' Lopez said, recalling the period of the South East Asia conflict during which some of the fiercest fighting occurred. 'American troops began pulling out afterward.'

'The tide of the war was changing,' Greene acknowledged. 'Public opinion and Congress were both favouring a pull-out of the conflict, something that occurred a few years later.'

'An American defeat,' Ethan said, knowing well as a former Marine the dismay US forces must have felt in retreating from a technically inferior enemy.

'What does this have to do with us?' Lopez asked.

'It's not what it has to do with you,' Jarvis said. 'It has to do with what happened to Major Greene next.'

The former soldier looked at Ethan as he spoke.

'We were pulled out of Vietnam in 1971,' he said, 'and brought back to the States. At that time, combat-experienced troops were flooding back to their barracks from the conflict and there was no shortage of manpower. So they start laying us off, ten to the dozen. Only way for me to avoid being tossed out onto the street was to sign up for what was called "special duties".'

Ethan leaned forward with renewed interest. 'Paramilitary work?'

Greene inclined his head. 'Working for the Barn, the Central Intelligence Agency. Those of us who signed up were retrained, taught to work in urban environments instead of those damned jungles. It was good work, covert intelligence gathering.'

'Until?' Lopez murmured.

Greene looked uncomfortable, frowning as he talked.

'It's hard to figure out,' he said. 'We were put on a watch detail for what we were told were suspected lead figures in communist organisations working within the United States. The brief was that elements of Russia's KGB had inserted small sleeper cells, groups of highly trained communist agents who lived and worked as Americans. Their placement was to create an enemy within, so that if in some future event Russia wanted to attack us, these sleeper cells could create havoc within the country's infrastructure, provide intelligence and so on.'

Ethan had heard of the long-running Soviet program that had placed countless Russians inside the United States, as well as other Western nations like the United Kingdom, France, Germany and Spain.

'They're still here,' Lopez said, 'so I've heard.'

'They are,' Greene confirmed. 'The CIA and other agencies pretty much know who the agents are now. But better than bust them wide open, they used to just keep an eye on what they were doing. Every now and again, they'd turn one or two of them into double agents. You'd have been surprised how much even the most ardent communist enjoyed living in a country where they didn't get their head chopped off at the slightest error.'

Jarvis gestured out of the window.

'It's reckoned that there may be several hundred loyal sleeper agents still living in America, although whether they will ever see the action they were trained for is doubtful.'

Major Greene nodded.

'We kept a watch on one of these suspected sleeper cells for almost two months and sure enough we began to detect suspicious activity, but none of it anything to do with monitoring US interests. All of the individuals seemed to us to be spending a lot of their time high on drugs.'

Lopez blinked. 'Seriously? The *Ruskies* were coming here for their hits?'

'They weren't Russian,' Greene said. 'One of the guys, after watching their odd behavior for a few days, decided to make a close pass on them when they were walking down a boulevard. They were taking with American accents, which you'd expect of well-trained Soviet agents, but he actually recognized one of them.'

'Who was he?' Ethan asked.

'His name was Harrison Defoe,' Greene said. 'He'd been a CIA spook working out of Singapore during the Vietnam War.'

Ethan stared for a long moment at the soldier, and then sat back in his seat. 'Joanna Defoe's father. This must have been after he served time in Singapore.'

'You know this man?' Major Greene asked in amazement.

Jarvis leaned forward on the table as he spoke.

'Joanna Defoe is Harrison's daughter and Ethan's fiancée,' he explained to the major. 'In 1967, Harrison had been a serving officer in the United States Army, working as a translator in Singapore. He was a languages expert and spoke fluent Cantonese as well as Vietnamese, working as part of an electronic-intelligence outfit tasked with monitoring Vietcong communications with sympathetic communist parties in the Malay. They worked on tracking funding and weapons smuggling that came up into Vietnam from the south, instead of the more normal route down from the Communist north and Russia.'

Major Greene took up the story.

'Harrison could talk to local people and so get information from the ground, which is the best way to find things out. But the people he was tasked with watching were largely well-known civilian figures discreetly supporting the communists. Popular with people in the region, if the American military had arrested them, somebody, somewhere, would probably know about it and expose them, losing the United States respect and support in the region.'

'So the CIA got their man Defoe to do their dirty work for them,' Lopez guessed.

'Pretty much,' Jarvis said. 'Ethan's sister, Natalie, uncovered much of this during her work within a much larger congressional investigation last year, before the CIA managed to get it shut down. Harrison was asked in 1967 by the CIA if he would like to use newly developed hypnosis techniques to expand his knowledge of Malaysian dialects. Over the next three months, he underwent numerous, extensive hypnotherapy sessions. His testimony says that he did indeed learn a great deal about various dialects but that also he began to develop an inexplicably strong sense of outrage toward communist businessmen in Singapore, especially those whom he knew had links to the Vietcong.'

Major Greene smiled bitterly.

'Like I said, the writing was on the wall by the time of the Tet Offensive,' he said. 'We were relying on carpet-bombing, Agent Orange and brutal jungle combat.'

'So you're saying that Harrison's CIA work was in fact MK-ULTRA, and that he was hypnotically induced to commit murder?' Ethan asked.

'Harrison Defoe shot four Malaysian businessmen outside a downtown restaurant in Singapore, and served three years in jail for the killings,' Jarvis said.

'And that's how we recognized him,' Major Greene explained. 'We were being pulled out of Vietnam, and boarded a transport plane that stopped over in Singapore. Your man Defoe got aboard with a diplomatic envoy for his ride home.'

'Harrison picked up a government pension and a Purple Heart,' Ethan said, dimly recalling what little Joanna had told him of her father. 'I think he spent a few years at Harvard teaching languages to students.'

Major Greene nodded. 'Which was where we set up our observation post. The student route was a common location for Russia to send newly trained sleeper agents, young and full of enthusiasm for Mother Russia.'

'But Harrison Defoe was no junkie,' Ethan protested. 'He was as cut-and-dried as they come. Far as I know, he liked a drink but nothing excessive.'

'And if those drinks were spiked with drugs?' Jarvis suggested.

'You think MK-ULTRA was still working on him?' Lopez asked, amazed.

'We kept a closer watch after that,' Greene said. 'We went beyond our remit to see if we could figure out why a patriotic educator like Harrison Defoe would be taking drugs. We pretty soon figured it out. The water supply to his apartment had been spliced with a canister that supplied a steady flow of LSD. We even caught the guys doing it on camera, filmed them sneaking in and topping up the canister.'

'The Barn.' Ethan guessed.

'Same department we were working for,' Greene confirmed. 'We even knew some of their names. My surveillance team was working for MK-ULTRA and didn't even know it.'

'Have you got that footage?' Ethan asked.

Greene smiled and reached into his pocket. He produced a small tape of 8mm film, a vintage 1970s magnetic recording that he handed across to Jarvis.

'It's all here,' he said, 'and the agents responsible are still alive.'

Lopez and Ethan exchanged a glance.

'This is it,' Lopez said. 'This is hard evidence.'

Jarvis smiled, clearly enjoying himself as he pulled from his pocket another piece of paper, this one sealed in a protective sheet of clear plastic.

'Better than that,' he said. 'I managed to obtain this with the major's help. This is a list of names found by the CIA in 1947.'

Ethan's eyes widened as he looked at the yellowing sheet of typed paper entrapped in the plastic sheath.

'What kind of list?' Lopez asked.

Jarvis held the sheet of paper up.

'It turns out that this sheet of paper was the catalyst for the start of MK-ULTRA's covert mind-control programs and the CIA's research into paranormal phenomena. It's extremely old, close to a century, and it concerns a series of events that occurred during the First World War. These names are those of young soldiers who died in their thousands during the Battle of the Somme, and who appeared thousands of miles away as crisis-apparitions to their families at the moments of their deaths.'

Jarvis looked at Ethan and Lopez directly.

'This document represents the first recorded evidence of life after death.'

# 11

'What's a crisis-apparition?' Lopez asked.

Major Greene looked uncomfortable, leaning back in his chair as though to distance himself from the conversation. Jarvis took his cue.

'It's a sort of ghost,' Jarvis replied. 'They've turned up throughout history when people have died, usually appearing to close family or loved ones as an apparently solid embodiment at the moment of death, which then fades away.'

'What the hell would the CIA be doing with a piece of paper like that?' Ethan asked. 'It belongs in a museum.'

Jarvis laid the delicate sheet down on the table as he spoke.

'It turns out that when the CIA started MK-ULTRA, they weren't just looking for strategically placed military personnel who were susceptible to things like hypnosis and such like. They were actively seeking out evidence of families who had a strong history of what we would call paranormal activity. The idea seems that they felt that anybody who might inherit a strong propensity for paranormal events would also be an ideal candidate for experiments probing things that MK-ULTRA was designed to look into, like remote-viewing.'

'What's remote-viewing?' Lopez asked.

'A failed surveillance technique,' Major Greene replied. 'The CIA started Project Stargate in the early 1970s and it ran until 1995, investigating the ability of people who claimed to be able to view places and objects thousands of miles away just by mentally focusing on them.'

'But it failed,' Ethan said.

'The project was *deemed* a failure,' Jarvis replied for the major, 'but not because the technique did not work. Individuals were able to view Russian missile silos and even objects in space. It's recorded in documents that have since become part of the public domain that one man identified that the planet Uranus had faint rings long before passing space probes were able to prove it.'

'So what went wrong?' Lopez asked.

'The intelligence received was reliable,' Greene replied, 'but the translation of that intelligence by the viewers was highly unpredictable. One remote-viewer gave an extremely detailed account of what was believed to be a missile silo being built in Russia, making drawings and such-like. The CIA devoted millions of dollars into physical surveillance of the site, until they realized that it was in fact a power station. The viewer felt that he was looking at large missiles; in fact, they were power conduits and ventilation shafts. That mistake revealed the flaw in using psychically adept civilians to visualize uniquely complex locations – they just couldn't be relied upon to accurately decipher what they were seeing.'

'So how does this tie in with us?' Ethan pressed.

Jarvis gestured to the list of names.

'All of these families independently reported experiencing crisis-apparitions during the First World War,' he replied. 'The CIA used this list and tracked down the families in the 1950s, targeting them as potentially viable subjects for experiments like Stargate and MK-ULTRA. This is the source document, the real-world evidence that set them on their course. It's likely that any family on this list may have descendants that were either hired by or experimented on by MK-ULTRA.'

Ethan carefully lifted the list off the table and scanned down the names. All of them were written in a flowing yet precise script. Given the time that the document was written and the location of most of the fighting in the First World War, it wasn't surprising that many of the names were British and French.

'Did we have troops fighting in the First World War?' Lopez asked.

'We did,' Major Greene confirmed. 'American Expeditionary Forces fought alongside British and French troops in the last year of the war.'

'However,' Jarvis cautioned, 'we can't use nationality to refine our search. Families have moved around, marriages have confused the lineage of inherited names. We could just as likely pursue an American on this list and end up with a descendant who has lived in Norway all their lives. A century has passed since the Great War.'

Ethan sat back for a long moment.

'So these crisis-apparitions,' he said, thinking out loud, 'are used as a marker to identify individuals or families susceptible to paranormal events. Then what? They haul them in and start some kind of weird brain reprogramming?'

'The MK-ULTRA and Stargate programs were many and varied,' Jarvis explained, 'covering every possible facet of extrasensory perception and mental manipulation, depending on what part of the program was being experimented on. Most of the cerebral programming was via hypnosis and forms of electroshock therapy, rumored to have been designed to create these unwitting assassins. Certainly, the actions of otherwise entirely sane and patriotic individuals suggests that they were under some kind of influence, whether by drugs or therapy.'

'You think that Joanna was a part of this, that she underwent some kind of programming?' Ethan asked outright. 'You think that because it worked on her father, the CIA might have assumed that it would work on her?'

'Perhaps,' Jarvis said nodding. 'She could even have been placed back into the population as a sleeper agent herself, primed to cause who-knows-what chaos when activated. But it's not for that reason that I've brought you here.'

Ethan instinctively looked across to Major Greene, who spoke quietly.

'My work with the CIA continued right up to my retirement, two years ago,' Greene said. 'As well as commanding an infantry battalion, I would often be asked to act as oversight for covert operations with the 24th Special Tactics Squadron, a paramilitary outfit that . . .'

'. . . supports the CIA,' Lopez finished the sentence for him. 'We know all about those guys. Bumped into some of them in Idaho a few months back.'

Greene looked at Jarvis in surprise, who nodded.

'Ethan and Lopez got into this whole mess when they were tracking down evidence of some kind of monster up in the forests of central Idaho. Turns out that the CIA's work in MK-ULTRA had extended well beyond anything we could have imagined. They barely got out of there with their lives.'

Greene looked across at Ethan and Lopez, and continued. 'Then you'll know that the STS are elite troops, highly specialized in both conventional and urban combat. You might also like to know that a small unit was inserted into Palestine five years ago, with a briefing to maintain surveillance on a pair of journalists who had been stirring up trouble in South America and who had recently arrived in Gaza City.'

Ethan felt his blood run cold as he sat bolt upright in his chair and glared at the major.

'You were watching us, even back then?' he asked in disbelief.

'We were watching,' Greene replied. 'And when Joanna got a little too close to uncovering the actions of a private arms company, Munitions for Advanced Combat Environments, our team was ordered to apprehend her.'

The rest of the room blurred in Ethan's vision, only the major's features and icy-gray eyes piercing his from across the table. Greene's words traveled toward him as though from down a long-distance telephone line.

'Our team abducted Joanna Defoe from a hotel in Gaza City. The CIA held onto her via militant groups paid to hold hostage Westerners who were considered "troublesome" by intelligence agencies here in the States.'

The major made no attempt to apologize for what he had done, his features calm and his hands folded before him on the table.

He was completely unprepared for Ethan.

The confined, imprisoned rage of thousands of days of *not knowing* swept up and through Ethan's body as though it had never left, as he lunged across the table and hauled the major out of his seat as though he were a rag doll. He didn't hear Lopez or Jarvis shouting at him as he dragged the major across the table and pinned the back of his neck against the edge, the older man's head hanging over it as Ethan drove his forearm down against the major's jaw.

Greene gagged as the back of his neck came under unbearable strain, his vertebrae cracking and his eyes swimming with panic as he realized that he was utterly defenseless against the sheer force and speed of Ethan's attack.

Jarvis stepped forward to free the major, but Ethan swiped the old man aside with his free arm as though he were barely there. Jarvis staggered backwards in surprise.

Ethan glared down at the major. 'Who ordered the abduction?'

Greene, barely able to speak and with his neck on the verge of being broken, struggled to reply.

'I don't know.'

Ethan leaned in harder and the major screamed and grasped at his hands. 'For God's sake, I don't know!'

Ethan leaned forward again, driven by something inside of him that was utterly devoid of emotion, of empathy and regret. The major's eyes widened in pain and the sudden realization of impending death.

A hand touched Ethan's face.

Softly, without force and yet a thousand times more powerful for it. It stayed there, unmoving, until Ethan turned his head. Lopez looked down at him, her hand cupping his face, and shook her head.

'Don't,' she said. 'This isn't the way and you know it.'

Ethan stared up at Lopez for a long moment and then he whirled away and released the major's head. He ran his hands through his hair as the older man rolled off the table and thumped down onto the thick carpet. Ethan desperately sought a vent for his anger, but found nothing. He couldn't even smash the place up, because some part of his mind remained annoyingly, stupidly sane and told him that it would achieve nothing. That grabbing the major had achieved nothing. The man had been here to help.

Ethan ran his hands down his face. In the five years since Joanna had vanished, he had believed that the raw fury, the sheer rage, that had festered within him due to being powerless to find her, had somehow abated. He had really believed that the corrosive anger was gone but now he realized that it had remained all along, just waiting for the catalyst it needed to unleash itself on the world around him.

'Ethan.'

He turned to see the major on his knees with his hands clasping his throat as Jarvis helped him to breathe. Lopez was watching him and perhaps for the first time since they'd met, he saw a shadow of fear in her eyes. She took a pace toward him, rested her hands on his forearms.

'Ethan, this is what I was afraid of. You've got to keep yourself under control because you can't finish this from a prison cell, okay?'

Ethan looked up. Jarvis was also watching him with a look of genuine caution on his features, as though Ethan were no longer an ally but more an enemy kept close.

'You done?' Jarvis asked.

Ethan looked at the major. Greene got to his feet, leaning against the table and recovering his breathing as he looked at Ethan.

'I suppose, in some way, I probably deserved that,' he managed to utter. 'We were abducting US citizens.'

'You didn't know that,' Lopez said. 'You thought that they were sleeper agents, right?'

'We had our doubts about the cover story,' Greene rasped. 'It bothered us all, but there was no real way of getting word out about the abductions without us all being thrown into military prisons.'

Some of the rage flared once more inside Ethan. 'So you let Joanna get thrown into one instead?'

'We had no idea what happened to her after she was picked up by the STS grab team,' Greene insisted. 'It was only when Doug contacted me and told me about his search for Joanna Defoe and that she was known to have escaped, that I felt it was worth telling all. But it's not without risk. I'm still bound by non-disclosure protocols and could be court-martialed if they find out I'm talking about this, especially to you.'

Ethan managed to get his anger under control and his brain back into gear.

'What did they do to her, for all of those years?' he asked.

'That much we don't know,' Jarvis said. 'But given the connections with the CIA, her father's presence in the MK-ULTRA program and Joanna's history of exposing governmental corruption, it's quite likely that the CIA would have at the very least tried to dissuade her from any further investigations upon her release.'

'Dissuade?' Lopez murmured bitterly. 'That mean what I think it does?'

Jarvis nodded.

'They'd have likely used any of MK-ULTRA's methods to alter Joanna's personality, to make her more pliable. That's why they're so keen to find her. Since she escaped, whatever they did to her she could now be using against them. She's walking evidence of everything they've ever done and she's on the loose.'

A cellphone trilled faintly and Jarvis reached into his pocket and answered. Moments later, he looked across at Ethan.

'Something's happened,' he said. 'We need to get back to the city.'

# 12

# KHAN YUNIS, GAZA CITY, PALESTINE

*3 years ago*

The room was dark. She couldn't see because of the blindfold bound tightly around her head, but somehow she knew. There was no way to mark the passage of time. Here and now was all that mattered. Nothing, and nobody else.

She had long ago paced the perimeter of her tiny patch of loneliness and knew it to be precisely eight feet square. She knew also that this tiny space was built deliberately to be small enough to feel claustrophobic, but large enough that she could not touch the opposing walls at the same time with her hands and feet. If her hands weren't tied, that might have allowed her to shimmy up to the small opening nine feet above her head where a faint breeze drifted in from outside, and the people who had incarcerated her here were clearly not willing to let that happen.

Her hands were bound behind her back with tough plastic cords, far too strong to break. The plastic had once cut deep and painful grooves into her wrists, but the skin there had long ago hardened against the constant rubbing of the cords.

She sat on a thin mattress that lay across two cardboard boxes stuffed with Styrofoam balls and crushed by the weight of her body. The simple bed presented nothing with which she could construct a weapon or means to escape the tiny room. A single door made of heavy wood and sealed with big iron locks sealed her in. She knew that on the other side of the door was a four-foot wide latch that dropped into its holders either side of the door frame, making breaking the door down an utter impossibility. She had glimpsed the outside once, when her captors had applied her blindfold too hastily and left a gap for her to see through at the bottom.

That one glimpse of light had sustained her for the past four months. It had been the first thing she had seen with her own eyes in almost a year, as she had shuffled on legs weak with fatigue brought on by her meager diet of rice and unleavened bread.

She had been moved, but only occasionally. When they had abducted her from her hotel in Jabaliya in Gaza a year previously and shoved her down into the rear footwell of a battered old car, they had driven her for more than two hours, presumably to make her think that she was being transported across the border into Egypt or maybe even Israel. But she recognized the odours and sounds of Gaza like the back of her hand and knew that she was being driven round in circles. Disorientation, then. A removal of familiar psychological anchors. Standard procedure for breaking down abductees and reducing them to compliant automatons.

She had been placed in the tiny room an hour later. No questions. No food. No water. Nothing.

And that was when she had really started to worry.

Terrorists working in Gaza would normally have placed great fanfare in capturing a Western journalist. Aware of the vast international outcry that would result from such an abduction, they would have milked it for every drop of recognition that they could achieve before the final, inevitable conclusion: a prisoner release or execution. But not here.

She received no communication from any of her captors or any other human being. Food was supplied to her through a hatch in the door, always when she was asleep. It was collected in the same way. When Joanna left the food tray somewhere in her cell, it remained there untouched until she placed it on the collection shelf on the door. The latrine was periodically sprayed with cleaning fluid via a hole in the wall above it that otherwise remained sealed.

There were no words and no sounds. Ever.

She eventually realized that she was alone in a building, and that her captors merely visited her to provide food and water, nothing more. Gradually, her hair matted against her head and her clothes chafed against her skin, which became oily and slick to the touch. The inadequate diet stripped the fat from her already slim frame as though her life was physically slipping away from her, until her muscles began to feel weak and she staggered weakly about her cell.

Occasionally, at random times to avoid patterns that she could track, men would burst into her cell. They would hold her down and roughly cut her hair and trim her nails to both maintain a basic level of hygiene and also to remove any possible means of tracking the passing of time: she knew that hair grew at about half an inch per month.

She struggled to maintain track of time, determined not to lose that most essential grip on reality, yet it became impossible. Her sleep patterns became erratic, switching to a natural body rhythm of thirty-six hours instead of the more familiar twenty-four, and the mental arithmetic to keep track of the passing days eluded her. Time became an illusion, each month blurring into the next, then each week, then each hour until she was finally struck with the realization that she did not know how long she had been a captive. It could have been days.

It could have been years.

With her grasp of the passing of time taken from her, so the slow but irrevocable loss of her sanity began. Despite knowing, for sure, that she must maintain her sense of self, she found herself in the bizarre position of watching her lose her own mind. She began talking to herself to ease the burden, trying to replace the human contact that was so vital to a healthy mind, but always there was the overpowering awareness that she was, in fact, talking to *herself*. The conversations began to lose direction, veering into uncharted territory like dreams half remembered until she couldn't recall whether she had been talking at all or the voices had been a product of her imagination. As the endless procession of immeasurable months drifted by in utter solitude, blind and deaf to all but her own sounds, her mind began to close in upon itself like an imploding star, shriveling and contracting until it finally blinked out into a deep and empty blackness.

The cold, silent universe that enshrouded her lasted for what felt like a millennia and yet may well have passed almost instantly. She did not sleep and yet her mind was utterly devoid of thought or awareness. She did not eat or drink. She did not move. She was both alive and dead at the same time, an empty shell of what had once been a human being now lying in her own filth and smothered with infected lesions and thick, greasy hair that stuck to her scalp like oily snakes.

They came, then.

When she did not eat or drink for several days, somewhere on the periphery of her awareness she sensed people around her. Voices coming as though from a thousand miles away and the sensation of movement, of rough hands.

She was hauled to her feet and pinned against the wall of the cell. Manacles were clamped to her wrists and ankles to hold her in place as she swayed drunkenly from a lack of spacial orientation and low blood pressure. The blindfold was yanked from her head, but the cell was poorly illuminated so that she could not see her tormentors. Her tattered clothes were stripped from her frame and a blast of water hosed across her naked body along with a handful of powdered soap tossed by one of her captors. The water and chemicals burned in her wounds as she hung limp from the manacles.

The men unchained her, dressed her in a fresh white jumpsuit and lifted her compliant body onto a gurney before strapping her blindfold back on. The wheels of the rattling gurney squeaked as they turned somewhere below, and for the first time in countless months she was wheeled out of the cell.

The journey was short, ending in another room. The sound echoes told her that the room was fairly small. A door closed behind her and she was lifted into a sitting position on what felt like a leather chair.

Then more voices, speaking Arabic.

And then a voice speaking English. With an American accent.

Pain, as a needle was slipped into her arm. A sudden jolt of energy as though adrenaline had suddenly flooded her system. Bright light as the filthy blindfold was hauled from her head, aching through her retina as she squinted against a bright orb that hovered above her. For a fleeting instant, a tiny voice buried deep in her subconscious believed that she was about to be liberated by her countrymen.

It took her only a few moments to realize that she could not move despite the resurgence of energy flooding her veins. Her eyes, so long accustomed to the dark, struggled to focus on her surroundings.

She was strapped to a chair that faced a television monitor. Headphones were in place over her ears and a single lamp above her created a halo of fearsome light that beamed down and blinded her to the rest of the room. She detected sterile odours, vastly different to those of her cell, as though she were in some kind of hospital.

'Begin.'

The single word, the first that she had heard clearly in what felt like a year but might have only been days sounded as loud as anything she had ever heard. She tried to turn her head toward it, but pads either side of her head kept it in place. She swiveled her eyeballs sideways, but they felt odd, stiff. She tried to blink and realized that she couldn't – her eyelids were taped open.

The television screen in front of her flickered, and then an image appeared of a group of what looked like Soviet soldiers standing to attention in front of a large missile carrier. Communist flags and banners rippled as a huge audience of soldiers stood to attention.

Even as her brain processed in a split second what she was seeing, a jolt of white pain surged like burning acid through her body. She cried out and her limbs writhed of their own accord as live current raged within her.

The image vanished and the pain ceased.

Her heart fluttered in her chest as she stared at the television screen. Another image appeared and she flinched, but this time the image was of Washington, DC, and the Capitol. A flush of warmth tingled through her body, a delirium of comfort, and she felt herself fall back into the warm, soft chair.

The screen snapped to an image of Islamic terrorists standing around a man kneeling before them, a black sack over his head and one of the terrorists holding a broad scimitar. The terrorist leaned down and drew the savage blade across the kneeling man's throat in a spray of blood as another surge of agony burned through her body like fire. She screamed again and writhed in the seat until the image vanished.

Somewhere in her mind she knew what they were attempting to do, but she no longer had the strength to resist them.

# 13

# HELL GATE, QUEENS, NEW YORK

Ethan peered out of the window of the SUV as it pulled into the sidewalk alongside an old chain-link fence that ringed a series of low warehouses on the cold shore of the East River. He climbed out and followed Jarvis to where police cars were parked outside the nearest warehouse, crime-scene tape fluttering across an open access door nearby.

'A crime scene?' Ethan asked Jarvis. 'What are we doing here?'

'The scene's being handled by detectives from the Fifth Precinct,' Jarvis explained. 'The same officers recently investigated the death of a man named Aaron Lymes, a retired CIA operative found murdered in his apartment. Turns out he served . . .'

' . . . in Gaza,' Lopez guessed. 'You think these guys know anything yet?'

'That's what we're here to find out,' Jarvis said.

A group of four detectives were standing outside in the lot, a tall man with rugged features and gray hair dominating them as he stood with his hands shoved into the pockets of a long black overcoat. He turned and looked at Jarvis as the old man flashed his identity badge.

'Doug Jarvis, Defense Intelligence Agency. This is Ethan Warner and Nicola Lopez.'

'Jake Donovan, NYPD,' the tall man said. 'We weren't expecting you guys down here.'

'We're here for the Aaron Lymes case. DIA has jurisdiction,' Jarvis explained. 'Lymes was a former CIA operative you found murdered downtown recently. We need to talk about it.'

'Is that right?' Donovan replied. 'Well, I tell you what. If you can explain this crime scene, then I'll talk to you about Lymes. Deal?'

Jarvis gestured to the warehouse. 'Deal. Something here not making sense to the CSI team?'

Donovan introduced his team to them: Karina Thorne, a young-looking detective, Glen Ryan, whom Ethan quickly deduced was a former soldier, and Neville Jackson, an African-American detective.

'Got ourselves a double homicide,' Donovan explained.

'What's the big deal?' Lopez asked.

Donovan looked at Lopez quizzically for a moment. 'Nicola Lopez, you say? Why do I know that name?

'Metropolitan Police Department,' Lopez replied, 'over in DC. I worked there for several years.'

Donovan nodded slowly as though trying to recall something. 'Didn't you blow some kind of corruption scandal in DC a couple of years back? Got yourself a hell of a reputation?'

'Reputation is one word,' Lopez replied with an easy smile, 'infamy's another.'

Donovan grinned back at her and then looked across at the warehouses that were now ringed with bright yellow police-cordon tapes. A forensics vehicle was parked nearby, and a small cluster of construction workers from nearby buildings were watching the police with interest.

'The feds would have been our first port of call here anyway so it's helpful you turned up,' Donovan said finally to Jarvis, 'because what we've got in there sure as hell doesn't make much sense to me.'

Lopez led the way. 'Let's go see what the fuss is about. You got up real early for a double homicide.'

Karina Thorne rested one hand on Lopez's arm as she passed, her features creased with concern. 'It's a bad one.'

Ethan glanced at Lopez as they followed Donovan's team across to the warehouse entrance, the two uniformed cops standing guard outside parting to let them through. Ethan whispered to Jarvis as they walked.

'What's the story with these guys?'

'Call came in,' Jarvis replied. 'These guys called the FBI about the killing of Aaron Lymes and the feds followed the new protocol and sent it on to us right away. We'll chat with them and find out what we can about Lymes' death, see if it yields any clues to Joanna's involvement or whereabouts.'

Lopez moved ahead alongside Karina Thorne. 'Forensics done a sweep yet?'

'All cleared,' Karina confirmed. 'Donovan got here first, then Nev Jackson worked the scene with the CSI guys. Not that they found much.'

Ethan heard their voices echo as they entered the cavernous warehouse. Shafts of pale morning light beamed weakly through windows thick with grime. The warehouse floor was stained with thousands of bird droppings and coated with dust, through which he could see several rows of footprints ahead of them that wound a trail back and forth toward the very rear of the warehouse. More faint footprints were to either side, where the CSI teams had walked around the originals to avoid contaminating them.

'Guns kill, then,' Lopez surmised. 'No contact.'

'No gunshots,' Donovan said over his shoulder at her, 'not with resulting wounds anyway.'

'Blades?' Ethan asked.

'You'll have to see it for yourself,' Donovan replied.

Ethan followed them to the rear of the warehouse, but, like Lopez, he came up short long before he reached the corner where the forensics team were still dusting down for prints and evidence around the scene of the crime.

The trail of footprints in the dust led to a scattering of more footprints, appearing to move in random directions all in the same area. Clearly, whoever had entered the warehouse had made their way to this corner before doing something on the spot.

Whatever that something had been, it hadn't ended well for the two victims now lying within ten feet of each other on the dusty warehouse floor. Ethan looked down at the body of one man lying on his side, his torso ending in a bloodied mess of congealing intestines, entrails and blood stains smearing the ground.

'Jesus,' Lopez murmured. 'Where's the rest of him?'

'That's where this starts to get interesting,' Donovan said, and gestured across to Ethan's right.

Ethan turned and saw some fifty feet away another smaller cordon of police tape and a lone forensics officer working on two long objects lying on the ground. Between the two locations was a faint splatter of blood droplets scattered in a thin line across the ground.

'That's his legs?' Jarvis asked in amazement.

'That's not all,' Donovan replied and gestured the other body nearby. 'This guy doesn't have a mark on him. We'll have to have it confirmed via autopsy but there are no visible wounds, puncture marks, contusions or any other visible sign of death.'

Ethan looked at the second corpse. The body was on its knees, crouched over with its elbows resting on the ground and the hands clasped across the chest. The dead man's face was pinned against the ground and locked in a gruesome rigor of agony, the jaw open and the eyes wide, the tongue hanging limp and dry between the lips.

'Looks a little like a heart attack,' Lopez suggested. 'He still in rigor mortis?'

'Coming out of it as we speak,' Donovan confirmed, 'but for some reason, he's still stiff as a board. Only thing the coroner can confirm at this moment is that he died in that position. Liver mortis shows he hasn't moved since his heart stopped beating.'

Ethan looked from one body to the next. 'Were any weapons recovered from the scene?'

'A pistol,' Donovan replied. 'Nine millimeter, an old Russian make, apparently.'

'Makarov?' Ethan hazarded.

'How did you know?' Donovan asked.

'Former standard Soviet sidearm,' Ethan explained. 'Very stable weapon, easily obtained on the black market, especially since the fall of the Soviet Union. Were these two guys criminals?'

'Ethan was an officer in the United States Marines,' Jarvis explained to Donovan, 'served with me on a couple of tours.'

Donovan nodded, looking at Ethan with renewed respect. 'Connor Reece and Wesley Hicks. Local hoods and petty thieves, not much between them but jail-time. They were known to us but didn't figure much on the bigger scale of things.'

'They do now,' Lopez pointed out, 'for somebody at least. Who the hell would rip a man in half just for the hell of it?'

'They did more than that,' Donovan said. 'Coroner gave the body a quick once over and said that virtually every bone in his body was broken, and that it likely happened before he died of massive hemorrhage.'

'Gangland beating got out of hand?' Karina wondered out loud. 'Maybe they got in with bigger fish and upset them.'

Lopez shook her head slowly. 'Doesn't make any sense. This guy's been ripped apart but there's no sign of any power tools, weapons, nothing. How'd they do it?'

'Indeed,' Donovan replied. 'Biggest problem we've got here is that both men were obviously murdered, yet the only weapon on the scene cannot have been used to commit the crime.'

Ethan frowned. 'You said that there were gunshots though.'

Donovan nodded, and his grizzled features seemed to pale a little. 'Five shots, all closely spaced.'

Lopez blinked, looking around her. 'Where's the mark then?'

Donovan slowly lifted his hand and pointed straight up.

Ethan craned his neck back and looked up to the warehouse ceiling, forty or more feet above their heads. There, needle-thin shafts of light pierced the dusty air in the ware house from five tiny holes in the roof. It took Ethan only a moment to realize that there were no walkways, no beams and no girders across which a potential killer could have been hiding when the shots were fired.

'That's weird,' Karina murmured.

'It gets even weirder,' Donovan said. 'Our heart-attack victim has powder residue on his right hand, suggesting that he fired the shots. But both of their prints were on the weapon. So he probably didn't kill his companion here and was instead firing at something else. Judging by what happened to his friend, we think that he was trying to defend himself against someone.'

'Or,' Lopez said, finding a more comfortable foundation for thought, 'this was drugs related. Maybe they were both high, got spooked into shooting at shadows.'

Donovan looked at Lopez. 'Drugs and shadows don't normally tear people in half.'

'No,' Lopez agreed, not bridling at the accusation of stupidity. 'But there's nothing to say that these two people died at exactly the same moment. The man who is in half may have died here first. His companion comes to find him, panics at what he finds and then starts shooting wildly.

Maybe has a heart attack. He could have had an existing condition that made him vulnerable to cardiac arrhythmia, common in cocaine users.'

Donovan conceded the point with an inclination of his head, but Ethan had already considered something else.

'The answers may lie in finding out why these two were here at all,' he said as something on the floor near the bodies caught his eye.

He carefully skirted the nearest corpse and knelt down alongside several deep grooves in the warehouse floor.

'Who called this in?' he asked, glancing up at Karina Thorne.

'Site manager,' Karina replied. 'Found the gate chains broke and the warehouse door unlocked when he showed up this morning to open the site.'

'I got here first,' Donovan added, 'and called the team in as soon as I saw these guys lying here.'

Ethan gestured down to the grooves in the floor.

'This warehouse is old and covered in dust from lack of use, but these grooves are fresh. These boys came in here looking for something, found it, and then got hit by someone. Whatever they found is now gone, taken by whoever walked out of here. Those footprint trails in the dust are moving both in and out of the warehouse.'

Donovan shrugged. 'The grooves in the flooring could be unrelated, maybe residue from recent storage operations. The footprints are interesting but still don't explain cause of death.'

Ethan stood up and looked about him.

'Cause of death is for the coroner,' Ethan said. 'My guess is that the footprints in the dust trail leading to this spot will hold some answers. Have forensics take a closer look and try to figure out who walked out of here last, then have the site manager give up any documents regarding users of this building in the last six months. If anyone's there it might be a lead, but this warehouse looks like it's been abandoned for a few years. Perfect place to hide things to be recovered at a later date.'

Karina Thorne frowned at Ethan. 'To do that, you'd need access,' she pointed out.

'Yes, you would,' Ethan agreed as he jabbed a thumb in the direction of the entrance door. 'Somebody had to cut the chains to the gate to get into the compound but there's no forced entry to the warehouse itself. Who would own one key but not both?'

'Maybe they picked the lock?' Glen Ryan hazarded.

'You see the size of it?' Lopez challenged him. 'It's turn-of-the-century and no evidence of tampering. They got in without a problem.'

'And with an empty warehouse inside, they had to be looking for something that somebody else had already left here. The question is: What?'

Donovan nodded, then cast a last glance at the grooves, before he turned to Karina.

'What do you think?

Karina shook her head, mystified by what she was looking at but, more, Ethan suspected, by the lack of evidence to support what had actually occurred.

'There's not much that we can do here until forensics finish their work and the medical examiner can get toxicology reports on the two victims,' she said. 'Right now, I don't have any explanation for how they could have died this way.'

Ethan glanced up at the five tiny bullet holes piercing the ceiling high above.

'Somebody does,' he said finally. 'Ultra-violent killings like these, with people torn in half, are usually the preserve of organized crime syndicates like the Mafia. But they don't bother with technical skill – they'd have just used a chainsaw or something. These guys were in fear of their lives from someone who had managed to get above them.'

Donovan turned away from the grisly remains. 'Either way, we need to figure this one out and fast. If the perpetrator strikes again, it could cause a media frenzy. I don't want them championing a vigilante killer.'

Donovan strode away, leaving Ethan and Lopez staring at the bodies.

'Hell of a way to go,' Karina uttered.

'They say crime doesn't pay,' Lopez shrugged.

Ethan glanced up again at the holes in the ceiling and saw a shadow hovering over them. As soon as he focused on it, the shadow whipped aside and vanished. In the empty warehouse, the sound of soft footfalls rushed across the warehouse roof.

'We're being watched!' Ethan shouted, and whirled for the exit.

# 14

Ethan sprinted past Donovan, who turned in surprise as he shouted out his warning to the police officer. The footfalls across the roof had been heading in the opposite direction to the warehouse exit, and Ethan already realized that he would be lucky to catch whoever had been watching their every move.

'Call for back-up!' he yelled to Jarvis as he ran through the warehouse door and vaulted down the steps. Lopez was in hot pursuit, with Karina Thorne close behind her.

Ethan turned right, guessing that the mysterious figure would probably drop down into the haulage yard behind the warehouse. He had seen trucks parked there, some loading and unloading inside a small parking lot with maybe a dozen vehicles.

'*Escape route*?' he yelled back at Lopez and Karina, who were also running hard.

'Anywhere off 26th Avenue!' Karina yelled back. 'Probably 4th onto 27th and they'll be gone!'

Ethan mentally pictured 26th Avenue running parallel to them to the south as he reached the back of the warehouse and slowed. A high chain-link fence lined the rear of the lot, shipping containers stacked up on the other side. Ethan's practiced eye scanned the fence line and saw a portion of the fence quivering from where it had been recently scaled.

He ran hard across the lot and leaped high up onto the fence, his sneakers finding purchase and his fingers gripping the thin metal links as he scrambled up over the top and jumped down onto the roof of a container that was slick with water and filth.

A man was sprinting across the parking lot ahead and below him, dressed in black and with a hooded top concealing his features. Light brown boots splashed through puddles of icy water as they fled.

'He's heading for 4th!' he yelled back at Karina.

The cop grabbed her radio as she ran and began directing Donovan as Ethan leaped down off the container and rolled onto the cold asphalt, Lopez landing alongside him and setting off like a scalded cat.

Ethan kept running but moved out to the right, hoping to cut the man off as they dashed out of the shipping yard and down 4th while Lopez stayed behind them. He dashed down 3rd Street, a hundred and fifty yards straight, his chest heaving and his heart thundering as he reached the end and turned left onto 26th Avenue.

He had almost made it to the Shop Smart on the corner of 4th when a small, battered-looking gray Pontiac screeched across the intersection in front of him and vanished away to the south. Lopez clattered to a halt on the sidewalk, heaving for breath as she saw him and shook her head.

'Car was parked on 4th,' she gasped. 'No chance.'

Donovan's car swerved out of 3rd Street behind them, and the cop pulled in to the sidewalk. 'Where'd they go?'

'South,' Ethan replied breathlessly, 'gray sixties Pontiac, pretty rough-looking.'

Donovan picked up his radio and called in a description for patrol vehicles to keep an eye open for the Pontiac, as Karina jogged up alongside them, her labored breath condensing in clouds on the cold air.

'Who the hell was that?' she asked.

'Probably our perpetrator,' Ethan replied, getting his breath back. 'Killers often return to the scene of the crime.'

'No, they don't,' Donovan said, getting out of his car. 'Unless they're serial killers looking to get off on how horrible their crimes are or how stumped detectives are in trying to solve them.'

'You think we've got a serial killer on our hands?' Karina asked. 'That's a big leap from the double homicide of two low-life criminals.'

'I didn't say that,' Donovan corrected her. 'It's not likely to have been the media, and who the hell else would get all the way up on top of that building to spy on us?'

Karina shot Ethan and Lopez a curious glance before she replied: 'I'll have somebody get up there and take a look, okay? Maybe see if there were any security cameras running, anything that can pick up their trail or identify them.'

Donovan nodded, got back into his car and drove off into the flow of morning traffic. Karina waited until he was gone before confronting Ethan and Lopez.

'You want to tell me who *you* think that was on the roof?'

Ethan raised a placatory hand. 'I don't know, okay? Nobody's informed the media and they're unlikely to stumble on this investigation by chance way out here on the docks.'

'Then, who?' Karina demanded. 'You guys turn up here and suddenly there are weird people in black hoods hanging around.'

'We don't know who it was,' Lopez replied. 'It's likely that it was somebody snooping around the crime scene for kicks.'

Ethan turned away from Karina in time to see Jarvis's black SUV sweep through the intersection and turn toward them. It performed a graceful U-turn across the street, its thick black tires squealing as it did so, and pulled into the sidewalk.

Jarvis climbed out. 'You find them?' he asked.

'They got away,' Lopez replied. 'Donovan's on the case right now.'

'You want to tell me what the hell's really going on here?' Karina demanded, eyeing Jarvis suspiciously.

'Your team is getting the support it needs to solve this case,' Lopez replied.

'I mean that goddamned warehouse!' Karina snapped. 'We've got two impossible murders, you guys turning up and taking over our cases and people photographing a crime scene that nobody but us should know exists.'

Jarvis stepped forward, taking over from Lopez.

'This is how we work,' he replied. 'Sometimes agencies have problems solving cases and they pass jurisdiction to us.'

Karina shook her head. 'The FBI haven't even visited this site yet, so how the hell would they know? How did you get jurisdiction of this scene and this investigation? Why are you here?'

Ethan looked at Karina and sensed that she was not the type to simply back down. If they didn't bring her in as an ally, sooner or later she would start digging and things would get even more difficult than they already were.

'It's complicated,' Ethan said. 'We're here to help but right now we need your help, too. Can we talk, later? We'll explain as much as we can.'

Karina looked from Lopez to Ethan to Jarvis and back again.

'Apartment 4B, Forton Place, Broadway,' she said. 'I get off at eight.'

As Karina turned and stalked away, Jarvis looked at Ethan and gestured to the SUV. 'We need to talk.'

Ethan got into the vehicle with Lopez as Jarvis climbed in behind them and shut the door.

'You're damned right, we need to talk,' Ethan snapped as the vehicle pulled away. 'There's a hell of a lot going on right now that doesn't make any sense. I thought you said that the CIA was off our case?'

'They are,' Jarvis replied defensively. 'I don't know who that was on the roof.'

'It could have been CIA,' Ethan said reasonably. 'You said it yourself: the CIA's director was at the meeting with you.'

'They're not on the scene,' Jarvis assured him. 'The director promised to pull his people off your tail just as long as we didn't make any further investigations into MK-ULTRA.'

'And you believed him?' Lopez asked. 'I wouldn't trust a spook as far as I could throw one.'

'Nor would I,' Jarvis admitted with a brief shrug, 'which is why you'll continue with your investigation.'

Ethan raised an eyebrow in surprise, as the SUV smoothly changed lanes. 'You're double-crossing them?'

Jarvis smiled thinly.

'The CIA has made a fifty-year career out of double-crossing people, so Director Steel's not likely to be shy of going behind my back. I'm not about to let this go until I have absolutely solid proof of CIA corruption or involvement, whether sanctioned or not, in the killing of American citizens. Right now, the evidence I have is circumstantial unless we can find somebody to testify to the Senate.'

Lopez leaned forward in her seat, a cynical smile slapped across her features. 'And once you have this evidence, then what? Somehow, I don't think you'll run screaming to the papers.'

'The evidence will be presented to a military court,' Jarvis said. 'Either that or it will be locked safely away at the DIA to act as insurance against any further inter-agency interference, from the CIA or anybody else.'

Ethan felt something uncomfortable slither inside him. 'And what about this case here: the two losers they found in that warehouse?'

'I want you to work with the police team and solve this case, while I find out what I can from Donovan about Aaron Lymes' death. It will look good back at the DIA that you're still actively on their side. Right now, half of the Joint Chiefs of Staff is entertaining the possibility that you two have been murdering CIA agents, remember?'

Ethan's guts felt as though they had turned to stone.

'I'm not doing this to suck up to a bunch of brass.'

'And what about Joanna?' Lopez asked. 'If we lose her trail, she'll be almost impossible to pick up again; and if we find her and the CIA are watching us, then they'll grab her and that's the last we'll see of her.'

'Not necessarily,' Jarvis pointed out. 'It's what she might know that scares them, and what she might do with that knowledge. If Joanna has done what they obviously think she has and gone underground on a mission to expose MK-ULTRA, then the CIA's mission is to stop her at all costs. But if she can be prevented from doing so, and we at the DIA hold any hard evidence she possesses, then she is no longer a threat.'

Lopez leaned back in her seat with a bitter chuckle. 'The DIA has its own get-out-of-jail-free card and we're all in the clear. You've got it all worked out, Doug, I'll give you that.'

'I don't know,' Ethan said, finally. 'The bodies in the warehouse could just be some sort of elaborate hoax to throw investigators off the trail.'

Jarvis shook his head.

'Unlikely. We'll have to get you both down to the Medical Examiner's Office as soon as possible to find out what the autopsy says. Even if it's not a case that warrants the DIA's involvement, it gives you a reason to stay in New York and any case you solve will increase your standing. Right now, you need all the support you can get.'

Ethan glanced out of the vehicle's window at the bleak winter sky and the cold gray cityscape of New York City. The huge metropolis was both the perfect place for a fugitive to hide and also the perfect hunting ground.

'Whatever the situation might be, this city's going to be a dangerous place until we resolve this situation once and for all. There's a possible assassin, fugitive and serial killer on the loose here all at the same time.'

'Then we'd best get to work,' Jarvis said. 'Stay close to Karina. Maybe she can help.'

# 15

# BROADWAY, NEW YORK

'We really appreciate this, Karina.'

Ethan watched as Karina handed them both a drink before flopping down onto a tired-looking couch. Her apartment was cramped and sparsely decorated, her salary as a detective probably only just allowing her to cover the rent. New York City was densely populated and the price of property was totally off the scale. Unless you were a celebrity or the Bronx and Harlem was your thing, everybody rented. People only went for mortgages when they were too old to live in the city, and then they bought places out to the north or over New Jersey way. New York City was a playground for the young, the successful and those who wanted to be. For the rest, it was just damned hard work.

'No big deal,' Karina replied. 'Not like I get many visitors, anyway.'

'Glen doesn't live here with you?' Lopez asked.

Ethan stared at her in surprise. 'How do you know that Glen's with Karina?'

'It's a woman thing.' Lopez smiled at Karina, who grinned conspiratorially back at her as she noticed Ethan's apparent discomfort.

Karina shrugged. 'Glen's as busy as I am, and he doesn't want us to move in together yet, anyway. Says it's too much *commitment* too soon.' Ethan noticed Lopez roll her eyes and glance in his direction, but he said nothing. 'And, on my own, I can't afford to do much but sleep and eat. Been here two years and all I've done is paint the walls.'

'Same for me back home,' Lopez said. 'I feel like I've only been out of the force for a few months.'

Karina nursed her drink as she eyed them both curiously.

'Yeah, what was the deal with that anyway?' she asked. 'I heard you were up for promotion after busting open some kind of big thing in DC, like Donovan said. Your name was big news for a week or two.'

'It's a long story,' Ethan replied for Lopez.

'Good,' Karina replied without hesitation and looked at Lopez. 'I like epics. Begin.'

'It's complicated,' Lopez replied. 'My partner and I in DC got involved in an investigation that was much bigger than we thought. Ethan here came in close to the end, but, by then, my partner had been killed.'

'I'm sorry,' Karina said. 'I didn't know.'

'A lot of the details were kept fairly quiet outside of local media,' Lopez said. 'I was offered promotion but turned it down and left the force. Ethan and I teamed up and we're private investigators, technically.'

'*Technically?*' Karina pressed.

'We work for the government,' Ethan said. 'We're subcontracted to a department within the Defense Intelligence Agency, which picks up criminal investigations that are passed over by other agencies as unworkable.'

Karina raised an eyebrow. 'Very Men in Black. So what brought you here? And don't tell me it was the Hell Gate case. You must have been in town before then, if you're from DC?'

'We're from Illinois,' Ethan informed her. 'Our work for the DIA takes us across the country.'

'You follow the news a few months back?' Lopez asked her. 'A Democrat Congressman sanctioned a congressional investigation into corruption within the intelligence community.'

Karina frowned. 'Sure, got shut down after a couple of months. Some poor guy died or something.'

'Quite a few people died,' Ethan replied for Lopez. 'We're investigating what happened.'

The decision to lie to Karina was one that Ethan and Lopez had debated on the way over. Ethan feared that exposing her to what was really happening could possibly make her a target. Lopez had admitted that was something she wished to avoid but at the same time was loathe to risk lying to a potential ally only for those lies to later be exposed. Ultimately, it came down to a practical requirement of their work with the DIA that they were already used to: tell as much of the truth as possible, in order to cover the lie.

'You're investigating your own people?'

Lopez nodded. 'But quietly. There's not much more we can say right now as this may lead to nothing but, because we need to be able to work without raising suspicions, we've had to travel incognito. We're subcontracted, so it's a little easier for us to investigate than putting actual government employees on the case.'

'So nobody knows that you're here?'

'Officially, we're on vacation from the DIA,' Lopez replied smoothly. 'Nobody knows we're in New York.'

Karina appeared to be wavering between excitement and disappointment. 'Jesus, I get to investigate drug-homicides and domestic assaults and you guys are going all Jack Bauer. There's no justice.'

'Believe me,' Lopez replied, 'it's not all satellites and car chases. Most of the time it's dead boring.'

'Sounds like it,' Karina said demurely. 'So you're here for how long?'

'We're not sure,' Ethan said. 'We did some work up in Idaho a few months ago that exposed an operation that was off the books. We're down here doing follow-up research to see if anybody else knows about their experiments.'

'Their *experiments*?' Karina echoed.

'It's not as exotic as it sounds,' Lopez lied. 'The trail led us to New York and we've got to do some digging around here. It's better that we don't broadcast our presence too widely.'

Karina looked at them both closely for a moment. 'You think that people might come after you? The same people that killed Aaron Lymes?'

'No, it's not like that,' Lopez reassured her. 'After what happened in DC, they're as keen to resolve this discreetly as anybody else, and Lymes is a separate case.'

'And yet you're hiding,' Karina said suspiciously.

'The CIA has burned evidence of previous covert operations before now in order to avoid public outcry and congressional investigations,' Ethan pointed out. 'Our job is to grab evidence before they have the chance to do that again. It's not us they'll target, but paper trails and safe-houses, stuff like that.'

Karina rubbed her forehead as though trying to clear her thoughts. 'So what's my role in all of this?'

'We need access to the police,' Lopez replied. 'Not personal access but an ear to the ground.'

'Are you looking for people?' Karina asked.

'Yes,' Ethan said. 'Right now, we're just trying to identify leads from older cases handled by our agency.'

Karina inclined her head. 'Okay, I get it. You can't go to the FBI or anything because that might result in your investigation getting noticed.'

'That's pretty much it,' Lopez said, nodding. 'Everything needs to be covert so that we don't spook anybody into closing up shop.'

'Why not just go public with what you've got?' Karina asked. 'It worked for WikiLeaks.'

'All sorts of reasons,' Lopez said, 'and look what happened to the founder of WikiLeaks when they went too far. Sure, we could go public with what's happened, and that might make it difficult for those responsible to cover their tracks without attracting attention and drawing suspicion down on themselves. But how many people have you seen die in the papers who claimed they were the victim of intelligence conspiracies or political hits, whose stories then vanished without trace? It happens all the time, but nobody really believes it.'

Karina's features paled as she looked at Lopez. 'You're talking about assassinations?'

'That's right,' Ethan confirmed. 'There's the former KGB spy in London, Alexander Litvinenko, who was murdered by an assassin using polonium-210, a lethal dose of which killed him via radiation poisoning. The Russians were undoubtedly behind it but nobody was convicted or faced charges and it's largely been forgotten.'

'Then there's Viktor Yushchenko, the former Ukrainian president,' Lopez added, 'who was the victim of an assassination attempt using TCDD, a potent dioxin used in Agent Orange. He survived but was permanently disfigured as a result.'

'Sure,' Karina admitted, 'but they're both being hit by Russian agencies, not people here in the States. I thought you said you weren't being targeted?'

'We're not,' Lopez said with an easy smile, 'and nor would anybody around us. But others might be, which is why we need to collate evidence and present it to the Pentagon before anything goes pear-shaped.'

'Look,' Ethan said, 'right now, we're trying to track down people whose families may have been of interest when the CIA's operations were at their height. There's hardly any names left on our list but one of them comes from New York City.'

'Where'd you get this list from?'

'My sister, Natalie,' Ethan said. 'She was working at the Government Accountability Office in DC during the congressional investigation. It was one of her colleagues there who was killed, shutting the whole thing down.'

'You think that was an assassination?' Karina gasped.

'We don't know,' Lopez said. 'Either way, it doesn't affect us as we're much removed from those events.'

Karina shook her head slowly. 'What's the name you've got?'

'Barraclough.'

Karina chuckled. 'That name, in a population of about nine million in the city alone and twenty million in the state? Good luck with that.'

'There's a narrower criteria,' Lopez told her. 'The individual almost certainly will have family members involved with the military, usually around the period 1950 to 1973. The CIA drew upon individuals who had unusual abilities when they were researching things like hypnosis, LSD, mind control and remote-viewing.'

'I've heard about stuff like that,' Karina murmured cautiously. 'I thought it was all just a myth, you know, conspiracy theories.'

'It's not a myth,' Ethan assured her. 'The program was called MK-ULTRA and is well documented by historians. The CIA has even apologized and paid compensation to the families of servicemen suspected to have died as a result of experiments conducted upon them without their knowledge.'

Karina thought about this for a moment and then looked at Ethan. 'So, how are you going to track this person down?'

Ethan shrugged.

'I guess we'll start at a hall of records and see if we can narrow the search down. Maybe, there'll be something about this Barraclough family that will stand out, something that made the CIA take notice of them in the first place. If we can identify the family then we might be able to track down surviving members, maybe even the person who was involved with MK-ULTRA themselves.'

Karina got to her feet and headed toward the kitchen, her empty glass in her hand.

'My mother once tried to track down our family heritage, going all the way back to the first colonial settlers,' she said as she walked past Ethan. 'Took her fourteen years and she still never managed to . . .'

Karina screamed and leaped backwards, as her glass crashed onto the kitchen floor and shattered into a thousand tiny crystals. Ethan leapt out of his seat in shock, his heart thundering against the wall of his chest as he whirled to see Karina staring into the kitchen, her eyes wide and her hand covering her mouth.

'*What's wrong?*' Lopez yelled, leaping to her feet.

Karina continued to stare into the kitchen, her face pale despite the warm glow of the lights. Ethan walked across to her side and looked into the kitchen, the room dimly lit by the glow from the lounge.

Something tingled across the base of his neck, raising hairs as though he had felt something unnatural hovering close by. He shivered involuntarily.

'I saw somebody,' Karina said. 'Clear as day, standing right there in front of the window.'

'Outside?' Ethan asked, confused. 'We're three stories up.'

Karina shook her head. 'Inside, right there.'

She pointed to the corner of the room. Ethan looked down at her and somehow he knew that she wasn't lying. But after what they had just been discussing, she could have gotten spooked and started seeing ominous shadows where there were none.

'You okay?' Lopez asked, joining Karina. 'You're shaking.'

Karina stared vacantly into the middle distance for a long moment, and then she turned and grabbed her cellphone from her pocket. Ethan watched as she speed-dialed a number and listened for it to pick up for ten long seconds.

She dropped the cell from her ear and glanced at the clock on the kitchen wall.

'I have to go somewhere,' she announced suddenly and strode toward a set of car keys hanging from a rack near the apartment door.

'I'm coming with you,' Lopez said, concern etched into her exotic features.

Ethan, with no real choice left in the matter, followed them out of the apartment.

# 16

The apartment Karina drove to was just a few blocks away, near downtown. Ethan sat in the rear seat and watched Karina's features in the rear-view mirror as she drove.

Karina Thorne was a tough cop. Had to be really, serving in New York City, where crime was almost as prevalent as people. Although things were far better in the city than they had been twenty years before, it was still rough territory at times and nobody donned police blues without a sturdy backbone to support them. Yet he had seen a cold flicker of fear in her eyes in the apartment.

Karina pulled up alongside one of the smarter apartment blocks and scrambled out of the car, Lopez and Ethan jogging to keep up as she launched herself up the entrance steps and jammed a finger against the door buzzer.

'What are we doing here?' Lopez asked her.

'Gut feeling,' Karina replied.

No reply came from the speakerphone set into the wall. Karina hit the emergency button and, moments later, the voice of a site manager croaked out of the speaker.

'Maintenance, how may I . . .?'

'Thorne, NYPD, one-seven-six-nine-two,' Karina snapped, flashing her badge at the small camera above the speakerphone. 'I think there may be an emergency, apartment six-Charlie.'

There was a moment's wait and then the door buzzed open and Karina pushed through.

'How come we haven't tried that before?' Ethan asked Lopez as they piled through and began running up the stairs two at a time in pursuit of Karina.

Karina hit the sixth floor at a run, dashing down a corridor and reaching the door of apartment 6C, just as the site warden stepped out of a nearby elevator; a portly man with receding gray hair and a thick moustache.

'What's the rush, officer?' he asked as he wobbled his way toward them.

'Non-responsive,' Karina replied urgently. 'Just open the door.'

The warden fiddled with his keys and slipped one of them into the lock, then turned it. Karina barged into the door, which snapped open three inches and then stuck fast on a security chain.

'Damn it, Tom!' Karina yelled. 'Open up!'

Ethan stepped forward and Karina ducked aside as he lifted one boot and slammed it into the door just below the safety chain. The door shuddered but held firm. Ethan leaped back and hit the door again with his boot, this time the chain straining as the wooden door frame splintered. Ethan stepped back and kicked again, and, this time, Karina slammed her shoulder into the door at the same moment.

The safety chain burst from its mount and the heavy door swung open and cracked against the wall, as Karina raced into the apartment with Ethan close behind.

The lounge was dark but for a single lamp that glowed in the far corner near the windows, the veils drawn tight. A large coffee table was stacked with photographs in their frames, all facing a long couch.

There, slumped across it, was a man Ethan judged to be in his early thirties, another picture frame lying across his chest. A half-full glass of milk lay spilled on the thick carpet and, alongside, it a scattering of pills and an empty bottle.

'Paramedics, now!' Karina screamed.

Ethan and Lopez dashed across the lounge, as the maintenance manager grabbed his cellphone. Karina reached the man first, reaching out toward him. A bright blue spark of electricity crackled up and snapped at her fingers.

Karina leaped back involuntarily as the bolt of static writhed and vanished.

Ethan stared at the body as a strange but somehow familiar smell tainted the air.

'Electricity,' Lopez murmured in surprise. 'You can smell the charge.'

Karina reached out again for the man's body, this time more carefully. No further energy hit her as she tried to drag the man's body off the couch and onto the floor.

Lopez helped her, checking for breathing and a pulse, as Karina rolled the man over.

'There's nothing, he's arrested,' Lopez said.

Karina responded instantly, starting cardiopulmonary resuscitation, as Lopez stood back and looked up at Ethan.

'You see that spark?'

Ethan nodded. 'Maybe static or something off the couch before he arrested.'

'I guess,' Lopez agreed, then looked at Karina. 'How did you know he was like this?'

Karina shook her head as she rhythmically compressed the man's chest. 'I just knew. I don't know how.'

Ethan knelt down alongside the man's body and rested one hand on Karina's, to stop her, before he leaned down and touched his finger to the man's neck. A faint pulse threaded its way past his fingertip.

'He's got a rhythm,' he said to her, 'but it's very faint.'

Lopez stepped aside as two paramedics rushed into the apartment, the maintenance manager following them and pointing at the man on the floor. Ethan glanced at the glass of milk and the pills nearby and touched a hand to the glass.

'He's an overdose,' Karina informed the paramedics desperately, 'arrested but we've got a pulse.'

'How long since he crashed?' one of the men asked.

Karina shook her head, but Ethan spoke for her.

'Five minutes, maximum,' he said. 'Bottle has pills left in it, the milk's still warm and we'd never have gotten a pulse back if he'd been down any longer.'

Ethan got out of their way and watched as they went to work on the man's body, slipping an intravenous line into his arm and preparing a stretcher. Lopez put her arm around Karina as the trauma of the day finally began to catch up on her. Ethan watched as her face began to crumple and she turned away from the scene, hiding from the light.

Ethan looked around the apartment, at the photographs stacked on the table and the one that had been resting on the man's chest. He guessed that it was Karina's partner, Tom Ross, who had attempted to take his own life. He could see it was an image of Tom, his wife and his daughter taken at close range maybe on a beach holiday in bright sunlight, all three of them smiling and laughing at the camera. As the paramedics hoisted the stretcher with Tom Ross upon it, Ethan could hardly blame the guy for wanting to quit. Ethan himself had lost his fiancée years before and he knew well the grief that such an event could generate, but to lose an entire family was beyond comparison.

'Ethan?' He turned to see Lopez looking up at him. 'I'm going to go with Karina to the hospital. Why don't you get on the horn to Jarvis from here, instead of using our cells, and find out what we're going to do? It'll help prevent anybody from tracking our movements.'

Ethan nodded, admiring her quick thinking.

'Sure, I'll catch you up later.'

Ethan waited until everybody had left the apartment except the maintenance manager, who looked questioningly at Ethan.

'I'm going to turn everything off in here before I leave,' Ethan explained to the portly man. 'I don't think Tom's going to be home for a day or two and he'll need some clothes for hospital, when he wakes up.'

'Right, sure,' the manager said 'I'll leave you to it.'

Ethan waited alone in the apartment until he heard the elevator door close further down the corridor outside. Then, he walked across to a telephone on a shelf near the window and picked it up. He dialed Jarvis's number from memory.

'*Jarvis.*'

Ethan hesitated for a brief moment before replying.

'It's Ethan. We got any news on the Hell Gate victims or Aaron Lymes yet?'

'*Nothing on the Hell Gate case,*' Jarvis admitted, '*but Aaron Lymes was murdered in his own apartment. Donovan's investigation concluded that he let his attacker in, believe it or not. If it was Joanna, she might have been able to win his confidence before overpowering him. Lymes was in his late fifties when he retired from the agency, so it's plausible.*'

'What was the cause of death?' Ethan asked.

'*Blunt force trauma followed by asphyxiation,*' Jarvis replied. '*Where are you?*'

'Been busy,' Ethan replied by way of an explanation. 'You remember what Major Greene said, about crisis-apparitions?'

'*Sure,*' Jarvis replied. '*Nothing I'd worry about. The CIA may have taken them seriously but, then again, they dropped oversized condoms on the Vietcong to try to intimidate them into thinking American soldiers were more manly.*'

'I wouldn't write them off so quickly,' Ethan said. 'Something just showed up at Karina's apartment and near scared the life out of her.'

'*Seriously?*' Jarvis replied. '*What happened?*'

'She spooked,' Ethan said, 'then came running over to her friend's apartment, the one who lost his family the other day. We found him lying on his sofa, overdosed on pain medication.'

'*Jesus*,' Jarvis replied. '*Maybe there's more to her than meets the eye. Stay close, Ethan, see what turns up.*'

'We're staying at her apartment for now,' Ethan said. 'She and Lopez hit it off pretty good.'

'*Perfect*,' Jarvis replied. '*How's her partner?*'

'Alive,' Ethan said. 'I'm heading down after them right now.'

'*Let me know what happens*,' Jarvis replied. '*Maybe one of them has something to do with MK-ULTRA. It would make sense. You followed Joanna's trail to New York and the killings certainly point in that direction.*'

'Not necessarily,' Ethan pointed out. 'We're assuming that Joanna's responsible for them but there's no hard evidence for that. It could even be a CIA set-up itself, using Joanna's name to cover their own clean-up operation.'

'*It's possible*,' Jarvis admitted. '*But I saw DCIA's face in that meeting with the Joint Chiefs of Staff. Something was making the fat asshole nervous, and, as much as I enjoyed seeing it, it's unlikely to be orchestrated by him.*'

'And what about Joanna?' Ethan asked. 'What if we do find her here?'

'*I can't do much until she shows up*,' Jarvis insisted. '*Let's do this one step at a time, Ethan. Right now, just concentrate on solving this homicide case. I've got you both a visit to Rikers Island in the morning, to see if the two thieves Donovan's team arrested on Williamsburg Bridge will identify their accomplices. The police didn't get anywhere. See what you can get out of them, because it will help your standing with the NYPD. We might need their help to locate Joanna before the CIA do, if she's in the city.*'

Ethan hesitated for a moment, before finally deciding that there was no real use in arguing further. If Jarvis had a solution up his sleeve to this whole damned mess, then he probably wouldn't reveal it until the last possible moment.

'I'll let you know what we find out,' he said.

Ethan put the phone back in its cradle, and was about to leave when he felt a tingling sensation creep across his shoulders, as though a gossamer web had settled on his skin. He turned, looking around the silent apartment for a long moment, before he finally shook himself out of it and shut off the lights. He closed the door to the apartment behind him, pursued by a strange and unsettling feeling.

# 17

# NEW YORK DOWNTOWN HOSPITAL

Lopez had never been a fan of hospitals, the clinical odour reminding her of the one time when she had been taken into an emergency room as a young girl, way back in the mountains of Guanajuato, Mexico. The experience had not been pleasant.

She sat on a bench alongside Karina, as orderlies, doctors, nurses rushed back and forth between the patients who shuffled or were being wheeled between wards. Karina remained silent, staring at the tired-looking floor tiles with her hands clasped together in her lap. Lopez watched her for a long time, before choosing her words carefully.

'How long have the two of you been working together?' she asked.

Karina blinked awake, as though emerging from a daydream, and looked across at Lopez.

'Just over a year,' she replied. 'Donovan hand-picked Tom to work with me.'

'He controls every aspect of your unit?' Lopez asked.

'Sure,' came the response. 'We work mostly homicide and each of us is a specialist. I work forensic and trace evidence. Glen handles firearms, Jackson's attached from vice, Tom usually covers victim and perp' histories and sometimes profiles. Donovan oversees and reports to the commissioner.'

'Tight unit,' Lopez guessed. 'Good idea in a big city. Should've tried it back in DC.'

Karina nodded slowly.

'It works well to have teams rather than just partners,' she replied. 'We have our own strengths and weaknesses, but the total is greater than the sum of its parts. We've cracked every case we've been handed except one since we formed – that's better than any other single unit in the city.'

Lopez nodded. 'Probably in the country,' she pointed out. 'There are always unsolved cases. Which one got the better of you?'

'Homicide in downtown, a gang-slaying between Crips and Surenos. We know who did it but we couldn't provide enough evidence to place them at the crime. Perpetrator got bail and took off into Mexico. Hasn't been seen since.'

Lopez took a chance and gave Karina a playful nudge. 'Should've called Warner & Lopez, Inc. They're amazing, apparently.'

Karina stared at the tiles for a long time. Lopez cursed herself inwardly. Then Karina spoke softly. 'I heard they were crap.'

Lopez looked at her as a tiny smile flickered briefly across Karina's lips.

'Miss Thorne?'

Lopez and Karina bolted upright from the bench as a doctor approached them. A warm smile told them all they needed to know before the doctor even spoke.

'He's in recovery,' she said. 'You got to him just in time.'

Lopez heard Karina let a sigh of relief spill from her chest as she reached across and hugged her. Karina returned the embrace briefly and then looked at the doctor.

'Is he okay? Awake?'

'He's conscious,' the doctor replied. 'Given what he's attempted, I'd suggest you go and see him now. In my experience, people who have tried to take their own lives feel extremely isolated and often embarrassed. The sooner that notion is taken from him, the sooner he can begin healing.'

Karina nodded, and Lopez guided her toward the nearby ward. A private room had been set aside for Tom, his standing as a police officer and the terrible loss he had endured warranting him special treatment until he was on the road to recovery.

Lopez followed Karina into the room and closed the door behind them.

Tom Ross sat on his reclined bed, his eyes open but drooping with fatigue as he looked at them both.

'Tom?' Karina asked in a whisper. 'You hear me okay?'

Tom Ross stared at Karina for a long moment and then replied with a barely perceptible nod.

'You're doing fine,' Karina said, perching on the side of Tom's bed and reaching out for his hand. 'We'll get through this, okay? I've got your back.'

Tom's dark eyes drifted across to meet hers and, for a long time, he said nothing. Then, as Lopez watched, he spoke in a quiet voice.

'How did you find me?' he asked.

'Came to check up on you,' Karina replied.

Tom's eyes flicked up to the clock on the wall, as though he knew she was lying. 'You'd only just left me.'

'It had been a couple of hours,' Karina said, 'and I was worried about you.'

Tom glanced back at her. 'Worried I might do something stupid?'

Karina looked at him for a long beat, then nodded.

Tom looked across at Lopez. 'Who are you?'

'Working a case with NYPD,' Lopez replied. 'In town for a couple of days.'

Tom looked at Lopez as though sizing her up, then looked back at Karina. He sighed softly.

'It was so easy,' he whispered. 'Once I decided to do it. So easy.'

Karina squeezed his hand. 'That doesn't mean it was right.'

'Right for whom?' Tom challenged her. Karina struggled to find an answer and, when she failed, Tom squeezed her hand back a little. 'You should have let me go, let me leave. I didn't want to be here anymore.'

Lopez caught the way Tom used the past tense, as though he had changed his mind since. Karina noticed it, too.

'Things change with time,' she replied. 'It's all just empty words right now, I know, but, someday, you'll be able to move on. You've just got to take it one day at a time.'

Tom shook his head.

'It'll be easier next time,' he said.

Karina's features became stern as she leaned toward him. 'There isn't going to be a *next time*, Tom. Okay?'

Tom looked at her. 'I saw something.'

Lopez felt a chill ripple down her neck and spine as Tom's softly spoken words drifted through the room around her.

'Saw something?' Karina asked. 'When? What do you mean?'

Tom's face looked both elated and haunted at the same time, as though he were struggling to decide whether he should speak at all.

'You have another friend in town,' he said finally, and looked at Lopez. 'A tall guy with light brown hair and a Chicago accent.'

Lopez felt another chill tingle across her shoulders and she shivered involuntarily as she replied. 'Ethan, my partner. How did you know?'

Tom looked at her, his expression serious now. 'He checked my pulse and told the paramedics I'd been out for no more than five minutes.'

Karina's jaw dropped as she stared at Tom. 'You were out cold,' she protested. 'Barely alive.'

Lopez stepped closer to the bed. 'Where were you, Tom?'

The young detective looked at her and smiled faintly.

'I was hovering above you all, up on the ceiling. I saw everything.'

Karina withdrew her hand from Tom's, as though his body had shocked her again, her features horrified as she struggled to comprehend what her friend was saying.

'What else did you see?' Lopez pressed.

'After that, I wasn't in the room.'

'Where were you?' Karina asked, overcoming her shock.

Tom shook his head as he replied.

'It's hard to describe, I don't know where I was. It was dark, totally black, but the blackness seemed huge, infinite. I was rising up, could feel myself going up and up, and then there was a light. It was so bright, brighter than the sun but I could look right into it.'

Lopez moved closer to the bed.

'The tunnel of light,' she said. 'You had a near-death experience, Tom.'

Tom looked at her, but he shook his head.

'Well, if I did, then the experience is highly overrated,' he replied.

'What happened?' Karina asked.

'I was floating up this tunnel,' Tom said, 'and I felt great. I can't even begin to describe it. It was as though every bad thing I'd ever done or seen or heard of suddenly was just utterly *gone*. I had no body but I could feel everything, could see everything, and there were people there waiting for me.'

Lopez shivered again.

'Friends?' she managed to ask; and then, more cautiously, 'Family?'

Tom looked at her and his expression of wonderment and joy faded away.

'They weren't there,' he replied, grief returning to stain his features. 'I could tell somehow that they weren't there, and then suddenly I could remember what had happened on the bridge, that I'd lost them, and then everything changed.'

'What changed, Tom?' Karina pressed.

'The tunnel of light faded away and I felt the darkness coming back. It was surging up toward me, cold and black and full of something I've never felt before.'

There was a moment's silence, as Tom sought the word he wanted, and then he looked at them both.

'Hate,' he said finally. 'Pure, undiluted, raw hate, more powerful than anything I can describe. I thought it would swallow me whole but it suddenly disappeared just like the tunnel of light did and, I was back in the apartment watching you all try to resuscitate me.'

Tom shook his head as he looked at Karina.

'I think I saw a little piece of Heaven,' he continued, 'and then a tiny fragment of Hell.'

# 18

# KHAN YUNIS, GAZA CITY, PALESTINE

*2 years ago*

'It's not working.'

The voice came from behind where she sat slumped in the chair, eyes staring blankly at the screen before her. A thin stream of congealed saliva lay drying on her chin. Her eyes were utterly dry and stinging painfully, but she felt removed from the pain as though it were a distant color or sound. She could not feel her arms, and, in her mind's eye, images flashed past continuously, even though the monitor before her was turned off. Those same images played all day in front of her, accompanied by fearsome jolts of pain delivered at cruelly random moments, and all night in her mind, awakening her as she jerked in expectation of electrical currents searing her body.

'Pull her out.'

The voices sounded as though they were part of a dream, monotone and indistinct, but, even now, she recognized them as American. From beyond the beam of light, she saw a figure approach, gray-suited. His face was long and sepulchral, his ashen skin matching his suit, as though he had been drained of color, and his expression as devoid of emotion as she was.

They had become more relaxed around her as time had passed, although, even now, she had no idea just how long she had been in captivity. There was no daylight, there were no clocks and the men using her for their bizarre experiments were extremely careful not to expose her to any sense of the outside world, be it through conversation or any other means.

She had lost all sense of her identity, long ago forgetting who she was, where she was, why she was there. Her memories had been scoured from her mind, leaving only the incessant flashing images grinding around the interior of her skull.

It had got worse when they had added video and sound. Her mind had been programmed to flinch at the slightest mention of terrorists, communism, socialism and a hundred other creeds and beliefs that clashed with the American Dream. She felt physical pain at the sight of images of wounded American soldiers or images of 9/11, even when no current was applied to her weary body. Utterly unable to sleep properly and exposed to countless hours of footage over immeasurable periods of time, she was now an empty shell, devoid of soul and spirit.

The gray-suited figure lifted off the headphones and unclipped the electrodes from her temples. As he removed the support pads, her head fell forward and her chin dug into her chest. Thick, lank hair spilled either side of her face.

'She's had it,' said another American voice. 'It was too much. I told you so.'

'Plenty more where she came from,' came the monotone reply. 'Give her to the doctor. There's nothing left of her for us to work with.'

'He won't be happy about that,' said the nearer of the two men as he lifted her unresisting body out of the chair and dumped it unceremoniously onto a gurney, strapping her in.

'Who cares?'

She was wheeled out of the room, back toward her cell. But this time, the two men pushed her past the cell door and on through the building to another room. Her eyes, dry and unseeing, could not focus properly on her surroundings. She was wheeled into the new room and heard the door close behind her.

A rhythmic beeping sound, that of a heart monitor, echoed slightly as though she was in a much larger room. Another figure, dressed in white, moved around her as she slowly focused.

'She'll see us.'

The voice came from her right and she swiveled her eyes to see the blurred images of the two men, both dressed in gray suits.

'It will take hours for her eyes to recover,' said the white figure as he moved to stand by her gurney. 'You have nothing to fear. I take it that she has been unresponsive to the programming?'

She felt a tiny pain in her right arm as a needle was slipped into a vein, and, within moments, she felt a strange surge of energy pulsing through her body.

'We completed the memory flush some time ago,' came the response. 'Cerebral reprogramming has proved positive but she has demonstrated no evidence of any ability to perform remote-viewing, precognition or any other extrasensory-perception tasks beyond those associated with chance. We're done with her.'

'And you've left her barely alive!' the white figure snapped. 'What use is she like this?'

'You're going to kill her anyway,' one of the gray suits said, shrugging.

'Temporarily,' replied the white figure.

'Whatever.'

The energy in her system flushed her senses, making her hyper-alert, and, as her eyes grew accustomed to the light, she saw the men come slowly into perfect focus. The adrenaline sharpened her thoughts and she did not look directly into the eyes of the two men, letting her gaze wander as though she were still blind.

One of them had dark, short hair, maybe late twenties, military-looking. A small scar on his left cheek, maybe a shrapnel wound from service in Iraq or Afghanistan. The second man in a gray suit was a taller and older. It was hard to avoid his cold gaze, but she managed to focus on his tie instead. His voice was utterly without emotion.

'Be sure that she is removed from play as soon as you're finished with her. We preserve security before any other considerations, including your insane little project. Is that understood, Doctor?'

The voice from beyond her line of sight replied calmly.

'It is understood. And it gets her out from under your skin, does it not?'

She tried to speak but her throat was utterly dry and nothing came out. She worked her jaw, trying to formulate words, but they would not come.

The white-coated figure emerged into view, and she saw a bright halo of white hair draped across an elderly face. The figure reached down and touched her arm. More pain, as another needle slid beneath her skin. She gasped, but no sound came out.

'Ssshhh,' the figure said to her, and touched a cold, dry finger to her lips. 'Save your strength. You're about to go on a journey you'll never forget.'

'Make it fast,' snapped the older gray suit. 'You're not done within six months, I'll ice her myself.'

The doctor glanced over his shoulder in irritation, but he nodded before he looked down at her and a chilling smile crept across his face.

'Now then, Joanna. I hope you've never experienced LSD before. I'd like this to be a uniquely maiden voyage for you into another world. Or, more accurately, somewhere else in this world.'

Joanna struggled to speak but her voice remained impotent. She felt the world around her begin to lose coherence as a warmth began tingling through her body, as though the doctor had injected her with a serious overdose of morphine.

The pain and the discomfort vanished as the last of her feeble resistance collapsed in the face of the drugs coursing through her system. With the last vestiges of her awareness, she saw the doctor loom over her.

In an instant, just before her senses disconnected from each other, she saw something that changed everything. In a flash that momentarily overpowered all of the suffering and all of the pain she had endured, Joanna knew how long she had been in captivity and knew how long it was that she had been experimented on. For a brief instant, that felt like the first ray of sunlight after an interminable darkness, Joanna remembered who she was again.

The doctor spoke.

'Joanna, my name is Doctor Damon Sheviz, and I'm going to take you to another plain of existence. You, my dear, are about to visit and return from the grave.'

Joanna's eyes flared in horror as the doctor went on.

'First, you will be anesthetized. Then, I will wire you up to a heart-bypass machine and you will receive heparin, which is made from cow's gut, to prevent blood clotting. Your heart will then be stopped via intravenously administered potassium chloride. Your body will be cooled over a period of about one hour to a temperature of around sixteen degrees Celsius, essentially as cold as a corpse. I will then drain the blood from your body and replace it with a chilled saline solution. By this time, you will be clinically dead, with no heartbeat, no blood and no brain activity. I will leave you in stasis in this condition for two hours, before reversing the process, returning your blood to your body, warming it and applying a small electrical charge to your heart to initiate rhythm.'

Joanna gasped but her throat was too dry and her muscles too weak to form words.

Damon Sheviz looked down at her and smiled.

'I expect that you have never had a near-death experience before,' he said. 'Trust me, by the time we're done here, you're going to have had many. You're going to meet God, Joanna, and I want to know what He looks like.'

The doctor's features swirled into a kaleidoscope of hazy colors, as Joanna Defoe finally lost consciousness, his words distant in her mind.

'Welcome to my Eternity Project.'

# 19

# ERIC M. TAYLOR CENTER, RIKERS ISLAND, NEW YORK CITY

'They ain't the talkin' kind.'

Ethan stood in a service corridor alongside Lopez as a duty sergeant signed them in and signaled a colleague sitting nearby in a small booth surrounded by bullet-proof glass. An electronic motor hummed as mechanical locks disengaged and a huge steel-barred door rolled open.

Located on an island in the East River between Queens and the Bronx, Rikers was a city of jails, with the Taylor Center, or '6 Building' as it was known, housing all adult and adolescent sentenced males. It was one section of a total population of fourteen thousand inmates, all awaiting trial. As new arrivals, the two men they had come to see were housed in the New Admissions cells, where they were kept in a sort of quarantine until the results of tests for tuberculosis and other diseases came back from dedicated labs.

Ethan walked with Lopez onto D-Block, a high-security wing of the center dedicated to holding high-profile inmates.

The block was deserted, the steel tables and benches bolted to the floor devoid of prisoners. All of them had been locked-down as Ethan and Lopez were brought onto the block.

'We're wasting our time here,' Lopez whispered to Ethan as they followed the sergeant onto the block. 'We should be looking for Joanna, not visiting deadbeats in jail. Jarvis is stalling.'

'For what?' Ethan challenged. 'Keeping us out of the way won't help our cause or his.'

'That all depends on what his cause really is,' she pointed out, and then looked at the sergeant. 'They had any visitors?' Lopez asked.

'Nope,' the sergeant replied, a burly man with a neck so squat and thick it looked like he'd dropped from between his mother's thighs and landed straight onto his head. 'No calls, no letters, no nothin'. They might be communicatin' with their cellmates for instance, but we don't see much of that in here as most cellies are strangers. Happens more in the prison population.'

Ethan looked at Lopez as they followed the sergeant across the block.

'That's unusual,' he said. 'Most all convicts would want to make a call or receive one.'

'Unless they're not expecting to stay long,' Lopez suggested.

'You kiddin'?' the sergeant asked over his broad shoulder as they walked. 'These two dudes were busted out on the Williamsburg Bridge, right? Caught red-handed. Ain't no jury in town gonna bail them.'

A crescendo of whoops and catcalls rose from the tiers nearby as the population caught sight of Lopez striding through the block below. Ethan glanced up and saw ranks of dark faces appearing at barred cell doors, all stained teeth, jaundiced eyes and orange correctional jumpsuits.

'C'mon up here, mama!' shouted one. 'I'll let you cuff me, honey!'

'Show us that touché, babe!'

Lopez glanced up at the incarcerated ranks above them, but she showed no indication of interest as she followed the sergeant through a door at the end of the block that led to a small corridor with three heavy security doors along one wall.

'Are our guys held alone?' Ethan asked, as the sergeant locked the door shut behind them.

'No,' he replied, and gestured to the farthest of the three doors. 'They're held in four-man cells, but your guy's tests aren't due back until this afternoon. They'll go on the block overnight, then they'll be on Twelve Main after that.'

Twelve Main was the high-security wing, where cells were walled with stainless steel to prevent the prisoners from ripping the toilets and sinks out to use as weapons. The sergeant walked to the farthest door and unlocked it, pushing it open as he led them inside.

Cuffed to a table inside were two men. One was a fairly mild-looking Caucasian of about forty years of age with shrewd, pinched features and quick eyes. The other was an enormous African-American with thick sideburns that lined his jaw like black scimitars and a shaved head and muscles that bulged from his orange correctional jumpsuit like brown footballs. Both men looked up at Ethan without interest, and then their eyes flicked to Lopez and stayed there.

The sergeant gestured to them.

'James Gladstone and Earl Thomas,' he introduced the two inmates. 'Gladstone's the big one, Earl's the brains. Ain't that right, fellas?'

Neither man responded, both still watching Lopez with hooded eyes. Ethan stepped forward, deliberately blocking their view of her as he leaned on the table. 'Get a good look, boys, because it's as close as you're gonna get.'

Gladstone turned his dark eyes onto Ethan and spoke in a voice so deep it sounded as though it came from the underworld. 'Un-cuff me, boy, and I'll rip your head off your shoulders and shit down your neck.'

Ethan smiled. 'Play nicely and you won't get a month in solitary. Understood, asshole?'

Gladstone strained against the steel cuffs, the metal cracking as it snapped taut. 'Only thing keepin' you alive is these chains. I'll see you when I get out.'

'Sure you will,' Ethan said, nodding. 'In about forty years, if you're lucky. You'll be able to throw your daddy diaper at me.'

Lopez walked up to the table, pulled out a chair and sat down. Ethan slid into the chair beside her and looked at the two men as Lopez spoke.

'Everybody can have their dreams,' she murmured to Gladstone, 'but we're here on business.'

Earl Thomas spoke for the first time, his voice soft compared to Gladstone's.

'We don't have any business with you.'

'That right?' Lopez asked. 'Strange, seeing as you're both looking at twenty-to-life without parole in a federal prison. In a couple of hours, your pre-trial arraignment will be the last chance you have to avoid that fate.'

'Even stranger,' Ethan added, 'considering you don't know who the hell we are.'

Earl smiled. 'Cops, or at least you are,' he said to Lopez and then turned back to Ethan. 'You, you're military, probably been out a few years.'

Ethan raised an eyebrow of genuine surprise. 'You're a smart man. Makes me wonder how you wound up in a place like this, being so clever.'

Earl said nothing in response, sitting with his arms folded in his lap, utterly unreadable. Ethan guessed that his big friend was considerably less well endowed with intelligence, and wondered briefly if they would be better served by splitting the pair of them up.

'How'd you make us?' Lopez asked conversationally.

'This guy's got army written all over him,' Earl uttered. 'Still fit, despite his age, and there's something about the way you assholes walk, like some drill sergeant's still got his boot up yo' ass, 'mongst other things. As for you, honey –' he smiled at Lopez – 'I can smell a cop just as easy as I can smell a rotting corpse. They're much alike.'

Lopez's expression didn't falter as she replied: 'Didn't do you much good on Williamsburg Bridge now, did it?'

'What do you want?' Gladstone growled, his huge fists bunched before him on the table.

'Names,' Ethan said. 'Federal prosecutor may be willing

to do a deal with you both, provide you reveal who you were working with.'

Gladstone leaned his big head forward, his shoulders bulging like boulders beneath the jumpsuit.

'Ain't no stoolie,' he rumbled at Ethan.

'You're looking at spending the rest of your life in here,' Lopez said, keeping her voice reasonable. 'Forty years.'

Gladstone's fearsome expression melted as he smiled at her, his teeth surprisingly white and his eyes sparkling with unexpected life as he replied: 'Maybe. Maybe not.'

'You won't get bail,' Ethan pointed out, ' and neither of you will see parole. This is it, fellas. You either cut yourselves a deal or they'll lock you both down and toss the keys.'

Gladstone glanced at Earl and the older man slowly shook his head.

'Like the man says, we ain't turnin' for nobody.'

Ethan sat back in his seat thoughtfully. Maybe there wasn't a brain behind all of this. Maybe it was Earl himself. But then why not try to create a character or finger an enemy for the bank jobs, at least try to get a break?

Lopez leaned forward on the table, her dark eyes focused on Gladstone's.

'You ever want to see anybody like me again,' she purred, 'you're gonna have to fold now. No sense in cutting your nose off to spite your face.'

Gladstone smiled at her. 'Ain't my nose I'm thinkin' of, honey.'

Lopez smiled back and then sat abruptly upright, cutting off Gladstone's enjoyment. 'That's my point,' she said. 'You don't talk to us now, all you'll ever be doing is thinkin' about it, so you might just as well cut it off. You opened fire on cops in the middle of a busy intersection and are up for half a dozen federal crimes. Life's gonna mean life. If you ever get out of here, it'll be in a wheelchair.'

Earl Thomas jabbed a finger at her.

'We ain't movin', sweetheart!' he snapped. 'So you can save your pretty chatter for all the slack-jawed faggots back on the block.' He looked her up and down, as though examining a vehicle. 'Besides, I don't do Latino.'

Lopez stood up, placed her hands on the table, and leaned closer to him.

'You won't be doin' anything for the next forty years, Earl. You're over, finished, history, except maybe for the young boys on your block.'

Earl cracked his cuff chains as he tried to stand, but the chains around his ankles kept him out of reach. He chuckled, his evil little eyes glittering at her.

'Be seein' you, missy.'

Ethan stood up and turned away from them both as Lopez spun to join him. The sergeant opened the door and followed them out into the corridor. Ethan waited until the door was shut again before he spoke.

'That didn't make any sense,' he said. 'They've got no reason to cover for an accomplice and every reason to try to shorten their sentence.'

'Maybe there isn't anybody else involved,' Lopez suggested. 'Or they don't know who it is.'

'I figured that,' Ethan admitted, 'but these guys should be clutching at any opportunity to get out of this. They're professional criminals facing life sentences – these people don't have loyalty to anybody but themselves.'

Lopez looked at her watch and shrugged.

'Well, they'll be on their way to the courthouse within the hour for their arraignment. We'd better catch up with Karina and see what happens to them at the court.'

# 20

# NEW YORK COUNTY SUPREME COURTHOUSE, NEW YORK CITY

'You sure you're up for this?'

Karina Thorne and Tom Ross stood in Foley Square and looked up at the towering edifice of the courthouse, a colonnade of ten fluted granite Corinthian columns looming over the busy street outside. The sky above was crisp and clear, the low afternoon sun flaring brightly between the nearby tower blocks that cast long blue shadows across the streets.

Tom Ross nodded. 'I want to see them pay for what they've done.'

Ethan and Lopez stood alongside them, and Ethan did not like what he was seeing. Tom Ross was Karina's partner, a trained, professional police officer and detective. But right now, he looked as though he was half dead. He was wearing a dark gray suit, neatly pressed, but it seemed to hang off his frame as though he had lost a lot of weight. His hair was roughly brushed into place but still managed to look disheveled, and his eyes were ringed with dark sclera, as though he had not slept in a week.

'They're going to be in there,' Karina said to Tom. 'The two men we caught on the bridge. This is their final chance to cut a deal.'

Tom nodded again, his sullen gaze fixed on the courthouse.

'I'm ready,' he said finally.

Ethan glanced at Lopez but said nothing as they walked across the street and up the steps toward the towering portico. Waiting for them at the top of the steps was the rest of the police team, Donovan at their head. The team fell in behind Karina and Tom as they walked into the cavernous interior and made their way to the main court itself. Ethan looked up as they passed between the columns, and saw words engraved into the stone facade above their heads:

THE TRUE ADMINISTRATION OF JUSTICE
IS THE FIRMEST PILLAR OF GOOD
GOVERNMENT

He wondered briefly if such noble sentiments extended to the Central Intelligence Agency or any of its paramilitary employees.

The interior of the courthouse was a massive rotunda with murals and friezes painted onto the walls and the dome high above. They walked through the rotunda and down a corridor to one of many courtrooms, each filled with a paneled bar at one end and matching rows of benches facing it. The far wall bore the motif IN GOD WE TRUST as Ethan, noticed sat down alongside Lopez, the police team sitting in front of them. A small crowd occupied the public gallery, probably families of people injured in the auto wreck on the Williamsburg Bridge.

The court rose as the judge entered and took his seat. Ethan sat down and looked across the court, as a lawyer stood to address the judge. As he spoke, so Earl Thomas and James Gladstone were led into the courtroom, both cuffed to cops. Every head turned to watch, and Ethan glanced at Tom Ross. He was staring at the two men, laying eyes on them probably for the first time in his life. His fists were clenched in his lap, the knuckles showing white through the skin. Karina sat next to him, and Ethan could sense that she was poised to restrain Tom if he leaped up in anger and tried to reach the two felons.

The lawyer, a tall, thin man with a hooked nose and fearsomely intelligent gaze, addressed the judge.

'Your honor, before we begin, I would like to request the opportunity to make an announcement on behalf of my clients.'

The judge, apparently surprised by the lawyer's request, nodded. 'Granted.'

The lawyer glanced at his notes before speaking.

'I would like to apprise you of a deplorable miscarriage of proper procedural justice by the New York Police Department in the arrest and detainment of my clients, that has hereby forced them to plea for charges made against them that are totally false. They have been charged with a federal crime, that of armed robbery of a premises insured by the

Federal Deposit Insurance Corporation, and also a capital crime, that of causing the automobile wreck on the Williamsburg Bridge that claimed the lives of seven people. I am here to contend that in both cases the charges are false and, in fact, orchestrated by detectives eager to secure convictions, with both of my clients innocent of involvement in the heist in question and, in fact, the victims of two professional criminals who escaped arrest on the day.'

A few of the police team rolled their eyes and Karina leaned in close to Ethan and Lopez.

'We see this all the time,' she said. 'They'll try to say that procedure wasn't followed so, therefore, the convictions won't stick, that there is no case to answer and that the judge should dismiss it. If he doesn't, they'll apply for bail and then try to delay the trial as long as possible. It won't work. We dotted every "i" and crossed every "t".'

Lopez frowned. 'How did those losers afford a top lawyer and not a state attorney?'

Karina shrugged but said nothing.

The judge looked down at the lawyer. 'Go on.'

The lawyer raised a sheet of paper in front of the court.

'The written statements as allegedly made by my clients to the police were unsigned, rendering them inadmissible in a court of law.'

Karina bolted forward in her seat as her jaw dropped.

'Is he serious?' Lopez asked her.

They were both drowned out by Donovan, who stood up and pointed at the lawyer. 'That's a lie. Both suspects signed their statements. We would not have let them leave the interview room without doing so.'

The judge glared down at Donovan. 'Retake your seat, detective, or I'll have you removed from the court.'

Donovan, fuming, sat back down, as the lawyer smiled coldly at him before continuing.

'In addition, closed-circuit camera footage of the entire incident reveals upon close inspection that the accused did not fire nor even possess any weapons. Both men contend that they were abducted by two professional thieves who hijacked their vehicle at gunpoint.'

A ripple of gasps flooded through the public gallery as the lawyer expertly related the sequence of events that had supposedly led up to the two suspects being dragged against their will into a violent crime.

Ethan looked across at Earl and Gladstone, who were standing next to each other. Both were wearing sombre expressions, their hands clasped before them in a display of subservience, dressed in ill-fitting suits probably hired or bought by the lawyer to give his clients a thin veneer of respectability. Both men made no attempt to look anywhere other than directly at the judge in the courtroom and studiously avoided looking at Ethan and Lopez.

'They're playing it smooth,' Lopez whispered.

'They're smart enough to hit armoured vehicles and banks all the way down the east coast,' Ethan said, 'and that makes them smart enough to play a judge and jury as best they can. Clearly, there's no evidence of them being in the area at the time of the other hits or it would have been presented by now.'

Lopez frowned.

'Then why, if they were involved from the start, wouldn't they give up the identities of their accomplices? They're screwed if they can't pull this off.'

The lawyer finished laying down his case as he gestured at the police officers behind him.

'What happened on Williamsburg Bridge was a tragedy, a loss of innocent lives in a deadly pursuit by New York Police Department detectives of highly dangerous, professional criminals. I ask you, your honor, to take a look at my clients and consider what was required of the men responsible for this complex, violent and reprehensible crime, then contrast that with the men you see standing before you today. Both of my clients have prior convictions, neither man is an angel, yet all of their crimes are misdemeanours, not painstakingly planned bank heists. It is understandable that the law-enforcement agencies of this city are desperate to locate and apprehend those responsible for the crimes, but I would caution that a heist of this complexity almost certainly had a plan for my clients' vehicle to be hijacked, and these two men were purposefully abducted and left to carry the sentence for a crime they did not commit.'

The lawyer glanced up at the public gallery, before he finished his closing speech.

'In short, your honor, I would ask that you refrain from sentencing these men to trial until further evidence comes to light regarding the heist itself as, I believe that, having reviewed the available footage, my clients have committed no crime at all and that their claims will be validated through further investigation.'

Lopez shook her head.

'They won't be able to hold them for long in jail without a trial date, and his case is strong enough that they'll probably get bail,' she whispered. 'Christ, they might even walk out of here as free men.'

Ethan glanced at Tom Ross, and saw that Karina was now holding his hand. Tom's jaw was hanging slightly open in disbelief as the judge spoke.

'I concur with your recommendation,' he said finally. 'Both of your clients will remain in custody within the jail system. Given the nature of the crimes concerned, I cannot with a clear conscience offer bail at this time until further validation of their claims can be provided. However, I will instruct the New York Police Department that they have a further forty-eight hours to either provide evidence of guilt or release your clients.'

The judge stood and the court rose in silence.

'I don't believe it,' Karina said as she turned to Donovan. 'What the hell's going on here?'

Donovan watched as the two suspects were led away, both of their faces shining with delight.

'I don't know,' he rumbled. 'But we've got forty-eight hours to figure it out and drag those sons of bitches back into this courtroom for a trial sentence.'

Glen and Jackson shook their heads in unison as Jackson jabbed a thumb over his shoulder.

'The other two got clean away,' he complained. 'Only way we can prove the involvement of those two losers is to catch them.'

'You haven't got CCTV of them leaving the bridge?' Ethan asked.

Donovan shook his head as they filed out of the courtroom and through the rotunda.

'The wreck and smoke damaged or obscured the images from cameras on the bridge,' he explained. 'Those on the south side didn't pick anything up, but the guys we're chasing are probably smart enough to avoid the cameras. Maybe they got under the bridge somehow, or even had another getaway vehicle waiting in support.'

'They plan ahead,' Karina explained. 'The gang has hit banks all down the east coast and nobody's been caught, except for the two men we've got in custody. Whoever the thinkers are behind these heists, they're smart enough to have planned for blockades around or on the bridge. Switching vehicles would have been an ideal way out.'

The sky outside was darkening as Ethan and Lopez walked down the steps outside the courthouse. Karina walked alongside Tom Ross, whose features seemed locked into a thousand-yard stare. With his family gone and the men responsible on the verge of walking free, Ethan began to wonder just how long it would be before Tom tried to take his own life again.

'Ethan,' Lopez whispered beside him.

Ethan turned to look at Lopez, who was staring out across Foley Square. 'Opposite side of the street, the boots.'

Ethan managed not to look across the street straight away, instead cupping his hands and blowing nonchalantly into them against the cold as he made a fuss of looking for a taxi. As he let his gaze sweep the street, he spotted Lopez's mark.

A man wearing a gray hoodie that concealed his features. Black jeans and tan leather boots, a black leather bomber jacket. The man was leaning against a streetlight and watching the courthouse, a heavy-looking digital camera held to his face as he snapped images. The brown boots he wore were identical to the ones worn by the person they'd chased out of Hell Gate the previous day.

'You think it's the same dude?' Ethan asked.

'Close enough,' Lopez said. 'You see him in the gallery inside?'

Ethan shook his head as Karina spoke to them from behind. 'I'm taking Tom home, okay? I'll see you guys later.'

Both Ethan and Lopez nodded, before Ethan looked down at his partner. 'Let's go,' she said.

Ethan turned and strode out across the street toward Foley Square.

# 21

Ethan walked not directly toward the photographer, but out to one flank as, across the street, Lopez did the same in a mirror-reflection of his movements.

The chances that the hooded figure was the same person who had been watching them at the warehouse on the docks was remote, but, if it was the same person, then Ethan very badly wanted to know who the hell he was. If the CIA was still on their tail, then they would probably have to flee the city, and Ethan wasn't quite ready to do that yet after what they had learned from Major Greene.

Ethan turned slightly as he moved behind the photographer, maybe twenty yards away on their right. Through the crowds, he saw Lopez mirroring his movements, starting to close in on their target.

And then, quite suddenly, the mark bolted.

The man leaped away from the post and launched into a full-blown sprint, dashing across the street away from Ethan and Lopez. Ethan raced in pursuit, headed south toward City Hall Park. Ethan saw the figure tuck his camera away into his jacket as he ran and then suddenly break away with a terrific burst of speed.

'He's headed for the park!' Lopez shouted.

Ethan dodged between startled pedestrians as he dashed down Park Row toward City Hall Park. The runner switched direction and dashed across Chambers Street, through the fully flowing traffic, a sea of flashing headlights.

Ethan sprinted hard as he watched the lithe figure vault across the hood of a taxi that screeched to a halt as angry voices bellowed. Ethan dashed around the taxi and through a flock of tourists that scattered out of his way.

He caught sight of Lopez running to his right, cutting into the park to intercept their quarry should he try to hide in the trees. Ethan could see the Brooklyn Bridge City Hall and other major buildings tucked away within the park as he ran.

The fleeing figure cut hard right and dashed down a pathway that led between the trees, the City Hall and the Tweed Courthouse, the low light and growing shadows concealing his movements. Lopez dashed out just in front of Ethan, agile but not quite fast enough to catch the fleeing figure ahead of them. Whoever it was, he was in supreme physical condition and with a long enough stride to outpace even Lopez.

The figure cut left and vanished into the shadowy trees. Ethan cursed mentally as he immediately dodged left on an intercept course where he thought the figure might be, then vaulted over a fence and into the trees.

Lopez hurdled the same fence further down and vanished into the darkness as Ethan slowed and tried to get control of his breathing. He glanced up at the sky above, now a flawless dark blue beyond the blackened morass of the trees. Winter had not yet robbed the branches of all their leaves, making the small park an ideal shelter in the fading light.

Ethan paused for a moment. He could hear the traffic and the pedestrians on the crammed roads and sidewalk, could see streetlights winking beyond the trees, but he could hear no sound of running. Smart move. He knew that the figure could simply change direction unobserved to re-join the crowds and escape.

Crouched slightly as he was, and searching desperately for some sign of their quarry, Ethan turned and saw Lopez silhouetted against the glow of the streetlights and traffic nearby. Ethan knew that their quarry had not yet escaped – not enough time to make it across to the main street opposite, Broadway.

Ethan moved parallel to Lopez through the darkness, trying to sweep through the trees and prevent the figure from doubling back on them. A parking lot ahead on the edge of the park led to a smaller park beyond, and he knew that if the figure got that far, they'd never catch him.

Ethan looked across at Lopez, his vision improving in the darkness as he began to pick out foliage and individual paths through the trees. Lopez was covering the area between himself and Broadway as Ethan focused on the trees between himself and the center of the park ahead, where a large fountain stood, the sound of trickling water just audible over the traffic.

Ethan looked up as he rounded a large tree.

Something dashed out in front of him and, as he opened his mouth to warn Lopez, a blinding flare of light blazed into his eyes as a camera flashed. In an instant, the world turned black as he threw one hand up to protect his eyes and reached out for the figure in front of him.

An iron-hard forearm smashed his hand aside and a heavy knee plowed into the side of Ethan's thigh as the figure rushed past him. He staggered sideways, blinded and off-balance as Lopez crashed through the trees toward him.

'*Where'd he go?*' she yelled.

Ethan pointed frantically behind him, toward the noise from Broadway, his eyes filled with sparkling blobs and whorls of color. He blinked as he heard Lopez run away from him, into the trees, and blindly fumbled after her, but he already knew that it was too late. The flare from the camera's flash had totally ruined his night vision. He stumbled his way to the edge of the park alongside the fountain and looked left and right, but both the mysterious figure and Lopez had vanished.

It was several minutes before Lopez jogged back to him and shook her head.

'Not a chance,' she said. 'He made the crowds before I could get anywhere near. He's long gone.'

Ethan shook his head in frustration. 'Who the hell is that guy?'

'Judging by the camera, they're press,' Lopez said. 'Although, I don't ever remember chasing anybody *that* fast from the media. They were running like their ass was on fire.'

Ethan nodded. Even encumbered by the heavy jacket and the camera, he'd given both Lopez and himself the slip.

'Don't know what the big interest in us is,' Ethan said, 'but I don't like it. CIA could have hired private investigators to look around for us.'

Lopez didn't look convinced. 'Doesn't make sense, they've got offices here in the city. They wouldn't outsource something as important as this.'

'As important as *us*?' Ethan grinned. 'Now you're putting us on a pedestal.'

'Just sayin',' Lopez replied. 'They've got their pants all twisted about us but I'd have thought they'd keep everything under wraps.'

Ethan turned as Donovan approached them, Neville Jackson alongside. Both of them looked as though they'd jogged across to the park, their breathing ragged.

'You want to tell us what that was all about?' Donovan asked.

'Bail-runner,' Lopez replied before Ethan could even formulate a response, 'recognized him and decided to give chase.'

Donovan eyed Lopez suspiciously. 'You recognized a bail-runner from thirty yards across the street in a hooded top with a camera stuck to their face?'

'It was the clothes,' Ethan replied for Lopez, 'the boots and the posture. Couldn't be sure, though, so we moved in for a closer look. Once they bolted, we gave chase. We could do with seeing any traffic camera footage there might be from outside the courthouse, maybe try to identify them.'

Donovan watched them both for a long moment. Ethan could almost see the chief's mind working things over before he spoke again.

'Best you give up the name of this supposed bail-runner,' he said finally. 'They've come a long way to be here from Illinois, but I'm sure Chicago's finest would love us to pick them up and ship them back to Cook County.'

Lopez snorted a laugh.

'Sure, and give up two thousand bucks? No way, skipper, that dude belongs to us.'

'Then there's nothing I can do for you,' Donovan replied. 'If you don't play ball, then why should I?'

'What's up?' Lopez murmured. 'Don't want two bondsmen busting perps on your turf?'

Donovan's jaw hardened slightly. 'The DIA might want you two hanging around, but I don't like outside influences, especially bail bondsmen looking to make a quick buck out of our work. You're here to assist with this investigation, not chase two-bit bail-jumpers, understood?'

Ethan leveled Donovan with a dispassionate gaze.

'That individual was present at the crime scene at Hell Gate. They may know something, maybe even have evidence.'

'A long shot,' Donovan insisted, then glanced across the park. 'I don't know what you two are really up to, but I'd hate to have to arrest you both for obstructing police business, if you see what I mean?'

Ethan chuckled bitterly but did not dignify Donovan with a response.

Donovan turned silently away and strode across the square with Jackson.

'Who pulled his chain?' Lopez wondered out loud.

'Who cares?' Ethan asked. 'And where the hell is Jarvis? We could have done with the vehicle support.'

'He had business in town, something about arranging a meeting with somebody?' Lopez replied.

Ethan turned and started walking. 'Come on, let's get back to the apartment. There's nothing more we can do here.'

Ethan's cellphone trilled in his pocket and he answered it, listening for several moments before shutting it off and looking at Lopez.

'Change of plan,' he said. 'The medical examiner's completed the autopsy on the two bodies from the warehouse at Hell Gate.'

# 22

# CHIEF MEDICAL EXAMINER'S OFFICE, 1ST AVENUE, NEW YORK CITY

'I hate these places.'

Ethan led Lopez into the uninvitingly blocky building on the corner of 1st Avenue, and headed for the reception desk. Flanked by two large flags and a mural on the wall reading, SCIENCE SERVING JUSTICE, the foyer had a hushed atmosphere that belied the gruesome goings-on within.

'I've seen a few, too, remember?' Ethan replied to her. 'Deep breaths, and all that.'

They were directed into the building to one of several autopsy rooms, where the bodies of people who had died in suspicious circumstances or without clear cause were brought to be dissected and the mystery of their deaths ascertained.

The medical examiner was a cheerful-looking man in his forties with a bushy moustache and bright twinkling blue eyes that belied the rigours of his job.

'Doctor Michael Freeman,' he introduced himself, with a

vigorous handshake, as Ethan and Lopez walked into his office. 'You're here for the Hell Gate bodies, right?'

'Got anything you can tell us about them?' Ethan asked.

Freeman chuckled as he nodded. 'I'll say.'

Ethan and Lopez exchanged a glance as they followed Freeman out of his office and through to the autopsy room itself, a windowless and clinical crucible of stainless steel and polished white tiles. Two gurneys stood in the center of the room, each bearing a glossy black bag that obviously contained a body.

'You were the investigating officers on the scene?' Freeman asked as he closed the door behind them.

'We were,' Lopez replied. 'NYPD had the case initially, but it got passed onto us shortly afterward.'

'I'm not surprised,' Freeman admitted as he unzipped the two body bags to expose the remains within, 'because these two are a real mystery.'

Ethan looked down and saw the two bodies from Hell Gate.

One, clearly Wesley Hicks, looked like he could almost still be alive but for the enormous blotchy purple bruise that covered his entire chest, stark against his pale skin. Connor Reece, however, was a mess of torn flesh beneath his torso. His legs and pelvis were laid out roughly where they should be, but the hideous damage remained obvious.

'You say you found these two in the warehouse, with nothing but a line of footprints leading to them?' Freeman asked.

'That's about the size of it,' Ethan admitted. 'Somebody walks into that warehouse, or so it appears, then kills these two and walks out again.'

Freeman humphed thoughtfully and then shook his head.

'Well, if somebody did this, then all I can say for sure is that they've committed the perfect murder.'

'How so?' Lopez asked him.

Freeman gestured to the corpses.

'For a start, there is no evidence of power tools, fingerprints or lesions, other than those that are obvious. Both of these victims essentially died instantly from their injuries, but neither shows any indication of blunt-force trauma, use of blades or gunshot wounds.'

'So how did they die?' Ethan asked. 'Somebody must have done this.'

Freeman shook his head. 'These two guys are in a warehouse, somebody arrives and kills them, then leaves. That's all you've got, right? No forensics?'

'Nothing,' Lopez confirmed. 'The site was clean apart from the footprints of the victims in the dust and those of the first officer on the scene.'

Freeman removed his spectacles and looked at them both.

'I hate to say this, given the scene that you found, but, in my professional opinion, there is absolutely no way that a human being could have killed these two victims.'

Ethan frowned. 'They're dead, aren't they?'

Freeman chuckled. 'Indeed they are, but they didn't die the way you think that they did.'

'Cut to the chase, Doc,' Lopez urged him. 'What happened to them?'

Freeman popped his glasses back on and gestured to Wesley Hicks.

'This man looks as though he has suffered an enormous blunt-force trauma to the chest, doesn't he? Something's slammed into him with enough force to turn his insides to mush.'

'So far, so normal,' Ethan agreed.

'Except that he has no broken bones,' Freeman continued, 'his skin was not damaged or even broken and none of his internal organs were damaged except one.'

'Which one?' Lopez asked.

'His heart,' Freeman replied. 'When I opened his chest to examine him, his heart had been crushed into nothing, a mess of tissue. The bruising you see on his chest isn't bruising at all in the classical sense: it's the result of massive internal blood loss. I scooped six pints of it out of his chest cavity.'

Lopez frowned as she looked down at the man's remains and the large 'Y' incision made by the ME on his chest.

'But he wasn't cut open,' she said.

'Exactly,' Freeman agreed. 'So how the hell does something crush a man's heart in his chest without even touching him? There was no evidence of an attack on this man at all, no defense wounds, no cuts or abrasions. All I found was trace residue from gunshots on his right hand and wrist.'

'He fired five shots,' Ethan confirmed.

'So something was there,' Freeman pointed out. 'Surely, he must have been close to his assailant for this kind of injury to have been sustained, so how come he missed with a gun?'

'He fired straight up into the air,' Lopez said, 'at the ceiling. It was thirty feet above him.'

Freeman looked down at the body and shrugged. 'Okay, well, maybe this guy was an extraordinarily bad shot, but it doesn't explain how he could have gotten this injury.'

'What about sound?' Ethan speculated. 'Could that produce injuries like this? Some kind of directed acoustic wave. That would account for the lack of forensic evidence.'

'Perhaps,' Freeman replied, 'but it's hard to explain the lack of damage to the rest of the tissue around the heart. And it certainly doesn't explain the other guy.'

Freeman turned to Connor Reece's body and gestured to the remains. 'So you found this guy's body lying next to the other one, but his legs were where?'

'Twenty yards away,' Lopez replied. 'Blood splatter indicates he was killed at the same spot, but, for some reason, the killer threw his legs across the warehouse.'

Freeman shook his head slowly as he stared at the corpse.

'Again, same problem with this guy: no evidence of use of tools, bite marks or anything to indicate how he was killed. He obviously died from massive trauma and blood loss, but I have no idea how it was done.'

'Something must have ripped him apart,' Ethan said. 'That must take immense force, right?'

'Tremendous,' Freeman agreed, 'but this man was not ripped apart.'

'*What?*' Ethan stared at the ME in amazement. 'He's in three pieces!'

Freeman nodded as he looked at Ethan.

'Yes, he is, but it's not because he was ripped apart. I looked at segments of his body tissue under a microscope and analyzed the tears. This man was forced apart from *within*.'

Lopez baulked slightly. 'You mean like an explosion?'

Freeman shook his head.

'Like a physical force,' he replied. 'That's what I mean when I say that no human being could have done this. I've seen some gruesome slayings in my time but this beats them all. Something took hold of this man, grabbed his insides and then forced them apart with enough energy to rip his legs off. Whatever is responsible, it's not a man.'

# 23

# EAST 120TH STREET, HARLEM

Jarvis pulled his car into the sidewalk and killed the lights and engine. A shabby chain-link fence ringed an abandoned lot to his right. As was his habit, he always pulled in with the sidewalk to his right. If anybody made for the driver's door, they would have to step out into the street, providing him with a warning.

Ahead were the soaring tower blocks of the Wagner buildings, one of the projects in Harlem. Although much improved from previous decades, the area was still impoverished and blighted by drugs peddled by street crews and unemployment. Jarvis kept a sharp eye open for the hoodies who roamed the streets of Harlem like packs of wolves and for young males hovering inside the entrance foyers to the various housing projects, watching for police. A white man sitting alone in a car in East Harlem would be dead in sixty seconds if he was spotted.

A figure crossed the street some fifty yards behind where Jarvis sat. Tall, dressed in a long black coat buttoned up against the bitter night cold. Jarvis tracked the man as he walked down the sidewalk toward the car, the skin on his face glowing a pale gray in the streetlights. The figure slowed as he approached the vehicle and a gloved hand reached out for the door handle.

Jarvis made no sudden moves as the door opened and the man climbed in. The door slammed shut and the man looked at Jarvis with gray eyes that matched his short hair. There was no expression or emotion on his face, as though the life had been sucked out of the man and a computer program put in its place.

'Mr. Jarvis.'

The man's voice was flat, monotone.

'Mr. Wilson.'

'What news?'

Jarvis scanned his rear-view mirror. 'You've been pulled from actively hunting down MK-ULTRA survivors, if you hadn't already heard.'

Wilson smiled without warmth. 'I've received contact regarding my new orders. I disagree with them, but it is not my place to oppose them.'

Jarvis nodded. 'Why did you pick Harlem?'

'Because it's the safest place in the city, for me,' Wilson replied. 'Law enforcement only come up here if they really have to, and most of the cameras were long ago vandalized by the worthless little thugs who populate these streets. Harlem is an intelligence blind-spot, Doug. I'm surprised you weren't aware of it.'

'Been out of the loop,' Jarvis muttered in reply, then looked at Wilson. 'How's the chest?'

It had been six months since Jarvis had last laid eyes on Mr. Wilson, lying as he had been on his back in a parking lot in Maryland, having been shot in the chest by Ethan

Warner's sister, Natalie. At the time, Wilson had been holding a gun to one innocent man's head while simultaneously trying to shoot Jarvis. Only Natalie Warner's courage in the face of fear had saved Jarvis's life. A wisely donned Kevlar vest had saved Wilson's, reducing the bullet's impact to heavy bruising and lesions, and the agent had managed to flee the scene before law enforcement had arrived. Jarvis did not mention that the blood sample he possessed belonged to Wilson, a critical link with the CIA's involvement in at least one attempted homicide of a US citizen.

'It's fine, thanks for asking,' Wilson replied. 'And the only reason you'll be able to tell your grandkids about it is because of this new deal you've struck. If not for that, Doug, I can tell you without a shadow of doubt that right now your heart would have stopped beating and you'd be lying here with your pockets being turned over by the natives.'

Jarvis looked at Wilson and saw there in his granite-hewn features an absolute resolve, entirely devoid of emotion. He smiled. 'I doubt that very much.'

Wilson's pistol was in his hand with ferocious speed and in utter silence, the barrel pressed against Jarvis's temple.

'Local mugging gone wrong,' the agent whispered, 'bullet to the head. No witnesses.'

Jarvis nodded slowly, still smiling.

'White man in a rough black neighbourhood,' he said, 'wouldn't stand a chance. The CIA would have to work carefully to cover up your identity.'

Wilson's eyes narrowed, and then his right eye flickered slightly as a tiny red light played across his face. Wilson's gaze flicked to the right, out of the windshield and into the darkness beyond. Jarvis held the smile on his face as he spoke.

'I know very well what you're capable of, Mr. Wilson,' he said. 'So you won't be surprised that I've taken every precaution and will continue to do so. I'm wired. Vest or no vest, just one little word will end this conversation badly, for you. You even look at me in a way that displeases me and you'll find yourself with an air-conditioned brain.'

Wilson glared back at Jarvis for a long moment and then slowly withdrew the pistol. It vanished beneath his coat.

'There,' Jarvis murmured cheerfully, 'that's much better. Shall we play nicely now?'

'You will deliver Joanna Defoe to me,' Wilson snapped.

'I will do no such thing,' Jarvis replied, enjoying himself immensely as he watched the infra-red beam of the sniper rifle playing across Wilson's chest. 'If she can be found I will lead her to you, but apprehending her will be your own responsibility. Fail, and you'll carry the can for it, not me.'

Wilson smiled bitterly.

'The deal was relayed to me in complete detail. Ethan Warner, Nicola Lopez and their families would remain unharmed, in return for Joanna Defoe. That's all there is to it.'

'All there is to it?' Jarvis echoed. 'Your people held Joanna Defoe for three years. She then escaped, and, despite the best efforts of the entire CIA, you've been unable to even locate her, much less apprehend her. The DIA isn't going to be able to just magic her into your hands. What the hell makes you think that she's in the city, anyway?'

'I have my resources.'

'They haven't done you much good then, have they?'

Wilson turned his head to look at Jarvis.

'I've spent the last two months tracking former members of MK-ULTRA and ensuring that they will not be testifying at any level their knowledge of CIA-sponsored paramilitary programs. Most of them were low-level players, not really worth hitting at all.'

Jarvis frowned. 'Then why take them down?'

'To leave a trail.' Wilson smiled coldly. 'Not one that Joanna Defoe would follow, but one that she could get ahead of.'

Jarvis felt a creeping sense of dread run cold through his veins. 'You killed them just to lure her in?'

'Like you say,' Wilson replied, 'nothing else was working. I silenced former MK-ULTRA assets in Iowa, Wisconsin, Indiana and Pennsylvania before coming here. If Joanna really is trying to track these people down, she will have seen the killings and immediately understood that the only way to stop them is to get ahead of them.'

Jarvis shook his head in horror. The whole charade by William Steel back in DC was an act. He had known that he was in no danger, happy to let Wilson kill former CIA agents and let either Ethan Warner or Joanna Defoe carry the can.

'You really are a product of something rotten in the CIA,' he said in disgust. 'You're like a disease, a boil that should have been lanced decades ago.'

'Sticks and stones, Mr. Jarvis,' Wilson said. 'Needs must, and whatever I have to do will remain out of the public record. Likewise, your knowledge of these events will also remain unknown as long as you want Warner and Lopez to remain alive.'

Jarvis gestured to the red light still hovering on Wilson's chest. 'Maybe I should have you finished off, just for the hell of it.'

'You think that this makes a difference to anything?' Wilson said, pointing at the light. 'You're going to either lose your two little puppy dogs or you're going to lose Joanna Defoe. That's the deal for your safety. You kill me, you're all done.' Wilson leaned closer to Jarvis. 'You think it isn't so, just tell your man to pull the trigger.'

Jarvis sat still for a moment before speaking.

'If Joanna Defoe turns up, I'll make contact. You'll need to tell me how.'

Mr. Wilson reached into his jacket pocket, producing a slip of paper. Upon it, Jarvis glimpsed a series of numbers, and at the top a New York Mega Millions lottery logo.

Several of the numbers were ringed in felt pen.

'Your lottery ticket,' Wilson said. 'The ringed numbers are a burner cell. I'll only take a single call from you on it before it's destroyed. Make sure it doesn't waste my time. You fail to deliver Defoe, I'll assume you've reneged on the deal and I'll take you down, understood?'

Jarvis didn't reply. Wilson tossed the ticket into the foot well and climbed out of the car. Jarvis waited until the door was slammed shut before he picked up the ticket. A disembodied voice spoke into a microphone tucked into his ear.

'You want me to take him down?'

Jarvis glanced up at a nearby tower block, where his man had installed himself an hour before the meeting.

'Yes, but, unfortunately, we can't. Yet. Stand down.'

Jarvis folded the ticket into his pocket, started the engine and drove away.

# 24

# NEW YORK COUNTY SUPREME COURTHOUSE, NEW YORK CITY

Maria Coltrane was not used to working alone late at night, but the unusually busy day and the extra workload it had entailed had forced her to stay inside the building long after most of her colleagues had left for home.

The usually busy halls, corridors and court rooms were silent and still, half of the lights extinguished. Those that still burned cast pools of light that glowed like enclaves in a dark universe as she walked down a corridor to a study on the fourth floor.

The footfalls of her heels on the tiles sounded hollow as she strode with a thick set of files clasped against her chest. Paperwork was not Maria's strong suit, and it had taken her an hour longer than usual to go through every single page of the day's transcripts and clerks' notes, scanning them into digital back-up files and storing them in a national database.

Maria pushed open the door of the study and walked inside. A large room with a long, central table, it was most often used by clerks to collate trial case files for attorneys as they prepared to prosecute or defend the legions of convicts churning endlessly through the legal system. The door whispered shut behind her, then clicked as the latch caught.

The windows looked out onto a darkened plaza between the court and Pearl Street, streetlights glowing and traffic lights flowing silently below. Maria watched the traffic for a few moments, feeling slightly more comfortable at the sight of so many people so close by, and then turned away.

She sat down at the table with the files in front of her and opened the first. All that remained for her to do was stamp each file as having been electronically archived, and then she could file them for recycling and leave the building. She methodically began marking each file and was halfway through when out of the corner of her eye she glimpsed somebody peek in through the door's window as though to wave to her or say goodnight. Maria glanced up and the stamp froze in motion.

The window was empty. Maria frowned, uncertain. Above her head she saw the lights flicker briefly. A splatter of rain hammered on the windows to her left, and she could just make out gusts of wind driving sheets of rain through nearby trees in the plaza.

Suddenly anxious that she might find herself in the building during a power-outage, Maria hurriedly stamped the rest of the files and then piled them up in a stack ready to carry down to the archive. She was busy piling them up when the lights flickered again. Maria hesitated, looking at the stack of files. The archive was in the basement and it would take her several minutes to travel down there, place the files for the archivist, return to the rotunda and exit the building. A long walk, alone through the building.

Rain drummed on the study windows again as though trying to beat its way inside. Maria decided that she would come in early in the morning and take the files downstairs then, when there were other people about. Although the court was not somewhere renowned for being spooky, something was already gnawing away at her nerves as she slipped her coat on and turned for the study door. The atmosphere had changed, as though suddenly charged. She could feel it somewhere on the periphery of her senses, like the feeling of being watched – tangible but somehow ephemeral, too.

Maria reached the door of the study and swung it open.

It wasn't a noise that caught her attention, more a soft fluttering of air pressure in the room as though somebody had opened a window. The change in pressure caused the small hairs on the back of her neck to stand proud and a tingling sensation to crawl like icy water trickling down her spine.

Maria turned to look back into the room as her chest seemed to suddenly freeze solid within her.

The files were lying open, scattered across the table in disarray, and the thousands of individual pages were fluttering upward toward the ceiling in a swirling vortex as though a tornado had swept into the room from outside. The countless pages spiraled upward and spilled out across the ceiling as Maria felt her legs quiver beneath her. She saw her breath condensing on the suddenly cold air and felt blind, primal terror cripple her limbs.

Maria staggered backwards out of the study and saw the door close in front of her, and then she turned and ran.

She dashed down the corridor, following it as it turned toward a pair of elevators, the doors open and inviting. Maria ran harder as the light around her in the corridor seemed to change. She looked back over her shoulder and saw the ceiling lights going out one after the other, accelerating toward her as though something was draining the power from them as it moved. In the flickering light, she saw air condensing into clouds of vapor that raced toward her, like the shockwave of an aircraft breaking the sound barrier. She felt her hair rise up as a static charge built up around her and the air froze.

Maria shrieked, the sound that came out of her throat sounding alien to her as she plunged into the elevator and hit the button for the ground floor. The doors slid shut as she watched the lights flickering out, the darkness and the demonic cloud racing toward her at impossible speed as the doors finally closed.

Maria stood inside the elevator, holding her face with her hands and listening to the sound of her heart hammering against the walls of her chest and her breath rasping through her throat. The elevator remained silent, the light still glowing in the roof, but it did not move.

'Come on,' she whispered, hitting the button again. 'Come on, *move*!'

She hit the Ground Floor button hard a third time and suddenly the elevator groaned as it shifted, but the movement was violent and caused Maria to stagger sideways. The lights flickered above her like strobes in a tiny, hellish nightclub as the elevator shrieked, a deafening cacophony of metal on metal. A wall panel beside her head burst inward as though something of unspeakable strength was trying to bludgeon its way in.

Maria screamed and hurled herself to the opposite side of the elevator, only for the panels there to jolt inward. She whirled and saw the rear wall crumple as the entire elevator suddenly began pushing in toward her, the floor beneath her feet crunching as the tiles split. She fell sideways and hit the elevator wall as it smashed inward, and in blind panic she began hitting the walls back.

'Help me! Somebody please help me!'

The walls crushed inward to the screech of rending metal as the translucent plastic light panel above her head shattered and crashed down upon her. The light sparked violently and shattered, spilling particles of searing-hot phosphor that rained down upon her hair and face and hands, scorching her skin.

In the pitch-black of the writhing elevator, Maria heard the doors buckle and warp as they were crushed inward. A faint glow of light spilled into the elevator from the corridor outside, the ceiling lights flickering wildly.

Maria launched herself toward the light and screamed at the top of her lungs for help, battering the immovable metal doors with her bare hands. Some distant, cowering part of her awareness saw the blood smearing the doors with each blow of her fists as the skin was flayed from her knuckles, smelled the acrid stench of scorched hair and skin that filled the elevator.

The entire elevator car crushed down around her, forcing her to her knees on the uneven floor as it jerked upward, and she cried out with the last of her will as the twisted, warped ceiling pushed down on her head, the jagged metal shards crushing down unbearably hard against her body and forcing her into an awkward crouch.

With her hands she gripped the doors and tried one last time to force them open, and managed to force her head through the gap.

'*Help me!*'

A pyramid of warped metal crushed down into her back and pierced the skin, driving her pelvis down onto the jagged elevator floor as shards of torn metal drove down between her ribs. Maria shrieked in agony and then something plunged through her skull with immense force and her world vanished into blackness.

# 25

# MANHATTAN

'So how's he doing?'

Ethan sat on the edge of a small table as Karina flopped down onto her couch. The tiny apartment glowed from the light of a couple of small lamps set into alcoves in the walls, the blinds drawn against the gusting wind and rain outside.

'Tom looks like death warmed up,' she replied. 'He must be exhausted, too. He fell asleep pretty much as soon as I got him back to his apartment.'

Lopez sat opposite Karina, her legs curled up beneath her on an armchair as she sipped from a coffee mug.

'You thought about putting him under surveillance?' she asked. 'After what happened today, he must be a risk again.'

'He's been a risk since the auto wreck,' Karina replied. 'Tom's usually full of life but the way he looks now I think he's still in shock. It's going to be a while before he shakes it off.'

'If he ever does,' Ethan said. 'I don't want to sound pessimistic, but the guy's just taken the biggest hit of his life. That kind of thing can take decades to get over.'

Karina nodded thoughtfully but didn't reply. Ethan was about to ask her about Donovan when Karina's cell trilled nearby on the table. Ethan reached across and grabbed it, tossing it across the room. Karina caught it deftly in one hand and answered.

'Yeah?'

Ethan could just about hear the reply buzzing from the cell, a male voice. Although he could not make out the words, there was no mistaking the veil of trepidation that fell across Karina's features. She clicked the cell off and leaped up off the couch.

'We've got a call-out,' she said.

Lopez stood up. 'Your man Donovan isn't taking kindly to us being here.'

Karina hauled her jacket on and grabbed her badge and her gun.

'I don't give a damn what he does or doesn't like,' she shot back. 'We're better off with your help right now than without it.'

'What's the call-out?' Ethan asked.

'Don't know if there's a crime yet,' Karina replied as she opened the apartment door. 'Precinct got a call about screams and possible gunshots from downtown.'

'How come the uniforms aren't handling it?' Lopez asked.

'Because the call came from the Supreme Court building,' Karina replied. 'Same place we were at this afternoon. Want to bet that your mysterious photographer might turn up?'

Ethan grabbed his jacket and dashed out of the apartment with Lopez.

*

Karina drove down to the court building through the rain and the flowing rivers of headlights cruising Manhattan's streets, the occasional blast of her siren and blue grill lights splitting the traffic down Broadway until they turned left and swung into the sidewalk alongside two police cruisers. The flashing lights illuminated the rain spilling from the inky-black sky above in sparkling rainbow halos.

Ethan and Lopez got out of the car to see Donovan glaring at them, Glen and Jackson alongside him.

'What the hell are they doing here?' Donovan demanded of Karina as she strode toward the court building. 'This has nothing to do with the Hell Gate case.'

'They're with me,' Karina snapped. 'What's the story?'

Neville Jackson replied as he picked up a carbine from the rear of one of the cruisers. 'Emergency call from the guy on the front door,' he said, 'heard what he thought sounded like gunshots and a lot of screaming from somewhere up on the fourth floor.'

'He heard that from the ground?' Ethan asked.

'Sound echoed down through to the rotunda,' Glen Ryan explained. 'The guard thought maybe somebody had broken in and was armed, and didn't want to play the hero without calling for back-up, in case he was outnumbered.'

'Smart move. He armed?' Lopez asked.

'Yeah,' Jackson replied, 'but only with a pistol.'

Donovan gripped a compact-looking automatic assault rifle, and gestured to Ethan and Lopez.

'You two stay to the rear. Let's move.'

Ethan and Lopez followed Donovan and the team up the steps into the rotunda, the circular hall filled with the sound of thousands of raindrops hammering the roof. A uniformed guard, his elderly face pinched with concern, hurried up to them.

'I haven't seen or heard anything since I called,' he said urgently, 'but I sealed all the exits. Whoever made all that noise is still inside the building. There's been some kind of electrical disturbance so the elevators are out.'

Donovan glanced at a nearby staircase. 'Any staff not yet accounted for?'

'Just one,' the guard replied, 'a junior clerk on the fourth floor. I heard screaming coming from somewhere up there.'

Donovan nodded. 'Stay here and cover the main doors. We'll check it out.'

Ethan watched as the guard jogged toward the main entrance. Lopez followed Karina and the team up the stairwell, their boots tapping softly as they hurried through the building.

'They could have moved to another floor,' Lopez whispered urgently to Karina. 'Your team isn't nearly large enough to cover the entire building.'

'The missing clerk is our priority now,' Donovan rumbled back. 'If they've taken a hostage and the kidnappers make a run for it, they'll still have to get past the guard downstairs. They won't get far and we'll have uniformed support outside within minutes.'

Lopez glanced at Ethan, who shook his head fractionally. There was no point in arguing with Donovan right here on the stairwell of a building that may be harboring an armed criminal.

Slowly, the team gathered in front of a door that led onto the fourth floor. Donovan gripped the handle as Glen Ryan, his rifle held before him, took up position. With practiced efficiency Donovan pulled the door open and Glen rushed silently through with Jackson right behind him. Karina followed them both as Donovan slipped into the corridor.

Ethan grabbed the door with one hand, waited five seconds to give the team time to get clear, and then followed them in.

The corridor was black as night, the only illumination coming from adjoining rooms with glass windows in the doors that allowed the faint glow of streetlights to permeate the gloom. Ethan could see the team making their way down the corridor, checking through the window of each room, before opening the doors and clearing each space, moving slowly and silently across the floor.

Ethan moved along behind them, nipping forwards as they split into two groups, each checking rooms on opposite sides of the corridor. He hurried forward with Lopez alongside him and rapidly checked the windows of the remaining rooms.

'Bingo,' he whispered, waving the team forward as they emerged from a pair of rooms two rows back. He pointed to the study room.

Donovan took the lead and the team silently entered the study, the under-slung flashlights on their rifle barrels sweeping the darkened room.

'Clear,' Jackson hissed.

'Struggle?' Karina whispered, looking at the files and sheets of paper scattered across the entire room.

Ethan shook his head in confusion, as did Donovan. If there had been a struggle, he would have expected to see files dropped in one particular area as the person holding them, presumably the clerk, had dropped them in favour of defending herself. But the papers, thousands of them, coated the entire floor like a sea of trash.

Donovan backed out and headed further down the corridor, with Karina alongside him. Lopez shadowed her closely as she raised her rifle, the flashlight beam slicing into the darkness ahead and reflecting off something metallic at the far end.

Ethan, just behind the team, hesitated as something odd began nagging at him. A strange sensation washed across his skin, as though static electricity was flaring off the walls and lifting the fine hairs on his body. He felt his ears twitch involuntarily, as though he were trying to listen to something behind him as a powerful compulsion to look over his shoulder swept through his awareness.

The corridor behind them was pitch-black, a mysterious void. Ethan was about to whisper a warning to the team when Karina's voice called out huskily.

'I can see someone.'

The flashlight beams caught on a face at the end of the corridor, somebody kneeling on the ground. Karina broke into a run, followed quickly by the rest of her team as they dashed to the elevator, the white beams of light dancing and reflecting off the doors.

Karina aimed her beam straight at a human face.

'Jesus!'

Karina staggered to a halt and collapsed backwards, landing hard on her butt on the carpeted floor of the corridor as her flashlight illuminated a face crushed between the warped and mangled elevator doors.

The features of a once-pretty blonde girl of maybe twenty-five were twisted sideways, her jaw shattered and yanked up across the side of her face. One of her eyeballs had burst inside her fractured skull, an arm dangling down to brush the floor beneath her.

'Goddamn,' Donovan said.

Glen Ryan played his beam over the elevator. The shaft itself was clearly visible around the elevator, which dangled from its cables within the shaft instead of hugging the walls. The entire car was crushed like a packet of potato chips, the metal warped and crunched as though hammered in a giant's forge.

'What happened here?' Karina gasped.

Ethan looked at the shattered hulk of the elevator. 'That must have been what the guard thought was gunshots,' he guessed. 'Somebody must have taken power tools to it.'

'Question is, who?' Lopez said, 'And where are they?'

Ethan felt again the overpowering desire to look over his shoulder. On impulse, he whirled, staring into the deep blackness behind them. Karina's flashlight beam spun to slice into the corridor, and, as Ethan glanced at it, he saw a galaxy of dust motes suddenly whorl away from them as though somebody had sprinted past.

'There's somebody behind us,' Ethan said.

# 26

The team's flashlights all spun and pierced the gloom back down the corridor. Ethan saw Karina point at the whirling cloud of dust motes.

'There,' she said.

Donovan aimed his rifle down the corridor, but the beam picked up nothing except the silent and empty spaces behind them.

'There's nobody there,' he said. 'We don't have time for this crap.' He turned back to the ruined elevator and then looked at Jackson. 'Call for back-up to sweep the rest of the building, and get forensics up here as soon as you can. We need this area sealed off until we can figure out what the hell happened.'

Ethan heard Donovan's words but they trailed off in his mind as he edged back down the corridor. Something in the air around him seemed off, a tension that charged his senses. He glimpsed Lopez alongside him, walking slowly and also gazing into the darkness. In the sweeping beams from the flashlights behind, he saw thin slivers of Lopez's long black hair dancing upward.

Ethan reached out and touched her shoulder.

'What?' she asked.

'Static electricity,' Karina said from behind them. Ethan looked at her as she followed them, her flashlight glowing through Lopez's hair. 'It's making your hair stand on end.'

Ethan searched the gloomy shadows. 'You can smell the charge,' he said, sensing a stale note on the air around him.

Karina gripped her rifle tighter. 'What the hell is going on here?'

Ethan shook his head as they crept forwards, sensing but not seeing. On impulse, he closed his eyes and stopped moving, just letting the strange, charged air settle around him. The darkness seethed and he felt something surge as though a live current had danced past high on his left. A brush of bitterly cold air seemed to suck the life out of the atmosphere.

Ethan's eyes flicked open as he turned and stared up into the corridor.

'It's up there,' Lopez whispered, looking in the same direction.

Ethan took a pace closer, the blackness as deep and featureless as anything he had ever known, and reached out.

A crash reverberated through the corridor as the crushed elevator suddenly tilted wildly and smashed into the shaft wall. Ethan's heart slammed inside his chest as he whirled to see the ruined car suddenly vanish from sight as it plunged downward through the shaft with a screech of metal scraping along metal. The elevator crashed into the basement, the sound of battered metal echoing up and down the shaft and corridor.

Ethan saw Neville Jackson staring at the shaft in disbelief. 'The cables were already severed,' he said.

'It must've been wedged in there somehow,' Glen guessed.

Ethan had only a moment to wonder how that was possible when the ceiling lights suddenly flickered into life and filled the corridor with blessed, warm light. Ethan looked around them as a sudden weight seemed to lift from his shoulders and the bitter chill vanished. He couldn't explain it even to himself, but a tension vanished from his chest as though somehow with the return of the light it had become easier to breathe. He looked at Lopez, whose dark eyes were shadowed with concern.

'Tell me I was just imagining all of that,' she said.

Ethan shook his head slowly and glanced at Karina. 'You, too?'

Karina nodded. 'Felt like somebody was standing on my shoulders. What's going on?'

Ethan turned, as Donovan, Jackson and Glen Ryan strode past, heading for the stairwell. 'Follow me, Karina!' Donovan shouted.

Ethan watched as Karina dutifully dashed away, then turned to Lopez.

'Something else is going on here, Nicola,' he said. 'I didn't imagine what I just saw and neither did you.'

Lopez shook her head as she gazed around the corridor. 'Damn straight. It's gone now, but that wasn't like anything I've felt since El Museo des las Momias back in Guanajuato.'

'The what?' Ethan asked.

'It's a museum back home in Mexico,' she explained. 'Whole bunch of bodies interred a couple of centuries ago in a cemetery where the families had to pay a tax to keep the bodies there. Nobody really paid, so the bodies were dug up. Some of them were mummified and were put in the museum. Point is, nobody goes in there, man, it's like a freak show. Disembodied voices, things moving about, you name it.'

Ethan felt a chill tingle across his shoulders.

'Your hair stand on end there, too?'

'No,' Lopez said with a slight smile, 'but myself and a few friends snuck in there one night and we snuck out again pretty damned quick. There are some things you don't mess with, and whatever was in this corridor felt just like that museum, Ethan, something that you want to get away from.'

Ethan turned as the lights of vehicles flooding into the plaza outside flashed against the rain-soaked windows.

'There's only one person that connects all of this,' he said. 'Karina.'

Lopez's eyes flared in alarm. 'Are you kidding?'

'No,' Ethan insisted. 'Think about what happened at her apartment, and now this. I've read before that paranormal phenomena often surround an individual. What if she's the cause?'

'You think that Karina squashed an elevator car,' Lopez said flatly. 'And tore a guy in half?'

'I don't know,' Ethan replied. 'I just know that we're going to need help with this one.'

'Jarvis?' Lopez asked as they walked toward the stairwell.

'Better than nothing,' Ethan replied. 'He'll be able to track down somebody who knows more about this than we do.'

'The Ghostbusters?' Lopez suggested with a twinkle in her eye. 'Maybe we can get that team off the television down here: Ghost Hunters, isn't it?'

Ethan grinned as he walked onto the stairwell, and then the grin vanished. Lopez almost walked into him as he froze but, even as she opened her mouth to remonstrate, she too fell silent.

The rain outside had stopped, the window opposite them streaked with a million droplets of water that clung to the surface of the glass and glowed in the light from the nearby street like a galaxy.

In the random raindrops was cast a pair of gigantic, symmetrical vortexes, as though Ethan were staring at water swirling down two opposing plugholes. The vortexes were slowly vanishing as the raindrops trickled down the window, giving up their fight against gravity. Ethan couldn't help the impression forming in his mind that something had passed through the glass.

Lopez stared at the immense pattern outside the window. 'Okay, I take it back. The Ghost Hunters would run like hell from this. We call Jarvis.'

Ethan nodded and continued on down the stairwell and through the rotunda. They walked through to the elevators, where a team of forensics and CSI officers were already swarming around the crushed elevator and the gruesome corpse pinned within it.

Beside them, being questioned by two cops, was the elderly guard who had called them in. Ethan made his way over, and, as the two cops moved off, he managed to grab the guard. The man was in his sixties and in reasonably good shape for his age. But his face seemed pale and his eyes glazed, as though he'd recently awoke from a deep but unsatisfying sleep.

'NYPD,' Ethan said, lying as though he did it every day. 'You got a moment?'

'It look like I'm going anywhere?' the guard muttered. 'I just finished talking to your guys, ask them.'

Lopez stepped in. 'Sorry, it's a double investigation, but we won't be more than a minute or two. You called the police after hearing gunshots, right?'

'Sounded like gunshots,' the guard replied. 'Then a whole lot of screaming. Like I said, I wasn't going up there with nothing more than my service pistol.'

Ethan nodded. 'I don't blame you. Thing is, we didn't find any evidence of weapons discharge up there.'

The guard sighed. 'Man, I heard a lot of damned loud bangs that I took to be gunshots. There ain't much else it could have been.'

Ethan looked at the elevator shaft down the corridor nearby and at the corridor that led to the stairwell, all the way up to the fourth floor.

'You really think that you could hear gunshots from the fourth floor?' he asked.

The guard glanced at the corridor and seemed to hesitate. 'Well, I guess, maybe.'

'But you said that the noises were loud,' Lopez pointed out. 'Damned loud, you said.'

The guard nodded but seemed confused. 'What are you saying?'

Ethan watched as the crushed and torn elevator car was hauled from the shaft by the police using canvass straps.

'You didn't hear gunshots,' he said finally. 'You heard the elevator car cables being snapped.'

The guard frowned and shook his head. 'Man, that thing only just came crashing down. How the hell could the cables have snapped and the safety devices failed all at the same time?'

Lopez looked at the guard. 'You tell us how a half-tonne elevator car can get crushed like a soda can without industrial power tools, we'll tell you how it came crashing down. Deal?'

'You notice anything strange happening while all that was going on?' Ethan asked.

'Strange how?'

'Odd,' Ethan pressed. 'You said there were electrical disturbances, things like that?'

'Sure,' the guard replied without hesitation, 'was bugging me for a few minutes before I heard the bangs. Lights were goin' on and off, phone lines messing around, that kind of thing. I figured it was the gales outside causing it.'

Ethan nodded and decided not to push any further. 'Thanks for your time.'

Lopez joined him as they walked toward the exit. 'Well?'

Ethan fished his cellphone from his pocket.

'We get Jarvis in on this,' he said.

'That's my boy,' Lopez said. 'Leaves us to find your little Miss Mysterious, right?'

Ethan stepped out of the lobby and onto the steps outside, the wind tugging at his hair and carrying with it a fine dusting of moisture. He could see veils of drizzle flashing past the streetlights as he lifted the cell to his ear.

And then he saw the man with the camera, standing this time further down the street, watching the police swarming around the entrance to the court. For a brief instant, his body primed itself automatically for flight but somehow he restrained himself and engaged his brain.

'Don't look or move,' he said to Lopez. 'Ten o'clock, fifty yards out.'

Lopez pulled her collar up about her neck against the wind and rubbed her hands together as she surveyed the street in a single sweep and turned to Ethan. 'Got 'em. How do you want to do it?'

Ethan dialed a number and put his cell to his ear.

'With help,' he said. 'Let's see if we can get *them* to make a mistake this time.'

# 27

# 5TH PRECINCT POLICE DEPARTMENT, NEW YORK CITY

The dawn labored its way across the city horizon as Ethan and Lopez leaned against railings outside the 5th Precinct station in Chinatown, the street still enshrouded in shadows. The air was cold and misty, only a few cars and delivery trucks cruising the streets this early in the morning.

Karina Thorne strode out of the station doors and jogged down the steps to meet them.

'What's the story?' Lopez asked her friend.

Karina rubbed her temples with one hand. 'I don't even know where to start,' she replied. 'Forensics finished with the elevator car. Fingerprints all over the inside of course, but not a single fingerprint on the outside, except a small number of residuals already matched to personnel from the company that services the elevator cars. All of them have perfect alibis.'

'You're saying nobody laid a hand on that car?' Ethan asked. 'What about the body of the woman?'

'Assistant clerk of the court,' Karina replied. 'Maria Coltrane, twenty-three years old. No previous convictions, born and raised here in New York. Forensics is done with her and so far there's nothing to show for it, but we'll have to wait until the autopsy's complete, which could take another day.'

'I don't think they'll find anything new,' Lopez said. 'She was crushed to death. It's what did the crushing that interests us.'

Karina looked at them furtively. 'This isn't right, Nicola. Something's going on here and it's bigger than us. Donovan and the rest of the team aren't listening.'

Ethan moved closer to Karina. 'Did the forensics guys say what happened to the elevator car cables?'

Karina nodded. 'They were ripped apart, not cut by a machine. One guy told us that the weight of the car isn't nearly enough to break those cables. And as for the car being crushed, nobody's got an answer.'

Ethan glanced up and down the street, one eye now open at all times for their mysterious stalker.

'We'll look into that,' he replied. 'The MO is similar to the murders down at Hell Gate Field, right? No forensics, no motive?'

Lopez nodded. 'Figures, but there's nothing to connect the dead clerk with the two losers we found in that warehouse. They couldn't be further removed from each other.'

Ethan saw an SUV pull into the street and cruise toward them.

'We'll be in touch,' he said to Karina. 'Anything else comes up, let us know. Okay?'

'Sure,' she replied. 'Where are you guys going?'

'Research,' Lopez replied as Ethan opened the SUV's back door. 'We'll let you know what we find out.'

Ethan climbed aboard the SUV with Lopez, the vehicle pulling smoothly away from the sidewalk.

'Morning,' Jarvis said as he twisted in his seat to look at them. 'What's the story at the courthouse so far?'

'No news,' Ethan said. 'Local police are stumped, no forensics, no evidence at all and certainly no suspects. Victims are currently assumed to be unconnected.'

'But the MO is the same,' Lopez added. 'Technically, they're both examples of a perfect murder with nothing at all to go on. I've never seen anything like it before.'

'So Ethan said,' Jarvis replied. 'And you said you felt as though you weren't alone?'

Ethan nodded and explained the unusual things that they had witnessed the previous night.

'Something's going on here and it may have something to do with Karina Thorne,' Ethan said.

'We don't know that,' Lopez protested. 'How about we stick to what we do know and save the speculation for later, okay?'

Ethan looked at Jarvis. 'What about our mysterious friend? Did you manage to follow him?'

Jarvis cast Ethan a hurt look. 'Seriously, you need to ask?'

'Who is he?' Lopez snapped.

'We don't know, yet,' Jarvis admitted. 'We spotted him right after you called me. I put one guy on the street and then stayed in the vehicle to back them up. The mark seemed to watch you both for a while, snapped a few pictures and then took off north. We followed him for several minutes but he kept his face well covered against the weather and observation. Stayed outside, too, never caught the subway or a cab.'

'The rough weather gave him a reason to keep his hood up,' Ethan speculated, 'and avoid being identified. Where did he go?'

'My man followed him as far as Central Park but was given the slip,' Jarvis admitted. 'It's his best guess that the mark realized he was being followed and took off at the first available opportunity.'

Ethan sat back in his seat in exasperation. 'Who the hell is this dude? He's definitely not CIA, they'd have shot or arrested us by now.'

'I keep telling you, you don't need to worry about them,' Jarvis insisted. 'They're not on your case anymore and won't be as long as I have something to do with it.'

Lopez gestured to the driver of the SUV. 'So where are we going now?'

Jarvis looked back at them. 'Your call last night raised a few questions at the DIA when I relayed the details of the case back to them. We're going to see somebody who might understand what's going on here.'

'I'll believe that when I see it,' Lopez murmured, 'literally.'

'We don't even *know* what we saw,' Ethan said. 'The whole event lasted seconds, and the spiral patterns on the window of the court could have been caused by some kind of wind effect. It was blowing a gale last night.'

'That's possible,' Jarvis agreed, 'but it doesn't explain what happened in the warehouse. If the two cases are connected, as you yourself said you suspected them to be, then the person we're going to visit might be able to explain how.'

The SUV drove north up onto Washington Square, pulling in alongside the New York University. The halls occupied one entire length of the block opposite the tree-lined square, a row of tall buildings with an almost Gothic appearance. Ethan got out of the vehicle with Lopez and followed Jarvis into the nearest entrance.

'I didn't think scientists at accredited universities did research into ghosts,' Lopez said to Ethan as they walked through the building, 'if that's what this is about.'

'They don't,' Jarvis replied, over his shoulder, for Ethan, 'at least not officially, but there are a few here who spend their free time chasing up reports of hauntings and similar phenomena. Most wouldn't talk about it but one seems happy to help in a murder case, albeit off the record.'

Jarvis led them to an office in the psychology department of the building and knocked before entering. Ethan and Lopez followed him into the small room, and found there waiting for them a surprisingly casually dressed woman. In her forties, with long black hair, wearing a short leather jacket, faded blue jeans and sneakers, Ethan figured that she was some kind of New Age lecturer, the type who somehow managed to be more cool than their students.

'Professor Amanda Bowen,' Jarvis greeted her with a shake of her hand, and introduced Ethan and Lopez.

'What can I do for you?' she asked Ethan and Lopez directly. 'Doug said that you had encountered something unusual during a murder investigation.'

'We don't know what we encountered,' Lopez replied. 'What we do know is that we now have three homicides, all of which have been conducted in a way that can only be described as impossible.'

'Impossible, how?' Professor Bowen asked.

Ethan explained the nature of each of the crime scenes, the lack of forensics and the circumstances in which each of the victims had died. Professor Bowen bore an expression of deep interest that slowly dissolved into something akin to fear as Ethan outlined the case. When he had finished, she looked at each of them in turn for a few moments, before speaking.

'And this event that you witnessed last night?' she asked. 'Did you actually *see* anything?'

Lopez shrugged as she replied: 'It's kind of hard to describe. We didn't see what it was, but we saw its effect on things like dust motes and falling rain. There was something there for sure, you could feel the drop in temperature and a sort of static charge on the air.'

Professor Bowen nodded, then turned to a bookshelf nearby and selected a weighty tome that she laid down on her desk in front of them. Ethan watched as she opened the pages and flipped through, before stopping on one page and turning the book toward them.

'You ever heard of one of these before?' she asked.

Ethan looked down at the page and felt something unpleasant ripple beneath his skin, cold and foreign.

The image on the page was reproduced, according to the caption beneath it, from an ancient medieval woodcut. The crude, heavy lines and simplistic visualization did little to deter from the apparent ferocity of the phantom shape that towered over a victim cowering on his knees. Drawn by the artist to resemble flames rising from a nearby fire, the spectral terror loomed over the man, who was clasping his chest and screaming.

Beneath the caption was the image title:

*An encounter withe the Wraithe.*
*Bulgaria, 1586*

Lopez looked up at Professor Bowen. 'What's a wraith?'

The professor gave her a worried look. 'Bad news, that's what.'

# 28

# 5TH PRECINCT POLICE DEPARTMENT, NEW YORK CITY

'Who are they, really?'

Karina Thorne stood in Donovan's office, aware of the eyes of the rest of the team watching her.

'I know about as much as you do,' she replied. 'Their boss, Jarvis, keeps his cards real close to his chest. But they're the real deal and they're helping us.'

'What about Warner?' Donovan pressed. 'He's trouble, isn't he? I can tell it just by looking at him.'

'I don't know,' Karina insisted. 'What difference does it make? They're here to help. It's not like we're making any headway without them.'

Donovan tossed a letter across his desk to face her. 'You got any explanation for this?'

Karina looked down at the letter. It was from the Federal Bureau of Investigation, who had originally automatically become a part of the investigation because the Pay-Go hit had been on a Federally insured property. Contrary to television cop shows, the FBI routinely assisted police on investigations and that assistance was generally gratefully received, their immense resources and ability to investigate across state borders an asset. But even before the New York FBI Field Office had been able to make an assessment of the crimes, the case had been subject to a jurisdiction request from an even more clandestine agency: the Defense Intelligence Agency.

'So what?' Karina asked. 'We know they got jurisdiction of the case, don't we?'

'Read further,' Donovan said, and tapped a lower paragraph of the letter with the end of a pen. Karina read down and quickly spotted the names of Ethan Warner and Nicola Lopez, both under the overall command of Douglas Ian Jarvis. 'You see who authorized the change of jurisdiction?' he asked her.

Karina looked down at the letter and felt a wave of disbelief wash over her. The signatures of some of America's most powerful military figures adorned the bottom of the letter.

'The Joint Chiefs of Staff,' she whispered.

'Jesus would be outranked by these guys,' Donovan said, tossing his pen aside. 'Who the hell are these people? This is a double-homicide case, now a triple. Sure, it's unusual and possibly even the work of a serial killer, but since when does the Joint Chiefs of Staff get involved in something like this? They're not usually interested in anything less than the invasion of entire countries.'

Karina looked straight at Donovan. 'More to the point, why are you so opposed to them being here? Who cares if it's FBI or DIA who are tackling the case? You saw what happened in the courthouse. We're out of our depth here.'

'We sure as hell will be, if we lose face to your new friends!' Donovan snapped. 'I had them checked out, Karina. They're nothing but bail bondsmen and bounty hunters, working out of a little office in Chicago. How the hell do people like that get involved with the DIA and JCOS?'

Karina frowned as she thought back. 'Didn't Jarvis say that he and Ethan served together in the Marines? Maybe they watch out for each other, got to work together on this?'

Jackson shook his head. 'Seriously? The DIA, with all of its resources, hires a couple of gumshoes out of Chicago and sends them all the way out here to work on this case? They came down here to talk about the death of Aaron Lymes, who we know was a former CIA man. Now they're taking over everything we're doing and I want to know why.'

'I don't know,' Karina insisted, and looked at Donovan. 'Why the hell are you giving me a hard time over this? It's not like I invited them in on the case.'

'But you invited them to stay at your apartment, so I heard,' Donovan snapped. 'Getting a little cozy with them, aren't you?'

'They're helpful,' Karina snapped. 'Which is more than you're being right now.'

'Helpful,' Donovan echoed, watching her. 'You want to know the most interesting thing I found out about them?'

'Amaze me.'

'Our new friends haven't been seen or heard of for six months. I called Chicago and asked them to send a squad car round for a look-see. There's no mountain of mail by the front door, so somebody's collecting it for them, and their homes are in good order. But they haven't taken a single phone call through their office in six months, nor have either of them made any credit-card transactions or used the cellphones they're contracted to.'

Karina's eyes narrowed. 'You've had the police on their case?'

'Damned straight.' Donovan nodded. 'Why wouldn't I, when they're sneaking around here? Now they're getting the backing of major military muscle and we don't know why. I don't know what the hell's going on here but I don't like it.'

'What the hell do you want me to say?' Karina asked. 'Sure, something's off about them but they're not obstructing us. Why the hell would you be so worried about all of this? I want as many people on this case as possible. You think the Chiefs of Staff will pull them off just because *you don't like it*?'

'I haven't asked them yet,' Donovan rumbled in reply. 'And this photographer who keeps following them? They tried to tell me it was a bail-runner. If so, it must be the dumbest criminal in history to keep hanging around the kind of people who will put them back in jail.'

Karina felt entirely unable to defend Nicola, but, at the same time, she genuinely had no idea what the hell was going on. Nicola's colleague, Ethan, seemed competent but troubled, as though he were on his own private mission.

'Honestly,' Karina replied, 'I haven't got a damned clue what they're doing. They've only been here a couple of days, for Christ's sake. I'll talk to them and try to find out what's going on, okay?'

'You do that,' Donovan shot back as he got up and grabbed his jacket. 'I've got enough to deal with here without having to keep an eye on your damned friends. The media's already suspicious about the murders and there's a growing concern that there's a serial killer out there. The mayor's on my ass to solve this. With the case in the hands of the DIA, we're powerless, it'll probably be solved without fanfare and it will look for all the world as though this department can't catch killers.' Donovan barged past Karina and headed out of the office door. 'There's no way I'm letting that happen, understood?'

Donovan stormed out of the office. Karina stared after him, as Jackson raised an eyebrow and turned to follow their boss out.

Glen Ryan leaned against the wall and folded his arms as he looked at her.

'He's got a point, Karina,' he said finally. 'This could really cause a major problem for the department. We need to be seen to catch this asshole ourselves, whoever it is, not be bailed out by the government.'

Karina shook her head. 'I don't give a damn about who catches the killer, as long as they're caught. What's the matter with you?'

'This is about more than just the case, Karina!' Glen snapped. 'This is about our jobs. There are cuts going on, in case you hadn't noticed? The economy's in free-fall and if we can't do our job then what's to stop the department just cutting us loose altogether?'

Karina rubbed her temples wearily. 'We'd have more money if you didn't insist on living alone.'

'Jesus,' Glen murmured, 'not this again. I like having my independence, okay? I don't want to be—'

'Tied down,' Karina cut him off. 'Sure, I know the tune, Glen, okay? But I barely earn enough to eat and I know you're in the same position. It makes sense, especially if this all goes south. You going to be able to keep your rent going without a job?'

Glen looked away from her for a moment, out of the window, as though seeking a distraction. 'I don't know.'

'Crap!' Karina snapped. 'You know. If you're this bothered about it then maybe we should just quit right now because we're hardly together except when we're working.'

'I don't want to do that,' Glen replied quickly.

'Then what the hell do you want? You haven't stayed at my place for days.'

Glen dragged a hand down his face and nodded. 'I know, I'm sorry, I've just been real busy, okay? Maybe I'll come over tonight?'

Karina stared at him for a long moment.

'Terrific,' she replied as she walked out of the office. 'You wait until I have people sleeping on my couch and *then* you want to come over.'

'Oh, for Christ's sake!' Glen almost shouted as he stormed after her. 'You want to send me a written invitation next time?'

Karina didn't reply as she stalked away through the station.

# 29

Professor Bowen gestured to the open page of the book on her desk as she spoke.

'A wraith is a disembodied spirit,' she explained, 'a ghost, but not the kind that you'd ordinarily think of.'

'There's more than one type?' Ethan asked.

Professor Bowen stepped away from her desk and gestured to the books lining her shelves in their hundreds.

'People think of ghosts and hauntings in much the same way,' she explained. 'They imagine translucent figures drifting down the halls of old houses, or maybe spirits interfering with household objects and such-like. But the supposedly paranormal aspect of existence is one that has been documented for centuries and is only really just starting to enter the public conscience as a real and tangible aspect of what it is to be alive.'

'Would a crisis-apparition have anything to do with what we've described?' Lopez asked.

Professor Bowen seemed surprised. 'You know about crisis-apparitions?'

'A friend of ours worked on a government project back in the 1960s,' Ethan explained. 'He was charged with studying crisis-apparitions that were recorded during the First World War.'

Professor Bowen nodded. 'There were hundreds of them and in many conflicts beforehand, but it was only during the beginning of the last century that reliable first-hand accounts were recorded in detail. But a crisis-apparition is usually a benign event, a loved one saying goodbye to a family member.'

Ethan glanced at Jarvis, who was listening intently but saying nothing. For once, it seemed, he was learning as they were.

'So wouldn't that consist of absolute proof that the soul, or spirit, or whatever, can exist outside of the body and brain?' Ethan asked Professor Bowen.

'It is evidence,' she replied, 'but not absolute proof. Science requires as proof something tangible, something that can be measured and quantified and replicated in a laboratory. A personal experience, even one that confirms knowledge of a loved one's death when there is no way of receiving that information by normal means, can only be judged by science as being *unexplained*. To just say something happened is not an answer, as no meaningful conclusion can be drawn from the statement and, thus, science has nothing to say.'

'But you think differently,' Lopez said.

Professor Bowen smiled. 'I think exactly the same. However, just because something remains unexplained does not mean that it cannot be provided with some evidence to support it. I've been researching things like out-of-body experiences, NDEs – that is, near-death experiences

– such-like for over twenty-five years and I can tell you two things for sure: one, that I don't know what it all means, and, two, it happens all the time and it's real.'

Ethan leaned against the office wall. 'The soul outlives the body?'

'I didn't say that,' she cautioned. 'Nobody knows. All of the world's religions are founded on the belief that there is life after death. It doesn't matter which god they purport to worship or what name they give to that afterlife, whether it's Heaven or Nirvana or Paradise: all faiths are void if there is no afterlife. Because we can say that nobody knows for sure if there's an afterlife, then the lie of all humanity's religions is exposed. But that doesn't mean that the afterlife doesn't exist, only that man's attempts so far to rationalize and justify their beliefs are utterly in vain.'

'How does this tie in with the homicides?' Jarvis asked.

Professor Bowen gestured to the image of the wraith in her book.

'There are stories from medieval times of what were called at the time "vengeful spirits". Supposedly the souls of those wronged in life, they would return from the dead to get revenge on their assailants. These spirits were renowned for immense strength and violence and formed the origin of *poltergeist* legends. But according to these old accounts, a poltergeist is nothing compared to a wraith.'

'And these things would actively hunt down enemies from their former lives?' Ethan asked.

'Supposedly so,' Professor Bowen replied. 'The only detailed account we have of a wraith comes from the diary of a man named Henry Wilberforce, a British Army Officer who served in India during the uprising of 1857. The insurrection was called The Mutiny, when Indian soldiers subservient to the British Crown rebelled when they were ordered to bite the paper off their ammunition cartridges, which they believed were coated in tallow. The use of the fat went against their religious beliefs.'

'The grease was made from tallow or lard,' Ethan said, recalling the event from history books, 'which derived from beef or pork respectively and, therefore, upset both Hindus and Muslims. The rebellion was eventually put down.'

'Precisely,' Bowen confirmed. 'During the conflict, many British prisoners were captured and were held in a place called the Black Hole of Calcutta, a prison so small, hot and dangerous that in one night alone only twenty-three of its one hundred forty-six prisoners survived, the dead victims of starvation, dehydration and the trampling of other prisoners.'

'Makes Cook County look like the Ritz,' Lopez observed.

'One of those survivors was Henry Wilberforce,' Bowen explained. 'Liberated by British troops, he went on to serve as a provincial governor. But immediately after the deaths in the Black Hole, he recorded that every single prison guard in the jail was murdered over the next few nights. Some were crushed to death, others torn limb from limb, others impaled at impossible heights and angles on trees and railings. Most people thought that the jail survivors were responsible, but all of them presented alibis and none could explain how the jailors had come to die in such extreme ways.'

'You're saying that somebody's ghost killed them?' Lopez asked.

'Nobody knows for sure,' Bowen admitted, 'but the event was recorded by Wilberforce as an example of an extreme supernatural event because one person actually saw the ghost that did it.'

'What did he say?' Ethan asked.

'Not much of any use,' Bowen replied. 'He died of shock soon after saying that they had seen the Devil himself lift a man off his feet and tear him physically in half. That victim was one of the jailors.'

'Wait one,' Lopez said. 'So you believe in this kind of phenomena, but you don't believe it at the same time?'

'It's not about belief,' Professor Bowen said, 'it's about evidence. You only have to search the Internet to find a thousand pages of claims of violent hauntings and terrible poltergeist activity. But a more patient search on each of the cases reveals that other people who lived in the same houses noted no such activity. The Haunting in Connecticut, the Amityville Horror, the Exorcist: all of them have been made famous through television and film, yet none of them have a shred of evidence to support the claims and considerable evidence showing them to be false. The house in the Amityville case has been occupied continuously since the family concerned in the book and film moved out, yet nobody has reported anything untoward as having happened within the property since.'

'But?' Ethan coaxed her with a smile.

'But,' she replied, 'as with so many supposedly paranormal events, a small percentage defies rational explanation. They stand up to scrutiny, are witnessed by people who make no attempt to gain financially or otherwise from their stories, and often have footage or audio recordings to support their claims. They're rare, but there, as I like to say.'

'Could they crush an elevator car or tear a man in half?' Ethan challenged her.

Professor Bowen sighed.

'I've never heard of anything like that,' she admitted, 'but, in 1967, in Rosenheim, Germany, scientists from the Max Planck Institute were called to a lawyer's office to investigate an immense surge of poltergeist activity. Drawers would open and close, lights would swing, printers would spill their ink, telephone calls would be made when there was nobody actually using a phone. One set of records shows the talking clock being dialed three times per minute, too fast for the mechanical dialing system of the phones of the time to handle. On one occasion, every light bulb in the building blew at once. Such events require huge amounts of energy and yet nobody was doing anything untoward. The scientists set up cameras and voice recorders to monitor events and recorded some of the only existing footage of things like pictures rotating on their hooks, far beyond the reach of the witnesses. They also noted that electrical equipment would falter and lights would flicker when a nineteen-year-old employee was in the building. They eventually traced the events to her and, when she was sent on vacation, the poltergeist activity ceased.'

'That's hardly the same, even if it is true,' Ethan said.

'On one occasion,' Professor Bowen added, 'an extremely heavy filing cabinet was witnessed to have been shifted across the office floor. It would seem that, as remarkable as it may appear, it is possible that this kind of energy can indeed be directed by poltergeist activity and to an extent that exceeds our own physical capabilities.'

'And you say that a wraith is worse?' Lopez asked.

'Much worse,' Professor Bowen confirmed. 'There is no precedent in modern times. The name derives from archaic Scottish dialect, meaning a ghost. However, most descriptions of a wraith suggest it's something like a poltergeist on steroids, extremely violent and utterly unstoppable. There are numerous references to witches in ancient literature that might in fact refer to wraiths, but nobody's really sure.'

Ethan glanced thoughtfully out of the window of the office.

'So you're saying that poltergeist activity is often attached to somebody who is alive, but a wraith is the spirit of somebody who is dead?'

Professor Bowen nodded. 'That is almost certainly the case. Poltergeists tend to be caused by the living, through means that we just don't understand that may involve an individual actually causing the entire disturbance themselves or being used as a channel for the events. It is often centered on troubled teenage girls, as in the Rosenheim case, or girls at about the age of puberty. Wraiths, on the other hand, are the spirits of the dead.'

Lopez looked at Ethan. 'That kind of rules out Karina,' she said.

Ethan shrugged. 'All of this is just based on hearsay. Like you said, professor, there's absolutely no evidence that there is an afterlife, anyway. So why should we even consider that this is the work of some kind of rampaging spirit?'

'That's not quite what I said,' Professor Bowen corrected him. 'Whatever you may or may not think about the after-life, the notion that we can exist independently of our bodies is a fact.'

# 30

'How can you say that?' Lopez asked. 'There's no evidence to support it.'

'Actually,' Professor Bowen replied, 'there is a wealth of evidence. There have been countless cases of victims of massive trauma finding themselves floating above their bodies as paramedical teams strive to save their lives. The experiences of people floating up through tunnels of light, meeting deceased family members and so on are common in the public knowledge.'

'No.' Lopez shook her head. 'I heard it was suggested that all such experiences were the result of lucid dreaming.'

'What's that?' Ethan asked.

'It's when you wake up *within* a dream,' Lopez said. 'The brain builds our world around us using what we see through our eyes. When we're asleep, it does so without information coming in, and we dream. That's why dreams can be so weird – the dream world is just the brain working alone. But some people train themselves to become aware when they're dreaming, and the result is the best virtual-reality in the world, completely indistinguishable from the here and now, except that there are no rules: if this was a dream, I could walk through that wall right now.'

'She's right,' Bowen said. 'Lucid dreams are remarkable, and the majority of all supposed alien abductions can be put down to people having lucid dreams without realizing what they are. If you don't understand them, they can be terrifying, as it appears to be absolute reality. Near-death experiences could plausibly fall into the same category.'

'It's still personal experience, though,' Ethan said. 'So it can't be proved. I thought that such experiences were thought to be the product of chemicals in the brain, or similar?'

'A chemical known as dimethyltryptamine, or DMT, exists in trace amounts in mammals, including humans,' Professor Bowen agreed. 'It acts as a psychedelic drug, if ingested, and has been repeatedly cited as the cause of both out-of-body experiences and near-death experiences, which in many cases are closely related to each other.'

'So can't DMT explain the experiences entirely then?' Lopez asked.

Professor Bowen inclined her head in acquiescence. 'That's not impossible, but the victims I'm referring to were clinically dead. They did not *have* any activity in their brains. Not only that, but the events they witnessed when floating above their bodies actually occurred and were not the imagined products of the release of chemicals such as DMT. There are multiple accounts of people recounting the actions of surgeons and nurses working to save their lives while they were clinically dead. How could they even see and hear, Mr. Warner, if their eyes were closed and their brains inactive?'

'More to the point,' Lopez challenged, 'how could they remember their experiences if their brains were inactive? I thought that if a person's cortex was completely shut down, it could not be reactivated, that they really would be dead?'

'Because you assume that the brain is the sole repository of memory,' Bowen replied to her. 'But what if the brain is in fact an antenna of sorts, a point of access rather than the home of memory? There are individuals who have fallen into icy water and been trapped for up to two hours, their bodies as cold as a corpse and their brains entirely inactive. Yet these people have been revived and made full recoveries. If their brain was dead and with it their memory lost, how could they have recovered in full?'

Professor Bowen gestured to newspaper cuttings tacked to the walls of her office.

'In 2006, a Japanese man named Mitsutaka Uchikoshi was stranded on a mountain in the depths of winter for twenty-four days. His core temperature dropped to twenty-two degrees Celsius and he ate nothing. It is believed he went into some kind of hibernation, because, after being found, he was revived in hospital and made a full recovery.'

She gestured to another cutting.

'Erika Nordby, a one-year old who in 2001 got out of her Canadian home on a bitter winter's night and was found hours later lying in the snow wearing only a diaper in temperatures of minus twenty degrees Celsius. Her heart had not beaten for two hours and she was clinically dead, so cold that her mouth was frozen shut and her toes frozen together. Yet when she was warmed by a hospital team, her heart spontaneously began to beat again on its own and, upon recovery, she showed no sign of brain damage.'

Professor Bowen turned back to face them. 'Both of these cases evidence the ability of the human brain to survive extreme trauma, with the cold likely responsible for preventing decay of otherwise dead organs and allowing them to return to life.'

'But doesn't that support a sceptical view of the soul and not a believer's perspective?' Lopez asked.

'At first glance, yes,' the professor agreed, 'until you think about it. It took extreme cold to achieve what survivors of near-death experiences achieved without any such support. The decay of biological organs occurs very quickly in a hospital bed at room temperature. Yet the subjects clearly recall details of their experiences and of the real world around them despite having no recorded brain activity.'

Ethan frowned. 'I thought that there were experiments done, where investigators secretly placed playing cards on top of cabinets in the hope that patients who had out-of-body experiences would spot them.'

'They did,' Professor Bowen agreed, 'but answer me this: If you were suffering from a potentially fatal trauma and found yourself floating above your own body while surgeons tried desperately to resuscitate you, would you be watching anxiously to see if they were successful or would you be busy examining the dusty tops of nearby cabinets?'

Ethan smiled ruefully.

'Fair point,' Lopez said. 'So you have evidence of life after death?'

'Direct evidence of a man who experienced not just a near-death experience and all of the classical signs that go along with it,' Professor Bowen replied, 'but who also underwent a physiological change as a result of the NDE.'

'What kind of change?' Ethan asked.

'The subject was a sixty-year-old man, whose experience was published in an extensive journal written by a British nurse who spent years documenting such events,' Professor Bowen explained. 'He had a profound out-of-body experience during a period of extremely deep unconsciousness and found himself floating above his own body. From there, he was later able to accurately describe the actions of the doctor and nurse caring for him at the time. He then rose up out of the room and traveled to what he described as a pink room, where his dead mother told him that it wasn't yet his time and that he had to go back.'

'Sounds like the effect of drugs,' Lopez surmised. 'If he wasn't clinically dead, how could his experience be defined as proof of an afterlife?'

'Because when he was in the pink room, what he described as a "messianic figure" touched his hand,' Professor Bowen replied. 'The subject had suffered from cerebral palsy all of his life, and, from birth, his right hand had been in a permanently contracted position. But following his experience, he was able to open and use his hand normally. There is absolutely no medical explanation for that.'

Professor Bowen stepped out from behind her desk and gestured to her bookshelves.

'Another case involved a fifty-nine-year-old woman who was admitted to a British hospital suffering from a severe asthma attack. She was in such distress and danger that she blacked out in the emergency room, but to her she didn't lose consciousness at all. She reported that she suddenly felt entirely calm and was looking down at her body on a hospital bed from above. She reported noticing a mousetrap discarded on top of a tall cupboard on one side of the room. Then a bright light appeared and she was drawn toward it. Figures appeared, as outlines, and she reported feeling incredibly peaceful, but the figures told her that she had to go back. Although she wasn't able to identify the figures, she reported feeling as though she knew them, like they were members of her own family.' Professor Bowen looked at Lopez as she went on: 'When she recovered consciousness, she reported the experience to a nurse, who checked the top of the cupboard in the emergency room and found the mousetrap.'

Ethan inclined his head.

'But what you're describing, even though they are true accounts with evidence, doesn't tie in that well with what we're encountering here in New York. This thing, if it really exists, is roaming the damned streets killing people.'

Professor Bowen glanced down at the picture of the wraith in the open book and sighed.

'There is a different kind of NDE,' she said. 'They don't get nearly as much attention, perhaps because they're considered somewhat frightening.'

'Frightening?' Lopez asked. 'In what way?'

'They start the same,' Professor Bowen explained, 'with the body rising into a tunnel of light, but then things start to change. There are a few variations: the first is that the ordinary process of rising up into the light is translated by the person experiencing it as frightening. The second is that the person finds themselves in an infinite void of blackness, utterly alone and isolated. There is no sense of time – they could have been there ten minutes or ten thousand years, but are unable to tell. The third, and final type, is an experience of being dragged down into an intensely cold darkness by ghoulish, demonic beings. These experiences are considered terrifying by those who witness them, and are accompanied by loud and annoying noises, the sense of many beings in extreme pain or distress, and a complete inability to prevent the witness from plunging into an abyss of misery and suffering.'

Lopez raised an eyebrow. 'I can see why that trip isn't advertised as loudly.'

'You think that people who have lived badly get the demon treatment, and those who have lived well head upstairs?' Ethan asked. 'Like heaven and hell?'

Professor Bowen shook her head.

'It would be nice to think so,' she replied, 'but studies have shown that there is no defined difference. Some people who have had more than one NDE have undergone both good and bad experiences. It seems to have more to do with the person's state of mind than any particular sense of judgment.'

'Which could rule out the afterlife evidence entirely,' Lopez pointed out, 'but not the ability of the soul to escape the body or the brain.'

'Exactly,' Professor Bowen replied. 'The experiences of what people are so tempted to call heaven or hell may simply be an extension of the person's psychological state at the time of death. A high percentage of attempted-suicide victims report distressing NDEs, which holds well with the hypothesis: they're unlikely to be in a healthy mental state when they decide to take their own lives. What really interests me is the fact that the consciousness does indeed seem able to escape the body and brain, and it's not just the person undergoing the experience that has witnessed this event.'

'What do you mean?' Ethan asked.

'Sometimes,' Professor Bowen countered, 'the experience provides knowledge that the recipient could not possibly have obtained through normal means.'

'Such as?' Lopez asked.

'They're called "Peak in Darien" cases, where a dying subject has a near-death experience and speaks to a family member whom they believed to be still alive but who now claimed to be dead. Upon recovery, they mention this strange meeting, and subsequent investigation reveals that the person in question has indeed died.'

'Have there been many of these?' Lopez asked, really interested now.

'Countless,' Professor Bowen replied. 'One early example was recorded by Doctor Henry Atherton himself in 1680. His young sister died after a long sickness. Attendees placed live coals to her feet to no response and saw no breath on a mirror held to her face. But the girl later awoke and reported a vision of seeing heaven and several people who had died, one of whom was thought by the attendees to still be alive. They checked it out, and found that the girl was indeed correct.'

'Anything a little more recent?' Ethan asked.

'There is the case of an elderly Chinese woman in the terminal stages of cancer who reported that her sister and husband visited her bed in visions, urging her to join them. She reported to a nurse that her sister was still alive in China, but they hadn't met for many years. The nurse told this to the woman's daughter, and was informed that the long-lost sister had died two days earlier of the same cancer, but the family had decided not to tell the patient to avoid upsetting her.'

Lopez shrugged. 'Okay, but there's still nothing here that we can use to try to stop whatever's killing these victims.'

'Yes, there is,' Professor Bowen insisted. 'I cannot speak for every paranormal event or haunting on our planet but, if there's one thing that I have discovered over the past twenty five years, it's that these things happen for a reason. The spirit of somebody is hunting people down and it must have some kind of goal in mind. You have three victims. Something must connect them, and, when you find out what that something is, you'll be one step closer to figuring out how to stop the wraith.'

Ethan raised an eyebrow. 'You think we can stop it? We can't even see it.'

'It's on a mission,' Professor Bowen insisted, 'just as some hauntings seem to involve spirits unable to move on from injustice and murder, so maybe this wraith cannot move on. It's your call – let the killings continue, or find out why they're happening and try to put a stop to it.'

# 31

'Tell me you've got something.'

Karina Thorne pulled out into the stream of traffic as Ethan and Lopez settled into the rear seat, the university disappearing behind them. Lopez had called her as soon as they walked out of the university, eager to share the new information. Jarvis had climbed into the front seat, but Ethan had noticed that the old man had remained mysteriously quiet for some time.

'We have,' Lopez replied, 'but you're not going to like it.'

Karina sighed as she glanced in the mirror.

'You've got fifteen minutes before we get back to the station. Shoot.'

Ethan filled her in on the details they'd learned from Professor Bowen. Karina seemed to take it all in well enough, but the response when Ethan was finished betrayed her disbelief.

'You seriously think it's a spook hunting down these victims?'

'Supposedly so,' Lopez confirmed, 'and it fits what we saw in that courthouse. There was something with us.'

'What the hell am I supposed to do with that?' Karina asked. 'Issue an arrest warrant for a poltergeist?'

'Maybe,' Ethan replied, 'but right now, we need to get back to the station and look into the case and see if there's a connection between the dead men in the warehouse and the dead clerk.'

Karina frowned.

'You think that Wesley Hicks and Connor Reece were with Gladstone and Earl Thomas, the guys who hit the Pay-Go and caused the accident?'

'Is there a reason why they shouldn't be?' Lopez challenged.

'Sure there is,' Karina replied. 'The men who hit the Pay-Go were hardened criminals, professionals, backed up by the two men we caught. Reece and Hicks were small fish, not the type capable of arranging a major heist.'

'There wasn't much major about the attack on the Pay-Go,' Ethan pointed out, 'in case you hadn't noticed. Brute-force impact to rupture the armoured truck was enough to extract the cash, wasn't it?'

'Sure,' Karina agreed, 'it wasn't graceful, but the men responsible would need serious connections or experience to make use of the money. The cases it's sealed into on those trucks are equipped with trackers and ink dispensers that allow them to be followed and render the cash useless if the cases are forced open.'

Ethan thought for a moment. 'I've read about the spate of bank robberies down the east coast. It could be a copy-cat robbery, somebody mimicking the original gang in the hopes of avoiding arrest themselves if the original gang ends up being caught.'

Karina shrugged. 'I guess, but that's speculation, and Donovan's not going to let you just walk in and start sifting through the evidence.'

'Donovan's not going to have much choice,' Jarvis said to Karina. 'He starts obstructing us, I'll have him removed from his office until we're done.'

'Jesus,' Karina muttered, 'this just gets better and better. He'll hit the goddamned roof if you try that on him.'

'It's not your fault,' Ethan pointed out.

'Tell Donovan that,' Karina complained. 'He's losing control of a case that could cost us our jobs now that the media's getting involved and budget cuts are being made. There's a good chance that the mayor will make an example of our unit if things don't turn out for the best real soon. Last thing we need is a serial-killer scare hitting the headlines.'

'Let me handle Donovan,' Jarvis said, as Karina turned into a parking lot near the 5th Precinct. 'I'll make sure he sees sense.'

Karina said nothing in reply as she parked and led them up into the precinct offices. They were halfway across the room when they spotted Donovan standing in the doorway to his office, glaring at them and beckoning Karina with one hooked finger.

'See what I mean?' she said.

They filed into the office, Ethan closing the door behind them, as Donovan sat at his desk, folded his arms and glowered at Jarvis.

'You want to tell me why you're really here, Mr. Jarvis? Right now, you're the asshole who's taken this case from us for no good reason that I can figure.'

'I am that asshole,' Jarvis replied. 'And you don't need to know anything else.'

Donovan stood up abruptly and towered over Jarvis. 'I've got ten staff working with me, all of whom might see their jobs on the line if we get chopped from the precinct, and I'm damned if I'm going to let someone like you come in here and steal this from under us—'

'Your jobs are safe,' Jarvis interrupted. 'Nobody's going anywhere.'

Donovan's eyes narrowed. 'You can't know that or force the mayor to secure our positions.'

'I can't control the mayor,' Jarvis replied evenly, 'that much is true. However, our presence here is covert. Any breakthroughs made during this investigation will be announced by yourselves, not us. So the faster we solve this case, the safer your jobs will be, agreed?'

Donovan, apparently stumped, seemed to lighten up a little. 'Agreed,' he said suspiciously. 'What's your interest in this?'

'A long-running investigation,' Jarvis said airily, 'the less about which you know the better.'

'I don't like being kept in the dark,' Donovan rumbled.

'You won't be,' Jarvis replied, 'as far as the case you're investigating is concerned. Right now, our priority is analyzing the closed-circuit-television camera footage obtained from the Williamsburg Bridge.'

Donovan raised an eyebrow. 'The footage? Why would you need that? I thought you were here for the Aaron Lymes' case?'

Karina stepped forward.

'They think that the two men we found in the warehouse on Hell Gate were involved in the auto wreck.'

Donovan appeared surprised. 'They didn't fit the profile of professional armed robbers.'

'It's not profiles we're interested in,' Ethan said, 'it's connections. All of the murders share similar characteristics that seem impossible, especially the absence of forensic evidence and the presence of extreme force. Maybe there's a reason why they were all targeted. Find that reason and we might just find our killer.'

Donovan appeared to consider this for a moment.

'That's a weak link by any stretch. There's a more likely scenario: our professional robbers use hired hands to do their dirty work and then silenced them afterward, permanently.'

'I doubt that a well-educated clerk would have much to gain from working with professional criminals, except to report them to the police at the first opportunity,' Ethan pointed out. 'And your theory doesn't explain how the criminals supposedly killed two men without leaving any evidence behind whatsoever.'

Donovan chuckled and shook his head.

'This case isn't going to be solved by two gumshoes,' he said. 'There's no link between these two murders and—'

'Yes, there is.'

The voice came from behind them all, and Ethan turned to see Tom Ross standing in the now open office doorway.

'Tom?' Donovan said in surprise. 'You should be at home.'

Karina hurried to his side. 'Tom, you shouldn't be here.'

'I'm fine,' Tom insisted to her with a faint smile. 'I want this case solved and any avenue of investigation is fair game for me right now. I've been able to dig up one piece of information that might be useful.'

'What's that?' Ethan asked.

'The connection between the two men found dead in the warehouse and the clerk.'

Donovan rolled his eyes. 'Go on, then, what's the story?'

Tom gestured to a picture board nearby, where images of the two dead thieves and the clerk were pinned.

'Those two men were involved in the raid,' he said.

'You don't know that,' Donovan insisted. 'Even we don't know that.'

'And that clerk,' Tom went on, 'was responsible for the paperwork assigned to the case. The signatures that failed to make it onto the statements must have been doctored, and that means that she must have been involved, because I won't believe that the two men we have in jail right now could have walked from the interview rooms without having signed and dated their own statements.'

'That's very thin,' Donovan pointed out, 'and speculative, too. There's nothing to suggest that the clerk was in any way involved in some kind of cover-up, or that there was one in the first place.'

Jarvis stepped forward. 'Worth checking out, though, don't you think? We'll need access to that camera footage.'

Tom looked at Karina in confusion. 'Who the hell is he?'

'Defense Intelligence Agency's handling the case now,' Donovan explained, then turned to Jarvis, 'not that we're happy about it. Okay, go ahead, but I want to be informed of anything that you learn. I can't imagine why a clerk would be involved with two dropouts.'

'That's why we're doing it,' Lopez replied tartly.

Karina turned to Tom. 'We've got this, Tom, really. You need to get some rest.'

Tom sighed. 'I need to do something to help. Sitting at home all day is driving me nuts.'

'And being here could compromise the validity of our investigation,' Karina replied. 'You know that. You're too emotionally invested. I'll keep you posted, on everything.'

Tom glanced at the team in the office and then reluctantly turned and walked away. Karina watched him leave for a moment and then turned to Donovan.

'I'm worried about him, he's not taking care of himself right now.'

Donovan glanced at Jackson, who'd just walked in. 'You want to keep an eye on him?'

Jackson nodded. 'I'll drop by, tonight.'

'I'll visit him tomorrow,' Karina added. 'He needs people around him as much as possible.'

Ethan stepped forward. 'The tapes,' he said to Donovan.

The chief pressed a button on his desk. 'I'll have them sent up.'

# 32

Ethan sat down behind a monitor that showed a grayscale image of traffic flowing across the Williamsburg Bridge on the day of the Pay-Go heist, Jarvis and Lopez standing behind him in an interview room.

'Quality's not great,' Lopez observed.

'Doesn't need to be for traffic observation,' Jarvis said, 'but, if we can place our two suspects in the morgue at the scene, then at least we're a little closer to solving this. I can get the guys in the labs at the DIA to clean up anything we find, enough for it to be admissible in court.'

Ethan spun the footage through, accelerating time to the moment of the auto wreck.

'We could do with Project Watchman right now,' he suggested.

Jarvis shook his head. Watchman was a covert government-funded surveillance program that Ethan and Lopez had encountered during a previous investigation in Florida, a series of KH-11 'Keyhole' spy-satellites providing a high-resolution three-dimensional virtual replay of the entire globe that a viewer could walk through. Essentially, the government could look into the past at any location on Earth or follow any individual, anywhere.

'My clearance is no longer sufficient to access Watchman,' Jarvis replied. 'Besides, we got control of this case because I asked for it through the Joint Chiefs of Staff. Our agency doesn't have any stake in these homicides, so we wouldn't have been able to use it anyway.'

'Clearance,' Lopez echoed his words. 'Stakes. People have died and your agencies don't give a damn unless there's something in it for them.'

'They're concerned with national security, Nicola,' Jarvis replied, 'not one-upmanship.'

'You expect us to believe that?' Lopez challenged. 'After what they pulled in Idaho and DC?'

Jarvis pointed at the screen. 'There, that's the flatbed, right?'

Ethan had already spotted the flatbed truck swerving violently through traffic on the outside section of the bridge. They watched as the truck raced beneath one camera and was picked up on the next as the image switched.

The pursuing police vehicle closest to the flatbed accelerated, and its front fender smashed into the truck's tail lights.

Ethan watched as the truck swerved, lost control and then crashed against the barriers guarding traffic against the long fall into the East River. It rolled violently, the two men in the rear tumbling out, and then it slid to a halt, balanced on the barrier.

'There's Karina and Tom,' Lopez identified the officers as they jumped from their vehicles.

The doors to the truck flew open as the two men in the cab leaped out, leaving their two accomplices lying comatose in the road behind them. Several shots were fired at the police, but the men had their backs to the camera as they retreated, their faces obscured. The truck lay with its chassis hanging over the precipitous drop and the balance altered as the men jumped free. Slowly, the truck tilted backward as the cases of money spilled out and tumbled away toward the river below.

'There goes the cash,' Lopez said wistfully. 'A few million bucks turned into fish food.'

'Come on,' Ethan snapped at the camera in frustration as the armed robbers disappeared from view, 'there must be a better angle than this.'

The cops whirled as, behind their vehicle, a huge tanker swerved as it tried to brake and avoid the suddenly stationary traffic, but then hit the cars in an explosion of shattered glass, smashed plastic and rending metal. The cops hurled themselves clear of the wreckage.

Ethan stared at the monitor in disbelief. 'Where's the next camera's shot? The one of them running down the bridge?'

'There aren't that many cameras on the bridge,' Jarvis said. 'There's this one on the overhead, plus the one that captured the first images, which is a surveillance camera on the north side of the pedestrian-and-pushbike path.'

Ethan sat back, feeling a sense of dismay as he saw the flames burning around the stricken tanker and the police struggling to both apprehend the two men lying in the road and free crash victims trapped in their vehicles.

'What about cameras in Manhattan and Williamsburg, coming off the bridges, and private security cameras?'

'I'll see what I can get,' Jarvis promised, 'but it'll take time. A lot of camera systems run a twenty-four-hour recording loop, deleting as they go. If you don't access the footage within that time window, it's lost.'

'And we're already forty-eight hours down the road,' Lopez muttered. 'That's sloppy. They could have pulled something by now.'

Ethan stared at the screen and rewound the images, playing them again. Something about the footage seemed off, somehow, but he couldn't put his finger on it.

'You know, these guys must have had some other way off the bridge,' he said. 'Police were already moving to block the exits on the Williamsburg side of the bridge into Queens, so traffic would have been stopped and searched.'

'The bridge was closed after the incident for over twelve hours,' Jarvis agreed. 'Caused havoc around Brooklyn.'

'Maybe they went into the water?' Lopez guessed. 'It's a hell of a drop and swim, but it's not impossible.'

'In winter?' Jarvis replied. 'I doubt they'd have made the shore before succumbing to the cold, and the currents would have dragged them far downstream.'

Ethan looked up. 'But if they'd *planned* for it? They might have got beneath the bridge, maybe stashed something there in case of the police blocking them on the bridge during their escape?'

Jarvis frowned. 'Seems a long way to go, and high risk, too.'

Ethan shook his head slowly. 'Something's just not right,' he said as he played the footage back: the chase, the crash, the confrontation, the truck spilling the cases from the rear and then the tanker hitting the parked vehicles as the thieves disappeared out of shot.

'Wait one,' Lopez said, and pointed at the screen. 'Wind that back a little.'

Ethan spun the footage back slowly and Lopez jabbed her finger at the flatbed's open passenger door.

'Stop there!'

Ethan froze the image. The two unidentified thieves were backing toward the camera around the front of the vehicle, their weapons aimed at the cops. Lopez pointed at the glass of the open passenger door. 'That enough to get a clear image?' she asked Jarvis.

Ethan smiled as he saw a vague reflection of the driver in the glass, the angle of the door reflecting his face.

'It might just be,' Jarvis said. 'Copy that image and send it to this address,' he said as he handed Ethan a card with an email address on it. 'They'll sharpen it up in no time and send it back here.'

Ethan tapped out a quick email and then sent the image as he looked up at Lopez. 'Not just a pretty face, then?'

Lopez smiled back at him and raised an eyebrow. 'Was that a compliment, kind sir?'

Ethan looked at Jarvis. 'If this does link the murders, then it changes everything. If we do have some kind of spectral murderer hunting down these individuals, it suggests that there's something much bigger going on here.'

'And that links it to the trial,' Jarvis agreed.

A few minutes later, the computer in front of Ethan pinged and an email notification appeared. Ethan opened the link and an image appeared.

The reflection in the car door taken by the traffic camera had been blown up to full screen and programs with complex algorithms used to enhance the pixelated image into something approaching clarity.

It only took a moment of observation for them all to nod together.

'That's Wesley Hicks,' Lopez said. 'Tom was right.'

Jarvis pulled out his cellphone. 'It still doesn't help the case against the two men in custody,' he said. 'They didn't fire at anybody and can still claim their truck was hijacked by Hicks and his accomplice.'

'True,' Ethan replied, 'but it gives us a lead to follow and it means we have leverage against Gladstone and Thomas, maybe enough to get them sweating a little because they won't know that Hicks and Reece are dead. How about we start searching the clerk's background and try to figure out why she'd be helping these losers.

'You think she'd need a reason?' Lopez asked. 'There were five of them in on this. That's close to a million each.'

'Of illegally obtained cash,' Jarvis replied for Ethan as he dialed a number. 'Come on, let's figure out why a law-abiding legal clerk would risk life without parole for these two assholes.'

'I've got a better idea,' Ethan said.

# 33

# KHAN YUNIS, GAZA CITY, PALESTINE

*1 year ago*

She awoke, but it was as though she were somehow still dreaming.

Joanna wanted to blink her eyes, but there was no means by which she could do so. From a milieu of colors and light, she focused on the scene before her, even though that scene was physically impossible.

She felt no fear. She felt no pain.

Joanna looked down at her own body as it lay far below her on a metal gurney surrounded by tubes and wires and electrodes and monitors. Her first instinct was to look at her face. She was shocked at how much weight she had lost, her eyes sunken into darkened orbits and her cheekbones visible beneath pale skin. Her hair looked lank and had been hacked short, but her expression was entirely calm, her lips relaxed and her eyes closed as though gently resting.

There was no sound, as though she were watching a silent movie in full color. Doctor Sheviz stood nearby, watching a monitor that was attached to electrodes placed on her temples that she guessed were recording brainwaves. All four lines were straight, registering no activity. She looked at the heart monitors, and saw no rhythm.

With a start of realization, she knew that she was dead.

And yet she was not dead.

The heart-bypass machine was filtering its chilled saline solution through her veins as she watched and she felt a mild sense of disgust at how her body was being violated by the insane man in the room with her. But rage would not come.

She saw Sheviz turn from the monitor to look at her body, saw him smile as he ran a hand through his thick white hair. As he dropped his hand, he knocked a pencil from the top of a desk to land on the floor. He bent down and picked the pencil up, then tossed it to one side on the desk.

Joanna felt something change around her. She looked down but she had no body of her own as she hovered above herself, as though she were a single point of light. The room around her seemed to lose focus slightly and then it began to draw away from her, as though she were climbing up into the night sky. She looked for the city lights but saw nothing but a darkness as deep as the universe.

She felt as though she were being watched, and turned.

Far away, in the darkness, she saw a pinprick of light that glowed with the hue of a rainbow, a pearlescent sphere that began to grow as though sunbeams were reaching out to her. She felt warmth permeate her soul and the endless interminable suffering that she had endured fell away like discarded clothes.

A thousand worries and concerns, the coalesced pressure of years of life, tumbled from her mind and spiraled away into the darkness behind her as the light grew stronger. It folded around her in a glowing blanket of warmth as every emotion that she had ever felt faded away into insignificance before a light filled with completely unconditional love. She felt herself smiling, felt unable and unwilling to resist the light as it grew brighter and brighter, blazing with the strength of a billion suns and yet as gentle as an angel's touch.

Through the brilliant light, she began to discern shapes, moving slowly and subtly. She could not identify them but, somehow, she knew that they were familiar to her, like long-lost memories plucked from obscurity. The figures became closer, as the light wrapped around her, and she felt as though she were as light as air, not a single concern or conflicting thought entering her mind.

The light softened and yet pulsed at the same time, as though it too were alive, a conscious being wrapping itself protectively around her. From the diffuse glow, one of the figures approached her, both solid and diaphanous at the same time, as though existing simultaneously on different planes. She could not distinguish any features in the figure, and yet she knew without a shadow of doubt that it was her father standing before her. Behind him was her mother, the knowledge of her identity a bond that nothing could break, not even death.

There were no words and yet she heard her father as clearly as if he had whispered directly into her ear.

'It is not yet your time.'

Joanna knew that he was right, knew that she would not argue nor struggle against his word, for he of all people knew what was right for her. But there was no denying the fact that she did not want to leave, did not want to abandon the peace that surrounded her. She could think of nothing in the world behind her that she wanted, nothing that she craved or yearned for. The callous nature of humanity had scoured her of the desire to live, and she wondered why on earth she had fought so hard to survive her incarceration at the hands of madmen like Damon Sheviz when she could simply have given up and come here just the same.

'Because it is worth it, to remain.'

The words, or the sense of them that reached her soundlessly, shocked her only because her very thoughts had been heard. Her silent yearning to remain, found its own answer.

'You will return, and we will be waiting for you.'

Joanna's heart filled with joy at such simple words, any fear of death long since evaporated and cast away by the light and the warmth. She was still reveling in its comfort when the light suddenly flickered and weakened, paling and running like a watercolor sketch in the rain.

Joanna felt something terrible wrenched from within her, as though a cold and dark hand had reached into her soul and ripped it bodily away. The warmth and comfort of the light vanished as a cold darkness swelled and overwhelmed her. She heard what she thought were her own cries echo bleakly through her mind, mingling with deep voices and strange noises that infiltrated and violated it.

'Can you hear me?'

The voice sounded deafening after the blissful silence.

Joanna blinked and harsh white light painfully pierced her eyes. Her skin felt cold, her body ached and felt as heavy as all the earth, as all the emotions she had left so far behind dragged her down with a weighty, lethargic gravity. She felt as though she was being drowned by her own existence and, before she had even realized it, tears were streaming from her face. Pain from the intravenous lines ached through her arms and her head began to throb from dehydration as she coughed a thin stream of bile that dribbled weakly across her lips.

Damon Sheviz leaned over her and dabbed away the saliva, his head blocking the light as he held her face in his cold, dry hands.

'Tell me, Joanna, what did you see?'

Joanna managed to focus on him, and through her tears rose a terrible rage that swelled through her weakened limbs and surged through her belly like fire.

Joanna snapped her head sideways, latched her teeth onto Sheviz's left hand and bit down with every ounce of the fury that had been locked away inside for so long. Sheviz's screams echoed out around her like wailing banshees, as her teeth sank through his flesh and tore a chunk of his hand away in a bloodied mess that spilled onto the tiled floor beneath her.

Joanna spat gruesome, metallic-tasting blood out of her mouth as she laughed manically through her tears.

'Go to hell!'

Sheviz hopped up and down as he cradled the tattered wound on his hand, tears flooding from his eyes as he glared at her.

'You first!' he shouted. 'This was just the first experiment, Joanna! I'll keep working on you until there's nothing left. I'll keep sending you to the edge of death until you tell me what you saw! Mark my words, your days are numbered!'

Joanna, her mouth still dripping Sheviz's blood, smiled through her grief.

'Do it!' she spat. 'I have nothing to fear.'

Sheviz stared at her for a long moment, his pain forgotten. 'What did you see?' he gasped.

Joanna held the smile on her face and, without a word, lay back on her gurney. Sheviz rushed to her side, his blue eyes wide and frantic, and then he scowled at her.

'You're lying!' he spat.

Joanna closed her eyes. 'You knocked a pencil off the desk while I was dead, picked it up and tossed it onto the counter, then ran a hand through your hair as you watched me.'

Sheviz's face plunged in shock and wonder as he grabbed her shoulders, his bleeding hand forgotten as he shook her.

'Please, Joanna, tell me what you saw!'

Joanna lay still and did not open her eyes as she replied. 'I really will die, before I tell you,' she whispered softly.

# 34

## MANHATTAN, NEW YORK CITY

'Seriously?'

Jake Donovan stood in his office with Glen Ryan, Neville Jackson and Karina Thorne, as Jarvis laid out what they had discovered.

'It's the only thing that makes sense,' he explained. 'Whoever is responsible for the murders is systematically targeting the people that they believe were involved, however indirectly, in the auto wreck on the Williamsburg Bridge.'

The lie wasn't a big one, but Ethan still marveled at Jarvis's ability to deceive with a conviction that was utterly convincing. The auto wreck wasn't their main area of concern, but Donovan didn't need to know that. Many times in the past, Jarvis had, in effect, deceived Ethan, although never with malice in mind. Lopez seemed less inclined to believe the old man right off the bat, but then she too was capable of the same kind of deception. Takes one to know one, Ethan reflected. He wondered just what else Jarvis might keep buried up there in his head, what secrets he may harbor.

'You want us to start digging into the clerk's private records?' Jackson asked them. 'She's just a bit player. How will that bring the men responsible for this to justice?'

'You've already found the four men responsible for the robbery,' Ethan reminded them as he tossed the black-and-white photograph of Wesley Hicks onto the table before them. 'Two are dead and two are in jail right now. This is Hicks, caught by the security camera on the Williamsburg Bridge.'

'There wasn't any footage of them up there,' Jackson uttered.

'Computer-enhanced reflection in the window of the flatbed,' Lopez replied with a bright smile. 'Having the DIA on the case helps enormously, don't you think?'

'So they're linked,' Donovan said. 'You think we might be able to dig something up on the clerk, maybe some kind of payment?'

'That was my next move,' Ethan said. 'Problem is, if the money all went into the East River, then it's possible that she won't have received any payment. It would all have depended on the robbery going down without a hitch or, at least, one of the robbers making it out with the cash.'

'Then what use is any of this?' Glen Ryan asked. 'Sure, it's good procedure to have the clerk checked out, but I don't see much chance of there being a paper trail. Dudes like the ones who hit the Pay-Go work with cash. It's not like they'd have sent her a check.'

Ethan shook his head.

'We don't make the clerk our priority,' he explained. 'The bank heist is effectively solved. What we do now is start thinking about who else could have been involved on the inside and whether or not they might be targeted by the same person who killed Hicks, Reece and the clerk.'

'You think there'll be more killings?' Karina asked.

'There's been no justice,' Lopez explained. 'The killings seem to be motivated by revenge. If it's gone down the way we think, then the four thieves would have hired the clerk to alter, falsify or just plain lose the statements, rendering them inadmissible in court. That would have created the first big stumbling block for a prosecution. The whole set-up would be there ready just in case any of the men were captured, slowing judicial procedure and perhaps, ultimately, getting them off the hook.'

'We're thinking that maybe this *is* the gang that have been hitting banks all down the east coast,' Ethan said. 'Just that the brains behind the Pay-Go heist isn't one of the actual robbers.'

Donovan raised an eyebrow. 'A sort of mastermind, staying out of the limelight?' he speculated.

'It fits,' Ethan said. 'The heists are meticulously planned and go off without a hitch. It was only bad luck that the flatbed lost control on the bridge, but Hicks and Reece got away even then, suggesting they'd planned for every eventuality that they could. The latex masks, the waiting perhaps for days for the armoured truck to turn up because they run deliberately changed routes each day – all of it suggests that somebody must be behind the team actually hitting the banks.'

'Okay,' Karina agreed. 'I can buy that. Question is. What do you want to do about it?'

Ethan looked again at the picture board in one corner of the office.

'My thinking is that the chain of corruption might be bigger than just the clerk. What if the whole team had been captured on the bridge, before the money cases could be opened? The organizer of this little masquerade would need a guarantee that the thieves wouldn't sell them out to avoid prison time. The mastermind would need a second line of defense, somebody who could keep his team of thieves out of the prison system.'

Jackson got it first. 'The lawyer.'

'Exactly,' Lopez agreed. 'His name was Eric Muir and he wasn't a state attorney, he was privately hired and likely not cheap. Where did the money come from?'

'The other bank heists?' Glen Ryan hazarded.

'Too soon,' Ethan said. 'They wouldn't have had time to launder the money. Unless, of course, the attorney was willing to consider cash.'

'If he's crooked then cash is the best way because the notes are so hard to trace,' Donovan agreed. 'Anything else, there would be a trail to follow.'

Ethan nodded in agreement. Fact was, so many criminals were too damned stupid to realize that keeping cash tucked in a safety box or similar was by far the best way to commit the perfect crime. Whether by fraud or outright robbery, thieves too often splashed their ill-gotten gains in ways that made them conspicuous and easy to trace: fast cars, casinos, drug deals that brought them to the attention of other police forces and so on.

But the smart man who carried off a decent take from a heist or fraud and ensured that their life changed as little as possible, at least on the outside, held a crucial advantage. Sure, you might still have to hold down a day-job to cover your tracks, but, if a successful heist netted a man a couple of hundred thousand bucks and he was smart enough to use it for all of his cash purchases, things like gasoline, food shopping, household goods and such like, then even if he spent a thousand bucks a month that cash would last him more than fifteen years. And that didn't even take into consideration the extra salary that would build up in his bank account, money that would otherwise have been spent on those same goods that could now be legally spent on the cars and casinos without attracting unnecessary attention. A wise man could double his available annual income for the majority of his working life off the back of a single successful heist.

'We follow the lawyer, Eric Muir,' Ethan said. 'If he's attacked by somebody, then maybe we get to catch our killer. If he isn't but evidence is found of him doing deals to get these convicts off the hook for a price, then we still win. Either way, I'd be surprised if this guy's completely clean: somebody had to hire him as the defense for this case.'

Donovan nodded. 'Agreed, we'll do it. You guys keep searching for evidence of this mysterious mastermind.'

Ethan shook his head. 'We'll all take part in the stakeout.'

'What for?' Donovan asked. 'It only takes two officers to keep an eye on one man.'

Ethan thought fast. He wanted to be on site, because, if the mysterious photographer showed up again, he absolutely intended to corner them once and for all.

'We don't know if he'll lead us directly to the main man,' he said. 'The more people we have on this the better, as it's our only lead. Besides, putting cops on it costs money. We're not on the department's clock, remember?'

Donovan shrugged and nodded, and Ethan turned away and walked out of the office with Lopez and Jarvis.

'This is getting in the way of things for us,' Lopez pointed out as they walked. 'Nothing's being done about MK-ULTRA or our friends at the CIA.'

'One thing at a time,' Jarvis cut in. 'Let's get this case solved first.'

'Nicola's right,' Ethan insisted. 'Have you got anything from Major Greene's list of names?'

'The team's on the case,' Jarvis replied, 'but these things take time. There's a hundred years to work through, much of it from time periods when documentation wasn't as prevalent as it is today. If there's anybody here in the city descended from people on that list, they'll find them eventually.'

'The CIA were tracking Joanna toward New York,' Ethan said, 'and are likely here already. Just because we're not under threat, doesn't mean they'll stop their mission. If we don't find her fast, they will, and everything we're trying to achieve will be over.'

'I'll stay on it,' Jarvis promised.

Karina jogged up behind them as they walked. 'Nice work back there. You want to tell me what you're going to do if this wraith thing of yours turns up and kills that lawyer?'

'We haven't figured that part out yet,' Ethan admitted.

'Well, you might want to start thinking about it,' she said, 'because, sooner or later, Donovan is going to realize what's happening here and, if he thinks you guys are crazies, he'll have justification for claiming back jurisdiction of the case. Just sayin'.'

Ethan looked at Lopez.

'Yeah,' she said, 'or he sees what we saw. Then he'll want us here.'

Jarvis stopped them both.

'Look, before we go see Eric Muir, why don't we take this to the people that we know for sure are involved?'

'Earl and Gladstone?' Lopez asked. 'I doubt we can do that without further compromising the case. If that lawyer is crooked and we lean on his clients, he'll use it against us in any trial and, besides, we already know that they're not talking. Identifying Hicks and Reece probably won't be enough to get them to sing for us.'

'This is DIA business, nothing to do with the police department, so we keep it quiet,' Jarvis replied. 'Why don't you pay them a visit and tell them straight that one by one their colleagues are being picked off by a crazed serial killer? Show them a few photographs of what's left of Hicks and Reece? Maybe that, along with the fact that the money all went into the East River, will be enough to tip them over the edge and finger whoever is actually behind all of this.'

Ethan looked at Lopez, who shrugged. 'I guess it's worth a shot.'

*

'What have you managed to dig up?'

Donovan looked Glen Ryan in the eye. The kid shrugged as he replied.

'Nothing. Out-of-towners, nothing to suggest they're up to no good here. Karina's not hiding anything as far as I can tell but we're not on great terms right now.'

Donovan turned his gaze to Jackson. 'You?'

'Plenty,' Jackson replied. 'They took off out of Chicago a few months back and somebody's been housekeeping for them, that much we knew. I checked the local rags for information around the time they cleared out, and guess what I found?'

'Tell me.'

'It was all over the news,' Jackson said, 'a major congressional investigation into corruption at the Central Intelligence Agency. A big government department in DC was running the show when suddenly two staff members were killed in suspected homicides. The investigation is shut down, the media goes quiet and everything's forgotten.'

'What's that got to do with Warner and Lopez?' Glen Ryan asked.

'Only the fact that Warner's sister was on the team that got hit,' Jackson replied. 'Natalie Warner. She too goes off the radar for a few weeks, but then turns up again after an internal investigation clears her of any wrong-doing. Point is, there was no need for her to disappear at all, seeing as she wasn't ever a suspect in the murders.'

Donovan stared thoughtfully out of his office door. 'Their man Jarvis works for the DIA,' he mused out loud. 'Maybe some kind of inter-agency-rivalry thing? The CIA tying up loose ends in some kind of cover-up?'

Jackson shrugged. 'Beats me. They're up to their necks in something, but, as it involves government agencies, there's never quite enough evidence to tie them down. You want me to call Langley and see what they say?'

Donovan thought for a moment, then shook his head.

'No,' he replied. 'I'll do it.'

# 35

# KHAN YUNIS, GAZA CITY, PALESTINE

*One year ago*

The experiments ceased, finally.

She had known they would, after the last had almost resulted in her dying for good.

The tunnel of light had not reappeared. Instead, Joanna had found herself sucked down into a gruesome, black, cold, timeless place, where every step was hindered by dense tangles of writhing undergrowth. Cruel, threatening creatures tracked her from the darkness, loud noises shocked her or ground interminably through her skull like a thousand fingernails dragged down endless chalkboards. There, in that seemingly endless pit of despair, she had felt something new and terrifying that had haunted her thoughts ever since.

Evil.

Like most adults, she no longer believed in monsters under the bed or ghosts haunting the darkened corners of lonely houses, but now she had a new appreciation of what evil truly was: the construct of our wildest and yet darkest fantasies, lived for real through the actions of those unable to contain them. Monsters, ghosts, gargoyles – all were the inventions of men designed to avoid facing the truth of what evil really was: their own actions.

Joanna had seen the evil lurking within her in her last voyage into her own soul, a beast of indescribable fury and strength that if unleashed would destroy the world just to see the sparks it made going up. There was no Satan but that which lived within her, and all other people, too.

For the first time, Joanna was relieved to have found herself lying on the cold gurney as her body was dragged back from the brink of oblivion once again.

Joanna Defoe remained in captivity, in the tiny cell in the darkness, although now she no longer wore the blindfold: only her hands remained bound. She sat on her mattress as the voice of Doctor Sheviz reached out for her through the hatch in the door.

'Tell me, Joanna. What did you see?'

Joanna remained silent. She ignored the question just as she had ignored it hundreds of times before. Doctor Sheviz had gone through alternating paroxysms of hatred, rage and desperation, but Joanna had never once faltered. Finally, after months of repeated experiments, the men who were funding the doctor's insane Eternity Project had demanded that he either obtain verifiable results or abandon the work.

To Sheviz's dismay and Joanna's veiled delight, he had failed. He had already made a fatal mistake and now deep within Joanna was forged a core of cold iron, hard and without flaws, impervious.

'Please, Joanna,' Sheviz whined through the hatch. 'Tell me what you saw. I know that you saw something, Joanna. I could tell, by your features, by your eyes. You saw things, tell me what they were!'

Joanna remained silent. Since Sheviz's failure, the men who she assumed were responsible for her abduction had gradually become more relaxed. The men in the gray suits, and there were several over the months that had passed, had spoken more openly around her. Sometimes, they had exchanged entire conversations right outside the door to her cell, their American accents and terminology as plain as the day was long.

Then, as now, Joanna had simply listened, all the while playing the part of a catatonic waif divested of both resistance and interest in the world around her. It had become surprisingly easy to adjust, to recover the spark of hope, ever since she had laid eyes on Doctor Sheviz months before on the gurney. What she had read there had provided her with the vital link to reality that she so desperately craved, the anchor they had tried to take from her. After all of the painstaking care they had taken to break her down into an emotional and physical blank slate, the insane doctor had eradicated all of it with one simple error.

The digital watch on his wrist displayed the time, the date and the year. As he had leaned over her, the sleeve of his white coat had ridden up his wrist and exposed the face of the watch to her at close range.

In an instant, Joanna had known how long she had been incarcerated, what month and day it was, what year it was. In a rush of awareness like the first stars igniting in a new-born universe, she had regained that which had been so brutally taken from her. Despite the crushing emotional trauma that she had endured since at the hands of Sheviz, she had looked forward to each and every visit, because each strengthened her awareness and her ability to maintain her fragile grip on the notion that she was still a part of a larger world and that there was still a future for her.

For the first time in years, she was able to think of *escape*. Three years, two months and seventeen days, to be precise.

'Please, Joanna. One last time: tell me what you saw.'

Joanna sat silent for a moment longer and then slowly turned her head. The desire to take immediate action, to escape this shadowy prison and simply breathe fresh air again was overwhelming, but that time was not now.

Sheviz's fanatically blazing eyes peered through the hatch as she turned to look at him and silently opened her mouth. Joanna croaked something unintelligible from her lips, tried to speak. No sound came forth.

Sheviz's face vanished from the hatch as he shrieked frantically at the guards outside. 'Open the door!'

The Palestinian gunmen, hired hands who were being paid to stand watch over the building in which she had been held for so long, hurried forward. She heard the jingling of keys, the heavy clank of the locking mechanism in the doors grinding around.

Joanna had been a pliant and comatose prisoner for many long, long years. The guards and the doctor had no fear of her. She liked that. The iron ball deep inside her pulsed into life as the door opened and Sheviz burst in, dropped to his knees in front of her and grasped one of her hands in his.

'Joanna, please tell me. What did you see?'

Joanna looked into his eyes but her awareness was directed at the two guards lingering just outside the room. Both looked young, fit and well fed. Both carried the ubiquitous AK-47 rifles clasped across their chests. At this close range, even the inaccurate Kalashnikov could not fail to miss her.

'What did you see?' Sheviz repeated in desperation.

Joanna focused on him again and a smile dragged itself onto her face, born of sweet and yet poisonous revenge. A word fell from her lips as soft as a whisper.

'Justice.'

Joanna sucked her stomach in as she flipped her head forward, her entire body jerking in a whiplash motion that smashed her forehead across Sheviz's face like a club. The doctor let out a strangled gasp of pain as he tumbled backwards and sprawled across the floor of the cell.

Joanna leaped up from the bed and jumped into the air, lifting both feet high as she plunged down and landed directly onto Sheviz's ribcage. She felt his ribs crack like dried twigs beneath her, just as the two guards raced into the cell and smashed her aside.

Joanna hit the wall hard, stars dancing in front of her eyes as her legs crumpled beneath her. She slumped down as she glared at the doctor with a savage smile plastered across her face.

Sheviz lay curled up into a foetal ball, weeping as thick blood spilled from his ruined face to pool in scarlet smears across the floor of the cell. Joanna watched as the doctor was dragged screaming in pain from the cell by the two guards and the door was locked behind them, sealing her in once more.

She got up, still reveling in the first act of defiance for years, and sat on her mattress. Her heart was pounding so hard inside her chest that she felt as though it were shaking her entire body. Her breath came in short, sharp gasps that she fought to bring under control.

Sheviz was finished with her, that much she knew. The men outside her room had spoken loudly enough that she knew the doctor had failed in his experiments and that her fate now lay in the hands of the CIA.

The CIA, she had deduced from months of overheard conversations, were working in conjunction with a powerful arms company called MACE, whom she had been investigating over claims of rigged ransom abductions, first in South America and now here in Gaza. When she got too close, they had decided to use a CIA grab-team loosely disguised as militants to abduct her. The CIA then took over, running its bizarre experiments on her and no doubt others. The family connection she had heard described long ago was her father, who had unwittingly been caught up in a program she had often researched: MK-ULTRA.

Her father, Harrison, had responded well to the experiments, which used drugs and other forms of mental suggestion, ending up in a jail in Singapore for three years for his efforts after he had abruptly shot four prominent Communist sympathisers during the Vietnam War. Joanna had guessed that the experiments were all an effort to try to 'program' her in the same way, and she didn't doubt that it would have worked were it not for Doctor Sheviz's sloppy mistake.

Joanna's resolve, strengthened since seeing the doctor's watch, had prevented her from slipping fully into a mental state entirely open to suggestion. But that did not mean that the doctor's experiments had failed entirely.

She curled up on the mattress, her mind filled with vivid imagery, sights that had changed her notion of what it meant to be alive. She had died during the experiments, and had seen a tunnel of light that had drawn her up into a place that was beyond imagination, beyond words, beyond anything that she could ever have conceived until she witnessed it herself. The darkness of her final visit was not enough to deter her, for she knew now that it was her own damaged soul that she was witnessing, not some place of suffering for the damned.

In no less than thirty-seven separate experiments, she had witnessed the afterlife. The very thing that Doctor Sheviz had sought confirmation of had been the very thing that had strengthened Joanna's resolve to the point that nothing could break her. Joanna Defoe no longer feared death and, in life, she had resolved to pursue one thing above all others: revenge. The cold iron ball in her belly pulsed again, fueled by the memory and the knowledge of the cruel resolve that lay within her, just waiting to be unleashed.

Damon Sheviz would not be fit enough to return for some time, due to the pain he would be suffering from his multiple fractured ribs. That meant that the CIA would probably seek to move or perhaps even terminate her.

Whatever they decided, when the time came, she would be ready.

# 36

## RIKERS ISLAND, NEW YORK CITY

'Ain't no talkin' me down!'

The bars of the cell were too solid to rattle as James Gladstone tried to shake them in fury, the guards nearby taking no notice as they patrolled the block.

'You're wastin' your time, man,' said Earl Thomas from behind him. 'We'll be walkin' from here soon enough, but those dudes –' he pointed to the guards with a cynical smile – 'they're the ones doin' life.'

Gladstone turned away from the bars to face back into their eight-by-twelve-foot cell. White-washed cinderblock walls, two bunk beds with reed-thin mattresses, a shared sink and latrine stared back at him.

'Man, I hate this shit.'

They had been incarcerated in the federal jail for little more than twenty-four hours, but Gladstone was already pacing up and down like an enraged, cornered bull. Six foot three and two-hundred forty pounds, he wasn't good with confined spaces. His glossy black face was bunched up like a prune, predatory eyes searching for someone, or something, to take out his frustrations upon. Earl, on the other hand, was half Gladstone's weight and barely five-nine. He rested back on his bunk and shrugged.

'Just gotta bide our time,' he insisted. 'Ain't nothing to worry about, long as the suit does his work right.'

Gladstone sneered at him. 'Mighty big gamble when we're looking at twenty-five to life.'

On the other bunk lay two scrawny prisoners, both wearing the same baggy orange correctional facility jumpsuits as Gladstone and Earl, both wearing the same anxious expressions. Their eyes were fixed fearfully upon Gladstone as he prowled up and down the cell.

'Man,' Earl said, 'just cool it, okay? You're doin' nothing but causing yourself more grief, gettin' all worked up.'

Gladstone's glare fell upon their two cellmates, who both looked away from him as though they'd caught the attention of a wounded tiger.

'Whatchoo lookin' at?' Gladstone boomed, pointing one heavily muscled arm at them like a shotgun. 'You want some?'

Gladstone reached the bunks in a single pace. His height meant that he was looking down at the man lying in the top bunk.

'I weren't lookin' at you man, 'kay?'

'You callin' me a liar?' Gladstone growled, one fist bunching into the size of a football.

Wearily, Earl dragged himself up into a sitting position on his bunk.

'Dude, seriously, let the kid go. You smash him to pieces, we'll never get out of here.' Gladstone's huge frame trembled with frustration as he realized that there was little he could do to vent his anger. 'James, stand down, dude.'

Gladstone backed off, lowering his fist, his jaundiced eyes fixed upon the two cowering inmates. The one on the lower bunk smirked at Gladstone.

'That's it, do as he says.'

The huge convict's eyes flicked down to the inmate as he sat on the bunk. Rage swelled inside Gladstone's immense frame as he struggled to comprehend what was happening.

'You talkin' down to me, boy?'

The inmate's smirk didn't slip. 'Sure I am. You got beef with that, *James*?'

The inmate spat the name as though it were an insult. Earl leaped off his bunk and grabbed Gladstone's arm.

'Don't!' he snapped. 'The little shit ain't worth it.'

'I ain't takin' nothin' from him exceptin' his life,' Gladstone growled.

'You can take it all right,' Earl said, glancing down at the smirking inmate. 'You think that because we're only on probation, we can't reach you, don't you?'

'It's a fact,' the inmate replied, flashing a grin of white and gold-capped teeth. 'You's got nothin' right now, so you'd best keep the peace here or I'll go squealin' to the watch about how's you and your dumb-ass friend here are beatin' up on us.' The inmate got off his bunk and grabbed the edge of the metal. 'All I gotta do is butt this rail an' you're goin' nowhere.'

Earl released Gladstone's bulging triceps and nodded.

'That's right,' he said. 'So go ahead, asshole.'

The inmate's smirk slipped as he frowned in confusion, but he didn't move.

'That's right,' Earl repeated. 'You see, you can't do nothin', because if you get us stuck here for any longer than we want to be, how long do you think it will be before James here gets hold of you?'

The inmate's gaze flicked back to Gladstone's giant frame as he realized his error.

'Imagine what will happen,' Earl said, 'if we were in this cell with you two assholes for a couple of years 'stead of a couple of days.'

Gladstone smiled as he stepped forward. 'Ain't that right, Earl.'

The inmate staggered back against the bunk. 'You do anythin', I'll scream anyways!'

Gladstone loomed over him, placed two giant hands on the inmate's scrawny shoulders and shoved him down onto his ass on the lower bunk.

'It's not me who's goin' to be doin' anythin' boy,' Gladstone rumbled. 'It's you.'

The inmate looked up at Gladstone in confusion. Gladstone reached up, shoved the inmate there aside and tore the sheets off the upper mattress, then turned and loosely tucked the sheet into the bars of the cell door. The sheet draped down, partially obscuring the cell from the view of others across the block.

'Don't disappoint me, boy,' Gladstone snarled.

Then, with one hand, he unhitched his pants and hefted himself free. The inmate grimaced and turned his head away. Gladstone grabbed his face in one giant hand and yanked it brutally back.

'Make it good,' he snapped, 'or I'll fuck you up fo' life, you understan'?'

The inmate slowly lowered his head as Gladstone guided him down.

The lights in the cell flickered, shimmering as Gladstone put a hand across the back of the inmate's head and shoved him all the way down. Earl looked up at the lights as the sound of muted gagging drifted across the cell.

Across the block, a handful of cell lights were also flickering intermittently but others further down the block remained on.

'What's goin' on?' Gladstone asked, his eyes closed but able to detect the flickering lights.

'I ain't sure,' Earl replied.

Earl walked to the bars of the cell as he looked out across the block. The body heat from a couple hundred inmates coupled with the lousy air conditioning meant that the block was frequently hot and always stank of a volatile fusion of stale sweat, urine and grease. But now the air was cold, bitterly cold, and Earl saw a cloud of his breath condense onto the air in front of him.

'What the hell?'

Earl was about to turn to Gladstone to ask him over to the bars when something plowed into his guts with enough force to propel him backwards across the cell. Earl hit the wall hard and his right leg smashed across the sink. The bone crunched loudly as his femur snapped under the impact and punched through his orange jumpsuit in a bloodied white stump.

Earl screamed as he slid not down the wall but up it, a terrific pressure collapsing his ribcage to the sound of fracturing bones.

Gladstone yanked the inmate off him and whirled to see Earl crunched up against the ceiling in a fetal ball, blood spilling from his ripped thigh around a jagged stump of white bone poking through his flesh. His voice shrieked across the block in a wail of indescribable agony.

'Jimmy! Get it off me!'

Gladstone's brain struggled to comprehend what he was seeing as he dashed forward and reached up for Earl. In an instant, Earl's body was hurled back across the cell and crashed into the bars loudly enough to ring in Gladstone's ears. Earl dropped onto the cell floor in a crumpled heap, the bones in all of his limbs smashed and his eyes wide but lifeless.

Gladstone dashed to the bars as whoops and shouts of delight echoed through the block. The mattress sheets were preventing the rest of the inmates from viewing the fight and they were clamouring for Gladstone to rip it down as he appeared at the bars and shook them with both hands.

'Get me out of here!' he bellowed.

The inmates, oblivious to his words, cheered and battered their cell doors with anything they could find as they saw the big man standing over his ruined, bloodied cellmate.

Gladstone turned and saw the other two men in the cell cowering on their bunks.

'How'd you do that?' he demanded.

'We din' do anythin'!' one of them shouted. 'Christ man, we din' move!'

Gladstone took a pace toward them, bunching his fists in rage as he reached out for them. He was stopped in his tracks as a bitter cold wrapped itself around him like a blanket of ice, snatching the breath from his lungs. Gladstone managed a brief cry of what might have been fear before he felt himself lifted off the cell floor and spun by the ankles as though he were a leaf in a gale. His deep voice screamed out above the roaring of the cell block outside.

'*Help me!*'

Gladstone's head smashed across the cell wall violently enough to shatter the side of his skull and spill the contents of his head in a fine spray of blood, bone and tissue that splattered the two cowering inmates nearby. His immense body whipped around, his ruined head clanging against the bars as thick splatters of blood splashed across the hanging sheets.

The raucous cheers in the cell block fell abruptly silent as the light from within the cell was masked by the gruesome splashes of fluid now staining the sheets and the walls of the cell with pink and red blotches. For the first time in living memory, there was no sound in the entire block as several hundred men stared in shock at the terrible orgy of gore spilling from the upper-tier cell.

An immense crash broke the silence as what was left of Gladstone's huge body slammed into the cell doors, his limbs flailing like torn sails, his head entirely missing and one of his thick legs severed above the knee.

A chorus of '*Jesus*' and other whispered profanities drifted up through the tiers as Gladstone's corpse slumped onto the cell floor. As the inmates watched, the sheets hanging from the bars of the cell suddenly billowed as though something had passed through like a scythe through wheat. A shape like a giant, demonic hawk imprinted on the fabric until it fell back down.

The sounds of violence and shouting had not alerted the prison staff to anything untoward.

The deep silence brought them running.

# 37

'We're here to see Earl Thomas and James Gladstone.'

Lopez spoke through the electronic voice system to the desk sergeant behind a Plexiglas-and-wire-mesh screen, as Ethan looked up at a bank of six television monitors wired to cameras in each of the nearby cell blocks.

It only took him a moment to see the medical teams dashing down one of the upper tiers, guards in uniforms standing back from an open cell as the medics dashed inside.

'Looks like you've got some action on D Block,' he warned the desk sergeant as he gestured to the monitor.

The sergeant looked up at it and frowned. 'You say you're here for Gladstone and Thomas? Well, that's their cell.'

Ethan looked at Lopez, and she turned to the sergeant. 'Get us in there, now!'

The doors rumbled open as Ethan and Lopez hurried through, two guards appearing as if from nowhere to escort them onto the block. The first thing that Ethan noticed was the silence as they walked, completely different to the cat-calls, profanities and insults hurled at them on their previous visit. They reached the cell, where a loose knot of guards were staring at something within.

Ethan and Lopez stood on the cell-block tier and stared into the now-open cell.

'Christ,' Lopez uttered.

The walls of the cell were splashed with what looked like gallons of blood, sprayed in enormous crescents across the walls and soaking thickly into sheets already stained yellow with age.

Two bodies were being wheeled out of the cell in bags as a blood-pattern analyst stood in the cell door and looked at the carnage around him. It was a measure of the violence within Rikers Island that an analytically trained guard was a permanent member of the uniforms. Homicide was not uncommon, especially on wings that housed the more dangerous inmates. Ethan had the brief impression of a spectator at a gruesome art gallery admiring a masterpiece.

'What do you make of it?' Lopez asked.

The analyst shook his head slowly as he looked around the cell, careful not to step inside it.

'I've never seen anything like it,' he uttered.

'Looks like a particularly bad knife fight,' Ethan said. 'Are we looking at arterial-blood splatter here?'

The analyst slowly shook his head as he gestured to some of the wide arcs of blood stretching across the cell's rear wall. 'These patterns are consistent with arterial blood, but they're far too broad and the splatter much too widely spaced to have come from severed arteries. These patterns are more consistent with a wounded body being hurled through the air.'

Ethan looked over his shoulder at the ranks of cells on the opposite side of the block. Dark faces were watching them in utter silence.

'The convicts here are pretty spooked,' Ethan observed.

'We've got witnesses who say that the two men were murdered right here in front of the entire block,' a nearby guard said. 'The cell was locked, but that sheet obscured the interior from the view of most of the rest of the block.'

The analyst stared at the cell for a moment longer and then turned to them.

'I saw the body of one of the victims before he was bagged,' the analyst said. 'What was left of him, anyway. He was a big man, maybe two-hundred fifty pounds. I saw the two survivors when they were being questioned, too. They couldn't have been more than two-hundred fifty between them.' He shook his head in apparent disbelief. 'You want to tell me that they picked that guy up and spun him around in this cell violently enough to tear his head off?'

Ethan looked at the bars of the cell. Amid the blood running down the bars and congealing in blackening puddles on the floor, he could see tufts of black hair and splinters of bone scattered across the floor of the cell.

'There's even small amounts of blood splatter down on the ground floor of the block,' the analyst said. 'The *far side* of the block. Whatever happened here must have been staged somehow. Maybe the guards were bribed to leave the doors unlocked and the whole block came in here, but then there would be clear evidence of their presence and that's what's freaking me the most right now.'

'No forensics?' Ethan hazarded.

'I don't know about forensic evidence here,' the analyst said. 'What I can tell you is that when I arrived here, the guards had kept the cell door locked to prevent any contamination of the scene. The other two men in the cell were huddled together on one of the beds, both of them crying like babies and staring at what was left of the two victims. Both of them were covered in blood, and the guards took that as evidence that they murdered their two cellmates. I can tell you that they couldn't have.'

'How can you be sure?' Ethan asked.

The analyst pointed to the floor of the cell.

'Because apart from the victim's, there are no bloodied footprints on the floor. Whoever committed this crime did so without setting a foot on the ground.'

Ethan turned away from the cell with Lopez. 'Let's talk to the two survivors, see what they have to say.'

They were led by two guards to the North Infirmary, a low-risk ward where a duty nurse was attending to the two inmates as they sat side by side on a bed. Both were silent and still, staring into the distance.

'Guys,' Ethan said as he approached.

Both men flinched as though shot, their eyes flicking nervously up to meet his. 'We din' do it,' one of them almost shouted at him. 'We din' do anythin'.'

Ethan raised his hands as Lopez took over.

'We're not here to charge you,' she said. 'Just tell us what happened, okay?'

The smaller of the two men shook his head. 'They don' believe us. We tol' 'em everythin' but they says we're goin' down for this.'

'Nobody's charging anybody just yet,' Ethan assured them. 'Just explain what happened.'

The older of the two men sucked in a quivering lungful of air before speaking.

'Gladstone was pushin' us around,' he informed them. 'Like usual. We were just mindin' our business, like, when all a'sudden the other one, Earl, gets thrown up against the wall. Broke his leg. Then he's up on the goddamned ceilin', man, all writhin' around, and, before we know what's happened, he hits the cell gate and breaks his neck. Just falls to the ground, dead.'

Lopez nodded. 'And the big guy, Gladstone?'

'Tried to help Earl,' said the smaller man, his eyes wet with tears that he made no effort to conceal. 'Got himself fucked up, too. Just floated right up into th'air and spun around like he was riding a bronco. Time it stopped, there was nothin' left, man. He got smashed to pieces.'

Ethan turned at the sound of approaching footsteps, and saw Donovan stride into the infirmary. The chief paused, seeing the interview in full swing, and leaned against the infirmary door as he listened.

Ethan leaned in close to them, dropping his voice.

'If the guards organized these murders, we can arrange to have you moved out so you can testify against them. This is your chance to come clean, fellas. You see any money change hands, any bribes, weapons, anything?'

Ethan had no power to pull the two men out of their cell

block, although he suspected Jarvis could probably arrange it, if required. If the two men were covering up for a gang slaying or similar, they could get themselves a ticket out of Rikers Island right here and now. It would be like their every Christmas all on one day.

He saw the two men calculate briefly, and then almost in unison they shook their heads.

'Man, there weren't no bribes, and I ain't just coverin' here y'understand?' said the older of the two. 'There was nobody in that cell but the four of us, and we were sitting on the damned bunk watching Gladstone and Earl die, thinkin' we were next. Jesus Christ, it was like they were killed by thin air.'

'You notice anything else?' Lopez asked. 'Anything at all?'

'Yeah,' said the younger inmate. 'It was cold, cold as hell. It ain't never felt like that on the block.'

'And the lights kept flickering out,' said the other. 'Like there was a disruption in the power supply or somethin'. Jesus, man, don't let 'em send us back to that cell.'

'I'll see what I can do,' Ethan lied smoothly.

Ethan stood back and walked out of the infirmary with Lopez. Donovan joined them.

'You want to tell me what the hell that's all about?'

Ethan didn't stop walking as he replied. 'Everyone involved in the heist is being hunted, and not by a human being.'

'That's ridiculous,' Donovan uttered. 'I've got a killer to catch and we need hard evidence to—'

'Go talk to the convicts on that block,' Lopez cut him

off. 'Couple of hundred hardened criminals stunned silent by what happened in that cell. You'll get your evidence there. We're going to keep a watch on Eric Muir. He's likely to be a target.'

# 38

# KHAN YUNIS, GAZA CITY, PALESTINE

*One year ago*

She knew that her ordeal would soon be over.

Joanna heard little through the door of her cell, the guards more wary after she'd smashed the doctor's face and check in, but she had managed to overhear snatches of conversation from further away in the building. The Americans visited only rarely now, maybe once a month, and their drawled-English voices were distinctive from the gentle lilt of Arabic.

Words, important words, had reached her. Old experiments over, new projects, huge discoveries in Israel's deserts, problems. One word stood out to her, mentioned several times by different individuals: MACE. She knew the acronym from her work in South America with Ethan Warner: Munitions for Advanced Combat Environments, a major arms developer and supplier she had suspected of running an abduction racket in Mexico City, snatching the children of wealthy businessmen and then providing specialist teams to 'find and rescue' the unfortunate victims once more. She had almost pinned them down when threats to Ethan's and her lives forced her to abandon the chase and them both to flee the city.

Now, the name of the company boiled through her mind.

Somehow, they were responsible for what had happened to her, she knew. The CEO of the company, an unpleasantly mercenary man by the name of Byron Stone, possessed close ties to the Pentagon and perhaps enough influence to persuade the CIA to pluck her off the streets of Gaza and help her to disappear for good.

Now, the snatched conversations and disconnected dialogue she overheard was sending her a warning loud and clear. Whatever was being worked on now did not involve her and that made her an inconvenience that would soon be removed, permanently.

The return of Doctor Sheviz a few days later confirmed her worst fears. His face had appeared at her door, smiling in at her with a look of smug satisfaction on his features.

'How's the nose?' she had murmured.

Sheviz's nasal bridge was even more hooked now than it once had been. The doctor's smile did not slip as his icy little eyes looked her up and down.

'Better now, thank you,' he said. 'But my condition will soon be of no consequence to you, I can assure you.'

Joanna shook her head, slowly. 'It's about time. I was getting bored. What's it to be now? Thumb-screws? Waterboarding?'

Sheviz's features glittered with malice.

'Oh, nothing so barbaric, my dear,' he replied. 'I have found a new use for my procedures, one where the outcome is not dependent upon your willingness to convey your experiences.'

Joanna managed not to betray the deep chill of fear that sank inside her.

'I wouldn't bet on that.'

'I would,' Sheviz had replied cheerfully, 'because you're not supposed to survive. Only the condition of your blood is important to me now, Joanna. You're to be a mere test subject.'

The doctor had smiled at her and slammed the observation slot closed. Joanna had wrapped her arms around her shoulders to fend off the chill that seemed to have enveloped her, and she resolved to find a way out of the building while she still had the chance.

That chance came just a few days later, when, to her surprise, she heard a rattle of gunfire from outside and the deep, reverberating thump of a rocket-propelled grenade that slammed into nearby buildings. A chorus of alarmed shouts and the sound of running boots echoed through the building, and, within moments, keys were rattling in the locks of her cell door.

Two men barged in, a third training a Kalashnikov on her as she was dragged out of the cell and hurried down the corridor outside. One of the men moved in behind her and grabbed her arms, forcing them together as he hurriedly bound her wrists with coarse rope as they rushed down the corridor.

Joanna pressed her clenched fists together for him, but angled them slightly apart and tensed her arms to produce a small gap between her wrists. The guard, concentrating on running and focused on the sound of gunfire outside, was either too busy to notice what she had done or more concerned with what was going on outside. Crucially, they did not make any effort to blindfold her.

She was hustled down a dusty stairwell that doubled back on itself twice before reaching a small foyer. Like many buildings in Gaza, the foyer was devoid of furniture or decoration, a shell of a building buried amidst so many others. More shouts from outside echoed through open windows, chattering machine-gun fire replying from nearby.

One of the guards reached a door and held onto the handle with one hand as he readied his weapon with the other. Joanna was jostled to the door, and all at once it was thrown open.

A brilliant-blue sky and blazing sun greeted her as she was shoved out into the heat, the searing air as fresh as roses to her and the caress of the sun as warm on her skin as her mother's touch had once been. Her captors shoved her to the right, circling the outside of the building as the gunfire nearby increased. Joanna stumbled along with them, loosening her bonds as she went.

A car awaited, a dusty dark blue sedan.

The men shoved her toward it, and then one of them broke free and rushed across the street, reaching out for a door. Joanna felt her bonds slip past her knuckles as she ran amongst her captors, and she looked sideways at the man carrying a Kalashnikov beside her.

A terrific impact thumped into her chest, and, in a flash of light and heat, she saw a white trail of smoke pointing directly at the sedan as it vanished into a fireball. The man holding the door was torn from it and hurled through the air to hit the side of the building, his arm still hanging from the car door as it was consumed by flames and smoke.

Joanna hit the ground on her back as thick black smoke filled the street. She rolled sideways and saw Israeli troops advancing down the street toward her, shifting from cover to cover and firing as they went.

Veils of smoke obscured them from her vision as she struggled to her feet.

The hard muzzle of an AK-47 jabbed her in the ribs and she turned to see one of her captors lying on the dust beside her, blood spilling across one of his eyes as he tried to force her to her feet. Joanna scrambled upright and, as the gunman stood, she shifted position into his blind spot and pushed the rifle aside with one hand as she stepped in and slammed her knee up into the gunman's groin with all the fury she had harbored for so many long years.

The gunman doubled over as a great rush of air blasted from his lungs. Joanna turned and rammed her knee up into the man's throat, collapsing it as he toppled onto his side in the dust. She grabbed the rifle's barrel, holding it to one side as she lifted one foot and smashed it down repeatedly across the man's face until the rifle dropped away and he lay silent and still before her on the ground.

Clouds of drifting smoke and the heat of the nearby flames spilled across her as she backed away from the body.

Then she turned and fled into the warren of Gaza's alleys and streets before the Israeli troops burst onto the scene. It was possible that they were her saviours, sent to liberate her, but, as her own government had to have had a hand in her imprisonment, so another government could not be trusted to have her best interests at heart.

Joanna kept running until she could no longer hear the sound of gunfire behind her.

# 39

# CITY UNIVERSITY OF NEW YORK SCHOOL OF LAW, LONG ISLAND CITY

The law school was on the corner of Hunter and 25th, a modern-looking building of glass and aluminum ringed by steel bollards. Ethan sat with Lopez and Karina in her car in a parking lot nearby, watching the building from one angle while Donovan and the rest of the team sat on 44th and watched it from another.

'He's been in there for over an hour,' Lopez said.

'He's a lecturer as well as a practicing attorney,' Karina replied. 'I guess the law is this guy's life.'

'The law?' asked Ethan. 'Or breaking it?'

'We don't know that for sure, yet,' Karina cautioned him.

A trickle of students were spilling from the main entrance, making their way out into the cold night air, some hugging friends goodnight as others lit cigarettes that flared in the darkness. Most of the lights in the building were out, except those on the third floor, where Ethan guessed the lecture had taken place.

'We told you what happened in the jail,' Lopez said to Karina.

'There were two other convicts in that cell,' Karina insisted. 'We can't rule out that somebody else got to them, maybe offered them huge sums of money to take down Gladstone and Earl. You think you can take the word of two inmates? Their rap sheet was a yard long.'

'Why bother offering money to take down Gladstone and Earl?' Ethan asked. 'Better to let the lawyer do his work and let them get out for free.'

'They didn't make anything off the Pay-Go raid, remember? The money went into the river,' Karina replied. 'Maybe the man behind it all gets greedy and decides to bump off the remaining two men on his team. Probably cost him less than hiring the goddamned lawyer.'

'It could have backfired,' Lopez suggested. 'If Gladstone and Earl were targeted, they may have been able to convince their attackers that they could lead them to more money than this mysterious mastermind was offering. Not to mention the fact that if their former boss was having them iced in jail, then why should he honor any payment to their killers?'

'Lopez is right,' Ethan confirmed. 'It's too messy and not in keeping with what these guys have done in the past. Something else got them in their cells, and from what we heard from the two convicts who witnessed the entire attack, I'd say it's our vengeful spirit.'

Karina snorted.

'You think that two convicts responsible for the murder of their cellmates are going to just stand up and say, "Hey, yeah, we did it!"'

'They could barely walk or talk,' Lopez pointed out. 'It takes a lot for guys like that to completely lose all thoughts of machismo.'

Ethan nodded. The two men who had survived the attack were known thugs and fraudsters, and, although they weren't exactly high-ranking criminals, they certainly had spent time in the prison system. They would have had forged into their psyche the knowledge that to show weakness, especially in front of other inmates, was to condemn themselves to a life of misery at the hands of others. Such people were referred to in Rikers Island as '*food*' for the bigger fish.

Yet the pair of them had been crippled by terror and had both wept openly in front of Ethan, Lopez and the other cops. These were not men covering up one of countless jail-based or gang-related homicides. These were men who had witnessed something terrifying enough to have scoured them of any sense of shame or pride. The last time he and Lopez had witnessed fear like that in men, it had been hunting down an unknown and savage creature in the backwoods of Idaho six months previously.

'Whatever got them,' Ethan said, 'can move at will and has tremendous strength. I don't think we're going to be able to protect Eric Muir, no matter where we send him.'

'If he's not guilty,' Lopez said, 'then we've got nothing to worry about.'

Ethan shrugged and was about to reply when up on the third floor of the school the lights began flickering on and off as though the power was going out.

'You see that?' Lopez pointed.

'I see it,' Ethan replied and went for his door handle. 'It's going down.'

'He could be turning the lights out!' Karina snapped, as Ethan opened his door and climbed out.

Before he could respond, the radio in Karina's car crackled.

'*All available units please respond, assault in progress, corner of forty-fourth and Hunter.*'

Karina cursed as she grabbed the radio microphone and yelled back. 'Alpha Team in position, moving now!'

Karina and Lopez leaped from the vehicle and ran with Ethan across the street, as Donovan, Glen and Jackson dashed across from 44th, their weapons already in their hands.

The students huddling around cellphones and cigarettes near the entrance leaped out of the way as the police team dashed through.

'Any other students in here?' Lopez asked as they ran past.

One of the young guys shook his head. 'We were the last out, except for the lecturer.'

Ethan dashed inside as a member of staff rushed toward them in the foyer with a phone clasped in her hand. She looked like a cleaner, gloves on her hands and a waft of something clinical surrounding her as she pointed back the way she had come, her face wracked with fear as she spoke in a foreign accent.

'Third floor!' she yelled. 'Something bad happen!'

'You see anything?' Donovan asked as he ran past.

'Mr. Muir, he screaming for help!'

The team dashed past her and ran for the elevator nearby.

'Don't use the elevators!' Lopez shouted.

Neither Donovan, Jackson nor Glen listened to her as they piled into the elevator and Donovan hit the button for the third floor. Karina dashed past the second available elevator and crashed through the stairwell door.

Ethan followed Lopez through the same door and they turned, leaping up the steps two at a time. Ethan dug in, his fitness now getting somewhere close to where it had been when he had served in the Marines, but he was still no match for Lopez. Several years younger and just as driven, she flew up the stairs and passed Karina.

Ethan sucked in a huge lungful of air and fought to keep Lopez in sight as he caught up with Karina. They turned the corner of the stairwell on the second floor and raced up the steps.

'She do this often?' Karina gasped as she struggled to keep up with Lopez.

'Sure, if there's a pay check at the other end,' Ethan wheezed.

As they reached the third floor, Ethan saw the lights flickering, the fluorescent tubes clicking as they fluttered on and off. Lopez hurried to the stairwell exit as Karina approached, her pistol drawn. Lopez grabbed the door handle and swung the door open as Karina rushed through and aimed down a corridor that flickered in the intermittent light.

Ethan followed Karina through as Lopez slipped into the corridor and quietly shut the door behind them.

The corridor led to a series of what were probably classrooms or lecture halls. Karina crept forward through the flickering pools of light toward a door that was open as though recently vacated. Most of the other doors were closed, nothing but inky blackness visible through the windows, but the open one cast a dim light from within.

A movement ahead in the darkness caught Ethan's eye and he momentarily froze. Karina hesitated, but then moved on as she recognized Donovan edging his way toward the shaft of pale light. The shaft flickered on and off like the lights in the corridor. Donovan pointed silently at the open door and Karina nodded.

Glen and Jackson fanned out in the corridor, ready to charge into the room as Donovan counted down on his fingers.

*Three*. Jackson raised his rifle.

*Two*. Glen Ryan crept up to the edge of the door, pistol in hand.

*One*. Karina aimed to cover Glen.

Donovan pointed into the room and Glen charged in first, followed by Karina, Jackson and then the rest of them.

Ethan and Lopez dashed into the room to see a lecture hall before them, quite large with a vaulted ceiling, a dais and lectern on one side and ranks of chairs on the other. The lights flickered ominously and the air felt bitterly cold as they all saw clouds of their breath condensing in the stuttering light.

But the room was empty.

'I don't see anything!' Glen snapped, sweeping the room with his pistol.

'Clear,' Jackson said, lowering his weapon.

Donovan slowed and looked at Ethan, who glanced at Lopez.

'Maybe he took off?' she suggested. 'Heard us coming?'

Ethan felt the hairs on the back of his arms stand on end and he shook his head.

'It's too cold,' he said. 'It's here.'

'What's here?' Jackson uttered. 'What the hell are you talking about?'

Ethan was about to answer when something dropped onto the carpet a few inches from where he stood. He looked down and in the flickering light saw a glistening droplet of fluid.

Donovan, Glen, Jackson, Karina and Lopez all looked down at the droplet at the same moment, and then all of them looked up into the lecture hall's vaulted ceiling.

'Oh, Jesus,' Karina whispered.

In the inky blackness above was the body of the lawyer, Eric Muir. He was spread-eagled across the ceiling, his body trembling as though in some kind of seizure. It took a moment for Ethan to realize what he was actually looking at.

The body was suspended in mid-air fifteen feet above the dais, hovering as though on a pillar of air.

# 40

'That's not possible!' Jackson snapped, a thin trickle of panic infecting his voice.

Donovan raised his pistol as a sudden agonized scream echoed out through the hall and Muir quivered with the seizures racking his body.

'Get him down!' Donovan shouted.

'Jesus,' Glen uttered. '*How?*'

Ethan was about to suggest grabbing some of the chairs to help reach the lawyer when a crackling sound like snapping twigs echoed around the hall. Muir's strained screams were cut abruptly off as his body jerked in violent spasms and then his body shot toward the ground as though he had been fired from a cannon.

Mr. Muir slammed into the carpeted floor with a deep, reverberating crunch that utterly shattered every bone in his body. Ethan saw his eyeballs plunge into their sockets and fluid burst from the cavities under the impact.

'Sweet Mother of Christ, what the hell is going on?' Jackson shouted and began backing away toward the door.

'Stand still!' Ethan snapped, pointing at him. 'It's not after us.'

Jackson froze.

The room remained silent but Ethan could still feel the bitter cold in the room as though his skin had turned to ice, the breath from all of their bodies condensing on the air as though they were in the middle of Central Park on a frosty morning.

'What is it?' Donovan uttered.

'Never mind what it is,' Glen growled. '*Where* is it?'

Ethan spoke as calmly as he could manage. 'It's called a wraith,' he said, 'a vengeful spirit.'

'No shit,' Jackson uttered, clearly disturbed. 'We need to leave, right now!'

'What do you mean, it's not us it's after?' Donovan snapped at Ethan.

Lopez looked across at him. 'That's what vengeful spirit means,' she said. 'It's out for revenge.'

Ethan slowly began backing toward the door. 'There's nothing we can do here. Call for forensics and an ambulance and we'll wait for this thing to clear out.'

The team stood immobile, looking desperately up into the darkness of the ceiling like blind men seeking an escape from hell.

'Stay calm,' Lopez said. 'Just back up and get out of the room.'

Ethan nodded. 'Trust me, there's nothing to be afraid of.'

The flashlight beams cut up through the darkness and Ethan caught a glimpse of clouds of dust motes swirling upward toward the ceiling as though a terrific updraft had swept through the room. He felt the chill in the air deepen as though energy was being sucked from the hall, and a spiraling vortex of moisture condensing from the air appeared above them, glowing in the pale light.

'What the hell is that?' Jackson shouted.

Ethan saw the cloud of moisture coil upon itself and, for a brief instant, he thought he glimpsed a horrific visage haunting the cloud, rage twisting its features. Then the vortex plunged down toward them as though unleashed from invisible manacles.

'Get down!' Karina yelled.

Ethan and Lopez hurled themselves aside as a mass of seething, freezing energy rushed across them. Donovan yelled out in alarm as he was hurled backwards out of the room, Jackson spun aside to hit the wall as Glen Ryan was flipped over and crashed onto the ground like a rag doll.

Ethan saw Karina try to get out of the way but, as the vortex blazed past her, she spun sideways and collided with the table in the center of the room, her head hitting the solid wood with a dull thump. She collapsed and hit the ground hard, her pistol falling from her grip.

Jackson let out a cry of terror and sprinted out of the doorway as both Donovan and Glen leaped up and fled the entrance to the room.

'Christ, it's after all of us!' Lopez shouted to Ethan, scrambling to her feet as she dashed across to Karina. 'Help me get her up!'

Ethan got to his feet and ran to Lopez's side, and together they hauled Karina's comatose body up. Ethan hefted her over his shoulder, all the while trying to spot the diaphanous mass he was sure was still hovering nearby.

'It went for *us*!' he said in disbelief.

'I don't think it's too picky about targets!' Lopez snapped. 'We've got to get out of here.'

Ethan hurried out of the doorway into the corridor, trying to see in the inky blackness.

'Let's get back to the stairwell.'

They were about to head left when a series of cries echoed down the corridor from behind them. Ethan froze as he heard Jackson's screams for help laced with horror.

'Dammit,' Lopez uttered, 'they took the elevator.'

A shockingly loud banging shuddered through the corridor as Ethan turned and followed Lopez through the darkness toward the elevators. The faint beams of flashlights bounced and jerked crazily in the darkness as they rounded a corner and saw the elevator ahead. The mesh doors were closed, Donovan, Jackson and Glen visible inside and trying to batter their way out, their breath condensing in dense clouds in the white beams.

'Get us out of here!' Donovan shouted. 'The door's jammed!'

Ethan set Karina's body down gently onto the carpet and then rushed toward the elevator. As he did so, the air turned even colder as though he had run into an icebox, the hair on his arms standing on end again.

'It's here!' he shouted to Lopez.

Ethan grabbed the mesh doors and tried to pull them apart but, although the doors were not locked, they would not budge, no matter how hard he pulled. Lopez dashed to his side and pulled with him, but the doors remained stubbornly closed.

Ethan let them go and stood back, staring at Donovan, Jackson and Glen.

'It's not letting you out,' he said finally.

A moment of silence filled the corridor, and then the ceiling of the elevator crashed inward as though hit by a giant hammer. The terrific noise smashed through Ethan's awareness and made him flinch. Another impact crushed the elevator's sidewall in like a paper bag and sent Donovan flying sideways into Jackson.

'Do something!' Jackson hollered.

Ethan looked desperately at Lopez, who was staring wide-eyed and in disbelief as the elevator began folding in upon itself, as though a giant, invisible hand were inexorably crushing it into oblivion.

Ethan grabbed the doors again and pulled frantically on them but he already knew that there was nothing he could do. He shouted into the elevator.

'What about the service hatch in the ceiling?'

Donovan looked up and shook his head. 'Too small! It's for emergency ventilation, not access!'

Ethan saw Donovan's normally stoic features crumble into genuine terror as the elevator crumpled and collapsed. The three men inside were forced together, shoulders packed against chests, faces grimacing with fear.

'Do something!' Lopez shouted at him.

Ethan stared at the dying men and grabbed his hair in helpless desperation as a razor-sharp shard of metal touched the surface of Jackson's face.

A deafening crash like a gunshot thundered out from the elevator and then suddenly all noise ceased. Ethan's ears rang as he stared at the elevator, the three men pinned inside it. Then, quietly, the lights flickered back on. Ethan blinked as he felt warmth caress his arms and face as though the bitter embrace of death had been snatched away at the last moment.

He turned and looked at Lopez, and then they both turned and saw Karina lying on the floor at the end of the corridor, a cellphone to her ear. Karina, her head smeared with a thick trickle of blood, dropped the cellphone and shut it off.

Ethan turned back to the elevator.

'What happened?' Glen Ryan asked.

'You got lucky,' Ethan said quickly. 'That thing obviously gets its juice from somewhere and it ran out of gas somehow.'

Donovan, his face pinched between the elevator wall and Jackson's shoulder, nodded as much as he could.

'You want to get us the hell out of here? It might come back.'

Ethan pulled his cellphone out of his pocket as he turned and walked back toward Karina. She slowly dragged herself to her feet, one hand holding her head.

'You want to tell me what that was?' he asked her. 'What did you do?'

Karina refused to look at him. 'Called for back-up,' she replied flatly.

# 41

The mirrored-glass exterior of the law school flashed with the reflections of dozens of strobe lights in a flickering kaleidoscope of blues, oranges and reds as Ethan stood with Lopez beside an ambulance.

The body of Muir, the lawyer, was wheeled into the vehicle by a pair of paramedics, his battered remains covered with a black body-bag.

From the entrance of the building walked Donovan, Jackson and Glen. All three of them were carrying water bottles and Jackson had a blanket draped across his shoulders. It had taken the fire service almost two hours to cut them free from the mangled wreckage of the elevator car. Donovan reached them first.

'Karina did tell you to take the stairwell,' Lopez pointed out.

'Noted,' Donovan snapped, clearly having been divested of every last shred of his sense of humor. 'Tell me, everything.'

'It's not of this world,' Ethan replied. 'We don't know how to deal with it yet.'

Donovan's features were creased with an anxiety that Ethan had not seen before. The solid rock that was the police chief was crumbling after what he had witnessed.

'You two know damned well more than you're telling me. I want to know everything,' Donovan insisted.

'So will the manufacturers of those elevators,' Ethan reminded him. 'That's two of them crushed by unknown forces in as many days.'

'Coroner's going to have a hard time explaining how the lawyer died, too,' Lopez said.

Donovan looked at the body thoughtfully. 'Suicide,' he suggested. 'Long fall.'

'Not long enough,' Ethan said. 'That ceiling was maybe twenty feet up. No way he could have got into that mess.'

'Then it stays with us,' Donovan insisted. 'We can't afford to create a city-wide panic right now.'

'We told you what it is that's doing this,' Lopez said, 'a vengeful spirit. It's called a wraith.'

'I don't give a damn what it's called,' the chief shot back. 'I want to know how it's stopped.'

'It isn't stopped,' Ethan assured him, 'until justice is done.'

'Justice?' Glen asked as he joined them. 'Justice for what, and how?'

'Whatever happened to that spirit,' Lopez said, 'when it was alive, needs to be corrected. It was wronged and it's seeking revenge.'

'For what?' Donovan asked, confused. 'Even if you're right, how can we know whose spirit it is or how it was wronged?'

Ethan turned to face Donovan directly, his face barely inches from the chief's.

'That's what's been bothering me ever since we got out of that building,' he said. 'This wraith, supposedly, only attacks the people who wronged it during life. So why would it be going after you three?'

Donovan looked at Jackson and Glen, and shrugged. 'How the hell would we know? Maybe a disgruntled criminal? Maybe somebody got put away for a crime they didn't commit and got iced while inside?'

'Doesn't match the hits on the clerk, the lawyer or the thieves,' Lopez pointed out. 'Fact is, the only thing that ties them all together is the Pay-Go robbery.'

Donovan's eyes narrowed suspiciously. 'That could mean it's the wraith of somebody killed on the bridge in the accident, maybe.'

Ethan nodded. 'Like Tom Ross's wife or daughter.'

'You think that's who's doing this?' Jackson uttered, his eyes wide like an animal caught in headlamp beams. 'Why the hell would they be coming down on us? That accident wasn't our fault.'

'They may not see it that way,' Lopez replied. 'You ever heard of a poltergeist that could be reasoned with?'

'This isn't a goddamned poltergeist,' Glen snapped. 'This is the mother of all weird demon shit!' He looked about for a moment. 'Where's Karina?'

'She's taking a break,' Lopez replied.

Donovan looked at each of them in turn. 'You've got jurisdiction of this case but not my officer. Take me to her immediately.'

'*Your* officer?' Lopez echoed. 'The same officer that we had to carry out of that hall after you took off with your tail between your legs?'

Donovan ground his teeth in his skull. 'I didn't see her go down.'

'Then you weren't paying enough attention,' Ethan snapped. 'You'll see her when she's good and ready, not before.'

Donovan fumed on the spot for a moment before he turned away and stormed across the lot between the fire truck and the ambulance. Glen Ryan looked at Lopez.

'I could do with seeing her,' he said.

'She could have done with you not high-tailing it out of there, too,' Lopez uttered, barely looking at him. 'She wants you, she'll find you.'

'Karina and I are none of your business!' Glen snapped as he pointed at her. 'You stop sticking your nose into it or I'll—'

Ethan's knuckles pushed against the base of Glen's throat as with the other hand he grabbed the younger man's wrist and spun him around. Glen hit the side of the ambulance and found himself pinned there, his face squashed against the cold metal. Ethan peered at him with interest. 'You'll *what*?'

Glen coughed as he tried to swallow, but couldn't.

'Let him go,' Lopez murmured. 'He's just a little boy.'

Ethan considered sending Glen sprawling onto the asphalt, but instead just shoved him sideways. Glen stumbled, rubbing his throat as he glared at Ethan.

'What goes around, Warner.'

Ethan smiled coldly. 'Ain't that right.'

Glen stalked off and Jackson looked at each of them in turn, before turning and hurrying away. Ethan looked at Lopez.

'We're not going to get much help from them now,' he said. 'This whole thing just got a lot more complicated.'

'We could still be wrong,' Lopez pointed out as they started walking toward Karina's car. 'Maybe this isn't about revenge.'

'You saw what happened to Eric Muir,' Ethan replied. 'It's too much of a coincidence. What bothers me more is that the wraith went for Donovan.'

'You think that he had something to do with this?'

'I don't know,' Ethan replied, 'but there's definitely something more going on than we know about, and I don't like surprises.'

They turned a corner alongside bright yellow police-cordon tapes and saw a television crew already setting up. Ethan caught sight of a photographer standing nearby, camera at the ready, looking toward the law school.

Ethan and Lopez had rounded the police tapes alongside a fire truck, and had been concealed from the view of the television crew and a handful of bystanders. The photographer, hood up and concealing their features, was side-on to them and had not seen them emerge.

'Get the car and follow me.'

Ethan launched himself into a full sprint, aiming directly at the photographer as he lifted his camera and took a shot of the ambulance leaving the site with the dead lawyer aboard.

Ethan's headlong dash alerted him. The photographer's head snapped round at the sound of approaching footfalls and instantly he whirled and took off down the street. Ethan sprinted past the television crew at full speed and barely ten yards behind the photographer.

He saw him slip his camera into a pocket of his thick winter coat, struggling to seal the pocket up as he ran out across 44th Drive and dodged past a slow-moving vehicle. Ethan hurled himself across the vehicle's hood as it screeched to a halt, sliding off and hitting the ground at a run again as he closed in on the wildly fleeing reporter.

The runner turned south, heading toward the Metro on Court Square as he cut across a tree-lined plaza and headed for Jackson Avenue. Ethan pushed hard, just a few yards behind now and closing fast. He reached out as they cleared the plaza, gambling that the runner wouldn't head right out across the lanes of traffic.

The runner suddenly slammed to a halt and ducked down, then jerked backwards into Ethan's path. Ethan stumbled as he tried to avoid him but the reporter's body crashed backwards into his legs and sent him flying over them.

Ethan hit the tiles of the plaza hard, rolling into his shoulder and coming up onto his feet in time to see the reporter dash between cars flowing south-west on Jackson. Ethan struggled on in pursuit, his joints aching from the impact as he fought to regain lost ground. Cars honked their horns as he ran across Jackson and into Court Square Park, a circular affair with a small clump of trees on the east side and cars parked along the sidewalk beyond them.

*Not this time.*

Ethan plunged between the trees in pursuit but this time he kept running, dashing through the copse until he burst out onto the sidewalk on the opposite side. He turned back, scanning the trees for his quarry to emerge.

A car's tires squealed as it turned onto Court Square, the beams flashing across Ethan as he stood on the sidewalk. He saw Lopez driving Karina's car and then pointed into the trees in front of him.

Lopez did not hesitate. She swerved the car up onto the sidewalk and switched on the high beams to illuminate the copse in bright white light. Ethan saw the trees glowing in the beams and then the figure that dashed from behind one of them, back through the treeline.

Ethan sprinted back into the treeline, hearing Lopez's car reverse off the sidewalk behind him as he ran, and he burst out onto Thompson Avenue only a few paces behind the reporter. They sprinted across the street and the reporter vaulted a chain-link fence into a courtyard filled with old vehicles.

Ethan flew lithely over the fence into the courtyard, just in time to see the reporter whirl and flick one foot out toward him. Ethan careered sideways, sweeping his right arm down and across to block the blow as he staggered off balance.

The reporter spun with surprising agility, one fist trying to catch Ethan with a back-handed punch. Ethan threw his left forearm up and smashed the wrist aside, regaining his balance as he drove his bunched right fist straight into the man's chest, just below his throat.

He heard a gasp of shock as the reporter was hurled backward by the force of the blow. He tumbled into the chain-link fence, one hand flying to his chest as he struggled to breathe. Ethan surged forward, driven by anger. He grabbed the reporter by the throat and pinned him against the fence, then reached up and yanked the hood aside.

The streetlights cast a pale glow down on the face that stared back at him, and, all at once, Ethan felt the air sucked from his lungs as the strength drained from his limbs. He staggered backwards as though struck, his jaw hanging limp and his eyes wide in disbelief.

The reporter was a blonde, her hair tumbling out from her hood, and her green eyes seemed dark in the shadows cast across her face by the streetlights above. But there was no mistaking her features, no doubt who she was.

Joanna Defoe stared back at Ethan, but she did not speak.

# 42

# 5TH PRECINCT POLICE DEPARTMENT, NEW YORK CITY

Donovan set his phone back down in its cradle and sat back thoughtfully in his seat.

It was late and the station was virtually empty but for the night crew manning the cells and the phone lines. It not being a weekend, evenings were generally quiet, even in New York City. Only the patrol officers would have their work cut out for them, an endless stream of gangland territorial disputes and domestic disturbances to field.

'What did the CIA say?'

Glen Ryan sat opposite Donovan. The younger man was intelligent, determined and committed to his job, but he was also vulnerable in his affection for Karina Thorne. Donovan was not sure just how much he ought to be telling him. Yet now there was another crisis. Jackson had been sent home a jabbering wreck. The events in the lecture hall had fractured his nerves and Donovan was not sure when he would return to work. Or worse, if he would fold under the pressure.

'They know about Ethan Warner and Nicola Lopez,' he replied finally. 'It was strange. I got bounced from one department to the next before I spoke to somebody.'

'What's strange about that?' Glen asked.

'Because each new office was higher than the last,' Donovan said. 'Then, they put me through to another number, and this guy answers. I'd called Langley, but this guy was here in New York.'

'So?' Glen said. 'The CIA has field offices in every city, right?'

Donovan shook his head. 'This guy was in a car and talking on a cell. Soon as the line opened he asked to meet me.'

Glen frowned. 'Somebody looking for Warner?'

'Maybe,' Donovan confirmed. 'And right now that suits me just fine.'

'You're going to sell them out?'

'Why wouldn't I?' Donovan asked. 'They're climbing all over our asses right now and we could do without the attention.'

Glen leaned forward on the desk. 'Right now, it's the DIA that's helping us with this investigation and also preventing the media from tearing us to pieces. That guy Jarvis has turned what happened at the law school into a whole big nothing. The media had packed up and gone within an hour of arriving.'

'They're digging around too much,' Donovan insisted. 'Sooner or later . . .'

'I don't give a damn!' Glen snapped and smashed his fist down on the chief's desk. 'You saw what happened. There's something out there and it's hunting us down! At least

Warner and Lopez seem to know something about it. Without them we'd probably be dead by now.'

Donovan looked at Glen for a long moment before he spoke.

'Glen, you saw what Karina did in that corridor, didn't you?'

Glen sighed and sat back, rubbing tired eyes with his fingers. 'I saw her do something,' he replied. 'I heard her say to Warner that she was calling for back-up.'

Donovan shook his head. 'I don't buy that. She could have called for back-up any time and she'd have used her radio not her cell.'

'Our radios were down,' Glen said. 'So were our cellphones for that matter, while we were stuck in that elevator.'

Donovan nodded.

'Seems like whatever the hell that wraith thing is, it only affects an area immediately around it. The lights flicker, batteries drain, shit like that. Maybe Karina was far enough away that her cell was working.'

'It fits,' Glen agreed. 'The lights were on outside the building and on other floors. Did you feel that cold, too? But that also figures if what Ethan said is right, that it gets its juice from something but that it can run out, too.'

Donovan thought hard. Karina had still used her cellphone and not her radio, which meant that she wasn't calling for back-up. Something nagged at him but he couldn't put his finger on it. With Jackson down for the moment, there was nobody else he could ask. At least, he figured, he'd get to know where Glen's loyalties truly lay.

'Glen, I need you to pull Karina's cell. We need to know who she was calling.'

Glen stared blankly back at Donovan. 'What the hell for? What does it matter who she was calling?'

'She's up to something, Glen,' Donovan replied. 'I don't know what, but whatever it is it's important enough that she would make a call whilst we were under attack from some godforsaken homicidal ghoul.'

Glen shook his head. 'I don't know. It was a panicked situation, she probably just grabbed the first thing that came to her mind and—'

'Glen,' Donovan interrupted him. 'If you're worried about upsetting her now, imagine what will happen if she, Warner, Lopez or Jarvis manage to figure out what really happened on Williamsburg Bridge.'

Glen sat silently for a moment and then dragged a hand down his face.

'If I try to pull the records, it'll show up,' he said. 'Easiest way to do this is for me to just take a look at her call list on the cell itself.'

'However you do it,' Donovan muttered, 'do it soon. We don't figure out a way to stop all this before they do, then everything we've achieved is for nothing.'

Glen stared at Donovan. His features paled slightly. 'You really think that this thing that's hunting us is the ghost of Tom Ross's wife?'

'I don't give a damn what it is!' Donovan snapped. 'Right now, all that matters is stopping it, understood?'

Glen got up out of his seat and looked down at the chief. 'What about this CIA guy? What are you going to say to him?'

Donovan grabbed his jacket as he stood and slipped it over his shoulders.

'I'm going to offer a trade,' he replied. 'I'll hand Warner and Lopez over to them provided that they get the DIA off our case here. Everybody wins.'

'But that doesn't remove our problem,' Glen insisted. 'Christ's sake, Donovan, we're being haunted!'

'Everything dies,' Donovan snapped, and jabbed his finger into Glen's chest. 'We use our brains to figure out how to kill it. It's not invulnerable – we've just got to figure out where it gets its juice from, okay? We solve that, then we finish this.'

Glen exhaled noisily, then turned and walked out of Donovan's office.

The chief looked at his desk for a moment and then rested one hand instinctively on his sidearm. He had no idea why a CIA agent would want to meet him in secret in the middle of the night way up in Harlem, but, after what Jackson had found out about the killings in DC, he sure as hell wasn't going unarmed.

# 43

Ethan stood on legs that felt as though the strength had been drained from them.

His heart fluttered in his chest as though unsure of whether or not to keep beating, and he reached out for something to steady himself as he released his grip on Joanna's neck. The chain-link fence rattled as he leaned on it.

'Hello, Ethan.'

Her voice reached him as though from another dimension, a voice that he had not heard for five years. Strange, how her face had been burned into his conscience over time but he had forgotten how she spoke, the slight southern lilt to her accent, the perfect pronunciation that had always eluded him.

He sought for something to say but he felt as though somebody had stuffed a sock into his mouth.

'Joanna?' was all he finally managed to utter.

*Idiot.* It wasn't like she could be anybody else. Joanna did not mock him, however. She nodded.

'You must have a lot of questions,' she said.

Ethan was about to reply when a figure vaulted over the chain-link fence and landed cat-like in the shadows.

Lopez stormed straight toward Joanna. 'Okay, who's the asshole?'

Ethan raised a hand to hold Lopez back, but it was still as if somebody had anesthetized his jaw. He couldn't speak. Lopez caught the atmosphere between them and slowed of her own accord, watching the blonde woman warily. 'Ethan?'

Joanna took a pace forward. 'I'm Joanna Defoe,' she said.

Lopez's dark eyes widened slightly and she glanced at Ethan before looking back at Joanna. 'Oh.'

Ethan managed to re-inflate his lungs and gain control of his wildly swinging emotions.

'Why are you here in New York?' he gasped, unable to think of anything more profound to say.

Joanna, keeping one curious eye on Lopez, answered: 'It's a long story.'

Finally, some of the emotions swirling in a silent maelstrom in Ethan's mind found their voice through anger as he broke through the shock and surprise.

'No shit,' he said. 'You're alive. You've been free for at least a year and you never made contact.' Joanna opened her mouth to reply but Ethan kept going. 'I spent years searching for you across half the goddamned planet and you show up here in New York with a camera and start shooting holiday pictures like nothing's happened? Where the hell have you been? What happened in Gaza? How did you get out of there and back home? Why didn't you call or make contact or . . .?'

'Because I couldn't!' Joanna snapped. 'I couldn't make contact, or call anybody or be seen wandering around. You don't know what's been happening, so don't judge me.'

'Don't judge you?' Ethan uttered in disbelief. 'I'm not judging anyone – I just want to know what the hell happened. You've been gone for *five* years, Jo, and you don't know what's been happening to me either.'

Joanna fixed him with a serious gaze. 'I've had other things on my mind.'

'So did we,' Lopez cut in. 'You can't expect Ethan to not be surprised when you show up with a camera having spent the last couple of days spying on us.'

'And who's *we*?' Joanna glared at her.

'Nicola Lopez,' she shot back, 'of Warner and Lopez Incorporated.'

'River Forest, Illinois,' Joanna replied with surprising speed. 'Former detective, Washington, DC, left the force after your partner was killed. Joined forces with Ethan afterward and set up as bail-bondsmen.'

Ethan's eyes widened with every passing word. 'How long have you been tailing us?'

'I haven't been tailing you,' Joanna insisted. 'You showed up here in the city just after I arrived.'

Lopez frowned. 'What brought you here?'

'Like I said, long story,' Joanna replied, 'and not for your ears, honey.'

'How about I tear your ears *off*?' Lopez growled.

Ethan stepped in between them. 'Easy,' he said, and turned to Joanna. 'Anything you tell me, you can tell Nicola.'

Joanna looked at Lopez for a moment. 'I see. Like that, is it?'

'Like what?' Lopez snapped and glanced at Ethan as she waved a thumb in Joanna's direction. 'You nearly had a breakdown over *her*?'

Joanna's features seemed to soften slightly as she looked at him. 'Seriously?'

'That's my long story,' Ethan shot back. 'Why are you here?'

Ethan and Lopez stood side by side, both of them wearing uncompromising expressions. Joanna stared at them both and then sighed.

'There are still people looking for me,' she replied. 'I've been tracking down what scraps of evidence I can find of a CIA project, looking for survivors.'

'MK-ULTRA,' Lopez said.

'How do you know about that?' Joanna asked in surprise.

'We know all about it,' Ethan replied. 'We know about your father's involvement in the project, the time he spent in a Singapore jail because of it, and that it's still going on. My sister nearly lost her life to the CIA because of it when they targeted members of a congressional investigation into "black projects" at the agency. Nicola and I have stayed off the grid for the last six months because of it, too.'

'I know,' Joanna replied. 'I lost track of you when you traveled to Idaho. I had to stay in DC.'

'You were there?' Lopez uttered with contempt.

'Of course I was there,' she snapped. 'A major congressional investigation into the same project that ruined my father's life and almost took mine? Where the hell else would I have been?'

'What?' Ethan asked. 'What do you mean almost took your life?'

Joanna glanced over her shoulder at the occasional car drifting past on the road, as though nervous of anybody and anything in the city.

'We can't talk here,' she said. 'There's too much ground to cover.'

'You think we're letting you go now?' Lopez almost laughed.

'It's not about letting me go,' Joanna insisted. 'I came here because there is at least one CIA assassin searching for me, and the only way I can expose the operation is to find people who were involved in it.'

'That's not surprising,' Ethan replied, 'considering how many former agents you've taken down in the last couple of weeks.'

Joanna scowled at Ethan. 'I haven't taken anyone down!' she snapped. 'Damned right, I cornered each and every one of them, forced them to talk and recorded their confessions on video. Sure, it might not be admissible as evidence in court and I sure as hell enjoyed scaring the life out of those bastards, but I didn't kill any of them.'

'You let them go?' Ethan asked, and was rewarded with a nod.

'I didn't want them dead,' Joanna replied. 'What kind of punishment is that? I wanted them alive, so that they could be tried and sent to prison for what they did. Somebody else has other ideas and has killed every agent I've spoken to.'

'But why would they do that?' Lopez asked. 'Killing off so many people associated with a single program would leave a pattern behind that law enforcement could easily track. It would bring them right back to the CIA, exposing them anyway.'

Joanna shook her head.

'Their murders could never be linked that way because all of the evidence from the original project burned in 1973;

there's nothing physical left. Whoever is hitting the former agents is clearing up afterward, leaving no trace. There's only been a single murder that made the news and that was covered up real fast.'

'Wisconsin,' Ethan agreed, and then raised an eyebrow. 'So how could you be tracking survivors down?'

Joanna smiled faintly. 'Because my father told me their names,' she replied simply, 'made me memorize them over and over again when I was a child. He used something called mnemonics, a memory trick that enabled me to memorize over a hundred names just like card sharks memorize an entire deck.'

'He took evidence with him?' Lopez asked. 'Before the papers were burned?'

'Memorized them in the same way,' Joanna replied. 'Kept them with him all that time he spent in jail in Singapore, and all the years afterward, until he passed them on to me before he died. He knew they'd come in useful if things went sour at the CIA. Just as damned well he did.'

Ethan struggled to keep up with the revelations.

'Then how come you're on their case now, hunting them down? What can you possibly do to help them?'

'I decided to start by hunting down every CIA agent I recognized from Gaza,' she said. 'Last agent but one is a man named Aaron Lymes, now retired. He lives somewhere in . . .'

'He's dead,' Ethan said. 'Murdered two days ago here in the city.'

Joanna looked crestfallen. 'They got to him first.'

'Who's the other agent on your list?' Ethan asked.

'I can't explain everything here,' Joanna insisted. 'Meet me in the morning, downtown. I'll tell you everything, okay?'

'We're going to need more than that!' Lopez snapped. 'Why were you following us?'

'Like I said,' Joanna replied, and then whirled and clambered up the chain-link fence before dropping down the other side. 'I'm not following you. I'm following the case you're on.'

'Why?' Ethan asked, deciding not to pursue her.

Joanna looked back over her shoulder as she walked away.

'Because one of the names on my list is serving on your team.'

Ethan took a pace forward. 'Tell us who!'

Joanna shook her head. 'No, not until I know I can trust you both. I'll meet you tomorrow morning at eleven at Bourne's Diner on Fulton Street. Don't be late.'

# 44

## HARLEM, NEW YORK

Donovan strode across the intersection between 7th Avenue and 112th and onto the boulevard, using a row of trees as a shield against surveillance cameras watching traffic behind him. His collar was up against the cold night air, and he wore a cap pulled down over his eyes as he walked.

The caller from the CIA had requested a meet in a vehicle, but Donovan had refused. He preferred to be on his feet with room to move. Although he did not expect the agent to suddenly turn and attack him, the speed with which the meet had been arranged and its covert nature had alerted his suspicions. Whatever he had stumbled on with Warner and Lopez was important enough to the agency that they were following up fast.

Donovan spotted a non-descript sedan parked beneath the trees, and, as he approached, a man climbed out from the driver's side onto the sidewalk and looked at him. The agent made no attempt to conceal himself, a shock of gray hair framing sepulchral features and cold gray eyes.

'Detective,' he greeted Donovan without preamble. 'Mr. Wilson. This way, please.'

The agent shoved his hands in his pockets as they walked, presumably to show Donovan that he was not going to attack him.

'Why the cloak-and-dagger routine?' Donovan asked outright.

'There's no threat to security in our meeting,' Mr. Wilson said. 'But I always prefer caution to carelessness.'

'Can't argue with that,' Donovan agreed and then cut to the chase. 'You're interested in Ethan Warner and Nicola Lopez.'

'I am,' Wilson replied. 'They are a thorn in the side of the CIA. I have been authorized to apprehend them for detention in a military prison.'

Donovan raised an eyebrow. 'Seriously? What did they do?'

Wilson's cold gaze turned to meet Donovan's as they walked. 'They got too curious.'

Donovan took the hint and refrained from asking what had attracted Warner's curiosity, figuring that whatever it was it was probably better that he didn't know.

'Do you know where they are?' Mr. Wilson asked.

'Right now, no,' Donovan admitted. 'But their boss has gained jurisdiction of a case we've been working on, a guy called Jarvis. Seems they're real interested in it.'

'What case?' Wilson asked sharply. 'How long have they had jurisdiction?'

'Twelve hours,' Donovan replied, 'and they're goddamned welcome to it. You wouldn't believe what's been happening.'

Wilson's expression did not flicker. 'Try me.'

Donovan shrugged as they walked and spilled the details of the case and of the bizarre nature of the killings. He refrained, however, from mentioning the fact that the killer may possibly be targeting members of his own team.

'Damn thing nearly killed us all,' he said as he finished. 'Sooner it's gone, the better.'

'Do you know the source?' Mr. Wilson asked.

'The what?'

'*The source of the anomaly?*' Wilson snapped. 'Do you know who's causing it?'

Donovan shook his head, wondering just what this man was pursuing. 'No. It was suggested that it could be the spirit of people killed on Williamsburg Bridge a couple of days ago. The murders didn't start until after that event.'

Wilson nodded as they turned the corner of the block. He kept walking and seemed to Donovan to be deep in thought.

'What do you want, exactly?' Donovan asked.

Wilson emerged from his reverie and looked at the police chief.

'You will keep me informed at all times of how the investigation is progressing. As soon as you know Ethan Warner's location, you will contact me immediately.'

Donovan considered the man beside him. Normally, if he had been spoken to in such a way, he would not have hesitated to pin the offender to the wall and remind them in no uncertain terms of their place in the pecking order. But now he hesitated. There was something about Mr. Wilson that suggested restrained violence, a man more than capable of defending himself. Donovan could not afford to take the risk that he would come off worse in a fight, not with everything else that was happening. The less attention he attracted, the better.

'Fine,' he replied. 'And what do I get for my efforts?'

'The gratitude of your country,' Mr. Wilson replied without emotion.

Donovan let a cold smile creep across his features. 'I've been serving the New York Police Department since I was twenty-two years old, pal, and I've had about my fill of my country's gratitude.'

Mr. Wilson stopped in the street and turned to confront Donovan. Wilson still had his hands in his pockets but he was also still wearing the same uncompromising expression. 'This is not a debate.'

'Yes, it is,' Donovan corrected him. 'Whatever's going on down here, I can tell from a lifetime's experience that it's off the record. You're not here to apprehend anybody, are you?'

Mr. Wilson did not respond, but he looked up and down the silent street as though checking for witnesses.

'I've got my people watching the cameras,' Donovan lied, and glanced across at the nearest intersection maybe fifty yards away. 'You pull anything here, it'll be on the news before dawn.'

Mr. Wilson looked back at Donovan, and his angular features cracked into a grin that was entirely devoid of warmth. A blade flashed in the pale streetlight as Mr. Wilson whipped the weapon up toward Donovan's belly, the serrated tip pushing against his jacket as he was propelled backwards against iron railings.

Donovan raised his hands in surprise, unprepared for the speed of Wilson's attack. The agent stared at him as though he were an insect caught between finger and thumb, only the application of a little extra pressure between Donovan's life and death.

'I know more about what you've been up to than you realize,' Wilson hissed. 'Whatever you've done, chief, will come out eventually, if I decide it should.'

'You've got nothing,' Donovan replied, managing to mask his fear. 'Empty threats aren't going to win you any friends here in the NYPD.'

'I don't make threats!' Wilson snapped back. 'I state facts. We already know about the discrepancies in the reports from Williamsburg Bridge, about how the robbery went down.'

Donovan's eyes widened as he looked at Wilson. 'How could you know about . . .?'

'We make it our business to know, because we have the technology to find out,' Wilson said as he pushed the blade a little harder against Donovan's belly. 'It's remarkable what a spy satellite can see. You fail to comply with our demands, then your little indiscretion will find its way to local media and from there to the courts.'

Donovan refused to cower. 'Then we have a bargain,' he replied. 'I'll bring you Warner and Lopez. You ensure that nothing, ever, gets exposed that shouldn't.'

Wilson did not withdraw the blade, as though sizing Donovan up. Fact was, Donovan figured that a compromise would likely be more convenient for the agent than icing a police chief and having to find somebody else inside the department to pressure.

'I see no need to disrupt the status quo,' Wilson replied finally as the blade vanished ghost-like into his sleeve. 'If you discover who the source of these . . . disturbances, is, inform me immediately. And I want you to keep your eyes open for a person by the name of Joanna Defoe. The FBI's missing-persons database will contain an image of her. If she should surface at any moment, contact me immediately.'

Wilson turned his back and stalked away, leaving Donovan against the railings.

'It's a person?' Donovan asked.

Wilson did not respond, but Donovan did not really need a reply. Although his common sense wailed to him that it could not be possible, somehow he knew that Mr. Wilson would not have asked if he did not believe it so. The CIA agent had listened to the description of everything that had happened in the case with complete attention.

Donovan realized that there was only one person alive who had a motive for the killings.

He started walking and pulled out his cellphone.

# 45

# EAST 79TH STREET, NEW YORK

Neville Jackson strode into his apartment block and headed straight for the stairwell, pursued by a deep sense of unease.

He wasn't the kind of guy who scared easily. He'd worked the streets of Harlem in uniform for years, then been assigned to vice and then worked as a detective. He was a born-and-bred New Yorker and took shit from no man. But what he had seen in the last twenty-four hours had ripped the gusto from his body and cast it to the wind.

He had spent the last hour just down the block in St. Monica's Church. First time in his life he'd walked inside the building and the first time in his life that he'd prayed. He wasn't religious, he just knew that whatever they were facing was not of this earth and he couldn't stand the haunting feeling that it was coming after all of them. Donovan. Glen. Him.

'Jesus.'

His voice echoed up the stairwell as he jogged the steps two at a time, making his way up to the sixth floor, where he shared an apartment with his girlfriend, Jenna. They'd been together for three years. He'd never figured himself as the type to settle down, especially as they didn't have enough money to start a family and could barely afford to live on the Upper East Side at all. But Jenna was all heart and he was making a little more money than she knew about, which was what haunted him as he walked toward their apartment door. The temptation to come clean was overwhelming, and he braced himself for whatever shit storm she would unleash when he'd finished explaining to her what had happened over the last two days. If his impromptu visit to the church had gained him anything, it was the knowledge that what they had done simply was not worth it. Crime did not pay.

It certainly wasn't now. No fortune was worth this.

Jackson felt his cellphone vibrate in his jacket pocket. He slipped it out and saw the screen glowing with an incoming call. Donovan's number. He fingered the answer button thoughtfully for a moment, then shook his head and shut the phone off. This was something that could not wait and he did not want to let Donovan have the chance to talk him out of it. Donovan was his boss, but Jenna was his life.

He slipped his key into the door and pushed it open.

The apartment, like most in New York, was compact. He walked down a short corridor, flanked by a bathroom and the bedroom, and then out into the living room.

'Jenna?'

A small hand-written note was waiting for him on a coffee table in the middle of the room. He picked it up as he felt a breeze coming in from the nearby windows, heavy curtains drawn across them. Jenna had gone across the block to a friend's place. Would be back in half an hour. Jackson shook his head and smiled. The fact that she could have left the note four hours ago obviously hadn't crossed her mind when she'd set off for Harriet's.

The breeze wafted cold air across him again and he looked up to see the curtains billowing in the breeze from the open window.

'For Christ's sake, Jenna, how many more times?'

Jackson tossed the note down and walked across to the window. Jenna had left them open a hundred times, preferring the fresh air, which was fine in summer but in the middle of November it was goddamned freezing.

Jackson reached up to pull the curtains aside, and even as he did so a tiny part of his brain registered that although the window was open, he could not hear the traffic down on the block seventy feet below.

His arms whipped the curtains aside and went numb as they did so. The window was firmly closed, sealed shut. Double-glazed panes blocked almost all noise but sirens from the city outside. His heart fluttered in his chest as he felt his guts sinking inside of him.

'Jesus,' he whispered. 'Please, no.'

The hairs on Jackson's neck stood on end as he felt the temperature in the apartment plummet, his breath condensing before him on the air. In the reflection of the room in the window before him, he saw the lights flicker and fade like distant lightning.

Jackson reached down for the pistol at his shoulder-holster but he knew that it was useless. There was only one possible way to save himself and that was to get out of the apartment.

His legs quivered beneath him and he felt his stomach loosen.

In his reflection he saw the lampshade hanging from the ceiling begin swinging gently as though something had brushed past it toward him. The cold became bitter and sharp as though it was biting into his skin, and with a sudden and complete certainty he knew that the wraith was not just in the room with him, but was directly behind him.

As terror constricted his breathing and threatened to paralyze his limbs, Jackson whispered a final prayer and then whirled.

He dashed forwards and hurdled the coffee table in a single bound, charging for the entrance hall and the front door. He was halfway there when something plowed into his chest as though he had been hit by a car.

Jackson's lungs convulsed as he was hurled backwards, his chin slamming into his breastbone as the impact threw him across the back of the couch to land hard on the floor. He rolled and hit the wall beneath the window, cracking the back of his head hard enough that stars danced in pulses of light before his eyes.

He staggered to his feet with his back to the window and raised his hands, looking uselessly across the apartment.

'Please, I didn't mean to do it!' The room remained silent but bitterly cold. His eyes searched desperately left and right, seeking a glimpse of his tormentor. 'I came here to put it right!'

His breath puffed in thick clouds before him as he hyperventilated, his heart pounding in his chest. Suddenly, the clouds of condensing vapor swirled before him and for a brief but horrific instant a terrifying visage glared back at him, a face both human and yet twisted with demonic rage, as though it had crawled from the darkest bowels of Hell itself.

Jackson let out a howl of terror and tried to run past the fearsome image. Something immensely powerful thumped into his guts and lifted him off the ground, his terrified scream cut short as the blow blasted the air from his lungs.

Jackson flew backwards and smashed through the glazed windows, shards of glass slicing through his body like scalpels as his head cracked against the window frame and shattered under the impact as he plowed through the window and out into the chill night air.

His body arced outward into the void amid a cloud of sparkling particles of glass and plummeted seventy feet down toward the brightly lit street below, before hitting the asphalt hard enough to shatter every single bone in his body and burst his skull like an exploding melon.

Cars tires screeched and several pedestrians screamed as the traffic crawled to a halt either side of the ruined corpse.

# 46

# ST PATRICK'S CATHEDRAL, MANHATTAN

'I don't know how this is going to help, Karina.'

Karina Thorne reached up and grabbed a solid iron door knocker, slamming it three times on the tremendous, ancient wooden doors. To Ethan, everything about the cathedral seemed to dominate the street before it. The doors themselves were probably forty feet high, ornately decorated, and the cathedral's facade and twin spires climbed high into the morning sky. Standing with Jarvis, Lopez and Karina, he felt entirely dwarfed by the building.

Karina looked across at Lopez. 'We need help, Nicola. We can't fight this thing on our own. It's not of this world.'

'Sure,' Ethan agreed, 'but the people that run these places don't have any answers either.'

'Monsignor Thomas is not your average priest,' Karina assured him.

The huge doors clicked loudly, and Ethan heard what sounded like a heavy iron bolt being dragged through its mounts, before a smaller door was heaved open by a young man inside.

'Miss Lopez,' said a young man, 'Monsignor Thomas is expecting you.'

Ethan followed Jarvis, Karina and Lopez inside as the man hefted the door closed behind them, the wood hitting the jamb with a dull thud that echoed around the cavernous interior of the cathedral.

Normally filled with tourists, the nave was empty this early in the morning. Chandeliers hung from lines that ran up into the enormous vaulted stone ceiling high above their heads, illuminating in a gentle glow the endless ranks of pews and the towering fluted columns that supported the roof.

Giant stained-glass windows set high into the walls glowed blue with the light from the sky outside, and the sheer audacity of the architecture and the complexity of the artwork forged into the stone walls took Ethan's breath away. He wasn't by any means a religious person, but the scale of what men could achieve in the pursuit of worship astounded him nonetheless.

'Built by men of power,' Jarvis said as they walked, 'when ordinary people were starving all around them. Such are churches. Building libraries would have served the people better.'

'Churches help people when they're afraid,' Ethan murmured in reply.

'Do they?' Jarvis challenged.

Ethan slowed as he walked, gently pulling Jarvis aside. 'There's something I need to tell you.' Jarvis looked at him expectantly. 'Joanna's alive, and she's here in New York.'

'You found her?' Jarvis asked, surprised.

'No,' Ethan admitted. 'She found us.'

Jarvis stared at him for a moment. 'When?'

'Hell Gate,' Ethan replied, 'and outside the courthouse. She was the reporter following us, Doug.'

'Jesus, Ethan, when did this happen?'

'Last night,' Ethan replied as they began walking again. 'Doug, she's not the killer we're looking for.'

Jarvis raised an eyebrow as he fell in step alongside Ethan. 'She would say that, and you'd believe her, Ethan.'

'She knew all of the CIA agents,' Ethan explained, 'cornered them all and gave them a good knocking about for information, but she left them all alive. She didn't want any of them dead because she wanted them to be put to trial for what they had done.'

Jarvis slowed, looking at Ethan as he walked. 'You're sure? Absolutely sure?'

'One hundred percent,' Ethan replied. 'It makes absolute sense, Doug. Her motivation is revenge, but she won't get that from murder and she knows it. She said that they all died within two days of her finding them.'

Jarvis stared straight ahead as they walked for a long moment before he spoke again.

'Where is she, Ethan?'

'I'm meeting her tomorrow,' Ethan said. 'I'll get more detail then, hopefully.'

'Karina.'

The monsignor's voice carried from the choir gallery at the front of the church all the way to where they were walking. Thomas stepped out into the nave and walked toward them, reaching out a hand for Karina who took it and smiled. Ethan and Jarvis joined her and Lopez as the monsignor looked up at Ethan.

'Thomas, these are friends of mine from out of town, Ethan, Nicola and Doug.'

The monsignor smiled at them both. 'Welcome, friends. Your call sounded urgent, Karina. What's happened?'

Karina gestured him to one of the pews. 'You might want to sit down for this,' she suggested. 'Ethan and Nicola will explain, because, right now, I don't know where to start.'

The monsignor's features creased with concern as he looked again at Ethan and Lopez. Ethan decided to let Lopez do the talking and leaned against a pew as she laid it all down for the monsignor. Step by step, she explained the course of events that had led them to seek out advice, relating the Pay-Go robbery, the accident and deaths on the bridge, then the murders of the thieves, the clerk, the convicts and the lawyer.

Ethan watched the monsignor closely as Lopez explained the details of the case. He betrayed no emotion, simply sitting with his hands in the lap of his ornate robes and absorbing everything that Lopez said. When she had finished, he let his head drop for a long moment before seeming to pick his words with care.

'And there can be no mistake?' he asked Karina. 'That you have all seen this anomaly, this spirit, and that it has killed?'

'You had to be there, Thomas,' Karina replied. 'There's no doubt about it, no trickery. This thing tears people apart as though they're made of paper, crushes hearts inside people's chests. I'd say that us being mistaken is now less likely than this thing being real.'

Monsignor Thomas nodded slowly and then took a deep breath.

'What do you want me to do?' he asked her.

'We need a way of stopping it,' Ethan replied for Karina. 'While there may be a reason that it's killing people, we need to let the law handle it. A vigilante poltergeist isn't what this case needs right now. We need answers, not corpses.'

Monsignor Thomas slowly stood from his seat, his hands clasped before him as he glanced across at the choir gallery glowing in the candle light and a huge golden crucifix suspended above it.

'There is so much that we do not know about our existence,' he said finally. 'Science has answered so much and will continue to do so, but there are some things that it is not equipped to measure. I fear that a phenomenon such as a wraith loose in New York City is one such event. You cannot defeat such a force of nature by strength, only by guile.'

'Force of nature?' Karina gasped. 'There's nothing natural about it!'

Monsignor Thomas smiled and shook his head. 'Isn't there? We call such entities *supernatural*, but only because our senses are not equipped to detect them easily and because they do not frequently interact with our world.'

'We need to stay in the here and now,' Ethan cautioned the monsignor, 'not get caught up in speculation about the afterlife.'

'I'm not talking about the afterlife, as you call it,' the monsignor replied easily, not taking offence. 'I'm talking about what we can detect, and how you might be able to use it to control this wraith.'

'Control it?' Lopez asked.

'Contain it, then,' the monsignor corrected himself. 'Put simply, our universe, whether you believe it was created by God or that it simply exists, is a universe of energy. That energy takes different forms such as heat, light, objects, gases and so on, but all of it is energy nonetheless. You have heard of Albert Einstein's Special and General Relativity, yes?'

Ethan blinked and almost laughed. 'You've studied them?'

'My PhD was in theoretical physics,' Monsignor Thomas replied without taking offence. 'As a scientist and a believer, I see no conflict between science and faith. For me, the one leads to the other.'

'So what does this wraith have to do with Einstein?' Jarvis asked.

Monsignor Thomas gestured to the candles near the choir gallery. 'Einstein worked out that everything is energy by asking questions about and studying the properties of light. One of the conclusions that he drew and that is little known is that, for his equations to work, he had to create an energy field that exists across space and time. It was once referred to, in ancient times, as the "*ether*", a field which would carry the passage of light. Einstein didn't believe in its existence or in the consequences of it being there: that the universe must be expanding due to this mysterious field of energy, so he fudged his equations to cover the gap. He later called it "*the greatest blunder of his life*".'

'So there *is* an energy field, all around the universe?' Karina asked, and was rewarded with a nod.

'It goes by many names, many of them associated with the strange world of quantum mechanics,' Monsignor Thomas replied. 'But essentially, it is the seething energy field of all atomic particles, invisible but constantly buzzing. There are particles popping into and out of existence in every square inch of our universe.'

Ethan realized where the monsignor was coming from.

'You think that's the fuel that the wraith uses to do what it does?'

'To a certain extent, yes,' Monsignor Thomas replied. 'But it will also be drawing energy from our everyday technology. Investigations into paranormal events around the world have documented many hundreds of times the draining of batteries in cameras or the fading of lights in the presence of paranormal activity, as though something is drawing energy from its surroundings to manifest itself.'

'The lights,' Lopez said, turning to Ethan, 'the lights are always out when the wraith is present.'

'Cellphones and radios fail, too,' Ethan agreed. 'But surely, there isn't enough energy in a cell battery or light bulbs to crush a half-tonne elevator car?'

'No,' Monsignor Thomas agreed, 'not nearly, but these devices are not the source of the energy, only a path to it, a conduit, if you will. The amount of energy in any atom, Einstein proved, is tremendous. If you doubt this then think about the power of our sun or a nuclear bomb. A single nuclear device can level cities and lay waste to entire regions.' He raised a clenched fist. 'Yet the bombs dropped on Nagasaki and Hiroshima at the end of the Second World War each contained a fuel cell for their destructive power no bigger than my fist.'

Karina glanced at his fist. 'That much power in that small a space?'

Monsignor Thomas nodded, lowering his fist and pointing at a small brass button on his robes. 'This button maybe weighs a couple of ounces,' he said. 'But if I took it and turned it into pure energy right now, it would vaporize this entire cathedral in a spherical explosion that would radiate in all directions at once, including straight up and straight down. The resulting shockwave would level the rest of the block, because the amount of energy in any object of mass is found by multiplying that object's mass by the speed of light, squared.'

Lopez blinked. 'That's a big number.'

'Big enough,' Monsignor Thomas replied, 'to crush an elevator car. I take it that it gets rather cold when the wraith is present?'

'Bitterly,' Karina confirmed.

'It is drawing from its surroundings,' Monsignor Thomas said. 'The latent heat energy lost from the atmosphere creates the chill that people often feel when in the presence of what we call ghosts. But a wraith's power would virtually freeze air if it lingered in one spot for long enough.'

Ethan looked around the cathedral for a moment and then was hit by inspiration.

'If we could take potential victims to a place where there were no electrical items, it would diminish the wraith's ability to attack them.'

Monsignor Thomas nodded. 'It's possible. Without a means to channel energy efficiently, the wraith's power would be greatly reduced, although it would still no doubt be able to manifest itself. And that's what bothers me the most about this case.'

'Why?' Karina asked.

Monsignor Thomas frowned thoughtfully. 'You say that you believe that this wraith is the spirit of a woman, or child, who died recently on Williamsburg Bridge?'

'My colleague's family,' Karina confirmed. 'Nobody else connected to this case has died, so we figure it must be one of them.'

Monsignor Thomas sat back down on a pew, his features now deeply concerned.

'What is it?' Ethan asked.

'I believe,' the monsignor replied, 'that you have made an error of judgment.'

'How?' Lopez asked.

'Well, I'm no expert on these phenomena, so rarely do they occur,' the monsignor replied, 'but I understood that crisis-apparitions only appeared to other people at the moment of death.'

'That's what we learned a while back,' Ethan confirmed. 'They were documented in detail during the First World War.'

'That's right,' the monsignor said. 'But if this was a haunting, then the wraith, or ghost, would be present on the bridge only. There are literally thousands of cases worldwide of roads haunted by automobile-wreck victims that periodically appear to drivers. Yet you say the wraith is moving freely, almost as if it is intelligent?'

'It seems to know where people are,' Lopez replied, 'if that's what you mean.'

The monsignor appeared to come to a conclusion, and he stood.

'Then you're looking in the wrong place,' he said. 'The source of this wraith must still be alive.'

# 47

The wintry morning air outside the cathedral seemed colder as Ethan jogged down the steps, with Lopez and Karina close behind.

'We should have thought of that,' Lopez said. 'Professor Bowen told us about that poltergeist case in Rosenheim, Germany, where the source was a girl who was alive.'

'I think we're out of our depth here,' Ethan replied.

'These crisis-apparitions appear when people have just died,' Karina said. 'Maybe somebody injured in the accident is in intensive care, slipping in and out of consciousness?'

Ethan looked at Karina. 'I think that you know more than that about what's happening.'

Lopez glared at Ethan angrily but he ignored her, staring at Karina until she let out a frustrated sigh and swiped a strand of hair from her face. 'I don't know,' she replied. 'It was just a gut instinct after what happened in my apartment the other night.'

'In the kitchen?' Lopez asked. 'What did you see?'

'I didn't exactly see anything,' Karina replied. 'I thought I saw a man standing there in the shadows, watching me, but it wasn't what I saw that mattered. It was a feeling.'

'You recognized the person,' Ethan said with a clairvoyant flash.

'I don't know,' Karina said, 'but it just felt like Tom was there. After what had happened that day, I got paranoid and decided to check him out. You know the rest.'

Lopez looked up at Ethan. 'He died on the floor of his apartment.'

'And then got resuscitated,' Ethan said. 'You think it's worth checking out the times of his cardiac arrest and the murders of the two guys out on Hell Gate Field, see if they match?'

Lopez nodded immediately, but Karina shook her head.

'Even if they do match, what the hell do we do then? We can hardly arrest Tom for the murders, he was dead on his goddamned couch! And what about the rest of the team? If it's Tom who's somehow behind all of this, then he's hunting them down, too.'

'For which there must be a reason,' Ethan said. 'Karina, we can't afford to just dismiss this, however crazy it might seem. If we can't rule out the possibility that Tom is somehow conjuring this wraith up, then we have to assume that, whether he knows it or not, Tom's our killer. He can't be prosecuted and the case would be thrown out by any self-respecting judge, so we have to deal with this ourselves. Where has he been the last two days?'

'Alone at home,' Karina admitted. 'But I've called him at least twice every day and he's always picked up. It's not like he's tearing around the city killing people. Christ, he's so depressed he can barely walk most of the time.'

'Check the times,' Ethan insisted, 'and then go and visit Tom, okay? I'll catch up with you in a while.'

'Why, where are you going?' Karina demanded.

'It's important,' Ethan replied. 'I won't be long.'

He turned and zipped up his jacket against the cold as he started walking down the sidewalk. He got ten paces when he heard Lopez jog after him and felt her hand on his shoulder.

Lopez looked at him. 'You want some back-up?'

Ethan shook his head. 'Probably better if I do this alone. We've got a lot to catch up on.'

'Yeah,' she replied, 'that's what bothers me. It's been five years, so you don't know anything about Joanna now, Ethan. She said it herself. Maybe you should take this a bit slower, a bit more cautiously.'

'Like you would?' Ethan asked with a smile.

'Your safety is paramount to me,' Lopez replied tartly, but there was a twinkle in her eyes. 'Most all times.'

'I'll be fine,' Ethan said. 'Just find out what you can about Tom Ross, and get Doug in on this. He might be able to match the name to our list.'

Lopez's eyes widened. 'You think?'

'It's exactly the kind of thing MK-ULTRA will be looking for. If there's a history of this in Tom's family, he might be more than just our killer. He might be a target, too. If the assassin that Joanna claims is following her identifies Tom, he'll be killed. We need Joanna on our side and Tom safe before we can finish this, okay?'

Ethan turned away. He could feel Lopez watching him as he walked, and wondered just what he was doing. Sure, he could hardly avoid meeting with Joanna: he'd been searching for her for five years. But so much had happened in between that maybe Lopez was right and there was nothing left for him to find.

The Metro took him south into downtown. He hopped off on Broadway and walked onto Fulton, the street lined with diners and pizza houses, small businesses tucked out of sight from the main streets. Truth was that in New York City there weren't very many places that a person could hide for long. Cameras were everywhere, many of them used by law enforcement to track vehicles and people, if the need arose. Joanna would be keeping her face out of sight, probably using a baseball cap and shades or a hood, maybe even a headscarf. Both he and Lopez had become fairly adept at avoiding cameras, using simple disguises over the past six months. Joanna would by now have perfected the technique.

As he walked he saw roadworks cordoning off part of Fulton, builders and street technicians digging holes and fiddling with scaffolding equipment. The large metal storage containers, each as big as an SUV, provided excellent shielding from the shops, bars and cameras on the opposite side of the street.

Ethan took the sidewalk behind the works, and soon found the diner that Joanna had mentioned, a small affair with maybe a dozen tables. This early in the morning, it wasn't easy to get a space, but he saw Joanna the moment he walked in. She was sitting facing the door deep inside the diner, far enough to avoid detection by any cameras outside, and to her back was the counter entry hatch: a quick escape route through the kitchen if anybody unfriendly tried to corner her inside.

Ethan unzipped his jacket and shouldered his way past truck drivers and construction workers tucking into breakfast, finally sitting down opposite her. She smiled and pushed a coffee toward him.

'Still two up and white?' she asked.

Ethan nodded, feeling a strange pang of nostalgia seep through his veins as he sipped from the cup.

He was seeing Joanna properly for the first time in five years, and he realized that the previous night had revealed only her identity and not her condition. While he could not doubt that she was superbly physical fit, her face now bore the weight of her years of incarceration. Gone was her smooth complexion. Her skin was creased around her lips and at the corners of her eyes, their once clear green appearance tinged with shadows. She was thinner than he remembered, the line of her lips harder and her cheekbones sharper. Her hair seemed more wiry than he remembered.

'You're staring at me,' she said.

Ethan blinked. 'Sorry, it's been a long time.'

'For me, too,' she replied. 'You're looking good, Ethan.'

He couldn't help the smile that broke across his face. 'You, too.'

'Bullshit,' she replied. 'I've aged ten years in five and it's not all down to bad coffee.'

There was a ghost of a smile on her lips as she replied, but it was muted by a flinty light of radicalism that glittered like distant lightning in her eyes. Whatever was going on behind them was vastly different to what Ethan remembered, and he chose his words with care.

'Tell me,' he said. 'Just tell me from the beginning what happened. I nearly drove myself into an early grave searching for you, Jo – it was like you disappeared into thin air.'

Joanna nodded slowly and set her cup down.

'I got jumped outside the hotel we were staying at in Gaza,' she began, 'if you could call it a hotel, what with the bare walls and that damned donkey outside.'

Ethan smiled involuntarily. 'The one owned by the guy hawking the mugs?'

'I *heart* Gaza City.' Joanna nodded, a smile breaking through like a ray of sunlight on a bleak winter's day. 'Never did ask him which part of that open prison he *hearted*. Anyway, four guys, real fast. I didn't even have chance to put up a fight before I was bundled into a blue sedan and whisked away.'

'Away where?' Ethan pressed.

'Not far,' she replied, and her features became sympathetic. 'It took a couple of hours to get there but they were just driving around in circles, and I was only ever moved once or twice in the whole three years, always ending up back in the same building. Truth is, I don't think I was ever more than a couple of miles from the hotel.'

Ethan felt tears pinch at his eyes but he refused to let her see them. 'I left you behind.'

'You did all that you could,' Joanna assured him. Her hand reached out and touched his, squeezed it briefly. Her skin was cool and dry, not soft and warm as it had once been. 'After I got away I started looking for you. It didn't take long to find the articles you'd written, the money you'd spent, everything. I know how hard you tried, Ethan.'

Ethan blinked hard, fighting off the grief that was swelling like a storm inside him.

'Then for Christ's sakes, why didn't you contact me?'

Joanna's expression changed to one of determination. The hand retreated back across the table.

'A lot happened, Ethan. There's still a lot that I don't understand, don't know. I couldn't trust anybody.'

'Anybody?' Ethan echoed in amazement. 'You couldn't trust me, even after all I'd done?'

'It wasn't you,' she insisted. 'It was everything, everyone, people connected to other people and on and on. By the time I actually tracked you down, I knew you were working for the enemy.'

Ethan frowned. 'The enemy? What are you talking about?'

'You're contracted to the Defense Intelligence Agency, right?' she asked, and, when Ethan nodded, she raised her hands palms up from the table. 'It was the CIA that pulled me off the street, Ethan. They've been looking for me ever since.'

'But why?' Ethan demanded. 'Why target you?'

Joanna glanced over Ethan's shoulder, around the diner, as though searching for prying eyes and ears.

'Because they were looking for survivors and relatives of MK-ULTRA, trying to remove evidence. They're doing it all the time, Ethan, right now, and whoever is responsible is likely to be close behind me because I'm a walking example of their experiments and I can identify those involved.'

*

'*Positive ID, repeat, I've got her visual. She's in a diner, on Fulton.*'

Jarvis sat in his vehicle parked almost a mile away from where his agent was walking. A small screen in the rear of the vehicle held a GPS indicator that flashed periodically as it moved down Fulton Street.

'Is Ethan with her?'

The voice in Jarvis's microphone was clear: '*Affirmative, Warner* is *with her. Positive identification as Joanna Defoe. You want me to stay on them?*'

Jarvis thought for a moment. The tracker he'd placed in the burner cell he'd given to Ethan was enough to ensure that he would remain under observation. Fact was, now that he had found Joanna, he would be unlikely to want to part company with her again. Considering their separate and yet closely tied missions, it was almost certain that they would work together.

'No,' Jarvis said. 'I don't want to risk one of them identifying you. Pull back now.'

'*Roger that.*'

Jarvis clicked off the microphone and watched the tracker's marker on the screen. Then he looked down to his side, at the burner phone he had been given by Mr. Wilson.

# 48

'They tried to program you?' Ethan asked.

'For two years.' Joanna nodded, sipping her coffee. 'The reason they picked me up is because of my father's connection to MK-ULTRA and because I was researching MACE, who were running an abduction-and-ransom scam beneath a veneer of military contracts.'

'I know,' Ethan replied, 'we busted them open in Israel three years after you vanished. The CEO, Byron Stone, died before he could be brought to justice.'

'Death isn't justice enough for that asshole,' Joanna snapped with uncharacteristic vehemence. 'I only wish I could have killed him myself.'

Ethan and Joanna, as well as being engaged to marry, had once worked together as journalists in South America for some years, exposing government corruption. While there, Ethan knew that Joanna had come close to exposing a major corporation's involvement in the 'abductions-for-ransom business' that had infected countries like Mexico and Colombia, but they had been chased away by death threats and the danger of arrest by local law enforcement. In Gaza, she had again come close to exposing MACE for deliberately organizing abductions, but this time their retaliation had been more definitive.

'So what was the CIA's connection to MACE?' Ethan asked.

'Covert,' Joanna replied simply. 'MACE was contracted through the Pentagon, but whatever Byron Stone arranged with the CIA was kept under the table. I never found any paperwork or evidence of CIA collusion until long after I'd actually been grabbed. But what I saw could blow the CIA wide open, even have it shut down.'

Ethan glanced around the diner as he spoke, as alert for eavesdropping as Joanna was.

'You saw what, exactly?'

'Saw and heard. They spent two years running all kinds of weird tests on me. Hypnosis, brain scans, stress tests, electroshock therapy, extrasensory perception analysis, psychokinesis, pyrokinesis, you name it. I really began to think that the people who'd picked me up were out of their minds. Sure, I knew about MK-ULTRA already, but this was totally insane.'

'They find anything?' Ethan asked.

'Wish they had,' she replied. 'If it had turned out I'd been able to set things alight without touching them, I'd have torched every one of the fuckers right there and then.'

'Electroshock therapy?' Ethan echoed as he digested what Joanna had said.

'They show videos,' Joanna replied, and she seemed to shiver slightly despite the warmth in the diner. 'Alternating images, some patriotic, others less so. The patriotic images turn up and they flush you with a bit of morphine, makes you feel all warm and fluffy. All's good. The others, they send a couple hundred volts through you.'

Ethan's throat swelled and he could no longer look at her as he averted his eyes and stared down into his coffee. 'How long?'

'About six months,' came the reply. 'Nine hours a day.'

Ethan wiped a sleeve angrily across his face, kept his head down. Joanna's voice reached him gently across the table. 'Stopped me from sleeping a lot, made me fear even seeing anything that wasn't American.' Her hand touched his again, and he looked up to see her smile faintly. 'Put it this way, I can't watch a Vietnam movie anymore without hitting the ceiling every couple of minutes.'

Ethan forced a crooked grin onto his face and tried to ignore the rage seething like acid through his veins. 'What else.'

'You don't want to know,' Joanna replied. 'I've moved on from . . .'

Ethan grabbed her forearm. 'What else?'

Joanna stared at him for a few seconds, and then replied as though she were talking about the weather.

'They killed me,' she said. 'Drained the blood from my body and replaced it with chilled saline. Kept me in stasis for an hour and then reversed the process. When I came to, they asked me what I saw. They were looking for evidence of the afterlife, Ethan. They called it the Eternity Project. They wanted to know the face of God.'

Ethan could barely speak as he looked at her. 'How many times?'

Joanna sighed. 'Thirty-seven, I think.'

Ethan kept hold of her arm. 'Jesus, I'm sorry.'

'There's nothing for you to be sorry about,' she insisted, and averted her eyes. 'Moving on.'

Suddenly, the creases marring Joanna's once, flawless skin appeared ominous. Ethan wondered at the terrors she had endured in that room buried deep in the volatile streets of Gaza City, but he knew better than to pry further. 'So you heard some stuff, later on?'

Joanna nodded. 'After a couple of years of doing these tests, they gave up. I suppose that, after seven hundred days, they'd finally realized they were pissing into the wind. I got moved back to my little cell without windows, while they figured out what to do with me.'

'MACE must have been long busted by then,' Ethan said, 'or at least on their way out.'

'MACE was only responsible for the team that grabbed me,' Joanna explained. 'The CIA took over from that point. Once they'd given up on the experiments, they relaxed a bit. The building I was kept in was secure enough, but the walls carried sound and the door wasn't sealed at the jamb. Sometimes the daft assholes had chats with each other right outside.'

'About what?'

'About Langley,' she said, 'about being back home, their wives, kids, that sort of stuff. They were as American as you and I, and any mention of Langley pretty much points the way. We were in the middle of Gaza, for Christ's sake. Who the hell else would be running a safe house there?'

Ethan nodded. 'Must have had people on the inside, though. Field agents would have stood out too much.'

'Probably. I saw these guys often enough, so they may have had their own way in and out of Gaza, probably at night. Point is, they were getting lax and eventually they screwed up enough that they got hit by Israel just as they were trying to move me to a new location. They hadn't bothered to liaise with Mossad or the Knesset, I suppose, and they also hadn't bothered to blindfold me.'

Ethan nodded. 'I know, I saw the hit.'

Joanna's eyes flared wide open. 'You were there?'

'No,' Ethan replied quickly. 'I saw footage of the raid, saw you on foot. You were gone before we could track you, but it was the first evidence I had that you were alive.' Joanna stared at her coffee as she digested this new information. Ethan looked up at her. 'What happened next?'

'Assan Muhammad happened next.'

'Assan?' Ethan finally laughed as an image of the rotund, cheery-faced trader they'd met in Gaza so many years before filled his mind. 'Is that old bastard still ripping people off out there?'

'Just like he's been doing since the time of the Prophet.' Joanna nodded, smiling. 'I found him where he always was and he got me out of there real fast. I was in a smuggling tunnel beneath Rafah and over the border into Egypt before nightfall and out of Cairo forty-eight hours later. I headed for Europe, and stayed in the United Kingdom for three weeks to get myself sorted.'

'Then what? You came home?'

'Right,' she replied. 'Started looking for you again and for the bastards who'd kept me locked up all that time. I knew there'd be a shit-storm brewing at Langley after I got away from them, so I just started listening in. Got myself a job in the kitchens of an out-of-town diner during unsociable hours, a small rent in DC, and kept watching and waiting. Sure enough, the spooks started hanging around our old house near Anacostia.'

'We were only there for six months,' Ethan said in surprise.

'Shows how desperate they were to find me. I guess they figured I'd come looking for you in all the old places.'

Ethan chuckled. 'Thought that maybe you'd left something tucked away there,' he guessed, 'buried evidence and all that?'

Joanna nodded. 'Dumb asses, the lot of them. I started shooting reels of them hanging around, identified the pool cars they were using, that kind of thing. They were maintaining low-level surveillance, using rookie agents, I guess, because they didn't have the manpower, so they were making a few mistakes here and there. Now and again, bigger fish would come visit them, and I recognized one or two faces from Gaza. It wasn't hard to link them all up and start putting together a piece on what was happening.'

'You publish it,' Ethan asked, 'under a different name? Or send it to England?'

'No,' she replied. 'I had a better idea: just stay under the radar and keep collating evidence until there's so much of it that it could never be denied. Especially, as I, the author, had effectively come back from the dead and could identify half of the men who had worked for the CIA out in Gaza. Those were the more experienced men but, of course, they always end up on home turf eventually, retired or whatever. I got a few of them on film.'

Ethan marveled at her tenacity and determination. 'So you've been doing this for over a year now?'

'Fourteen months,' she replied. 'But it's getting harder. They're cracking down, and the number of survivors of the original MK-ULTRA is getting less and less. We need to find one alive and get them to do a disappearing act all of their own, or everything I've achieved so far will be for nothing.'

'How many CIA agents have you leaned on?' Ethan asked.

'Five,' Joanna replied. 'Some broke quicker than others, but they all spilled their guts when I got the power tools out.'

Ethan blinked. 'Literally?'

Joanna's gaze was hard and steady. 'Just like they taught me all that time in Gaza, it's the threat that's more effective than the action. I gave each of them a good beating, enough that they didn't doubt I'd go all the way. Once I got the tools out, they blubbered like little children and told me everything.'

'Enough to hold a case in court?' Ethan asked.

'I doubt it,' she replied. 'Evidence obtained under duress and all that, but I know far more than I should about it all. The director must be quivering in his boots.'

'He is,' Ethan confirmed.

'You've spoken to him?'

'My boss has,' Ethan said, nodding. 'He thought that William Steel was afraid of being hit by an assassin. Seems like his biggest fear is you managing to drag him into a courtroom: he must have ordered the hits on the CIA agents you targeted, and must also have allowed you to be subjected to these experiments. That gets out, he's done, totally. He'll spend the rest of his life behind bars.'

'That's the plan,' Joanna replied. 'What have you been up to here?'

'We've been doing something similar,' he replied. 'MK-ULTRA has been largely shut down but its legacy is right across the country. There could be hundreds of American citizens out there who have no idea that they've been experimented on, living here and in foreign countries. Just because the CIA has finally mothballed the program doesn't mean that it doesn't have the capacity to now use the assets created by it.' Ethan looked up at Joanna. 'Maybe even you.'

Joanna smiled bitterly and shook her head.

'They tried cerebral reprogramming,' she said, 'spent weeks showing me those hours of images and footage, trying to desensitise me to violence or provoke outrage by showing me images of corruption and police brutality in the Middle East and using those damned electrodes.'

'It didn't work?' Ethan asked.

'Not even close,' Joanna replied. 'The thing was, I'd already seen it all and knew about it. It's not like my father, who went straight from college and linguistics school into the army and off to Singapore. Times are different now. People have much better knowledge of life overseas: we have twenty-four-hour news, a free media. My father probably fell for these experiments because his knowledge of the world was not as extensive as mine. All that I got from it was a better idea of how to shoot dramatic photographs.' She smirked. 'Would have cost me a couple of thousand bucks for a course like that back home.'

Ethan gave a rueful shake of his head. 'You've handled everything that's happened better than I thought possible,' he admitted.

'Maybe, but otherwise, they were doing their job well, almost totally ruined me through isolation and sleep deprivation, until their idiot doctor showed up to run the experiments. He wore a watch and I caught sight of the date and time. Gave me the anchor I needed to hold out.'

'You get a name?' Ethan asked, his fists clenched on the table.

'Sheviz,' Joanna spat. 'Damon Sheviz.'

Ethan looked at her for a long time and then a grim smile crept across his face. 'Well, I can tell you that Damon Sheviz met a prolonged and painful demise at the hands of Bedouin tribesmen out in the deserts of Israel a couple of years ago.'

Joanna's eyes flared in amazement as she looked at him. 'You knew him?'

'Found him on my first case for the DIA,' Ethan explained. 'He was by then using a similar experiment that he used on you, to try to clone the blood of another species to create hybrid embryos.'

'He said something about that,' Joanna said, thoughtfully. 'That he'd only need my blood and that I no longer needed to survive the experiments. What species was he trying to clone?'

'You don't want to know.' Ethan said as he leaned close. 'Did you learn anything that we could use to bring them down?'

Joanna shook her head. 'They weren't *that* slack,' she admitted, 'but I do have my secret weapon.'

'The names you memorized?'

Joanna nodded. 'Not all of the names were tracked down by MK-ULTRA, due to the age of the list they were using from the First World War. I've managed to follow a trail out here, which tied in nicely with my search for Aaron Lymes.'

'You found somebody?' Ethan asked in amazement.

'Not yet,' Joanna cautioned. 'The list of names refers to people who have been dead for many years. It's tracking down their descendants, the ones who were experimented on, that's hard.'

Ethan nodded. 'You have the same list as we do, compiled from the experiences of families during the First World War.'

'Crisis-apparitions,' Joanna confirmed. 'But I may have gotten a little further than you in identifying living descendants. I managed to track a family name from England in the early 1900s through family trees and records. Their name was originally Barraclough, but only the daughter of the family survived.'

'Yeah, that's the name we foud. You tracked them all the way here, to New York?' Ethan asked.

'Sure did,' she acknowledged. 'The daughter married a wealthy businessman by the name of Wilbur Thompson and they had three children, two of them girls. One girl married but died of pneumonia in her early thirties, without having had children.'

'And the other?' Ethan asked.

'The other was a Mary Thompson, who moved to New

York at the age of fifteen with her parents, just before the first shots of the Battle of Britain and the Blitz, after France fell to the Nazis in the Second World War. It seems her folks feared that the United Kingdom would fall, too, and decided to get out of dodge. They settled in Manhattan and the daughter married in 1965.'

'Who did she marry?'

'A New York police sergeant by the name of Harold Ross. I've been tracking his family down.'

The name bounced around the inside of Ethan's mind and finally he had confirmation of his worst fears.

'My God, it's Tom.'

'Who's Tom?' Joanna asked. 'You've already found the family?'

Ethan got up from the table. 'We need to leave, now.'

# 49

# EAST 79TH STREET, NEW YORK

Police cordons fluttered on the bitter breeze as Donovan climbed out of his car. The traffic on 79th was being diverted through the block past the apartments, the rush hour causing havoc nearby. In the middle of the sidewalk was a large white tent that rumbled in the wind as though breathing. A forensics vehicle and a couple of men in white jumpsuits were flanked by beat cops guarding the cordon.

Glen Ryan appeared from the tent and dragged one hand across a face taut with anxiety. He saw Donovan coming and hurried toward him.

'Jesus, it's happening,' he snapped. 'It's happening to us.'

Donovan raised a hand to slow the young officer down. 'What's going on?'

Ryan took a deep breath and gestured over his shoulder with a jab of his thumb. 'Jackson took a dive.'

Donovan hesitated on the sidewalk and then craned his head up to the soaring apartment blocks high above. There, several stories up, he saw a shattered window with bright yellow police-cordon tapes criss-crossing the gaping hole.

'From up there?' Donovan uttered.

'Yeah.' Ryan nodded. 'If a job's worth doing . . .'

Donovan started walking again, toward the white tent, Ryan alongside him.

'He didn't jump, boss,' Ryan said.

Donovan tried not to betray a response but he shook his head involuntarily. It wasn't worth the effort of even trying to deny the obvious. Jackson was head-over-heels for his girlfriend, loved his job and had no history of depression. All that Donovan knew for sure was that their encounter with that damned *thing* the previous night had shaken Jackson up far more than any of the gruesome, countless homicides they had dealt with over the years.

'I don't know,' Donovan replied finally, as they reached the tent. 'But it wouldn't have been like him.'

'Not like him,' Ryan replied flatly. 'No shit.' Donovan turned for the tent, but Ryan grabbed his arm. 'He didn't jump. Forensics will tell you.'

Donovan frowned and pulled the tent flap aside as he ducked in.

A lone forensics officer was taking samples from Jackson's body. Donovan swallowed a dense bolus of vomit that lodged briefly in his throat. Jackson was sprawled on his back, his skull flattened against the asphalt and his eyes vanished from their sockets. Thick blood had leaked from his shattered skull and from deep lesions in his skin, soaking his clothes where his body had burst like a balloon. His form seemed oddly shapeless and deflated, as though the skeleton within had simply crumpled, and a lake of fluids stained the sidewalk.

Donovan looked at the forensics guy, who was staring up at him.

'Anything?'

The officer shook his head. 'We've got trace samples from at least thirty different people, but as he's a cop that's not surprising. Can't make any comment about who might have done this but they sure as hell gave him a shove.'

Donovan looked at Jackson's ruined body. 'How do you mean?'

The officer gestured to the body.

'We found glass embedded in what's left of his skull. We'll have to confirm but it seems to match the glass in his apartment windows, which means he went straight through them at some velocity. People who are intending to commit suicide through a fall would normally bother to open the window first.'

Donovan thought for a moment. 'Maybe he just lost it, had a severe breakdown and hurled himself straight through the glass.'

The forensics guy chuckled bitterly. 'Maybe at a stretch, except that he could not have *just* thrown himself out of that window. In free-fall the human body attains a maximum velocity of about a hundred twenty miles per hour. But the injuries this guy has sustained are consistent with an impact at more like twice that speed.'

Donovan stared at Jackson's corpse. 'You mean he accelerated?'

The forensics man stood. 'Beats the hell out of me, but this guy dropped out of that window like he had a motor on him. Last body I saw that looked like this was in the front seat of an airplane that went into the ground vertically. There wasn't much left to look at.'

'How fast was Jackson going when he hit the sidewalk?'

'Best guess,' the forensics officer hazarded, 'about two hundred miles per hour.'

'Physically impossible then,' Donovan replied.

The forensics man nodded. 'Don't envy you solving this one, guys. Either this guy was Clark Kent on a bad day or he was murdered.'

Donovan walked out of the tent with Ryan close behind him.

'It got him,' Ryan insisted. 'Whatever this thing is, it got him and it'll be after us next.'

Donovan sucked in a deep lungful of cold air and looked about him thoughtfully.

'All of the victims have been iced at night,' he said.

'Great,' Ryan replied, 'that gives us a few hours to get packed and get a flight the hell out of here.'

'We're not going anywhere!' Donovan snapped, and jabbed a thick finger into Ryan's chest. 'Running won't achieve anything, except to expose us even more.'

'I'd rather give it a try than facing that thing!' Ryan shot back. 'Jesus, Donovan, it's killing us!'

'It's Tom, you asshole!'

Ryan stared at him for a moment in blank disbelief. 'Tom? What the hell are you talking about? Most of the time, he can barely walk and talk. Jackson would have pulverized him.'

'He's not doing it himself exactly,' Donovan growled. 'I don't know how, but he knows what happened and he's bringing us down one at a time. We stop Tom, and this ends.'

Ryan's gaze flickered as he digested what Donovan was suggesting.

'What do you mean, *stop* him?'

Donovan shoved one big arm across Ryan's shoulders and steered him out of earshot of the nearby police and forensics team. 'Tom knows, Glen. He knows what happened and he knows that we're implicated.'

Ryan shook his head in disbelief. 'But how? How could he know and how the hell could he be doing this? All of the victims have died in ways that no human being could achieve. And what about Karina? How come she hasn't been attacked?'

Donovan slowed as he considered that fact, and the answer came quickly.

'Because she wasn't in on it, Glen. We knew we couldn't trust her. Did you check her cell, find out who she called when we were in the law school?'

Ryan swallowed thickly, ran his hand across his face again as he nodded. 'She called Tom Ross,' he admitted. 'I don't know if he answered or not but somehow the call stopped the attack. Jesus, Donovan, we can't fight this.'

'We can fight this, because we can fight Tom. Without him, this all goes away.'

'You sure?' Ryan snapped, facing Donovan. 'You sure that this goes away? If Tom's got somebody else pulling the strings for him, then how do we know that it won't get even worse when we've arrested Tom?'

Donovan's rugged features creased into a smile that matched the bitter wind blustering down the street around them.

'Because whatever Tom's doing, it doesn't involve another *person*. Nothing else makes sense, Glen. Somehow, God knows how, Tom's doing this himself. Karina's call to him must have interrupted whatever the crazy asshole's doing. We've got to stop him before the sun sets tonight because it's just you and me now.'

Ryan glanced up at the morning sky and Donovan could tell that to the kid the rest of the day now looked impossibly short.

'But how do we stop him?' Ryan asked. Donovan did not reply, simply staring at him until the kid finally got it.

Ryan gasped and turned away. He shook his head.

'It's the only way,' Donovan insisted.

'We didn't mean for this to happen!' Ryan whispered. 'It wasn't supposed to be this way! It's not our fault his damned kid and wife turned up on the bridge, not our fault that it all went sour!'

Donovan's expression remained stony and impassive. 'I don't think that Tom sees it that way, Glen. Would you have, if Karina had been killed?'

'Oh, God, Karina,' Ryan said. 'How the hell are we going to explain this to her?'

'We're not,' Donovan growled. 'Nobody knows now and nobody knows ever. We deal with Tom and then we bury it, understood?'

Ryan's face collapsed into a tortured rigor of dismay and torn loyalty. 'She'll see through it, Donovan. She won't stop until she gets to the bottom of it all.'

The line of Donovan's jaw hardened. 'Then she'll have to be silenced along with Tom.'

Ryan stared at Donovan in horror, but he did not move from the spot. Donovan knew that despite what he was suggesting, Ryan just did not have the guts to come clean to Karina or hand himself in. He was a puppet, dancing to Donovan's touch.

'Get in the car,' Donovan ordered him. 'We need to find Karina, and where we'll find her, we'll most likely find Tom.'

Ryan stared at Donovan for a long moment, and then, like an automaton, he walked to Donovan's car and climbed in.

# 50

## 5TH PRECINCT POLICE DEPARTMENT, NEW YORK CITY

'Are you sure about this?'

Joanna stood with Ethan on the sidewalk outside the precinct, her hand on his forearm as she hesitated at the steps.

'The police are not the enemy,' Ethan replied, 'at least, not all of them.'

'That's not very reassuring.'

Ethan offered her a smile. 'We're here under the jurisdiction of the DIA. Nobody's looking for you, least of all in this station, okay?'

Joanna sighed and followed Ethan into the building. They made their way up to the offices and Ethan showed his identification to an officer before requesting access to the archivist's files he had previously viewed.

'What are we looking for?' Joanna asked as they waited.

'Evidence,' Ethan replied in a whisper. 'I'm not quite sure what, exactly, but there's got to be something on the tapes we're about to see that will expose corruption within this department. Trouble is, I can't admit to anybody here that that's what I'm looking for.'

An officer approached them with a disc. Ethan took it and walked across to the small room nearby that contained chairs, a table and a television with built-in DVD player. He shut the door as soon as Joanna was inside and then set up the disc to play.

Joanna watched as a fuzzy black-and-white image of a traffic intersection appeared.

'Fill me in,' she suggested.

'Armoured car robbery,' Ethan replied. 'The vehicle outside the Pay-Go on the corner of the intersection will get hit by a truck, busting it open. There'll be a gunfight between cops staking out the Pay-Go and the thieves, who will then escape in a pickup onto Williamsburg Bridge. That truck will then crash on the bridge and ultimately cause a pile-up that claimed several innocent civilian victims, including the wife and daughter of one Tom Ross.'

Joanna nodded as she watched the screen. 'The guy I've been searching for.'

'The same,' Ethan replied.

A huge Kenworth appeared on the screen and plowed into the armoured car. Ethan watched as the armoured car was split open and spun sideways across the sidewalk as the Kenworth smashed into the Pay-Go store. The armoured car then hit a fire hydrant and launched a pillar of white foaming water into the air.

'The hydrant leak's blocking the view,' Joanna said.

'Which is what's bothering me,' Ethan replied. 'Look, there are the cops moving in. Now, watch the big guy.'

Ethan followed the movements of Donovan as he ran across the intersection, his pistol raised and pointed at the crashed vehicles. Moments later, he vanished behind the pillar of water and the crashed armoured car.

'He can't be using that water as a shield,' Joanna said. 'There will be other cameras and he couldn't have known that the hydrant would blow.'

'I don't think that he's hiding,' Ethan replied. 'But look how he's sent all of his colleagues toward the Pay-Go. He's separated himself from his team.'

'Why?' Joanna asked.

'I don't know,' Ethan said. 'It bothered me when I first viewed the footage, but I couldn't think why. My problem is that there's no tactical advantage in doing so. In fact, with one gun where he is and the other three officers approaching the Pay-Go from the front, it means that he's almost forcing the thieves to move toward him.'

Joanna shrugged. 'Maybe that's what he wants?' What if he's covering them instead of attacking them? You said that this is about corruption – is it him you think is up to something?'

'Maybe,' Ethan replied, 'but I just can't figure out what.'

They watched as the thieves dashed for the pickup truck that appeared nearby, the cops' heads all down under blasts of automatic fire. The truck's tires spewed smoke as it accelerated away toward the Williamsburg Bridge, and Joanna pointed to a pile of boxes in the back.

'That the money?' she asked.

Ethan nodded. 'Aluminum cases, about a quarter million in each.'

Joanna leaned back in her chair. 'It's possible the driver and one other could have pulled up and loaded the cases in just a few seconds, but they would have been right in your man's line of sight.'

Ethan nodded. 'They could have fired in his direction, kept his head down. He's only got the wreckage of the armoured car for cover.'

'Too close,' Joanna replied. 'They'd be unloading it just feet away from where he's standing and couldn't fail to miss.'

The images switched to the traffic cameras high on the bridge as the truck swerved between other vehicles. A police sedan, its hazard lights just visible flashing through a grill above the front fender, pursued them.

'Here comes the crash,' Ethan said.

They watched as the truck was hit by the pursuit vehicle, lost control and crashed violently. The police sedan screeched to a halt nearby, the cops tumbling from it with their weapons aimed as the truck, its rear hanging precariously out over the bridge's ruined railings, spilled the money cases to fall out of shot toward the East River.

Then the fuel truck plowed into the stationary traffic in a tangled mass of crushed metal and burgeoning flames.

'Jesus,' Joanna uttered.

The cops apprehended two of the dazed thieves on camera.

'Where'd the other two go?' Joanna asked.

'Escaped,' Ethan replied. 'Maybe had another vehicle on the bridge, we thought, but nothing got picked up at the blockade on the east side of the bridge.'

Joanna sat staring at the screen for a long moment.

'Wind it back to the crash,' she said. 'When the flatbed lost control and busted the railings.'

Ethan used a remote to wind the footage back, and then advanced it at half-speed. Joanna leaned forward, watching closely as the vehicle hit the railings, careered into the other side and then finally spun out of control, before smashing through the railings and coming to an abrupt halt, side-on to the flow of traffic.

The silver cases tumbled from the rear of the flatbed.

'You said they grabbed twelve cases,' Joanna said.

'Yeah,' Ethan agreed, 'twelve were taken from the armoured car. Two were recovered from the flatbed, and one more from the shore of the East River a couple of hours later. The other nine were lost in the river.'

Joanna shook her head.

'What if they never made it into the truck?' she said. 'What if the truck was a deliberate diversion? Wind the footage back to the Pay-Go attack.'

Ethan wound the footage back and watched as the Freightliner was hit and the fire hydrant blew. The flatbed pulled away and raced off camera. Joanna grabbed the remote and paused the footage before re-winding a frame at a time. The flatbed inched back into view, two of the thieves sprawled in the back.

Joanna froze the image and pointed at the screen.

'There's the answer to your mystery,' she said.

Ethan leaned forward and peered at the pixelated image of the truck. There, the two thieves were lying on top of no more than three or four cases.

'The majority of the cash never made it onto the flatbed,' Joanna said. 'And the big cop you pointed out didn't join the pursuit on the bridge. So what was he doing?'

Ethan sat back in his chair and cursed himself for not realizing it sooner.

'He loads up the remaining cases into another vehicle, maybe even his own, and then controls the scene before other police arrive. The entire stake-out, Karina said, was based on a tip-off from an anonymous informer who approached Donovan. Maybe there was no informer, and the whole thing was set up so that Donovan could take the cash himself. He's a cop and could have gained access to the codes necessary to break into the cases and bypass the security devices, if required.'

Joanna frowned thoughtfully.

'But what about the fall-guys in the truck? If they were involved, they wouldn't just let themselves get caught like that?'

Ethan shook his head in wonderment.

'Nearly four million bucks is a lot of cash, if you know what to do with it. Four thieves, three cops, a lawyer and a bank clerk. That's nearly half a million dollars each, split evenly, in hard cash. Sure, the identity numbers on every note would be black-marked by the Federal Reserve, but with three billion notes passing through the system every day, the chances of them being picked up are tiny.'

'They could also be laundered,' Joanna suggested, 'passed on and generally mixed up in the system. If everybody involved was smart enough, the money would never be traced to individual owners.'

Ethan turned to Joanna.

'Maybe Donovan's original tip-off was genuine, but instead of locating and arresting the gang as they fled south, he instead manages to contact them and offers them a deal. A sure hit on a bank or armoured truck, in return for the police failing to arrest or charge them.'

'Half a million bucks a piece or near enough, plus what the gang had already accrued,' Joanna said thoughtfully. 'They could high-tail it out of America and never need to worry about money again.'

Ethan nodded, warming to the idea. 'They organize the hit, and all goes well enough until the auto wreck and two thieves get caught.'

'Donovan employs a crooked lawyer and a cash-strapped clerk to help in return for a slice of the profits,' Joanna added. 'Donovan probably worked out how to hit the armoured car himself – they're incredibly tough and only a high-speed impact by something as large as that rig, hitting it dead center, would do the job.'

'Spilling the contents out into the road,' Ethan said.

'Which was why he chose that Pay-Go,' Joanna agreed. 'It faces the intersection and the armoured car parks right outside, side-on to traffic coming off the Williamsburg Bridge. The rig hits the armoured car, and Donovan uses the chaos and pursuit to conceal the thieves loading cases onto *his* car as well as the flatbed. 'But what does Donovan do with the cases?'

Ethan thought back to the Hell Gate homicide scene.

'The warehouse out on the docks,' he said. 'Donovan must have dumped a few of them there for Reece and Hicks to collect afterward. I found grooves in the floor, like something heavy had been dragged before the two men were killed. Donovan probably found them the next morning, maybe checking to make sure they'd been collected, and removed the cases from the scene when he found the bodies of the thieves. More profit for him and no connection to the incident on the bridge or the Pay-Go hit. That's why the thieves got into the warehouse without busting the door, but had to break the chains on the gates. Donovan could get a duplicate key made because the locks were an old style, but to leave the gates open would alert the site manager.'

Ethan looked at the screen for a long moment. 'But all of that still doesn't explain how the two remaining thieves got off the bridge.'

Joanna stared at the screen before answering.

'What if Donovan's not the only one involved?' she asked. 'What if the whole team's in on it?'

Ethan looked around at her. 'You think it's possible? The more people in on it, the less cash for each player and the greater the chance of exposure. Besides, Karina seems arrow straight. And why would the wraith be hunting them if . . .?'

Joanna's green eyes blazed with realization.

'What if it's only a couple of them, and your friends Karina and Tom don't know about it?'

Ethan felt his throat go dry as he considered what Joanna had said and what Karina had told them about the robbery. 'Jackson was in another vehicle, waiting to cover them if the thieves got away.'

Joanna looked at the screen beside them. 'What if he wasn't where he said he was? Anything went wrong, he could just show up and collect anybody forced to flee the scene.'

'We don't see him,' Ethan realized, 'because he was on the other side of the bridge. He wasn't waiting to back them up on Delancey, he was in Queens on the east side of the bridge, backing up the thieves. That's why the escapees never showed up at the roadblock: Jackson got them out and back into Manhattan, heading in the opposite direction.'

'Donovan obtains the footage of the *east* side of the bridge,' Joanna finished for Ethan, 'and probably conveniently loses it. He covered all of their tracks. But what's he doing now?'

Ethan stood up urgently.

'He's finishing the job,' he replied. 'If he's worked out that Tom's behind the revenge killings, then he'll try to have him iced.'

'These are revenge killings you've been investigating? How could this Tom guy have done those things?'

Ethan grabbed his cell and dialed Lopez's number as he led Joanna out of the room. 'I think we're about to find out.'

The line buzzed in his ear, a strange clicking sound. Ethan looked down at his cell and frowned.

'Line's out.'

Joanna grabbed it from him and listened to the tone for a moment before she shut the line off. 'Electronic scrambling,' she said. 'Your phone's being jammed.'

'But how can it be jammed when it was Doug who . . .' Ethan stopped walking as he stared down at the cell in his hand. A cold dread settled on his shoulders. 'Oh, no.'

Joanna looked at Ethan for a long moment as she connected the dots.

'Your man's not what he says he is,' Joanna said. 'I bet that if you call him though it will connect, no problem.'

Ethan felt almost physically sick as he realized that Joanna was right. The burner cell Jarvis had given him was not just for contact, but to keep tabs on him.

'He's probably had me followed,' Ethan realized. 'Probably knows where we are right now.'

'He's controlling you both, Ethan,' Joanna said. 'Probably always has been. Now do you understand why I couldn't trust anybody?'

'Christ,' Ethan said. 'Do you have a cellphone?'

# 51

## EAST VILLAGE, NEW YORK

'Tom? Open up!'

Karina Thorne and Nicola Lopez stood at the entrance to the apartment block as Karina rang the buzzer to Tom's apartment for the third time. They waited, but, once again, there was no reply.

'Dammit,' Karina uttered. 'If he's taken his own damned life again, I'll kill him.'

'When did you last call him?' Lopez asked.

'Last night, about maybe ten o'clock. He seemed fine, at least as much as can be expected after all that's . . .'

Karina was interrupted by the door's security system buzzing. She pushed against the door handle and it slid open. Lopez followed her inside and together they jogged up the stairwell, neither of them even looking at the vacant elevator car waiting nearby.

Karina got to Tom's door first, knocking only to find it already open. She burst in, with Lopez just behind her, in time to see Tom slump back down onto the couch.

'Jesus, Tom,' Karina uttered. 'You had me worried.'

The apartment was dark, the blinds drawn. Lopez could smell the stale air, the faint odour of unwashed plates drifting from the kitchen.

'Christ,' Karina snapped. 'You need to clean up here, Tom.'

Karina reached up and yanked one of the blinds open. Bright light burst into the apartment and illuminated Tom Ross's face. Lopez froze as she looked at the young police officer as he sat staring blankly before her.

He looked as though he hadn't eaten for days and his eyes were darkened orbs ringed with bruised sclera. His hair was in disarray and his shoulders were slumped as though he no longer had the energy to support his own body.

Karina rushed to his side as Lopez threw open a window to let some fresh air into the apartment.

'Tom, can you hear me okay?' Karina asked, throwing one arm across her partner's shoulder as she sat down.

Tom nodded without replying, staring at his feet. Lopez wasn't sure but it looked like he hadn't changed his clothes since the last time they'd visited him, his shirt heavily creased. She looked around the apartment and noticed instantly that the clock on the wall had stopped. The time on it read 10.37. The analogue hands could not reveal whether the clock had stopped in the morning or the evening. She glanced across at a digital clock on the oven in the kitchen. The clock flashed 00.00, as though it had lost power and had yet to be reset.

'You had a power outage?' she asked Tom.

Tom blinked up at her vaguely but didn't respond. Lopez walked across to him and reached down to his left wrist. She pulled it up and looked at his watch, a silver analogue. The hands were frozen in place at 10.37.

Tom looked vacantly at his wrist.

'What's been happening, Tom?' Lopez asked him. 'Where were you at 10.37 two nights ago?'

'Back off!' Karina snapped, glaring up at Lopez. 'He's been through enough.'

'This isn't going to go away, Karina,' Lopez shot back. 'Either we figure this out or the killings won't stop.'

'What killings?' Tom asked, looking up at Lopez and Karina in turn.

'Since you got out of hospital,' Karina explained, 'several people have died, all of whom appear to have a connection to the robbery and pursuit on Williamsburg Bridge.'

Tom squinted at Karina for a moment. 'What does that have to do with me? I haven't left the apartment since I came down to the station.'

'That's why we're here,' Lopez said. 'Tom, you said that when you overdosed, you were floating above your body and that you went up into a tunnel of light. Has that happened before and again since?'

Tom's already pale features blanched. 'No, it hasn't. Not exactly.'

'Not exactly?' Lopez pressed. 'Can you remember any dreams or anything from the times when you've been asleep, since the accident?'

Tom stared at her like a little boy wrongly accused of stealing sweets. 'Sure I've had dreams,' he replied. 'Horrible dreams of being in the dark, with no sense of time and surrounded by . . .' His voice faltered.

'What?' Karina asked.

'Rage,' Tom said finally. 'I keep seeing elevators in my dreams, and strangers' apartments.' His voice seemed to fall away in horror as he spoke. 'God, it's always so cold in the dreams.'

Lopez looked at Karina for help, and, reluctantly, she took hold of Tom's hands and held them tightly as she spoke.

'We have evidence, of a kind, that all of the people who have died may have been involved in some kind of corruption. It's as if this thing is hunting them down, one by one.'

Tom stared at Karina. 'What *thing*?'

'A wraith,' Karina said, 'a sort of poltergeist but much worse. Think of the Blair Witch on anabolic steroids and speed. It's tearing people in half, literally.'

Tom Ross looked at them both for a long beat. 'You think that I'm doing it?'

Lopez took control of the conversation. She knelt down in front of him, bringing her eyes to his level and softened her voice.

'Tom, when you overdosed, the main reason that Karina came here so quickly was that you appeared to her in her kitchen. It was like a vision and it happened the moment you died. That's called a crisis-apparition, a last fleeting glimpse of the dead person's soul before they go wherever the hell it is we go when we die. Is there anything like that running in your family, Tom? Is there anything that might cause you to somehow be able to attack people even when you don't know you're doing it, like when you're asleep?'

Tom stared at the floor for several moments before he spoke.

'My great-grandmother,' he whispered. 'My mother once told me a story about how my great-grandmother, Pennie Barraclough, claimed to have seen one of her sons at the moment he died, out in some great battle in France during the First World War. She was thousands of miles away when it happened.'

'That's a crisis-apparition,' Lopez confirmed. 'There were many of them during the Great War. Has anything like that happened to you since?'

Tom sat still for a moment, and then he appeared to go white as a sheet as though the blood were draining from his body.

'I haven't been sleeping properly,' he said. He looked down at his watch. 'The clocks keep stopping and I keep having to re-set them.'

Lopez looked up at the clocks again, the one on the wall and the digital display on the oven. Another display on a DVD player near the television was also flashing zeros at her.

'How many times has this happened?' she asked him.

Tom frowned as he struggled to remember. 'Four,' he said finally.

Karina looked at Lopez. 'That blows your theory. There have only been three murders.'

Karina's cellphone buzzed in her pocket. Lopez watched as she picked up the call and switched it onto speakerphone. She put one finger to her lips as she set the phone down on the table.

'Yeah, what's up?'

Lopez heard Donovan's voice on the other end of the line.

'*We've figured it out, Karina. We think that Tom's doing this but he doesn't know it. There was another murder last night.*'

Karina's eyes flared in alarm as she looked at Lopez. 'Do we know who was killed?'

'*It was Jackson,*' Donovan replied. '*Got hurled out of his apartment window and hit the sidewalk at about two hundred miles per hour. Forensics said it's not physically possible to fall at that speed unless he was being forced downward by something.*'

Lopez glanced at Tom, who looked as though he had been slapped across the face.

'How can you tell that Tom's involved?' Karina pressed.

'*These things only happen at night,*' Donovan replied. '*Either somehow he's doing it or he's getting somebody else to do it for him. Either way, we've got to bring him in. I figured you'd rather talk to him first, give him a chance to alibi out or at the least explain himself.*'

Karina's eyes narrowed. 'What did you have in mind?'

'*Call him,*' Donovan suggested. '*Tell him that we need to talk to him and bring him up to Hell Gate. We can't interview him at the station without arousing attention, so let's keep this to ourselves. If Tom alibis out, all's good. If he doesn't, we can pursue it without risking him being arrested or charged.*'

Lopez caught Karina's eye and slowly shook her head.

'Why the big interest in helping Tom now?' Karina pressed. 'Yesterday, you wanted to string him up.'

'*Yesterday, Jackson wasn't dead!*' Donovan snapped. '*We can't deal with this in the normal way, Karina. Christ, it's hardly a normal situation! Can you get Tom to Hell Gate or not?*'

Lopez shook her head again. Karina spoke toward the cellphone.

'We'll be there. We'll find Tom and meet you, before sunset at the latest.'

'*Good*,' Donovan replied, '*keep him out of sight until then*.'

Lopez turned off the cell and shot Karina a concerned look.

'The law can't sort this, Karina.'

'Then the law can't hurt Tom, either,' Karina replied tartly. 'What would they charge him with? Homicide by psychokinesis?'

Lopez looked Karina in the eye.

'And if Joanna Defoe successfully goes public with evidence for MK-ULTRA? Then there'll be grounds for a prosecution, no matter how bizarre it might seem. Maybe there'll be evidence there that this kind of thing really *is* possible.'

Karina was about to reply, but Tom Ross cut her off.

'I can speak for myself,' he uttered, and looked at Karina. 'We can't run from this. We have to face it down.'

Karina shook her head. 'How?'

'We need to get out of here,' Tom said, 'fast.'

The phone in the apartment suddenly trilled. Karina looked at Lopez, who shook her head. 'We don't know who it might be.'

Karina thought for a moment, and then dashed across the lounge and picked it up.

'Tom Ross's house.'

'*Karina?*' came Ethan Warner's voice down the line. '*Listen to me and do everything I say*.'

# 52

## HARLEM

Mr. Wilson sat in his non-descript sedan and ignored the cold seeping through the vehicle and his bones.

As a covert agent, he had spent countless hours sitting immobile in cars, watching, waiting or simply sleeping. Often, there was no alternative, the risk of identification in motels too high. Instead, a deserted and trash-strewn service alley on Harlem's south-side off 8th Avenue served as the perfect anonymous staging post. He could reach Queen's via Randall's to the east, or head directly south toward Manhattan at a moment's notice while remaining unobserved and undetected.

There were no cameras or pedestrians. Ironically enough, he was only a couple of blocks from a police precinct building, but there was nothing of interest to them where he sat. A handful of vehicles were parked behind service shutters for businesses that faced the main streets either side of the block, plus a couple more vehicles long abandoned and coated with a thin film of dust splattered with raindrops.

His cellphone vibrated on the passenger seat next to him and he reached down and pressed the answer button. The line connected via a small speaker plugged into his car, allowing him to answer without picking the cell up.

'Wilson.'

The voice of Douglas Jarvis answered. '*I have them.*'

'Where?'

'*I don't know where they're headed yet. All I can be sure of is that Joanna Defoe and Ethan Warner are together as we speak. Nicola Lopez is not with them right now, but it's only a matter of time.*'

Wilson nodded. Today had turned out better than he could have expected. With both Warner and Defoe searching for the same person, the descendent of the long-dead soldier Barraclough, it was now simply a waiting game. As soon as they found their mark, Wilson would be in position to complete his mission. Two birds, one very violent stone.

'What direction are they currently headed?'

'*Stay where you are. Every indication suggests they'll move north out of Manhattan. I'm tracking them as we speak.*'

'Keep me informed.'

'*Your director lied to me*,' Jarvis said. '*He lied to the entire Joint Chiefs of Staff, too. Joanna Defoe hasn't killed anybody, you did. Steel's afraid of prosecution and . . .*'

Wilson cut the line off and then dialed another. An automated voice answered, and demanded a code from him.

'Wilson, eight-eight-one-five-nine-three-alpha.'

The line clicked and, moments later, the Director of the CIA, William Steel, picked up.

'*What news?*'

'They're within reach,' Wilson replied without emotion. 'Chances are they'll be neutralized before tomorrow morning.'

'*Take your time, and don't underestimate either Warner or Lopez,*' the director warned. '*We thought they were dead in Idaho and they returned. We'll finish this properly this time.*'

Wilson's expression betrayed a hint of disgust that flickered behind his eyes. The director was safely tucked up in his office in Virginia, not hunting down American citizens in the field. There was no *we*.

'What about Jarvis? He knows that Defoe is innocent of the slayings.'

There was a moment of silence before the director replied. '*Accidents happen.*'

Wilson shut the line off and started the engine, before he looked at his watch. It was half three in the afternoon and already the bleak gray horizon was touched with streaks of fiery gold where the sun was sinking into the west between tenement blocks.

Wilson pulled out and dialed another line. This time it was Donovan who answered.

'Where are you?' Wilson demanded without preamble.

'*The east side,*' Donovan replied, his tones equally crisp and uncompromising. '*I've been in contact and they're on the move. The person you've been looking for is Tom Ross, a police officer.*'

'Where are they going?'

'*Hell Gate Field,*' Donovan said. '*The subject is with a woman, Lopez, and another of my team, Karina Thorne.*'

'Good,' Wilson replied.

'*Too many people are getting involved,*' Donovan insisted. '*We can't wrap this up quietly if half the damned city knows what's going on.*'

'Then you had best hurry to ensure that nobody else turns up!' Wilson snapped. 'Get there ahead of them and secure the area. I'll join you shortly.'

Wilson shut the line off and turned southeast toward Randall's and Queens. With luck, he would be there in time to close the last couple of blocks on foot. He knew the area only because of the crime scene that Warner and Lopez had been poking their noses into. Remote and full of nothing but old dock buildings and small-holdings. Deserted at night.

Perfect.

Doug Jarvis sat in the rear seat of an SUV and stared at his cellphone for a long moment. There was no doubting that Wilson would double-cross him – the CIA man's sole purpose was to clean up the mess that his bosses back at the Barn had created over the past four or five decades.

Jarvis was not idealistic enough, and more than cynical enough, to know that there was no point in expecting the CIA to honor its side of the bargain and leave Warner and Lopez alone. Joanna Defoe, likewise. All of them represented a clear-and-present danger not just to the security of CIA operations but to the agency's very existence. It was one thing to blow the whistle on malpractice or corruption, but another entirely to expose several decades of cruel and unusual punishment meted out to innocent American civilians. The backlash, even from the hawks in Congress and the Senate, would be unprecedented.

Jarvis's dilemma came not just from his loyalty to Ethan and Nicola. It was far more complex for him than that. His problem came from his equally powerful sense of loyalty to his country. The needs of the many. A United States of America without the protection offered by a Central Intelligence Agency able to operate freely beyond the reach of congressional scrutiny was an America vulnerable to attack from afar. Like all Americans, he knew all too well the consequences of failures of security, of letting foreign nationals with a taste for martyrdom cross onto American soil to launch their suicidal campaigns of hate and mayhem. With the CIA disbanded or broken up piecemeal into fragmentary offices of impotent agents handcuffed to everything from worker's rights to anti-discrimination and goddamned health and safety laws, a significant fraction of America's ability to analyze, conclude and act upon foreign intelligence would be forever lost. And along with it, American lives.

Jarvis stared out of the windows of his vehicle as it drove through the crowded streets of Manhattan, the agent at the wheel instructed merely to cruise close to the Williamsburg Bridge. Thousands of citizens crowded the streets, bustling back and forth as they went about their daily lives, blissfully unaware that disaster could strike at any moment, just as it had done before. For most all people, it always happened to the other guy. The bombed-out apartment building in another city. The explosives in a parked vehicle reported on the television. The IED that decimated a platoon of Marines by a roadside in Sangir. Distant, something that could be discussed at arm's length.

Until it happened on their doorstep, as it had in New York City in 2001. Then everybody's attitudes changed.

Jarvis was protecting Ethan and Lopez because, frankly,

he gave a damn about what happened to them. But as a patriot and a servant of the United States, he was also obliged to give a damn about the other three hundred million countrymen who relied upon men like him to make the right decision, no matter how hard it might be, time and time again.

He looked at his cellphone one last time and then dialed a number. The line picked up on the first tone.

'*Ethan.*'

'It's Jarvis. Get yourself to Hell Gate right now.'

'*Donovan's corrupt,*' Ethan informed him down the line. '*The whole team may be responsible for what happened on the bridge.*'

'*I know,*' Jarvis replied. '*Bring Lopez and Joanna, and Tom Ross, if you can. We'll take them into protective custody from there. It's time to bring this all to an end.*'

There was a pause on the line, and then Ethan's voice came through.

'*Understood. We're on our way.*'

Jarvis shut the line off and tried to ignore the waves of self-loathing churning through his guts. It was the only choice he could make, because he never really had one.

He hoped that Ethan and Nicola would understand, one day.

# 53

'What kept you?' Lopez asked. 'And why the hell did you call Tom's apartment and order us to come here?'

Ethan and Joanna hurried across the street to where Karina, Lopez and Tom Ross were waiting for them beneath the bare branches of trees lining the sidewalk.

'We were working things out and didn't want to be tracked,' Ethan replied. 'Karina, Tom, this is Joanna. She's on our side.'

Tom and Karina glanced suspiciously at Joanna, who kept her gaze fixed on Tom as she spoke.

'I've been looking for you for a long time,' she said.

'Why's that?' Tom asked, his voice feeble and barely audible above the sound of the traffic hustling past.

'To stop you having to go through what I had to,' she replied.

Tom Ross squinted at her without really understanding. Karina turned to Ethan.

'We can chat about old times over coffee when all this is over with,' she said quickly. 'Right now, we've got to figure out what the hell Donovan's up to.'

'Already done,' Ethan replied. 'He's behind everything: the Pay-Go hit, the hiring of the thieves, bribing both the clerk and the lawyer to assist him and corrupt the court hearing. He's engineered the whole thing and, by now, I'm pretty sure he'll know that we've busted him.'

'You got evidence of all that?' Karina challenged. 'You go in there and accuse Donovan of all this without something solid and we'll all go down.'

'It's him, all right,' Joanna insisted. 'The whole event on the Williamsburg Bridge was a set-up. But the auto wreck screwed everything up for them, and they've been trying to fix it ever since.'

'But how could Donovan have done this without the team noticing?' Karina protested. 'Surely, one of us would have realized what was going on?'

Lopez looked at Karina for a long moment before she replied. 'Karina, the whole team was in on it. You and Tom are the only ones they didn't cut in.'

Karina stared at him for a long time before she replied. 'Glen?'

'All of them,' Ethan confirmed. 'That's why the wraith is hunting them down but hasn't directly attacked you or us. Donovan made sure that you were positioned furthest from the Pay-Go truck when it went down. He then covered the two thieves driving the flatbed truck. They loaded most of the cases into Donovan's vehicle, or maybe even another one parked ready, then took a few cases with the flatbed as a diversion. Earl and Gladstone sat on top of them in the back of the flatbed to conceal how many cases were actually there. Donovan then controlled the scene at the Pay-Go and made sure the remaining cases disappeared real fast.'

'And the thieves who escaped from the bridge?' Lopez asked.

'Jackson,' Ethan said, 'who was most likely waiting in Queens and helped Reece and Hicks switch sides on the bridge and high-tail it back the way they had come. With the auto wreck taking up everybody's attention and the police blockade on the east side of the bridge, it's the only plausible way they could have escaped.'

Ethan noticed that Tom Ross was staring vacantly into space, his dark eyes filled with an emotion that Ethan didn't want to check out. Karina turned away from them, her hand flying to her mouth, and he heard the name she whispered in horror.

'Glen.'

Lopez stepped forward and placed a hand gently on her shoulder. 'You couldn't have known, Karina. Nobody could have known how this would turn out.'

Karina shook her head. 'It's why he wouldn't move in with me, until this was all over. He kept talking about money worries. I thought he was in debt or something and couldn't understand why he wouldn't move in with me to save money, why he was so distant all the time. But all this time, he was planning a goddamned heist with Donovan.'

'Donovan had it all worked out,' Joanna said. 'All we've got to do now is bring him in.'

'Not that easy,' Karina said as she swiped a sleeve angrily across her eyes. 'Donovan's just put out an APB on you both.'

'*He's done what?*' Ethan snapped.

Karina gestured to Ethan and Lopez. 'Claims that the two out-of-towners must somehow be tied into all of these murders. You guys showed up in the city at the same time the murders started, have been staying at my apartment and have visited Tom Ross twice. You've both had access to police officers on the team, one of whom is now dead, and now it seems that you have government agencies interested in questioning you about events that occurred several months ago in Idaho.'

Ethan stared at Lopez, who shook her head in disbelief.

'I know,' she said, 'I couldn't believe it either. He's got to have spoken to somebody high up, somebody with enough weight to pull this off.'

Ethan nodded, thinking furiously. If Donovan had somehow managed to look them up, maybe contacted police departments in Chicago or Idaho, then he might have attracted the attention of government agencies. The National Security Agency's immense wire-tapping and surveillance could have detected keywords or vocal-resonance signatures, which would have flagged alerts up at the Barn and quite possibly at the FBI. Inter-agency alerts would have brought the traces to the attention of those concerned at the CIA or perhaps even MK-ULTRA, if they had a dedicated complex.

Amid the seething digital maelstrom of communications, the names of Ethan Warner and Nicola Lopez could have landed right on the doorstep of the very people they had been trying to avoid.

'It's worse than that,' Ethan said. 'The cell that Jarvis gave me is being monitored by him.'

'So?' Lopez asked.

'I couldn't call you directly to warn you about Donovan,' Ethan explained. 'That's why I called Tom's apartment instead and I used Joanna's cell. It's a burner, too.'

Lopez stared at Ethan for a moment. 'I told you so.'

Ethan nodded. 'Even now, after all that's happened, he's playing us.'

'You think he's in with Donovan?' Karina asked.

'No.' Ethan shook his head. 'He'll be playing a much bigger game,' he said as he looked at Joanna. 'He said repeatedly that we wouldn't be tracked by the CIA because he'd cut a deal. I think I know what he traded.'

'Me,' Joanna guessed. 'Only way he can protect you is to sell me out.'

'But how would he know you're even here?' Karina asked.

Ethan retrieved from his pocket the burner cell that Jarvis had given him and turned it over. He prized the back cover free and peered inside. A small, glossy black device lay taped to the battery pack, which was only half the size it should have been.

'It's got a bug in it,' he explained to Lopez. 'GPS tracker, very small, very sophisticated. Enough to track me in case Joanna showed up. Jarvis knew that our paths might cross on this eventually. He's probably had somebody tailing us since we met him at the motel.'

'Son of a bitch,' Lopez uttered. 'He's always got a motive. We can't trust him, Ethan.'

'There isn't anybody else we *can* trust!' Ethan pointed out.

A silence hung in the air for a moment around them, and then Lopez stepped slowly forward and looked up at him. 'We trust each other,' she said simply.

Ethan stared at her for a long moment, and then Joanna stepped forward alongside Lopez.

'And me.'

Karina looked at him and nodded. 'We're all in this now. Let's do it our way.'

Ethan's gaze fell on Tom Ross, who seemed to have returned to the present as he looked at his four companions. As if finally realizing all that had been done and all that had happened in the last three days, he stepped forward with a glitter of new resolve, burning like a distant star in his eyes, as he looked at Joanna.

'What do you want with me?' he asked.

'To expose what the CIA has done to me,' Joanna said. 'You're the wraith, Tom, but what's happening to you is similar to something that they did to me. Been having any bad dreams lately?'

Tom swallowed. 'Like what?'

'Like being alone in the darkness, hunted and angry, for what feels like a thousand years but could have been moments? They're called near-death experiences, Tom, and I suspect you've been having quite a few.'

Tom held Joanna's gaze for a moment before he spoke.

'It's time,' he said softly, 'to finish this. All of it.'

Ethan looked at each of them and felt his shoulders fall. 'Okay.'

'Donovan wants us to meet him at Hell Gate,' Karina said. 'Says he wants to work this all out. If I can speak to

Glen, I might be able to turn him, get him to come clean and end all of this. Christ, if this wraith is hunting for revenge then he's as much of a target as Donovan.'

'It's too dangerous,' Lopez insisted. 'Donovan's not going to fold now. He's in this for the long run.'

'It's the only way,' Karina insisted. 'Donovan won't try to attack me if Glen's there, he wouldn't just stand by and do nothing.'

'We need to protect Tom,' Joanna said. 'It's him they're after. Their biggest threat now is the wraith, not us. First chance they get, they'll ice him and then run.'

Ethan nodded slowly and handed the bugged cellphone to Karina. 'Then we'd better make sure that doesn't happen.'

# 54

## HELL GATE, QUEENS, NEW YORK

Jarvis watched through the tinted windows of his vehicle as he drove slowly along 26th toward the shoreline. He was alone this time, knowing what was at stake and what he intended to do. If his own people saw that he was willing to sacrifice allies in order to achieve agency goals, it might bring their own loyalty into question.

Besides, this was personal. Jarvis wanted to finish this himself, not hide behind his men.

Despite the galling sense of betrayal that seethed like an infection in Jarvis's guts, he knew that this was the safest way. If he let Wilson come alone then the agent would almost certainly take the opportunity to eliminate Ethan, Lopez and most probably Joanna Defoe and Tom Ross, too. But this way was safer, with Jarvis on the scene and ready to intervene should Wilson even think about taking down Jarvis's people.

The plan was simple: Tom Ross into protective custody; Ethan and Lopez out of the city; Joanna Defoe into the hands of the CIA and Donovan under arrest.

He glanced at Ethan's tracker. Moving north, toward Hell Gate.

Jarvis's vehicle pulled into the abandoned lot, the nearby warehouse looming against a dark gray sky of scudding clouds, the afternoon light fading fast. A faint drizzle dusted the windshield. Another of New York's vigorous nor'easters would hit the mainland within the hour and darkness would fall.

He pulled up discreetly alongside the warehouse, turning around so that the vehicle pointed back toward the exit but was out of sight of the main lot, and shut the engine off.

Jarvis watched the rain spill in ripples down the windshield and the wind rumble and gust past outside. Another vehicle turned into the lot, a low-slung sedan that swung around and parked out of Jarvis's view. Jarvis wasn't close enough to see the faces of the two men inside, but he guessed by their silhouettes that he was looking at Donovan and Glen Ryan.

Jarvis climbed out of his vehicle, pulled his collar up against the bitter wind gusting off the East River, and walked to the edge of the lot for a clearer view.

He saw the tiny, unmoving shape of a man standing amid small trees on one side of the lot. Invisible, unless you were looking for him. Wilson was taking no chances, remaining under cover until the last moment. His actions confirmed Jarvis's suspicions. Apprehending Joanna Defoe was of prime importance to the CIA's director, and yet here was Wilson all on his own. Instead of sending a small army of agents, one man was taking all the chances. William Steel was keeping the entire event off the books at the CIA, doing everything possible to cover his own ass. That put Wilson at a disadvantage, and he knew damned well how Wilson would deal with that. Shoot anybody who crossed his path, in order to achieve his objective. Then, this would all be over.

They waited.

Finally, a black suburban pulled into the lot. It advanced slowly, lights blinking out as it pulled up and the engine stopped.

He watched as the driver's door of the vehicle opened and Karina Thorne climbed out. Jarvis waited for the others to climb out of her vehicle, but nobody appeared.

'What the hell?'

Jarvis waited, staying out of sight as he watched Karina approach Donovan's vehicle, and was plagued by the knowledge that Ethan had lied to him. Jarvis knew with utter finality that he had lost the trust of his most valuable asset.

Karina walked slowly toward the parked vehicle and saw Donovan and Glen sitting inside. The two men opened their doors and got out, both squinting against the gusts of drizzle sweeping the lot.

'Where are they?' Donovan demanded as he shut his door. 'You said we would meet them all here.'

'Change of plan!' Karina snapped back. 'We know, Donovan. We know everything that you've done.'

Donovan said nothing in reply. Karina switched her gaze to Glen, who shook his head.

'You've got it all wrong, Karina,' he said quickly. 'This was all supposed to be . . .'

'Shut up!' Karina shouted. 'We're done, asshole.'

Donovan chuckled bitterly and shook his head. 'You can save the theatricals, Karina. We're *all* done here now, so we might as well figure out a way to resolve this situation. What's your cut?'

'What?'

'Your cut?' Donovan repeated. 'How much do you want?'

Karina shook her head. 'That's all this is about for you, isn't it?' she uttered. 'Money and how much you can get out of it. I'd rather die than get a single dollar of your blood money, Donovan.' She leaned closer to him, her eyes boring into his. 'You're done. Whatever happens now, there's no way that you can get out of this. Warner and Lopez aren't here because they're already in police custody, having solved the mystery of what you did on that bridge. They're filling in your superiors on how it was done.'

Donovan's eyelid twitched as he ground his jaw in his skull.

'Warner and Lopez are history,' he murmured. 'The CIA is hunting both of them. They'll be apprehended within hours and that's the last you'll see of them.'

'Their boss at the DIA is protecting them from . . .'

'He's protecting them from nothing!' Donovan roared back. 'There's a CIA man who is operating outside his agency's jurisdiction. He doesn't give a damn about who lives and who dies, just as long as his mission is complete.'

Karina's eyes narrowed as a chill ran down her spine. 'How do you know that?'

Donovan smiled cruelly. 'We had a little chat the other night.'

'You sold them out,' Karina whispered in horror. 'Is there nothing that you won't stoop to?'

'Nothing,' Donovan replied without remorse, 'just as long as it keeps my back clear. So now, Karina, you need me because I'm the only one who can identify the agent before he strikes.'

'Jarvis knows who he is,' Karina shot back. 'He'll ensure that no harm comes—'

'Jarvis is out of the loop and of no concern,' Donovan interrupted her again, and jabbed a thumb in the direction of the black SUV parked across the lot. 'They don't give a damn about him or his two little helpers. As soon as this is resolved to their satisfaction, he'll be out on his ear. This is already over, Karina. We've won. All the CIA wants is Tom Ross and some woman called Joanna Defoe, God knows why. We hand them over, then this is finished.'

Karina peered at Donovan. 'And what happens when the sun goes down?' she asked.

Donovan grinned again, a brittle smile that conveyed no hint of warmth. 'I don't give a damn, because the first thing I'm going to do is board a flight the hell out of here, until it all blows over.'

Karina looked at him for a moment longer and then shook her head.

'We both know that won't happen,' she uttered. 'You're here to kill Tom, aren't you?'

Donovan inhaled deeply, looked at Glen, and then shrugged. 'Have it your way, Karina.'

Donovan yanked a pistol from beneath his jacket and whipped it toward Karina with incredible speed.

'*No!*'

Glen whirled and stood between Karina and the pistol. Donovan glared down at the younger man.

'Time to choose sides, Glen,' he shouted. 'This is it. Are you going to waste your time watching out for Karina or are you going to get a grip on your life and start looking out for yourself?'

'This isn't the way to do it,' Glen said, raising his hands. 'We start shooting people, we're screwed for life.'

'We're already screwed for life!' Donovan yelled at him. 'They know, Glen. We don't make our way out of here, it's twenty to life in a security-max facility. You made your choice, son, when you started working with the rest of us on this. You didn't care about Karina then and you shouldn't now.'

Glen's features twisted in a fury of regret and indecision as he glanced over his shoulder at Karina.

The gunshot snapped out over the wind and Karina flinched in shock as she saw the back of Glen's jacket flutter as the bullet whipped through trailing a fine spray of blood. Glen whirled and stared at Donovan in disbelief, and then his legs quivered as he fell sideways onto the cold, damp asphalt. Glen's eyes flew wide and he looked down to see a thick, dark stain spread across his shirt as blood spilled from his fractured heart.

'God, no!' Karina shouted as she leaped forward and dropped to her knees alongside Glen.

Glen's mouth hung loosely open and the light in his eyes flickered away. Karina felt tears spill from her eyes as she held him. A faint, breathless whisper fell from his lips.

'I'm sorry.'

A rush of air spilled from Glen's lungs and his body fell slack as he died.

Karina felt the hard, uncompromising barrel of Donovan's pistol stab into her side, and turned to look up into his cold eyes as the chief glared at her. With his free hand, he pulled a cellphone from his pocket and dialed a number. When a scratchy voice answered, he spoke angrily.

'It's a bust,' he said. 'They're not here.'

'*I know*,' came the response. '*Use her to find out where they are*.'

Donovan looked up, scanning the lonely parking lot for any sign of the CIA agent, but he could see nothing. He shut the line off and dropped the cell into his pocket, and then yanked Karina to her feet as he kept the pistol pressed against her side.

'Get in your car, Karina!' he snapped. 'We're going for a ride and you're going to tell me where.'

'You can go to hell,' Karina snapped.

Donovan grinned cruelly down at her and jammed the pistol up underneath her jaw.

'I'd say that's for certain, so I've got nothing to lose. You going to join me, or are you going to lead me to where Warner and Lopez are hiding?'

# 55

# ST PATRICK'S CATHEDRAL, MANHATTAN

The cathedral glowed with a galaxy of candleflames as Ethan hurried between the pews toward the altar. Lopez followed behind him, with Joanna shepherding Tom Ross along at the rear.

Monsignor Thomas was waiting for them, his expression etched with deep concern.

'Where is Karina? he asked.

'Acting as a diversion,' Ethan replied sharply. 'We don't have much time.'

The monsignor looked at Tom Ross, taking in his darkened eyes and haggard appearance, and then he appeared to take a step back in fear.

'This,' he uttered, 'this is the one?'

Ethan nodded, and looked back at Tom. The young man he had once been was swiftly vanishing, as though he were physically being drained of life by every passing moment. His shoulders were slumped, his skin pale and sheened with a clammy sweat and his head hung low as though too heavy for him to bear.

As Ethan watched, Joanna levered Tom carefully into a pew and the young man slumped there, his eyes drooping. Joanna lifted his chin and slapped a hand across his cheek, the slap echoing up into the vaulted ceiling above.

'Stay awake, you hear me?' she snapped.

Tom Ross blinked and managed to keep his head up as Ethan turned back to the monsignor.

'I want you to go to the fuse box and shut off all the power,' he said.

'The power? What for?'

'A precaution,' Ethan replied. 'I think you know what for.'

The monsignor nodded fearfully, his gaze switching between Ethan and Tom Ross. 'Yes, everything will be off. The candles will be enough illumination.'

'Is there anybody else in the building?' Ethan demanded.

'No,' the monsignor replied. 'I have sent everybody home.'

'Good,' Ethan said. 'Then you had best leave, too, before anything happens.'

The monsignor looked at Tom and frowned. 'But I do not know this man. Why would his wraith attack me?'

Ethan looked down at the monsignor. 'Man of the cloth or not, can you stand there and tell me that you've never done anything wrong in your life? Never lied, stolen, cheated or deceived?'

The monsignor swallowed indignantly. 'I am a man of God.'

'Like that means anything,' Lopez uttered with brittle humor.

'Have you ever lied, stolen, cheated or deceived?' Ethan repeated. 'Because if you have, then this wraith might decide that it doesn't like you.'

The monsignor's defiance crumbled and he handed Ethan a set of heavy, archaic iron keys. 'To the main doors,' he said. 'Lock them after me.'

With that, Monsignor Thomas hurried away through the cathedral. He walked behind one of the huge columns, and Ethan heard a metallic-sounding door or panel being opened. Moments later, all of the main lights in the cathedral shut down and the muted hum of extraction fans faded away, to be replaced by a deep silence. The entire cathedral was filled with an ominous combination of flickering candlelight and deep shadows rising up into the huge vaulted roof above.

Ethan turned to Joanna, who gestured at Tom Ross.

'He's not going to be hanging around much longer, not in this state,' she said. 'He's no good to me dead.'

'He's going to be a bigger problem than that if he passes out,' Lopez shot back at her. 'This is about more than your damned revenge.'

Joanna raised an unconcerned eyebrow at her. 'Is it?'

Ethan was about to interject when he heard the cathedral door slam with a boom that echoed through the cathedral. To his surprise, he saw the monsignor reappear with his hands in the air. Behind him walked Donovan, one arm holding Karina Thorne as the other pressed a pistol into her side.

'Too late,' Ethan said.

Donovan prodded the monsignor toward the altar, keeping Karina close as he reached them and looked at each of them in turn.

'Well, isn't this cozy?'

'You're through, Donovan!' Lopez snapped. 'Whatever you do from here on in, you're going to spend the next few decades behind bars.'

'Is that so?' Donovan said. 'Then where are the cops? Why haven't they arrested me, especially when I'm driving about in my pool car with my police radio. Strange, I haven't heard anybody calling for my arrest.'

Ethan frowned. 'Good question. Want to reveal?'

Donovan sneered at him.

'None of your goddamned business, Warner. Now, this is how it's going to go. You're going to hand Tom Ross over to me. In return, I won't put a bullet in Karina's skull. Simple enough for you all?'

Lopez stood protectively in front of Tom Ross.

'He's not going anywhere,' she snarled. 'I don't know what you've pulled but you won't get away with it.'

'I've already gotten away with it!' Donovan shouted, his voice echoing back and forth through the cathedral. 'We're done here.'

Ethan raised his hands in placation, keenly aware that he wasn't armed. 'This isn't the way, Donovan. Killing Tom isn't going to stop this. You think that if he's dead his wraith isn't just going to hunt you down anyway?'

Donovan shook his head.

'It'll damned well hunt me down if he stays alive, so I'm willing to take the chance.'

Lopez shook her head.

'This thing hunts down injustice,' she said, 'and punishes it violently. The only way for you to end this is to come clean, Donovan. You go to the police, confess, reveal everything and it might just let you live.'

Donovan looked at her for several long seconds and then suddenly he burst out laughing.

'You two kill me, really,' he uttered. 'Sure, maybe I'll avoid death, only to be sent into a prison where I'll be the biggest walking target they've ever seen. A former detective now incarcerated on the block. I won't last more than a week, genius, so I'm not losing much by standing here telling you to either hand Ross over now or I'll start putting holes in Karina.'

Ethan was out of ideas and about to consider charging Donovan when the cathedral door clattered open. He saw Doug Jarvis appear at the rear of the cathedral with a pistol aimed toward them.

Ethan stared in silence as Jarvis edged his way toward them.

'Don't move,' Jarvis said firmly, 'any of you.'

Ethan glanced at Donovan, who had turned slightly to confront the new arrival.

'You're done, Jarvis!' Donovan snapped. 'Drop the gun.'

Jarvis continued moving and shook his head. 'You're not giving the orders here, Donovan. You're already up to your neck, don't make it any worse.'

Donovan sneered a grin at Jarvis. 'I've got myself nicely covered.'

'And I,' Jarvis said smoothly, 'have you nicely surrounded.'

Ethan heard a small scratching sound behind him.

Donovan shifted position again in surprise as he looked past Ethan to see a tall, sepulchral figure stalking toward them from behind the fluted columns, a pistol held firmly in his grip.

Joanna took a pace backward and gasped, and Ethan guessed that she recognized the man from her incarceration in Gaza. Ethan recognized him from years before, a de-brief after his chaotic first investigation for the DIA.

'Wilson,' he uttered.

# 56

Ethan watched as Jarvis and Wilson slowly maneuvered through the cathedral to flank them, and felt a hollow pit form low in his belly.

Donovan whirled, stepping back with Karina still in his grasp so that he could keep everybody in sight.

Wilson stopped near the altar, casting his icy gaze at each of them in turn, before speaking to Jarvis. 'Perfect,' he uttered.

Lopez glared at Jarvis. 'You son of a bitch, you sold out.'

'There was a price for protecting you from the CIA,' Jarvis sighed. 'Their price was Joanna Defoe.'

Ethan felt every fiber in his body prime itself for action. For a moment, nobody else existed in the room but Jarvis, as the weight of the old man's betrayal crushed down upon Ethan's shoulders.

'You knew, all along,' Ethan uttered. 'You guided this whole damned thing. You knew who Tom Ross was, didn't you?'

Jarvis shook his head as he replied. 'I've told you, Ethan, many times now, that sometimes decisions have to be made for which there can be no good outcome. My choice wasn't a choice at all. It was to protect two people instead of just one, yourself and Lopez instead of just Joanna. We traced Barraclough's family to Tom Ross not long before you did, as we knew that Joanna would turn up sooner or later.'

'That's why you kept disappearing after we got to New York,' Lopez said in dismay. 'You've been going behind our backs.'

'I've been doing my job,' Jarvis shot back.

Joanna Defoe stepped forward fearlessly, glaring at Wilson. 'And now?'

Wilson looked at her for a moment and then down at Tom Ross, who was watching the whole exchange through hooded eyes.

'You come with me,' Wilson replied without emotion. 'We can't have you running about with all that you know, can we? Don't worry, you won't be harmed. We just need to ensure that you forget about everything.'

'You really think that I'm going to believe that?' Joanna snapped at him. 'After everything you bastards did to me?'

'I don't care what you believe,' Wilson replied. 'It's not a choice, it's a requirement. You're coming with me.'

'Like hell!' Ethan snapped, taking a pace toward him.

Wilson reacted instantly, moving his pistol with fluid speed and aiming at Ethan. Joanna swung an arm out to stop Ethan in his tracks, her gaze still fixed on the CIA agent.

'And what about him?' she asked, gesturing at Tom.

Wilson, the pistol still trained on Ethan, looked down at Tom.

'I think that it would be safer for all of us if Mr. Ross were to have a very long rest.'

Karina squirmed against Donovan as she shouted, 'Leave him alone. Donovan's already killed Glen.'

Ethan shot a glance at Donovan.

'Crap,' Donovan uttered. 'The kid shot himself.'

Jarvis's voice reached them from nearby. 'That's not what I saw, back at Hell Gate.'

Karina's eyes flared in surprise and rage. '*You were there?* And you didn't do anything?'

'Not our place,' Wilson said, answering for Jarvis. 'It's your mess, you clean it up.'

Donovan appeared equally surprised, and suddenly unsure of who was backing whom as he looked from Jarvis to Wilson and back again. He was struggling to hold onto Karina and trying to keep his pistol both in her side but also available in case Wilson sought to betray him. Ethan looked at Jarvis, who was standing with one hand holding his pistol and the other down by his side.

Jarvis wriggled the fingers of his free hand. Resting on the outside of his pants, Ethan realized that the old man was signaling him. Three fingers. Three seconds? Three minutes? Ethan glanced around the cathedral but could see nothing untoward.

Donovan yanked Karina sideways and shouted across to Wilson.

'Finish Ross, and then we can deal with the rest of them.'

Wilson glanced down at Tom Ross, who was now being shielded by both Lopez and Joanna. He smiled bitterly as he swung his pistol to aim at them.

'Is this going to take one bullet, or three?'

Ethan looked at Jarvis and saw a finger disappear into his pants pocket. *Two.*

'Go to hell,' Joanna shot back at Wilson.

'Just shoot them both!' Donovan yelled. 'Get it over with!'

Jarvis retracted his last finger out of sight. *One.*

Wilson shrugged and shifted his aim to Joanna. 'Suit yourself.'

Wilson squeezed his trigger.

The gunshot was deafening as Jarvis fired. The shot hit Wilson high on the back of his right shoulder in a puff of blood and he staggered sideways, his own shot flying high into the vaulted ceiling above them.

Jarvis threw himself backwards across nearby pews as Ethan launched himself at Wilson.

The agent's pistol whipped around to face Ethan and discharged just to the left of his head as he smashed the weapon clear and crashed into Wilson. The gunshot rang in Ethan's ears as they plunged onto the polished stone flags of the cathedral.

As he hit the ground, Ethan saw Karina Thorne's head jerk backwards and crunch Donovan's nose against his face as he aimed at Jarvis. The pair of them fell backwards as Donovan's shot missed Jarvis and flew high to dislodge a sprinkle of stone from a nearby column.

The bullet ricocheted and crashed through one of the huge stained-glass windows, a shower of multi-colored glass fragments tumbling from the heights to sprinkle the stone floor of the cathedral in shards of glinting light as the entire window shattered and collapsed inward. Whorls of rain poured down into the cathedral from the darkness outside, glowing in the light of the candles.

Wilson hurled Ethan off of him with impressive strength despite his injury, then rolled away and brought his pistol to bear as Ethan scrambled to his feet and swung a boot at the weapon. The impact against his wrist caused Wilson to cry out in pain as the pistol was whipped from his grasp and skittered away across the flags between the pews.

Wilson leaped cat-like to his feet as Ethan fired a left jab at his eyes, a practiced hand scything Ethan's blow to one side as Wilson drove his left elbow in behind Ethan's ear. Ethan twisted aside, the blow glancing off his skull as he slammed his right knee up into the agent's belly.

Wilson growled as he folded over but he did not fall, folding his arms around Ethan's head and twisting violently. Ethan felt bright pain pulse through his neck and his body spin uncontrollably as he was flipped over and crashed down onto the flags on his back.

He glimpsed Wilson's face twisted with malice as the agent lifted a boot and brought it down toward Ethan's face.

Ethan swung his right arm across and the boot slammed instead into his shoulder as Wilson staggered off balance. Ethan lurched upright and drove a bunched fist into Wilson's groin with as much force as he could muster.

Wilson gagged and staggered backward as Ethan got back onto his feet, his shoulder throbbing with pain and his lungs heaving for air. Wilson glared back at him, coming forward again with his fists raised.

'That's far enough,' Lopez snarled.

Ethan turned to see her holding Wilson's pistol. He was about to smile when he heard a squeal of pain and turned to see Donovan scramble to his feet, blood caking his face as he aimed his pistol at Tom Ross and Joanna. Karina Thorne was on her back on the flags, blinking as though coming awake from a blow and powerless to intervene.

Joanna hurled herself at Tom Ross and collided with him as Donovan fired.

The gunshot thumped into Tom as he staggered off the pew and dropped to his knees clutching his belly. Joanna landed alongside him and stared in dismay as Tom rolled over and sprawled across the stone flags.

'No!' Karina scrambled across the flags past Donovan and grabbed Tom's shoulders as tears spilled from her eyes to splash across the fallen man's cheeks.

Ethan saw the kid stare up at Karina, fear poisoning his expression, and then his eyes finally closed and his body fell still.

For a moment, the cathedral was silent.

Donovan lowered his pistol, a grim smile on his face. 'It's done. He's not getting up from that.'

Ethan stared down at Tom Ross's body and then across at Lopez. Both of them looked at Jarvis, who was standing amidst the pews nearby.

Wilson stood glaring at Lopez.

Donovan turned and aimed at Lopez. 'Lose the piece, Chiquita.'

Lopez glared at Donovan with unconcealed hatred, but she slowly lowered the weapon. At Donovan's gesture, she slid the pistol across the flags to Wilson, who lithely scooped it up and aimed it at Ethan.

'All's well that ends well,' he uttered with a grim smile, and then looked at Joanna Defoe. 'With me, now, or I'll perforate your friends here.'

Joanna Defoe stood back from Tom's body and turned to face Wilson.

'If I come with you, will you guarantee everybody else's safety?'

'Don't do it,' Ethan said to her.

Wilson's smile vanished. 'You have my word,' he replied.

Joanna stepped out into the aisle, the veils of rain falling from the shattered window behind her and glittering in the candlelight like a silent diamond waterfall. As Ethan watched, and Joanna took a step away from Tom's body, so the falling rain suddenly rippled as though a wind had gusted through it.

Ethan felt his throat constrict as the falling rain suddenly folded in upon itself and began rising up instead of falling down.

# 57

Ethan took an involuntary step back as Karina Thorne jumped to her feet like a startled cat and retreated from Tom Ross's body. The falling rain swirled and folded upon itself as though rising on invisible thermals, spiraling and coiling like flocks of tiny glistening birds wheeling in tight formation.

'I thought you said the power was off!' Lopez yelled at the monsignor.

'It is!' he shouted back in horror, his eyes transfixed by the swirling apparition before them.

Ethan saw Wilson aim his pistol at the writhing mass of water vapor as it swelled above them. From the roiling core spread what looked like two vast wings, as though the wraith were some kind of avenging angel. The millions of droplets of water sparkled in the candlelight above them like a veil of diamonds caught in a sunbeam as Ethan felt the air turn bitterly cold, the spiraling rain-drops turning to frosty crystals, until the wraith's hellish form was, for a few moments, visible as it loomed over them all.

With a dawning realization, he looked at Tom Ross's body and saw the blood staining his shirt. He had been hit low in the belly, a certainly fatal wound without treatment. But in the candlelight, Ethan saw the glistening fluid gently changing shape, the reflections of the light subtly altering in a slow rhythm as Tom breathed.

A rippling shower of tiny blue sparks of light leaped to and fro across his body, as though he were enveloped by a static charge. Karina Thorne was staring not at the wraith rising up from his body but at the bizarre sparks.

'Get away from him, Karina!' Lopez warned her.

Wilson's aim dropped as he saw the sparks leaping across Tom's body, and Ethan hurled himself at the agent before he could fire. Ethan crashed into him and they collided against the rock-hard pews, the pistol trapped between them.

Lopez leaped over Tom Ross's body and swung a hard right into Donovan's jaw, which sent him reeling backwards down the aisle. The officer tripped over Ethan's boots and sprawled onto the flags as Ethan struggled to disarm Wilson.

The agent's near-suicidal determination was no longer enough to sustain his ageing muscles and blood loss from his wound, and Ethan's relative youth began to turn the tide in his favour. Wilson's wrists gave in before his spirit did, and Ethan twisted the pistol from his grasp just in time for Donovan's fist to crack across his temple.

Ethan spun away, his vision starring violently as he crashed down onto the flags. He blinked as his vision returned and saw Donovan aiming the pistol over his head at Tom Ross. Karina tried to throw herself in front of Tom, but Ethan could already see that she wouldn't make it.

Donovan looked up at the swirling mass of writhing rain hovering over Tom's body. It remained in place and did not move, as though watching the officer. Donovan sneered at it.

'Night-night!' he snapped, and squeezed the trigger.

Ethan flicked his boot up and connected with the pistol just as the shot rang out across the cathedral. The weapon jerked upwards, the shot flying high, and in an instant the seething mass of energy raced toward Ethan and Donovan.

Donovan fired at the wraith in desperation just as it plowed into him and sent him spinning through the air to crash into the pews nearby. Ethan rolled away and saw Donovan's pistol clatter onto the flags. He leaped up and dashed toward the weapon, as Wilson aimed at Joanna.

Joanna dove behind the pews as Wilson fired three shots that clattered off the altar's ornate marble surface, spraying chips and clouds of marble dust into the air.

Ethan grabbed Donovan's pistol and aimed at Wilson, who dashed across the cathedral and ducked behind one of the huge fluted columns. Ethan aimed at the spot where he had vanished, but turned as a shriek of agony echoed out across the cathedral.

Ethan turned to see Donovan's body being dragged across the stone flags at high speed, his face contorted in pain. His body hit the altar hard and was flipped up on end before he crashed down onto his back, his limbs hanging loose over the edges.

'Help me!'

Ethan scrambled to his feet, staying low enough behind the pews to avoid being shot by Wilson, and ran toward

Tom's body. He was halfway there when he heard a loud cracking sound.

He looked up, and saw the huge golden crucifix suspended above the altar shudder as its guide-lines were snapped. The immense object plummeted downward, and Ethan heard a fearsome scream just before the object plunged down through Donovan's chest and embedded itself into the marble altar with a deafening crash.

The sound echoed across the cathedral like a clap of thunder, rolling away into the distance as Ethan stared at the gruesome corpse now lying on the altar, Donovan's face staring lifelessly at them, his tongue hanging limp from his slack jaw.

The veils of frost and rain swirled upward again, and, as Ethan watched, so he saw the terrible shape converge in the center once more above Tom Ross's body. It surged upward, and then raced down toward Doug Jarvis.

Ethan dashed the last few paces across to Tom's body and dropped down as he punched the comatose officer in his wound.

The thump cracked across the cathedral and Tom Ross jerked awake and sucked in a huge lungful of air as pain convulsed across his body. Ethan saw the writhing cloud of rain dissipate and fall gently down around where Jarvis crouched with his hands over his head. Ethan reached down and pushed against Tom's wound, stemming the blood spilling onto the stone flags.

Karina Thorne dropped onto her knees alongside Tom and grabbed his hand, already slick with blood from his wound.

'It's okay, Tom, stay with me, you're going to be fine.'

Lopez and Joanna hurried to Ethan's side.

'Wilson's disappeared,' Lopez said, gesturing over her shoulder. 'I guess he got spooked.'

Ethan nodded and looked down at Tom Ross.

His skin was even paler now, his eyes sunken into their orbits and his breathing irregular. A thin sheen of sickly sweat glistened on his forehead.

'Ten minutes and he'll go into toxic shock,' Ethan guessed. 'The bullets perforated his stomach and the contents are leaking into his bloodstream.'

Karina looked up at Monsignor Thomas, who was cowering behind the knave. 'Call 911, right now!'

The monsignor nodded and dashed away. Karina looked back down at Tom. 'Stay with me, Tom, you're going to be fine, okay? Just hang on.'

Tom looked up at her, and then his head turned to see Donovan's lifeless corpse dangling from the altar. He swallowed thickly and then looked back at Karina. Slowly, he reached down with his free hand and began pushing Ethan's hand away from the wound.

Ethan looked into his eyes. He saw no evidence of delirium. Despite the terrible fatigue clouding Tom's expression, he saw somewhere deep inside a resolution he had seen before only rarely, on the battlefield when the injured knew that they were lost.

'No,' Karina whispered, clutching Tom's hand tighter. 'Just hang on a little longer.'

Tom looked at her and breathed a reply that sounded as though he bore the weight of the world upon his shoulders. 'I don't want to.'

Tom pushed Ethan's hand away again, and, this time, Ethan released the wound. Fresh blood spilled onto the flags and he heard Tom's breathing begin to falter.

Lopez joined him and watched in silence as Ethan stood up and backed away from Tom's body. Lopez leaned in close, her voice a whisper.

'What if he dies and that thing comes back, permanently?'

Ethan shook his head. 'I don't think it works like that.'

Tom's eyes began to droop, and, as Karina held his bloodied hands, so his chest gently sank as his final breaths escaped wearily into the cathedral's cold air.

Then, slowly, Tom's eyes opened again and he looked up above where he lay. For a brief moment, a little life returned into them, and Ethan saw the faintest ghost of a smile curl from one corner of his lips.

Karina held Tom's hands as his eyes closed and he exhaled a long, slow sigh. His hand fell from Karina's grasp and slid gently onto his stomach, and Ethan knew that he was gone.

Karina remained kneeling alongside his body for several minutes in the silence of the cathedral, until wailing sirens brought the outside world noisily back into her life.

Ethan turned to Lopez. 'Where's Joanna?'

Lopez looked up and around the cathedral and shook her head. 'She was right here. Where's Jarvis, for that matter?'

Ethan turned to where Jarvis had last been, but there was nobody there.

## 58

# DEFENSE INTELLIGENCE ANALYSIS CENTER, JOINT BASE ANACOSTIA-BOLLING, WASHINGTON, DC

*Two days later*

'I don't like this at all.'

Nicola Lopez paced up and down in the small briefing room, radiating tension. Ethan sat in a chair, with his hands in his lap, watching her walk up and down.

'How can you just sit there like that?' she demanded.

'Standard procedure in the military,' Ethan replied. 'Hurry up and wait.'

Lopez scoffed and continued her pacing. 'They're conspiring,' she decided. 'They've asked us to come over here so they can figure out a way of getting us into some goddamned Supermax prison or something.'

'It would have been easier to just arrest us on sight,' Ethan pointed out, 'and spirit us away than let us travel all the way up here.'

'Jarvis is up to something,' Lopez said, changing tack. 'He betrayed you, you know that? He sold out on Joanna.'

Ethan did not reply. Fact was, he knew damned well that the only way Wilson could have found them was if Jarvis had revealed her location. Ethan felt surprisingly unperturbed by what Jarvis had done. The old man had been given an impossible choice, and had done his very best to protect as many people as he could. The fact that Joanna was alive seemed to have finally divested Ethan of the bitterness that had festered inside of him for so many years. It had always been the *not knowing* that had poisoned his life, had erased so many weeks and months and years in a paroxysm of hate and regret. Now, *knowing* had extinguished those emotions and others, too.

'He betrayed us,' Lopez repeated, bending at the waist and getting in Ethan's face. 'I said he would, and he has.'

Ethan looked up at her. 'He betrayed Joanna, not us.'

'*There's a difference?*' Lopez snapped.

'Joanna is Joanna,' Ethan replied, 'and she'll be fine now. We're us, and we'll be fine, too.'

'Seriously?' Lopez uttered. 'You think they're just going to let us walk, after all that's happened.'

Ethan didn't doubt it, although he didn't bother elaborating to Lopez. She had made up her mind that they were doomed to incarceration and solitary confinement in some CIA black prison in Eastern Europe, or similar, and wouldn't be persuaded otherwise by his hunches. But the fact was that MK-ULTRA now had nothing remaining to hide, except its chief assassin, Mr. Wilson. While Ethan seriously doubted that the CIA would willingly hand over their loyal killer after so many years of service, it seemed unlikely that he would be able to continue working.

A door opened nearby and Jarvis stepped out, closing it behind him and walking toward Ethan and Lopez. Ethan stood up as Lopez got straight into Jarvis's face.

'Spill it!' she snapped.

Jarvis looked at her without concern, and smiled.

'The Joint Chiefs of Staff have all concurred that your work here was of the highest order and that the witch-hunt orchestrated by the CIA was severely misguided. All operations against you have been officially terminated.'

Lopez took a pace closer to him. 'What about that asshole, Wilson?'

Jarvis glanced at Ethan. 'That particular asshole is now retired, after I *accidentally* put a photograph of him into the hands of police departments in Washington, DC, New York City, Ohio, Wisconsin and Atlanta.' Jarvis rolled his eyes. 'Butter fingers.'

'What photo?' Lopez pressed, not willing to back down yet.

'Taken by Ethan's sister six months ago, in DC,' Jarvis explained, 'when she was being followed by members of the CIA while working at the Government Accountability Office. I also added some shots taken by an associate of mine, down the barrel of a sniper rifle. Needless to say, I didn't mention that to the police.'

Ethan began to feel the tension in his shoulders slip away. 'Non-disclosure agreements all round?'

Jarvis nodded. 'Witnesses to the events in the cathedral have all signed their respective documents, with one exception.'

'Joanna,' Ethan guessed. 'She took off.'

'As did you,' Lopez pointed at Jarvis. 'Mighty surprised you didn't see her.'

'She's quick as a cat,' Jarvis replied. 'If I knew where she had gone, I would have tracked her down by now.'

'She's good at lying low,' Ethan said. 'But she hasn't made contact with us either. What's the JCOS's decision on her?'

Jarvis shrugged. 'If she's willing to testify, behind closed senate doors, obviously, then those responsible for her imprisonment and treatment can be brought to trial.'

'But then that would expose the CIA's director to homicide and treason charges,' Lopez uttered. 'Like that's going to happen.'

Jarvis nodded apologetically toward Ethan. 'If they agree to put to trial former CIA figures, then it defeats the whole purpose of protecting the CIA's presence and operations. It can't end well.'

Ethan nodded, guessing the rest.

'So, as long as she stays quiet, she'll be likewise left alone. That's the deal.'

'That's about it.' Jarvis nodded.

'And what about us?' Lopez demanded.

Jarvis's smile returned. 'Fully re-instated to the Defense Intelligence Agency, as am I, with all security clearance restored. We're back in business, which is just as well because a situation is developing in Nevada that I think you'll be interested to . . .'

Ethan raised a hand to stop Jarvis. The old man stopped talking, looking at Ethan and Lopez in turn. Ethan spoke quietly.

'We're done, Doug,' he said. 'We're heading back to Chicago.'

Jarvis stared at them for a long moment, before speaking to Lopez.

'Look, if you think I was betraying you then that's not the case, I was just . . .'

'Trying to do the right thing,' Lopez finished the sentence for him. 'We know, but doing the right thing routinely either puts us in danger or screws somebody else, Doug, and we're tired of it.'

'Nobody said this life was easy,' Jarvis replied, and looked at Ethan. 'But it's a damned sight better than the place I dragged you from, Ethan. Remember that, all those years ago? The tenement block, the drinking and brawling?'

Ethan nodded, briefly recalling the bitter years spent watching life pass by his crucible of pain and loneliness.

'I do,' he replied, 'and I'll be forever grateful. But I've paid my dues, Doug, several times over, and Nicola's done enough. Everything we've seen has told us over and over again that if we keep playing this game then, sooner or later, one of us is going to die.' Ethan walked to join Lopez's side. 'And neither of us wants that to happen.'

Lopez looked up at Ethan as a bright smile spread across her features, and she glanced over her shoulder at Jarvis as she spun to walk away down the corridor.

'It's been fun,' she said, without an ounce of emotion. 'Goodbye, Mr. Jarvis.'

Ethan watched her go and then turned back to his mentor.

'What are you going to do instead?' Jarvis asked Ethan with a wince. 'Spend your days plucking losers out of the gutter for a couple hundred bucks a shot?'

Ethan shrugged. 'I guess. We've got a lot of catching up to do, but it's what we want, Doug. We're damned lucky to still be alive after what the DIA's put us through. Right now, a few simple bail-runners seems like a great deal. We're going home.'

Jarvis stared at him for a long moment, before replying: 'I can't believe you're walking away from this.'

Ethan stuck his hand out and Jarvis shook it reluctantly.

'Good luck, Doug.'

Ethan turned away, but Jarvis's hand on his arm restrained him. Jarvis reached into his pocket and retrieved a small roll of 8mm film. He pushed it into Ethan's hand.

'More use to Joanna than it is to me,' he said. 'It's Major Greene's footage of the CIA agents splicing Harrison Defoe's water supply with LSD. Just in case.'

Ethan looked down at the film in his hand and managed a grin. Then he turned and walked away from Jarvis without looking back.

# 59

# CHICAGO, ILLINOIS

The surface of Lake Michigan churned up white crested rollers that were whipped away by the gusting wind as Ethan jogged near the shore along an old beaten track that led to Rocky Ledge Park.

It had taken a couple of weeks to settle back into things. Lopez had managed to get back in contact with her family in Mexico and send them some much-needed cash after her long absence. Ethan had visited his parents and sister, and had been able to inform Natalie that she no longer needed to worry about CIA assassins knocking at, or indeed kicking down, her door.

Ethan didn't know what had happened to Mr. Wilson, but, this time, he felt sure that the remorseless agent would no longer be a CIA-supported asset. It was a fact that, despite his relentless nature, Wilson was a loyal servant of the CIA, and if he had been called off and retired then he would not have resisted. It wasn't a personal thing for people like him, merely duty. Although Ethan despised the man with all of his heart, he knew that he did not have to worry about the agent becoming embittered and hunting him down.

He turned onto Rocky Ledge Park, maintaining an easy stride, going for distance rather than speed. It was a measure of his cautious nature that, since working for the Defense Intelligence Agency, he still wore earphones when he ran but he did not play any music. Just in case.

It was that caution that allowed him to hear the footfalls rapidly approaching from behind. A sprinter, moving fast, closing on him.

Ethan let his left foot hit the sandy earth as normal, but, as his right struck, he turned it sideways and let his leg fold at the knee like a giant coiled spring, ready to hurl himself back at his attacker and catch them unawares.

The jogger jerked left and a hand skimmed the top of his head as it flew past, a bright smile and a plume of blonde ponytailed hair flashing by.

'Not bad.'

Joanna Defoe kept moving as Ethan started running again and moved alongside her.

'Nice of you to show up,' he said between breaths. 'But you could have just waited for me out here. I thought for a moment that you'd high-tailed it out of all of this for good.'

Joanna didn't reply. Ethan looked at her for a few moments before speaking.

'Nothing to say for yourself?'

Joanna shook her head.

They ran north onto Lake Shore Drive, maintaining the same steady pace in perfect formation until Ethan's legs started to ache and his breathing started to rasp in his throat. Joanna accelerated ahead slightly and turned, running up a shallow hill that ended overlooking the shore.

Ethan ran up behind her and stopped, pressing his hands onto his knees and recovering his breath. He looked up at her and saw a faint smile on her lips.

'Just pretending that the last five years hadn't happened,' she said finally.

Ethan stood upright and looked out over the lake. 'Yeah, me too I guess. But it did happen.'

Joanna nodded but said nothing more, drinking from a water bottle she carried in one hand.

'You know that you're in the clear, don't you?' Ethan said. 'You don't have to run anymore.'

'I know,' she replied. 'Just haven't got used to the idea yet, is all.'

Ethan watched her for a few long seconds, wondering if they would still have been together if she hadn't been abducted in the middle of one of the most dangerous cities on earth. If they'd finally have got married, had kids, settled down. Somehow, he knew that whatever they had once shared was long gone, that too much had happened since for either of them ever to revisit the past, because it would never be the same again.

'Where will you go?' he asked her.

Joanna finally turned to face him. He could see in her expression that she was surprised by his directness, but that she was also as resigned to the situation as he was.

'Not Chicago,' she replied, 'too many memories.'

'That's why I came back here.'

'I didn't mean it like that,' she said. 'I need to leave it all behind, start again. It's just too painful right now to think about everything those bastards took from me, all those years that we could have been . . .' She cut herself off and swiped a strand of blonde hair away from her face and forced a smile onto her features. 'And you've got Nicola now, anyway. I have the suspicion she'd be a bit of a handful, if I got in her way.'

Ethan smiled, nodded. 'She has a way with people.'

Joanna looked briefly out across the lake, and then back at Ethan. 'It was good to see you again. I'm glad you found your way, despite everything.'

'You, too.' Ethan nodded. 'And don't go hungry or anything, okay? You know where we all are if things get tough.'

Joanna smirked. 'Tougher than four years in a Gazan prison cell?'

'You know what I mean.'

Ethan reached into his pocket. He pulled out the roll of 8mm film that Jarvis had given him and held it out to her.

'What's this?' she asked.

'Footage,' Ethan replied, 'shot by a team from the 24th Special Tactics Squadron attached to the CIA. It shows them tampering with the water supply to your father's apartment, injecting LSD into it. Proof enough for a trial and insurance against any kind of hit. My guess is that the Director of the CIA, William Steel, will be made aware that this evidence exists. I saw on the television a few nights ago that he had decided to retire from his role. I think that we both know what that means.'

Joanna stared down at the roll in her hand, speechless. She looked at Ethan in wonderment.

'How the hell did you get hold of this?' she asked.

'Honestly?' Ethan replied airily. 'You know, it must be my age, but I just can't recall who gave it to me.'

Joanna smiled and looked again at the roll of film, before she tucked it into a pocket and turned to face Ethan.

'Take care of yourself, okay?' she said.

'What I'm best at,' Ethan replied. 'You, too.'

Joanna leaned forward and kissed him on the cheek. Then she turned and, without another word, she jogged away. Within a few minutes, she had vanished ghost-like into the city, as though she had never existed, still a distant memory in Ethan's mind.

Ethan jogged back to his apartment and took a long, hot shower, running through his mind everything that had happened in the past week. He felt strangely detached from events, as though so much had happened after so long a wait that his mind wasn't prepared to accept it. He had searched for Joanna for years and then suddenly she had reappeared. Yet, within days, she was gone again. The burden of regret was definitely lifted from his shoulders and the bitterness had dissolved into warmth that permeated his soul, but in the wake of her final departure was the feeling that tomorrow was an unknown. With his life's goal now resolved and having officially parted company with the DIA, he realized that he didn't know what to do next.

Ethan drove to the office he rented with Lopez, pulled up outside and sat silently in his car, looking at the building. The afternoon sun was setting to the west and he could see that the office light was on. Lopez was still there, probably calling every police department in the state to catch up on the names of bail-runners sought by the courts.

Ethan got out of the car and walked across to the door, punched in his access code and entered the building. Lopez was sitting behind her desk, gripping her phone tightly and jabbing a finger in the air while talking to the unfortunate person on the other end of the line.

'. . . you'll pay our fees on time or you'll wake up tomorrow morning to find me standing over you with a goddamned bat in my hand, you feel me? You've got twelve hours.' She slammed the phone back into its cradle. 'Have a nice day,' she added laconically as she looked up at Ethan. 'Well?'

Ethan eased into the chair behind his desk. 'Everything's going to be fine.'

'Joanna?'

'We crossed paths,' he replied. 'For the last time, I think.'

'I'm sorry,' Lopez said, and Ethan could tell that she meant it.

'It's been a long time coming. It feels okay.'

'You sure?'

'I'm sure.'

'Good.'

Ethan looked at her quizzically as she began shuffling through the mountain of paperwork on her desk. 'Good?'

'Good.' Lopez nodded, still smiling. 'You and I have got months of work to catch up on, and you were never any good while half your brain was focused on Joanna. At least now, I'll have your full attention.'

'*You'll* have it?'

'Damned right,' she insisted. 'No more Jarvis, no more DIA and no more Joanna Default – as I've come to think of her.'

'Joanna Default,' Ethan echoed. 'That's nice.'

'You know what I mean.' Lopez flashed a bright smile as she tossed him a thick wad of folders, each bearing the name of a down-and-out bail-runner loose somewhere in Illinois. 'Your cases. And I'll need you to book a reservation for us both for dinner this evening.'

Ethan gaped at her. 'Dinner? We've never gone to dinner before.'

'That's right,' she agreed, 'we've always had carry-out, eaten at our desks, or grabbed morsels while running all over the goddamned country for the DIA. I've had it with fast food, so you're taking me out to dinner. Somewhere nice. I like Mexican, if that helps. Any questions?'

There was a self-satisfied little smile coloring her features as he stared at her.

'Sure, I guess.'

'Thank you, kind sir.'

'And we're going to get on with all this, just like that?'

'Just like that.'

'And you don't want to talk about going back home to Mexico, or how we're going to survive without the extra work from the DIA and pay our rents, or . . .?'

'We'll survive, Ethan,' she said. 'That's what people like us do. In fact, without Jarvis sending us to near-certain death every few months, we'll probably thrive, know what I mean?'

Ethan sighed. 'Yeah, figures.'

'Good,' Lopez replied brightly. 'I'll get coffee and donuts. You figure out which one of these losers we're going after next and we'll get on the case. Any further questions?'

Ethan almost laughed, but he shook his head and flipped a mock salute. 'No, ma'am.'

Lopez grabbed her keys and sauntered toward the office door. He called after her as she walked out.

'Hey, you sure this is what you want?'

Lopez looked back over her shoulder at him. The smile was still there, but it seemed calmer, more content than before.

'Sure I am. You?'

Ethan thought only for a moment longer. A normal life, one that neither of them had been able to enjoy for years. No-brainer. 'Yeah, definitely.'

Lopez hurried away as Ethan pulled out his cellphone and scrolled down through his contacts menu. He found the entries for Doug Jarvis and Joanna Defoe and deleted them.

# ACKNOWLEDGEMENTS

Throughout the writing of these books I have owed an immense debt of gratitude to my literary agent Luigi Bonomi and his team at LBA, who discovered me as a writer and helped me become a successfully published author, in doing so changing my life beyond recognition and helping a long-held dream come true; to the publishing team at Simon & Schuster who all work so hard to develop and promote the series; and to my family and friends who all champion my work so enthusiastically. I also would like to mention the fans of the books who so often contact me with kind words and who follow my journey as an author through my website, Twitter and Facebook pages. Without readers all authors would be redundant and every one of you makes this author's work worthwhile.

In addition, for much of the revelatory detail in this novel I am indebted to Dr Penny Sartori. An immensely experienced Intensive Care nurse, Penny was awarded a PhD for her extensive research into near-death experiences. In 2008, her academic monograph "*The Near-Death Experiences of*

*Hospitalized Intensive Care Patients: A Five Year Clinical Study*" was published. It was from this reference that I obtained many of the genuine near-death experiences referred to by characters within this novel, and Dr Sartori's detailed study remains a unique and remarkable investigation into a phenomenon that fascinates all who encounter it.